The Fallen

Jennifer Wherrett

First published by Jennifer Wherrett 2018
www.thelady.com.au

ISBN: 978-0-6482977-0-3
Library data available from the National library of Australia

Cover design: Graphics by Sally
www.graphicsbysally.com.au

Typesetting by Publicious Book Publishing
Publicioushed with the assistance of
Publicious Book Publishing
www.publicious.com.au

Contents

Author's Note

Writing connects me to that highest part of my consciousness, but it also connects me to other higher-conscious beings with whom I have the privilege and pleasure of Working, hence my dialogues, particularly at the beginning of many of my stories. Now, to speak to them, as I would speak to any incarnated being, I write. I might write a question on a loose sheet of paper, and they will answer me. The flow of communion, not to mention communication, is something I can highly recommend. It is, in fact, one of my most favourite things. I have never thanked them publicly but they know my gratitude runs very deep. I could not have done this without them . . . any of it.

And so, "The Fallen." These stories deal very specifically with my very early incarnations – those lives that shaped the path I would walk in future ones. The order of these stories as they are presented here does not align with the chronology, or the timing, of when I lived them. Rather, the order of the stories represents the path my Process took me in leading me through the memories, and, therefore, in dealing with the whys and wherefores of those specific lifetimes. In terms of linear time, Kiaara lived first, Kalistäe second, and Elyra third, but in terms of my own personal chronology, Kalistäe lived first (Faerie), Kiaara lived second (The Fallen), and Elyra lived last (Oracle of Light), if you want to know.

And, as usual, I capitalise the first letters of certain words – like Process and Purpose and Work and Separation – to denote these as higher-dimensional or metaphysical (whichever term you prefer) concepts, and to distinguish them from ordinary lower-dimensional meanings and definitions.

Jennifer
August, 2017

Oracle of Light

Buried in the Sands of Time

When first she came upon it, she took a long moment to recognise it for what it was. And so, she was standing right in front of it before she knew she had found it. She certainly hadn't known what it was as she approached it, nor had she known she'd been walking towards it. She had, in fact, been thinking she was horribly lost, and so she had mentally been trying to make her way back the way she had come just to make sure she **could** find her way back, her pace slowing markedly as she concentrated on mentally retracing her steps. She could not allow herself to get lost in this place. To do so would potentially court real danger, especially since no one knew where she was . . . no one at all.

She had come half way around the world to seek this place out, having seen it in her visions, both now, as it was in the present, and as it had been in the past. When the visions had become so strong they'd started completely taking over her physical sight, at inconvenient times and places, she knew what it meant, and so, without questioning or hesitating, she had bought herself some new, appropriate clothes, packed a suitcase, booked a flight, and left without telling another soul. What would be the point? They would either have tried to talk her out of it, and she may or may not have been swayed, or they would have told her she was a fool. Either way, they would not have understood the urgency she felt or the raw, driving need to be back here now that she remembered it. She had long ago grown tired of trying to explain herself to others anyway, others who, bound as they were by lower-dimensional mindsets, simply were not capable of understanding, so this time she simply hadn't bothered.

In a way, they would have been right in telling her she was a fool to come here by herself. It was a risk even coming to this country at all at this time because never, in all of its sometimes-turbulent history, had Egypt been in such chaos and turmoil. It was a cruel twist of irony, really, she thought, given the absolute importance, and the recognition, for that matter, the ancient Egyptians accorded the Law of Maat – the idea or principle of cosmic order, truth and justice that, if upheld and honoured, kept chaos at bay. It had even been a vital function of the Pharaohs themselves to honour Maat and uphold her law. How they would turn in their graves if they could see their land now. Because chaos ruled. Egypt had, now, lost all sense of itself. Like flotsam and jetsam, it rolled with the tide of whatever was driving it at any given moment in time, with no direction, no leadership, no heart, at the mercy of the elements, so to speak. And so, it was, as a country and as a culture, at the mercy of the corrupt and of corruption itself. The Law of Maat was no longer even acknowledged in this land, or in any modern land, for that matter, to humanity's very great detriment. How typical it was for modern humanity to look back at its own history with arrogant eyes, as if the ancients were so much more primitive and ignorant so that their wisdom could simply be disregarded as if of no import. Oh the irony, because the truth was exactly the opposite, of course.

And then, as if travelling on her own, as a lone woman, to a country where political and cultural unrest and upheaval was the order, or lack thereof, of the day, she'd had no idea where the site of her visions actually was. She had travelled here purely on instinct, knowing, somehow, that the site was south of Cairo. How far south, she hadn't known, so she'd organised to stay in a motel as far south as she dared travel whilst still within easy reach of the city and the Australian Embassy. And then, with the help of the motel employees, she'd managed to hire a reliable car so that she was independent and didn't have to rely on anyone at all, especially the local taxis. But with only a crude map as a guide, she'd still had to heavily rely on instinct – a good thing as it had turned out because here she was, standing exactly where she wanted to be standing. It was as if the temple, in calling to her, was also guiding her. She certainly thought so.

But what it was that made her realise she had found the site was not the recognition of it visually, but, rather, a recognition of its energy and the way she responded to its energy. The sensation of resonance was very powerfully familiar. So powerful was it as it coursed through her that she had stopped and looked around, wondering what it was that was generating the sensation within her. And that's when recognition had begun to dawn, and she realised she had stumbled onto it without knowing. There were certainly no signs, nothing to indicate a vast and ancient temple existed here, at the site. It was in the middle of nowhere, surrounded by a motley and sparse collection of buildings that, together, formed a small local village.

When realisation hit, finally, properly, she stood stock still, rooted to the spot in shock, and, despite the relentless heat, pulled the front of her light cardigan closed around her and folded her arms together in front of her – an unconscious gesture of self-protection. And then her eyes swept over the landscape, noting and absorbing every detail, from the golden sands that buried the site, to the few palms that dotted the landscape, and, of course, the sparse ruins of the vast and ancient temple. The more she absorbed, the more she recognised the temple itself despite the fact that most of it was either missing or buried in golden sand.

As she took it all in, she realised the cluster of buildings – a few huts and houses and rusty old tin sheds – that surrounded the site effectively hid it from those who did not know it was there. But the buildings, and, in fact, the village itself, only came up to a certain point. The village did not actually touch the site, or the temple itself, at all. And because the village had grown up around the site without touching it, the temple itself sat in the very epicentre, the very heart of the village, like the perfectly calm eye of a small but powerful storm. Turning a full circle as she registered the fact of the village not touching the site, she felt as if she was standing in a vortex of energy that the locals had either consciously or unconsciously recognised and stayed away from, out of respect or fear, or perhaps both. That's exactly why a small part of the temple could be seen above the golden sands, because the village that had grown up around it, surrounding it, had not been built over the top of it, thereby covering it and forever hiding it.

So, why, then, if the temple had never been properly hidden, had no one ever excavated it? Had the village unwittingly protected it, or had the temple protected itself? The village was not that old, or it didn't appear to be old, but she had no doubt that there had been some settlement here for hundreds, even thousands of years, so that this relatively-modern village was built on older ones. She wondered, then, if the villages that had existed here for aeons had been attracted to the temple's energy, the villagers settling around the temple for that reason, thereby forming at least part of its protection. Many of the temples of the ancient world, she knew, had been marked, deliberately, so that their power had been rendered dormant, the energy they harnessed and emitted effectively switched off so as to block their effect on humanity. But they of the darkness had missed this one. She smiled. How had that happened?

Keeping her arms folded close to her body, she stepped closer and closer still, walking up an incline, the impacted sands of this ancient desert forming a mound around the ruins of the ancient temple. The temple had been enormous once, and the footprint formed of the surrounding buildings of the village reflected that, even highlighted it, because they formed a perfect frame for it, as if the villagers had built their houses as close as possible to the site without actually touching it, like standing just beyond the reach of a wave. The great hall of the temple had been far longer than it was wide – an enormous rectangle – with massive, tall, thick pillars, their tops carved in the stone to form closed lotus flowers. The pillars had been as tall as a two-storey building once, their circumference, or their width, too big to wrap one's arms around so that one's fingers met on the other side. The pillars had framed the rectangular hall on every side, holding up the dark, beautiful, thick, carved-wood ceiling. There was no sign of the temple's ceiling now. It had disappeared long ago, probably way back in the mists of antiquity, long ago lost to the temple. And most of the pillars had also long gone.

At the top of the mound, she stood in front of the set of pillars on one of the longer sides of the rectangle, but the pillars on this side had all but gone. Only their stumps remained, just visible in the golden sand, some higher than others. And around the stumps were bits of stone, again, some bits bigger than others, where the pillars had broken apart and rolled away from the row. Some of the broken stone was large enough to sit on, some of it no bigger than a closed fist. She wondered what it was that had broken apart the pillars on this side of the hall. Was it just time itself? She thought not because the pillars on the other side of the hall were still largely intact, forming a long line, like a row of powerful soldiers standing at attention awaiting their orders. Courtesy of the row of pillars on the other side of the hall remaining intact, the temple's width and length could easily be perceived and identified. Most of the pillars on the other side were still there, although some were missing, and some were half missing. Of those that were still fully intact, only the top half could be seen, their lotus flowers still closed to the elements, and the other half was buried under the golden sands of Egypt's ancient desert.

Unfolding her arms, she moved, walking over the top of one set of pillars to stand in the centre of the great rectangular hall. And once inside the boundary formed of the pillars, her vision altered. Blinking, she turned in a circle, seeing not the sands of an ancient desert, but the beautiful, polished, coloured squares of granite – brown, orange, cream, yellow, pink – of the temple's floor; seeing not the broken and missing pillars of the ancient ruin, but the tall, strong, intact, polished-granite pillars of the temple as they had once been; and, raising her eyes, seeing not the bright-blue sky above her, but, rather, the dark, heavy, beautifully-carved wood of the temple's ceiling, its carved beams forming large squares that perfectly reflected, in size and shape, the large squares of the polished granite floor. The temple had been spectacularly beautiful in its day – a true work of art – an edifice to the skill of the ancient artisans who had built it.

Blinking again in the over-bright sunlight, the vision of her physical sight once again re-staked its claim. She took off her sunglasses and looked down one end of the rectangle, and then, turning her head, she looked up the other end, wondering which end had been the temple's entrance and which end had, effectively, been the temple's inner sanctum, its sacred heart – a raised polished-granite dais the size of a large room upon which sat a stone bowl full of pure water. Knowing instinctively which end was which, she walked towards the end of the rectangle she now faced, knowing it had been the temple's sacred heart. Again, the energy felt different at this end, and the closer she walked to it, the stronger was the feeling.

She reached a point where the energy was at its strongest. How she knew that, she could not have explained if asked. She just knew that beyond the point where she now stood, the strength of the energy would start to wane. She wondered if the bowl was below her feet, buried in the sands of time, hidden from modern eyes. Or had it, like the ceiling, long gone, taken long ago to be used for some other mundane purpose. She hoped not, but the only way to know for sure was to dig.

Is that what she was here for? To dig?

Wrapping her light cardigan around her again, she realised she'd not once stopped to consider her reasons for coming here. It was kind of absurd, really, now that she thought about it. Why had she come? Why had she travelled all this way? Had she come just to stand in an ancient ruin, even if that ruin had once been home for her, her refuge, her very point and purpose of existence?

"Why do you wear white?"

Not expecting anyone else to be on the site, and not having heard anyone approach, she turned quickly at the sound of the heavily-accented voice. An old man was standing a few metres behind her, his body bony and stooped with age, his hair and beard pure white and hanging in wisps over his shoulders and chest. He wore old, brown, leather sandals and an old, long, brown tunic that almost reached his feet. And in his hand, he held a long staff. Curiously, though, in this sun-drenched land of dark-skinned, brown-eyed people, his eyes were blue – eyes that resembled the bright-blue sky on a cloudless day – a strange colour even for those cultures where blue eyes predominated – and his skin was pale as moonlight.

"Such pure white they are, too, your clothes," he observed, looking her over even as she looked him over. Indeed, he was right. She wore long, tailored white-linen trousers, a long, light, white cardigan, white-leather shoes, and a white silk scarf wrapped around her head and shoulders, hiding her hair and partially hiding her features, although her green eyes were revealed by the removal of her sunglasses. Only the fitted, sleeveless, turquoise blouse she wore broke the monotony of the white of her outfit.

"How is it you speak English out here, in the middle of nowhere?" she asked him. "And you speak it well, too."

"I speak many languages," he replied.

"How did you know to speak English to me, then? I could have been French or German. Why did you not speak either of those languages to me?"

He shrugged. "Maybe you have the look of the English about you," he said.

She raised her eyebrows, smiling ever-so-slightly. "But I'm not English," she said. "I'm Australian."

"No," he said, surprising her, "you are not Australian. You were just born there."

Her smile deepened. She knew he was absolutely right. "My father told me exactly the same thing once," she said.

"Then he sees truth, does your father."

"Not as much as he should have, or could have."

They looked at each other as a small silence descended upon them. And in the silence, a torrent of questions flooded her mind. She inclined her head. "Where did you learn English? Do you live here? Have you always lived here?"

He chuckled appreciatively and then closed his eyes and raised his face to the sun. "Ah, I can feel the movement of your thoughts even from here." Still with his eyes closed, he raised a hand, fingers splayed, palm down, and moved it from side to side, the gesture graceful despite his obvious very great age. "How they ebb and flow, your thoughts, like moving water. Ever was it so." He dropped his hand and opened his eyes to look into hers again. "I will strike a deal with you, my Lady. You answer my question, and I will answer all of yours, including those you have been asking yourself, for that **is** the reason you are her, after all."

She took a moment to absorb that and to acknowledge the goosebumps, despite the heat, that covered her body from head to toe. Although not entirely conscious of it at this early stage, she knew exactly who he was. Her sluggish conscious human mind was struggling to accept the truth of him, but her deeper mind knew perfectly well who and what he was, and was very comfortable with the knowledge. Such is the inherent contradiction of human existence, the fractured nature of it.

"All right," she said, somewhat tentatively, "we have a deal. The truth is, I don't wear white, as a rule. It doesn't actually suit me. But when

I knew I was coming here, I bought myself a whole lot of new clothes because I knew I had to wear white here, in the temple. I just had to."

"Ah," he responded, nodding, "and do you know why?"

"Because I always did . . . I always did. I never wore anything else."

He grunted in reply this time and, bowing slightly, asked, "Would you be my guest and join me for a cup of fine Egyptian coffee?"

She didn't tell him she only drank decaffeinated coffee. Egyptian coffee was far too strong for her even though she did like its sweetness. "It would be my pleasure," she said instead.

He turned and walked the length of the rectangular hall, his staff tapping a staccato beat on the dirt floor as he walked. Following him, she noted that they left the temple in the proper way, through its entrance, despite the fact of them being able to just walk through the broken ruins. She followed him a short distance to a small house made of white stucco, or what looked like white stucco, with no windows, only large, square holes in the walls, and thick thatch on its roof. It looked, from the outside, as if it would be small and very dirty inside, but upon stepping through its front door, she was pleasantly surprised by its interior. Far from being dirty, the single room was clean, and it was light, airy and spacious, and smelt faintly of incense. The terracotta tiles comprising the floor were covered by a large, beautiful carpet, patterned in many colours, the most prominent of which was red. In the middle of the carpet was a small, round, low brass table, and bright, colourful, plump cushions surrounded the table, scattered haphazardly. In the corner of the room, a small pot-belly stove already heated a kettle of water, and a wooden bed, covered in colourful blankets, was pushed against one wall of the small room. Above it, a pile of old books and scrolls and parchments filled and covered a wooden shelf. She frowned when she saw the blankets scattered haphazardly on the bed, wondering why they were needed, even though the temperature was significantly cooler in the small room.

"It gets cold here at night in the winter," he told her, as if he'd read her mind perfectly, which he had. He had laid his staff on the carpet beside the brass table when he walked in, and now he had his back to her, making preparations on a small, square table beside the stove, obviously preparing their coffee. "Please," he said, turning slightly to look at her over his shoulder, "make yourself at home," and he indicated the cushions scattered around the table on the floor.

"Do you mind if I take off my scarf and cardigan?" she asked him.

"Of course not. I do not adhere to the religious and cultural traditions of the people who currently inhabit this land, dreadful as those traditions are. So go ahead. As I said, make yourself at home."

She did as she was bid, unwinding her scarf and sliding her cardigan off her shoulders, putting them both with the sunglasses on the end of the bed. Then, choosing a plump cushion on the other side of the table from where he'd laid his staff, she dropped onto it and sat cross-legged, making herself comfortable as instructed. She watched him prepare their coffees and then bring them, on a tray, to the table, obviously having no trouble carrying the weight of the tray and its contents. All of these little anomalies were adding up, forming a very interesting picture, so that she knew exactly what her first question would be. She waited while he put the tray on the floor beside the table, sat cross-legged on a cushion of his own, and then brought two beautiful, tiny cups and saucers from the tray to the table, followed by an equally beautiful coffee pot. Still she waited to ask her questions while he poured the hot coffee into the cups, his hands steady. And then she reached over to take her cup from him when he offered it.

He raised his cup to her. "Shalom, mika," he said.

She hesitated. "Two very different languages," she observed quietly. And then she, too, raised her cup. "Shalom," she echoed.

They both sipped the coffee. As she expected, it was strong but surprisingly sweet and spicy at the same time. Intrigued, she took another sip. The coffee was quite lovely, not hard to drink at all.

"Very nice," she complimented him and took another sip.

"Thank you."

"Are you incarnate?" she asked somewhat flatly, her tone utterly devoid of emotion.

He paused in the act of taking another sip of his coffee. "Good grief no," he said. "Why on earth would I want to do that? I doubt I could think of anything worse . . . well," he said, rethinking, "maybe I could think of a few worse things. But not many."

She smiled briefly, quickly and genuinely at his response, but, then, she frowned. "You've been here all this time?" she asked him quietly.

He raised his eyebrows at her. "All this time? You are projecting your sense of time onto me, I think. I am not subject to the constraints of linear time as you humans are. But, yes, I have been here for the duration of the temple's existence. I am its Guardian, after all, so where else am I to be?"

"Do the locals know you are here?"

"Of course." He put down his cup and spread his hands out beside him. "They built this house for me, and they leave me offerings at my front door. Not that I eat. I've no need of food, but I do love to partake of the coffee, and I quite like having the blankets. I appear to them, the villagers, like a wraith, a glimpse seen here and there as if I am a mirage shimmering in the bright sunlight. Most of them have seen me, so they know what I look like. And the wisest of them know I am the temple's Guardian." He smiled, and his smile twinkled in his eyes. "They cannot handle any more than a glimpse. It frightens them. They believe their offerings placate me, which, of course, is true, and they know their assistance in the protection of the temple also placates me. They believe if they look after me, I will look after them, which is also true, to a certain extent."

She listened to his answer with interest. So, she had been right in thinking the villagers had protected the temple.

"Why can I see you, then, as if you are really, fully here?"

"Because I **am** really, fully here, and because you can handle the truth of me. You alone, of all souls, know the truth of me."

Tears pooled in her eyes and she lowered her little coffee cup to its saucer. "I remember you," she told him. "I've been trying to work out how the memory of you fits into the chronology of my other memories . . ."

"Then do not try to work out the chronology of your memories. You are binding yourself up in a false mindset where time is concerned. If it helps, think of all those lives as happening at once after you fell, culminating in this life."

"After I fell? So the life I lived here was after I fell, not before?"

"Of course. As you will see. You will recognise the same dynamics in the life you lived here, those same dynamics you have come to know well, I think."

She nodded. "What did I call you so I may call you the same now?"

His eyes twinkled with a smile. "You called me Elijah. I do not know what you are called in this life, mika, and I do not want to know. I only know you as Elyra because that was your true name when you lived here. But I only ever called you mika – dear one or dearest in the ancient language of Khem. So I will continue to call you that, if you do not mind."

"Elyra," she repeated. "That was my true name in that life? I like it. No, I do not mind. You may call me whatever makes you most comfortable, and I will call you Elijah. Our names hold the 'El' that refers to Light," she observed.

"Indeed. Of course. For good reason, as you no doubt remember."

She shook her head. "With the exception of the temple itself, which I see very clearly, my memories of that life are not clear . . ."

"Ah," he said knowingly. "Well, I suspected as much. Why else would you be here now?"

"To remember? Is that why I'm here?" She laughed, and he could not help but respond with a smile. Ever was it so. Her laugh powerfully held her Light, and it was impossible for one such as he not to respond to it. "I was right, then," she said. "I am here to dig, just not in the ancient sands." Sobering, she continued, "Truth be told, I just obeyed my intuition on this. I came half way around the world to a country where women really should not be alone, to find an ancient temple I wasn't sure still existed at all and certainly didn't know the location of. It is as if it called to me, the temple. It called and I came, just as soon as I possibly could. As its Guardian, you must know why."

"Of course I know why. But I know, not because of my connection to the temple, but because of my connection to you. And I would say it is not so much the temple that has called to you, but, rather, you who has called to the temple. You require its help, mika. Do you know why you would require the temple's help at this time in your life?"

She nodded once, definitively. "I need to know who I was . . . who I am."

"Yes, Lady of Light, you need to know, once again, who you really are, and you need to reclaim your full heritage. You need to step, once again, into your own powerful, higher-dimensional Light. It is time, and you are ready. But first, you need to remove the shadows within you that smother and contain your Light. You need to set your Light free.

"Now," he said, his eyes twinkling at her, "may I suggest you finish your coffee. It will facilitate your visions. You will find it will help to take you back there, to that life you lived here so long ago . . . if we must speak the language of linear time. First, we will look at the events that ended your life – the story of that particular life you lived – because there is pain there and we both, you and I, need to deal with that. If we do not resolve it, it will interfere with what we must now do together, and we cannot allow that. Then, once we have revisited the story of that life, we will focus on what you were and what you were able to do. Is this all right with you, mika?"

She nodded as she picked up her coffee cup. "Yes, that is perfectly all right with me. You will guide me, then?"

"My guidance is assured. I will not leave you even for a moment. I will be right beside you, so hold the knowledge of that close, and be not afraid, mika, my dearest."

She smiled her gratitude as she replaced her cup on its saucer, having drained its contents, but already, her vision was shifting and changing, and her eyes were refocussing to make the adjustment to what she was seeing.

He wasn't at all surprised by how quickly she was able to shift her focus and alter her sight. He knew what she was capable of, even if she didn't. In truth, she could have done this by herself, but there was a reason she had come to seek his assistance to go back there, and he was inordinately grateful because, in truth, it was wonderful to see her again and to be in her company – his version of heaven. Although bound not by time, he had still awaited her return, patiently protecting and guarding the temple, because he had known she **would** return. Her return was written in the very stars themselves. In a very real sense, she was as bound to the temple as he was, although not, of course, in quite the same way. That is why she had, actually, had no trouble finding it, despite having to come half way around the world to do so.

He, too, allowed his vision to shift and alter so that he joined his vision with hers. He wasn't looking forward to revisiting the trauma and grief of the events in that past lifetime, but he **was** looking forward to seeing her as she could be, her powerful Light filling the temple once again.

Oh, yes, he was very much looking forward to that . . . .

~

A Cloak of Raven Feathers

She connected her vision to that life she lived in the past at a point just after dawn so that the temple, while not full of the darkness of night, was also not yet full of people. As such, the atmosphere was peaceful and calm, the temple was full of silence, and the energy that filled it was pure. She stood close to the stone bowl of water on the dais, resting her fingertips on its edge, and Elijah stood opposite her, minus his staff. She was dressed in her white-linen trousers and turquoise blouse, and he wore his long, brown tunic and old, leather sandals, although the tunic was no longer old, at least in the way it looked. He was no longer stooped with age, and bony. Instead, he stood straight and tall, taller than she was, and his pure-white hair and beard were thick and full, his hair weaved into a plait down his back, and his beard long, reaching his chest.

They both exchanged smiles.

"You look very handsome," she complimented him.

"Why, thank you, mika."

"So this is how it is to be, then?" she asked him, referring to the fact of them being there as observers.

"Yes, mika, this is how it is to be, and this is how it must be, as you will come to understand. You must see what happened beyond your death, so for this memory, we will look on as not-quite-dispassionate observers. Remember, I will be by your side every moment. You have but to reach for me should you need to do so."

She nodded, once, definitively, as was her way. "I will remember. No one can see us, then?"

"No one can see us, not even those sensitive enough to perceive what is beyond the physical sense of sight. But you . . . or, rather, she, Elyra, will sense you, no doubt. You and she are, after all, very sensitive, not to mention attuned to the energies in this place, so she will sense something added, something altered. We shall see how that affects her."

"You don't remember?"

"I did not observe her with you here, so I am ignorant as to how she responded to your presence. I confess I am looking forward to observing her reaction to you."

Again, she nodded, slightly, and then she looked around her, at the temple's beautiful interior. "Ye gods, Eli, but it is breathtakingly beautiful, is it not?"

"It is indeed breathtaking. Go, mika, you have time. Wander around and take it all in. Enjoy being wrapped and immersed in its energy once again. I will await you here."

She did as she was bid, her fingers sliding off the stone bowl as she turned towards the dais' stepped entrance. She walked slowly down the few steps onto the temple's floor, and then wandered. She didn't know or care where she wandered. She just walked wherever her vision took her next as she drank in and absorbed every detail of the temple's very great beauty.

At first, as her eyes raked the heavy, ornate, carved ceiling, she turned in circles, craning her neck backwards, and sometimes walked backwards, completely unaware that she did so. The ceiling's heavy beams formed large squares of carved wood that perfectly reflected the large, polished-granite squares of the floor, and there was such exquisite detail in the wood carving, mostly of flowers, ferns, palms and creeping vines, but, occasionally, a beetle or a butterfly, a tiny bird, a serpent or a spider was carved into the wooden foliage. After a while, she lowered her vision, looking down at the polished-granite floor. Each large square of granite was a different colour – brown, orange, pink, golden yellow, cream – some with flecks of different colours in them, some pure in colour. The squares were outlined, separated and framed by a fine line of gold, but the floor itself, when one cast one's gaze over it as a whole, was seamless. Raising her vision again, she wandered over to the pillars on one side of the rectangular hall, reaching out to touch the polished pink granite of one of the pillars with affectionate fingers, looking up at the closed lotus flower at its top.

Courtesy of its size, its thick wall of pillars, and its dark wood ceiling, the temple's interior was dark. But beyond the pillars, there was bright sunlight, so that the sun's light lit the interior more and more powerfully as the sun rose to its zenith, although at this time of the day, just after dawn, the temple was yet to be lit by the power of the sun's light.

And then, the first of the people began to flow through the line of pillars at the temple's entrance. She saw them as soon as they started to come and so she knew it was time to take her place beside Elijah on the dais once again, there to watch her own unfolding story.

She and Elijah stood together on one side of the dais and watched the activity in the temple as the sun moved higher in the sky, its light changing the ambience in the temple's interior, and then as it reached its zenith and began to move lower in the sky. Throughout the entire day, they watched, every now and then speaking, either making some comment on what they were seeing or she asking him a question and he responding. Most of the time, though, they stood in silence and just watched.

When the first of the people had begun to flow through the entrance, they had watched Elyra walk through the line of pillars near the dais and then step up onto it.

Elyra. That was her name in this life.

She whom Elijah called mika looked at Elyra closely when she first appeared, knowing in an instant who she was. Initially, she couldn't help but observe and note both the differences and the similarities in their appearance. Whereas she had long, dark-brown, curly hair and green eyes, Elyra, the person she had been in the lifetime she was observing, had long, straighter hair that was so dark it was almost black, and her eyes were grey. Both were tall and slim, their limbs long, and so, had they stood right next to each other, they would have been exactly the same height, their eyes on exactly the same level, and they were, very possibly, the same weight. If anything, Elyra was slightly slimmer.

"You are always tall in your incarnations, mika," Elijah said, knowing her thoughts. "It is essential for you to be tall because you **are** tall, and you could not allow yourself to be reduced."

She who watched nodded silently, understanding, knowing the truth of that, without taking her eyes from Elyra. It was strange to be watching herself so clearly, so closely, in another body, another incarnation. Always, until now, she processed her memories of past lives by placing herself in them, by looking out at the landscape she was in through her own eyes. This time was different. This time, she retained the essence and the knowledge of who she was in her current life whilst watching herself in a previous incarnation. This time, she was outside of herself, and the sensation took some getting used to.

For she who watched, it was, at first, hard to make an assessment of Elyra's beauty objectively, or with a disconnected perspective. But the more she watched, the more she thought Elyra was, indeed, beautiful. Elyra moved with an innate grace that heightened her physical beauty, and, of course, the clothes and adornments she wore also heightened her beauty. But she was beautiful, and would have been so even without the adornments of the priesthood.

"Of course she's beautiful," Elijah commented, "just as you are. She, like you, holds her beauty within her, and she, like you, holds her power in her beauty. So it radiates out of the centre of her, as it does for you. You are absolutely no different in that sense."

His words made her focus on Elyra anew, with a slightly altered perspective. As the temple's oracle, Elyra wore pure-white clothes – a sleeveless white gown, the bodice of which hugged her body to the top of her waist from where it fell in flowing folds to the floor. The material of the gown was soft and fine so that when she walked, the skirt billowed out around and behind her, and it was so long she had to hold it clear when she ascended the steps onto the dais. Over the gown, she wore a sleeveless, floor-length coat, if it could be called that, of white material that was so fine it looked as if it had been spun out of spider's web and did nothing at all to hide the gown underneath it. It, too, billowed out behind her when she walked. At the top of the coat, a wide collar of gold, lapis lazuli, turquoise and red stones kept the coat in place, and around both her wrists, she wore matching wide bands of gold and stone. The ornamentation, accoutrements of a high priestess, would have been heavy, such was the amount of gold and stone in them, but Elyra wore them as if they weighed nothing at all. On her feet she wore simple leather sandals, and her dark hair had been woven into small but elaborate braids that swung down her back, almost reaching her lower back. Each braid was bound at its end with threads of gold.

"Do they not cut their hair?" she whispered to Elijah when she saw other priestesses, even though there was no need to whisper. She whispered not so as not to be heard but, rather, in deference to her surroundings. The whole scene was just so powerfully . . . spiritual. She felt a stirring within in response. She missed and mourned places like this – places in which she truly belonged – places in which she made perfect sense.

"No, mika," Elijah said, answering her question, not bothering to whisper himself. "The hair is symbolic of one's spiritual essence, one's spiritual strength, and, in the case of those powerful enough, like Elyra, the hair holds one's own psychic energy."

"Oh. That must be why I've stopped cutting my own hair," she observed, sounding somewhat puzzled.

"No doubt."

Throughout the passing day, she watched Elyra with the people who came seeking spiritual guidance and help. Some of the people brought offerings with them, items of cloth, perfume, oil, food, jewellery and coin, and some of the people brought nothing with them at all. The offerings were accepted graciously, the priests and priestesses of the temple carrying them away as soon as they were offered, to some place beyond the boundary of the pillars. Elyra never touched the offerings, and regardless of whether or not the people brought offerings, she gave them all the same compassionate attention. Throughout the day, a constant stream of people came, seeking whatever it was they sought from the oracle, and even though the temple was never empty, it was, at times, more crowded than at other times. Sometimes, with some people, Elyra smiled and said but a few words. Sometimes, she offered them her hand, touching them on the face or the arm, smiling at them as she spoke at length to them. Sometimes, she engaged in a dialogue with them, obviously asking them questions and awaiting their response, and sometimes, although much less often, she embraced them.

A couple of times, she who watched wondered and would've asked Elijah the questions that were swimming through her conscious awareness, but Elijah always shook his head, and at one point, he said,

"We will address the specifics of what she is when we talk about what we see in this vision, mika. For now, you must bear witness to her story, for there is much to discuss when the vision has run its course."

She accepted that, nodding, but she still asked him one very important question. "This is the closest I have come to my true Self in my incarnations, isn't it? Of all the lives I have lived since I fell, this is the closest I've been to my truth, I mean."

"Yes, mika, 'tis so," he answered gently.

And so, she continued to watch. Elyra never took a break, not a real break. Once or twice, she sat on the stone bench that almost completely framed the dais, resting her feet and her legs. But she didn't sit for long. Twice, a priestess brought her a plate of dried and fresh fruit, olives, bread and dipping oil, and a goblet of water, but other than these small respites, she worked with the people who came seeking her assistance.

Every now and then, fairly regularly, in fact, often between people but sometimes with people, she glanced over her shoulder in the direction of the two who watched her, looking their way with slightly narrowed eyes but not focussing on them.

"I told you she would sense us," Elijah said, when she'd glanced their way for the dozenth time. "She feels the pull of you, mika, the resonance, but she does not recognise her energy in yours. Do you know why?"

She who watched nodded slowly. "Everything I have experienced from her life to mine has altered my energy, my essence, dramatically, powerfully. I almost certainly carry within me more shadow dynamics than she did. The effect is like an entirely different energetic signature vibration, a different energetic imprint."

"That is so, mika, although your energetic vibration is not entirely different from hers, just a little bit different, certainly different enough so that she does not know who you are."

At one point, when Elyra sat to eat the second plate of food brought to her, she did not take her eyes off the place where the two stood watching her. She held the plate in her lap but moved her eyes, looking around them and at them and above them, and then, when she had finished the food, she handed the plate back to a priestess and stood for a moment facing the two. She spoke, softly, gently, in a language she who watched did not understand. But the words resonated within so that she knew exactly what Elyra had said.

"I can see you. I do not know why you are here, but I can see you."

She who watched swallowed nervously. There was power in this woman she was looking at, a power that felt alien to her. The power radiated from her, and it changed the way she appeared. She who was watching frowned, but Elijah put his hand on her arm, calming her, warning her, and so she neither moved nor responded to Elyra's words, and Elyra dropped her eyes and went back to the people who awaited her.

"You must not make contact with yourself, mika. We cannot, must not interfere," he said quietly. "We are here only to observe. That is very important."

She instinctively sensed the truth of that. What must be in the life she was watching had to be, and must not be changed or altered even slightly. To do so would change not just this life she was watching, but everything beyond it, too, including her own life. And even though she was powerful in both lives, such change could potentially be very dangerous . . . very dangerous indeed.

Pain.

Elijah had said there was pain in this life she was watching. She all but snorted cynically as the thought occurred to her. How typical of her lives, she thought, that this one, too, was tragic and traumatic. Had she ever lived a normal, happy life? Perhaps so, which was exactly the reason she did not remember it. She did not need to remember such a life.

But her thoughts generated a question that she could not hold to herself.

"Why does she not sense what is ahead?" she asked Elijah. "If there is pain ahead for her, why does she not sense it?"

"She is not that kind of oracle, mika."

"What kind of oracle is she, then?"

"She is not a future oracle. Rather, she sees the source, the cause, of the **present**. In that sense, she sees the past, not the future, as do you, mika. Have you not noticed that about yourself? You see the past, well into the past, actually, rather than the future. But you Work with the present. That is the way you read the cards, is it not? You and Elyra both possess an innate ability to set people's feet upon the path of their highest potential. In that sense, the oracle energy you both radiate is that of healing and guidance and counsel. As I said, mika, we will look more closely at what she is and at what she does later, when we leave the vision. Be patient, beautiful Lady."

She nodded her acquiescence.

As the sun moved lower in the sky, its ability to light the temple also waned, weakened. Slowly, as afternoon morphed into the onset of dusk, the temple was plunged into darkness. Still, the people came, and so the priests and priestesses of the temple brought in torches on tall stands to light the dais and the area immediately around it, and to light the space between each pillar from the entrance to the temple's sacred heart. The priests and priestesses moved around the torches like silent wraiths, tending them to ensure they continued to give off light. The light from the torches was very effective, but a different light was cast through the temple's interior space and over its floor. The floor changed colour as a result, and it became a canvass of interplaying light and shadow. Distracted, she who was watching focussed for a long time on the altered beauty of the temple's interior, especially its floor, and so she took a while to realise the steady flow of people coming through the temple's entrance had slowed to a trickle. And then, even as she watched, the flow of people ceased altogether.

She started to turn towards Elijah to make a comment about the effect of the torches, but a movement, a different movement at the temple's entrance caught her attention. Comment forgotten, she turned back quickly to focus on the movement that had caught her eye. Men, soldiers, perhaps a dozen or so of them walked through the pillars at the entrance and then formed a line across the temple as they walked towards the dais. Watching them approach, she was sure they weren't conscious of forming a line, but it was intimidating nonetheless. Force of habit, she thought. They were dressed identically, their long, brown cloaks billowing out behind them as they walked, and their booted feet sounding like the percussion section of an orchestra, pounding out a rhythmical, near-identical beat as they walked up the great hall, towards the dais.

Elyra had seen them at exactly the same time, and so, the two women watched the men approach, the same statue-like stillness holding them in place, the same silence wrapping around them both like an invisible cloak. In that one elongated moment, as they watched the soldiers approach, they were both completely connected. They were as one, but neither knew it courtesy of their consumed focus, their eyes never leaving the line of men approaching the dais.

Unconsciously, she who watched moved to stand near Elyra at the front of the dais so she could better see the soldiers, and, without realising it, as a gesture of solidarity and protection. And why not? After spending a day watching Elyra, she had come to like her . . . . a lot. Later, with time to contemplate the images of the vision, she would connect with the realisation that she liked herself in this other incarnation, and the knowledge would hearten her, even generate a kind of joy within her. Now, though, she was unaware of the undercurrents and the underlying dynamics within and between her and Elyra, and so she stood beside her other incarnation in a state of unawareness. In response, Elyra, feeling the presence beside her, glanced sideways, briefly, swiftly, and she spoke softly in that same language.

Again, the words resonated within, so that she who watched knew what Elyra said.

"Be calm. I know of these men. They mean me no harm. They are the king's personal guard. They are men of honour, hand picked for that reason."

But there is danger here, she wanted to say in response. Only the soft touch of a hand on her arm silenced her.

Elijah had moved with her when she stood beside her own incarnation, and she could feel his vigilance, his heightened tension, and the innate warning he held within him, communicated through his touch. For the entire day, he had been relaxed beside her, enjoying himself immensely. But now, both relaxation and enjoyment had vanished as quickly as if with a snap of a pair of fingers. Partly in response to what she sensed in him and partly in response to what she was seeing visually, her heartbeat quickened and, with it, so, too, did her breathing, despite Elyra's reassurance. Her mouth was dry and her hands clenched involuntarily at her sides, her nails digging into her palms, for she, and she alone, was at the mercy of the fear dynamic within her. Elyra was not. She who watched sensed the danger . . .

indeed, she **saw** the danger, but Elyra did not. It was, in fact, one of the very reasons Elyra could not sense who she really was. It was, in fact, one of those very same shadow dynamics that caused the energy within them both to be slightly, subtly different.

Fear.

Fear pounding through her veins like blood. Fear filling her lungs like breath, increasing her heartbeat. Fear pulsing through her muscles, clenching and tensing them. Fear flooding her body, causing her pain. Powerful fear. And not just fear of one single thing. There were many things to fear in this unfolding story. She didn't need to process the images in this vision to know that here was the source of some powerful shadow dynamics within her. She recognised them.

Again unconsciously, she uncurled her fingers and laid her hand over Elijah's. In response, he turned his hand over and held hers tightly, his fingers wrapping around hers.

"And so it begins," he said softly, deliberately warning her. "It would be prudent, from now on, if you hold my hand, mika. I will guide you through this. I will take you where you need to be. Do not let go."

She nodded, not once, as was her way, but many times, quickly.

When the line of soldiers reached the dais, they stopped, and only one, the one in the very middle of the line, stepped forward. He, like the others, wore a long, brown cloak over thick leather armour, leather wrist bands, dark-leather trousers, and thick boots. A long sword was strapped to his hip, and the handle of a knife protruded from the top of one boot. These men did not follow the trends of the king's court where long hair, even for men, was the fashion of the day. Their hair was cut short and, rather than being clean shaven as per current fashion, their beards were neatly trimmed but thick and full. His hair was as dark as Elyra's, almost black. He was tall, and he was powerfully muscular courtesy of years of balancing in and controlling chariots, and wielding swords, bows, and other weapons. He stepped forward, closer to the dais, and kneeled on one knee, the scabbard of the sword scraping the granite as he went down. He placed his hands flat on the floor on either side of him, and he bowed his head.

"My Lady," he said in that same language Elyra spoke.

Again, she who watched could not understand the language, but the words were just there, inside her conscious mind so that she knew exactly what they were saying. Was it memory that made it so? She couldn't tell.

"I thank you for your homage," Elyra said to him, looking down at him from the edge of the dais, "but I am not a god. You need not kneel before me."

Without standing, he raised his eyes and looked up at Elyra. His eyes were dark, but dark though they were, his eyes were not cold, and nor did they hide his expression. "Are you not?" he replied, his tone conveying the fact that he was making a point rather than asking a question.

The impact of the eye to eye contact combined with his words was powerful, and both women, both incarnations, felt it. It rocked them both on their feet. Elyra remained outwardly calm, but she who stood next to her knew she was not so calm within. The only outward sign she gave of any inner disturbance was a tiny movement of her hands so that she lightly touched and held the fine material of the coat she wore over her gown, holding it between her fingers. She who watched noticed the small movement because she, too, did a similar thing when pushed out of or beyond her zone of comfort.

Both women, as connected as they were, knew that Elyra had never, never responded to another soul the way she was now responding to this one. Although she saw uniqueness in each soul she interacted with, each with his or her own beauty – a beauty she tended to discover and uncover the more she delved and probed – and each with his or her own unique foibles, people still tended, at the same time, to be the same to her, and, ultimately, she responded to each soul accordingly. Unique they may be, those souls who came seeking her counsel and guidance, but they were not powerful. Not so this soul now kneeling before her. There was a beauty and a power in this soul that she had never encountered before – a beauty and a power that matched hers, had she but known it. This soul's beauty was powerfully, powerfully attractive. And so, for the first time in her life, Elyra responded to the soul kneeling before her not as a high priestess but as a woman.

"What can I do for you?" Elyra asked him quietly.

He stood, unconsciously resting a hand on the hilt of the sword at his hip.

"My name is Andular," he said. "I am cousin to the king, his brother and his friend, his loyal servant. I command his personal guard and his army. I have come to seek your aid, my Lady," he said. "The king is ill. The king's own physicians have been unable to help him, and so we have sought the help of soothsayers, wise men and women, and healers, all to no avail. I would not ask this of you unless absolutely necessary, but I would ask that you come with us to see the king. We need your help."

Both women could see and sense the truth of his words. He was, indeed, the king's cousin, the son of the old king's sister, and he was, indeed, the king's loyal and faithful servant, with no designs on the throne for himself. The two – the king and this cousin – had grown up together, and they had always been inseparable, like brothers. This man, they could see, served the king with every breath he breathed, and with his own very life. The command of the king's personal guard and the army was reward for that same loyal and faithful service. Indeed, there was none the king trusted as he trusted this man who stood before them. As such, only one as loyal as he could be implicitly trusted with such a command.

"What makes you think I may succeed where those others have failed?" Elyra asked him.

He hesitated. "I had a dream," he said simply.

"A dream?"

"The gods told me in the dream that you were the one to relieve the king of the burden of this illness, this madness that has taken hold of him."

"Madness?"

"Yes, my Lady, madness."

Both women suddenly had a sense of what they might be dealing with, and, as such, both women knew why the gods had told him Elyra could and would be the one to help the king with the curse that had befallen him.

"You wish me to leave the temple?" Elyra asked him. "You cannot bring the king here?"

"Nay, my Lady, 'twould not be wise to bring the king here. It would be difficult for us to bring him here, and I would not want the people to see him in such a state. I do not want anyone to witness the king's affliction if they do not need to. I am afraid it is you who must come to him."

As if materialised out of the air itself, Elijah was suddenly standing on the other side of Elyra. She who watched turned her head slightly to make sure he was, also, still standing beside her even though she could still feel his touch. When she turned, they exchanged a knowing glance.

"No wonder you have awaited me," she said. "You knew I would come back, one day, because you saw me."

He nodded, a small smile curving his mouth. "Indeed," he said simply.

The Elijah of the past, distinguishable only by the colour of his long tunic – the one beside her wore brown whereas the one of the past wore pure white – looked down at the man petitioning the temple for help.

"'Tis not wise for the oracle to leave the safety and sanctity of the temple," he said, sounding like the voice of authority, his words ringing with disapproval. "And yet you come here to petition for that which would see her taken from her place of sanctity and safety. You are an initiate, are you not, warrior? So you are aware that the darkness scrabbles for a foothold, the means of spreading its poison over this land, this city and its people. The oracle prevents this, and the darkness likes not the threat of her. It awaits only an opportunity like this to see her snuffed out as if she was but a flame on a candle."

Andular stood his ground as he looked at the temple's Guardian. "The darkness does indeed seek a foothold over our land and our people. But if we cannot heal the king of the madness that has taken hold of him, then I fear the darkness will have found a very effective foothold, despite the presence of the oracle."

He shifted his eyes from Elijah to Elyra.

"I and my men will protect you, my Lady. You will be under my personal protection whilst ever you are not in the temple. You have my solemn word on that."

In response, Elyra raised her eyes, breathing deeply as she looked out, over his head, at the interior of the temple. She who watched felt Elyra's absolute reluctance to leave the sanctuary of the temple, but still, she watched Elyra turn towards the Elijah who stood beside her.

"I must do this," she said softly. "He is right. If the darkness controls the king, it controls us all."

Elijah bowed low to her as if letting her know he would surrender to her judgement, and when he straightened, he held in his hands something long and as black as midnight, as black as pitch. She who watched stared at it, trying to work out what it was. It was laid across his arms, and it was thick, but it looked like a pile of black feathers. He moved it, handling it with great care, holding it lengthwise and gently shaking it out. At last, she realised what it was. A cloak of black feathers. A cloak of raven feathers.

He moved again to drape it over Elyra's shoulders. "If you must do this, mika, then this will protect you," he said as he turned her so he could do up the tie. "If you are to leave the temple," he said quietly, "the cloak will protect you. It will contain your Light and so it will shield you from their sight. It will hide you."

The impact of his words generated such a powerful realisation within her that it rocked her – she who watched – on her feet as if she had been punched and was reeling backwards. Her already-pounding heart increased its beat, feeling uncomfortable in her chest, and she suddenly felt slightly queasy.

"Oh shit!" she said, the words breathy but loud nonetheless. "Oh god! No."

Closing her eyes tightly, as if bracing against pain, she bowed her head, and in response, Elijah's fingers tightened around hers.

"I know, mika, I know," he said quietly. "We will address the issue of the cloak later, when we have time to talk, I promise you. For now, you must remain connected to Elyra's story. You must see what happens next."

Again, as she had before, she nodded and forced herself to open her eyes and look up.

When the cloak sat comfortably on Elyra's shoulders, the Elijah of the past, the one in white, pulled the hood over her head, hiding her features, and he pulled the cloak closed in front of her. She was completely covered by the cloak. To the one who watched, Elyra had become a mass of ravens' feathers, dark, dark, dark . . . . She could not take her eyes from the cloak. It was the strangest thing she'd ever seen – ugly and oh-so-beautiful at exactly the same time. But the workmanship was exquisite.

She watched as Elyra descended the stairs to join the captain of the king's guard. And then she watched as the two, with their escort, walked the length of the great hall, back to the entrance. The cloak was long so that it trailed Elyra as she walked, the swishing noise it made joining the beat of the soldiers' footfall beside her.

The Elijah in white also watched Elyra leave the temple, and then he turned towards the two who watched and bowed his head at them both. When he straightened, he looked at her and smiled that same twinkling smile she knew so well.

"You'd best leave here as well, methinks. There is much for you to witness, mika," he said.

"Yes, there is," the Elijah in brown said beside her. "Come, mika, I know where they are going. I will take you there."

As if in the blink of an eye, they were both standing just inside and beside the door in a different place, a room with white walls, its floor covered in similar terracotta tiles to those in Elijah's small house. She looked around, getting her bearings, absorbing the detail of her new surroundings. The room was not small. On the contrary, it was enormous, and it was full of people. So large was it that it comprised a few different sections, each section with its own purpose and function, the purpose fulfilled and evidenced by the furniture that filled the space. In one section, there was a large table surrounded by straight-backed chairs. In another section, in the very centre of the room, a large, beautiful carpet covered the tiles, and on every side of the carpet lounge chairs faced each other with a low table between them. On the white wall as you walked in, half a dozen large paintings hung in a line, effectively turning the wall into a gallery. The paintings were bright and beautiful, a colourful contrast to the white wall behind them. A balcony ran the length of the wall opposite the room's entrance, although there was only one entrance to it from the room – a double, glass door, currently open, allowing in the cool night air, which was as well because the room was stifling, overcrowded with people as it was. Over in the far corner of the room, on a raised dais of darker, brown tiles, was a large, wooden, canopied bed covered in fine white linens. Soft, white curtains, closed over the few windows in the room, billowed high into the room, caught as they were on the evening breeze.

Absorbing the details of the room as she was, she knew they were in someone's bedroom, someone's suite, actually, because the room was far too impressive, too sumptuous, just to be called a bedroom. And it wasn't hard to guess whose suite it might be.

As if in direct confirmation of her thoughts, the double wooden doors of the room's entrance opened beside her, and the captain, his men and Elyra walked in. Elyra, still covered completely by the cloak of raven feathers, hesitated when she walked through the door, taking in the scene at a glance. She who watched could feel Elyra's disapproval – an echo of her own – but where she had only the power to observe, Elyra had the power to alter the dynamics in the room. And so she did, immediately.

"You will need to clear the room," Elyra said to Andular.

He nodded, and within but a handful of moments had accomplished exactly what she asked. She stood near the paintings, looking up at them, deliberately turning her back on the people as they shuffled out through the open doors of the room's entrance, many frowning their reluctance to leave. She could feel their reluctance, and, tight-lipped with disgust, she knew it was born not out of concern for the king but, rather, out of a disappointment to be missing the show that was bound to follow, as if it was their right to watch.

When the room was both clearer and quieter, she turned away from the paintings towards the middle of the room, surprised when she saw a handful of men still remained. Even without knowing them personally, she could sense the importance they placed upon themselves. She knew not their role or function at court, and nor did she care. It made no difference to her. They were not welcome to witness what was to come.

"All of them," she said clearly, definitely. "Everyone is to leave except you, Andular. I will need your help."

Andular repeated her command to those who remained, and then he gave the order to his own men to guard the door and make sure no one entered without his express permission. Looking offended and affronted, those same handful of men who had remained reluctantly left the room with Andular's men.

The room was, now, not just clear of people, it was clearer and cleaner and calmer in terms of its energy, and it was quieter. She who was watching unconsciously took a deep breath, feeling the effect for herself of the clearer, quieter room. And, with the room clear, at last, she could see the king, the only other person in the room, as could Elyra. Both women, both incarnations, focussed on him exclusively, and both frowned in concern at what they saw. Elyra moved further into the centre of the room, lifting her hands to remove the hood of the cloak so she could see the king more clearly.

He looked like Andular. So much alike were they physically that they really did look like brothers. Like Andular, the king was tall and slim, not as muscular, and his hair was dark, almost black. Unlike Andular, the king wore his hair longer in accordance with the fashion of his own court, and, also unlike Andular, his chin was clean shaven as per current custom. Both had dark eyes to match their dark hair. But there the similarities stopped. The king was pacing, restless and agitated, and he was completely unaware of anyone else in the room. Back and forth he paced, sometimes pacing from one side of the room to the other, sometimes pacing but a handful of steps before turning back to pace the other way. His head was inclined slightly, as if he was listening to something no one else could hear, and he was muttering, as if speaking to someone no one else could see. And all the while he paced, he frantically worked the tips of his fingers together, as if he was untangling a very tangled, imaginary ball of yarn. It was the action of extreme agitation, stress and distress. And, of course, complete loss of sanity.

All four people left in the room, the two who were there in reality and the two who were merely observing through vision, watched the king for a long drawn-out moment, none of them moving.

"Ye gods," Elijah said softly, "he is resisting it. He is fighting it, but at what cost? 'Tis his resistance that is causing this madness. Andular came for help just in time, it would seem. Any longer and the king may have been lost forever."

She turned to him in surprise. "Of course," she said. "You did not see the king like this originally because you did not accompany her. Only she came to attend to the king."

"Just so. She told me, though. Still, 'tis worse than I thought. It has a very great hold on him, but at least it is not controlling him. He is not allowing it."

She knew to what he was referring, and he was not referring to the madness itself. When the king turned to retrace his steps, she who watched could see, clearly, the darkest of shadows behind him – a shadow that stood behind him, tainting the air behind him, rather than lying, as it should have been, or as a normal shadow would, across the floor. It was taller than he was and it obviously had a very strong hold on the king. It was not letting go any time soon. No wonder all those others had not had any success healing the king. She thought she could make out a tall cloaked figure in the shadow, a cloaked figure standing behind the king, but she could only see it when she didn't focus on it directly. She kept glimpsing it out of the corner of her eye . . . as did Elyra.

"How did this happen?" Elyra asked Andular without taking her eyes from the king. Frowning her concern, she followed him with her eyes as he paced back and forth. Glancing at Andular as he stood right beside her, she added, "This does not happen for no reason. Someone, or something, has exposed him to an unimaginable darkness . . ."

"That would be his mother," Andular said, sounding bitter. "She is a practitioner of the dark arts, although no one knew that when the king was a child. She took him with her, when he was young, to attend rites and rituals, and she made him swear on his life not to tell anyone."

Elyra took her eyes off the king and turned to look at Andular. "What kind of rites and rituals?"

"The kind that gave him nightmares, for years. The gods alone know what he witnessed. He would never speak of it to me. And we never had secrets from each other. He told me he would not speak of it to me for my sake, not for his."

Elyra made a clicking noise with her tongue, an expression of sympathy and extreme displeasure. "How could a mother expose her own child to forces of darkness like that? Did the old king know?"

"No, he had no idea. It was only through the concern and the courage and the suspicion of the king's old nursemaid that it all came out. She went to the king herself and told him of her concerns, and the old king took her seriously. He conducted an investigation of his own into the affairs of his own wife, his own queen, and it all came out. Before that, he'd had no knowledge of what she was, but when it came out, she was exposed for what she was. She, like you, is a high priestess, but, unlike you, she is a high priestess of something dark and dangerous. She is your opposite, my Lady, your absolute antithesis. Do you remember many years ago, the city mourned her death and attended her funeral?"

"Yes, I remember."

"Did you attend? I do not remember seeing you there."

"No. The queen was no friend of the temple. She had made that very clear, very early on, and now I understand why."

He nodded his agreement, his own understanding. "Well, she did not die. Unfortunately, she lives even now, although she is forbidden contact with the king. She was banished from court and now lives under permanent house arrest far from the city." He nodded towards his cousin. "I have no doubt this is her doing, no doubt at all."

Elyra nodded. "This was planned, even back then. 'Tis the way they work." She turned, again, to watch the king. "What is his birth name, the name you would have used when you were boys?"

"Ahmose."

She undid the tie of the cloak at her throat. "Can you help me take this off? I need to set free my Light, and the cloak hides me. The king needs to see me."

He complied, reaching up to take the cloak off her shoulders and then laying it gently over the back of one of the lounges.

Satisfied the cloak would not be damaged where it was, Elyra turned her full attention to the king once again.

"Ahmose," she said softly but firmly.

The king did not so much as miss a step, nor did he cease working his fingers, and nor did he stop muttering.

"Ahmose," she said again, unperturbed by his lack of response. And then she said his name again and again, her voice gentle but unyielding and firm.

"Ahmose," she said again for the dozenth time.

This time, the king hesitated before he turned to pace in the other direction, and he ceased muttering.

"Ahmose," she said again.

He was standing with his back to the room, and, therefore, with his back to everyone watching him, facing the door of his balcony, although he did not see anything through it. This time, when Elyra said his name, he stopped working his fingers, although he still touched the tips of them together. His head was still inclined, but now, for the first time since they had witnessed his agitation, he was still, if not calm.

"Ahmose," Elyra said again. "Look to the Light," she said, knowing she had his attention. "Look to the Light."

No response. The king stood still.

"Ahmose, turn around and look to the Light. Hear my voice, look to the Light."

She, too, was unmoving, still, standing right where she was, knowing she could not go to him without hurting him. Only he could come to her.

The king's eyes were unfocussed, but, slowly, ever so slowly, he turned so that he faced her.

"Good," she said. "Very good. Now, walk towards the Light."

His eyes still unfocussed, his head still inclined, his fingertips still touching, he took a small, unsteady step towards her, as if the step was hard for him, as if he was fighting himself to take the step.

"Good," Elyra said again. "Walk towards the Light, Ahmose. Keep walking. Keep walking."

He took a few more unsteady, seemingly-reluctant, shaky steps, his eyes still unfocussed, his head still inclined. And with each step he took, she matched him, stepping towards him every time he stepped towards her.

"Keep walking, Ahmose. Walk towards the Light," she said as she stepped. "Keep walking towards the Light. The Light will save you. The Light will free you."

When the distance between them was but a few small steps, she raised her hands, spreading them out wide beside her.

"You have done well, Ahmose. Now, reach out and embrace the Light. Embrace the Light." No longer soft and gentle, the tone of her voice was commanding now. "Embrace me," she commanded him.

Shaking with the effort, he, too, spread his hands, separating his fingertips. Taking another, firmer step, he reached for her, and she stepped into him, catching him and wrapping her arms around him. The shadow behind him pulled back in a sweeping motion, as if it had been sucked into a vacuum, and it screeched in pain as it released the king. Its screech filled the room, echoing off the floor and walls, and then both it and its screech vanished as if it had never been.

In Elyra's arms, the king lost consciousness and collapsed where he was. Holding him as she was already, she tried to support him, but she wasn't strong enough. Andular moved like lightning to catch him, and, together, she on one side and he on the other side, they lay the king on the floor. On her knees beside him, she cradled him like a mother holding a beloved child, holding him close.

"He will be all right," she said, soothingly, to Andular. "Just give him a moment."

For a long time, the king lay in her arms, unconscious, but then, he began to stir, moaning softly at first. She spoke to him, softly, gently, soothing him.

"It's all right, Ahmose. It's over now. You are safe. You can return. It's all right. You are safe now."

She who was watching the unfolding events, whispered to Elijah as she watched, "I really like her."

"You aught to," Elijah replied. "She **is** you."

Almost unconsciously, she shook her head. "No. I am nothing like her. I could not do that."

"Mika, you are exactly like her. Have you not banished darkness once already? The demon was attacking your nephew, I do believe. But you were holding him while he slept and the demon could not abide your Light so it vanished in the same way this one did. Do you remember?"

"I remember."

"The only difference between the two of you is that she is more knowledgeable about what you're truly capable of. Thus, she does what she does consciously, while you do what you do **un**consciously. That's all about to change, though."

She glanced at him, taking her eyes off the scene before them, her eyes questioning, but then the king stirred and awakened, drawing her attention once again.

Elyra helped him sit up, but the first person he saw was Andular who was leaning over him.

"Ands," he said, reaching up to embrace his cousin. "Gods, man, it's good to see you again."

"It's good to see you again, too, my friend," Andular said, returning the embrace.

When they pulled apart, the king became aware of Elyra kneeling beside him.

"Ahmose," Andular said, "this is the oracle of the Lady Is't (Isis in Greek). She has banished the darkness that had a hold of you."

Sitting up by himself now, the king looked at her, bowed his head and placed his hand flat over his chest. "My Lady. I am indebted to you. You have freed me from a nightmare."

"No, your majesty," Elyra said, "my Light is freely given. You owe me nothing. But this is not quite over yet. I need to show you how you may protect yourself."

For the next couple of hours, she did exactly that. At the end of the canopied bed, she drew an imaginary circle on the floor with her fingers, making sure the king knew exactly where it was, and instructing him to allow no one to step into or over it, not even to clean the floor.

"It may appear to others as though nothing is there, but the circle is real. It is very much there. You must protect it, and you must be the only one to ever step into it."

She performed a ritual spell of her own, imbuing the circle with her own Light and power so that it would protect the king. Finally, she showed him how to step into the circle and, once inside it, to imagine himself surrounded by and bathed in Light, as if he was standing under a powerful light. She made him practice over and over and over again, not satisfied with his earlier efforts. Gradually, his visions became stronger, and he was able to surround himself with powerful Light and hold it. She instructed him to stand in the circle at the same time every day, preferably in the mornings.

Throughout all of her instruction, Andular stood, shrouded in silence, watching them both, his eyes following their every movement.

Absorbed as she was, she who was watching was surprised when Elijah said beside her, "Come, mika, her work here is done. We must return to the temple. You must witness what comes next."

Again, as if in the blink of an eye, the king's suite was gone and they were, again, surrounded by the beautiful interior of the temple. The torches were still burning, casting their light over the temple's floor, causing that same interplay of light and shadow. Elijah still held her hand tightly, and they were not on the dais but, rather, below it, standing on the temple's floor.

"Phew!" she said, blinking as she regained her equilibrium and got her bearings and balance once again. "That was intense, Eli."

"Yes, that was intense, mika. But you have not yet seen it all. Brace yourself, my dearest one. There is more to come, and what is to come will cause us both great pain."

"Are we not going to take a break?"

"We can take a break if you would like to, but I would rather get this all over and done with now."

She pursed her lips. "Oh, dear. That bad, eh?"

He nodded. "Yes, mika, that bad."

~

A Glimpse Across Aeons of Time

B oth she and Elijah watched, then, as Andular and Elyra re-entered the temple. Elyra was once again covered in the cloak of raven feathers, the hood pulled up to cover her face and hair. Instead of leaving her at the temple's entrance, as his men did, Andular walked the length of the great hall with her. Again, the feathers of the cloak swished against the granite behind her as she walked. Neither of them spoke. They walked in silence, and she who watched could see that they were both tense, both worried about what might or might not come next.

When they reached the dais, they stopped, as one, and faced each other, both obviously reluctant to leave each other. She lifted her hands and removed the hood of the cloak, and as she lowered them again, he took one in his own hands.

"Do you never leave the temple?" he asked her.

"I have everything here I need, so I do not need to leave the temple."

"So how am I to see you again?"

"You may visit me here, any time you would like to."

"At the end of the day, when your work is done and my work is done." He sounded flat and frustrated. "My days stretch ahead of me now, and they seem dull and colourless without you to fill them."

She smiled. "If you visit me here at the end of each day, then you will have something to look forward to each day. And so will I."

This time, it was his turn to smile, and smile he did. He smiled into her eyes. "May I know your true name, my Lady?"

"My name is Elyra."

She who watched worked her bottom lip with her teeth, wanting to warn them. Seeing her distress, Elijah thought it prudent to distance them both from the unfolding events of Elyra's story. So he took her through the next months quickly, allowing her only brief glimpses of Elyra's and Andular's developing relationship.

So she saw them sitting on the steps of the temple, on the other side of the long line of pillars, the torches once again in place, darkness around them, sharing a plate of fruit and cheese and bread as they talked and laughed and shared their experiences of their past. She heard snippets of their conversations, so she witnessed him asking Elyra when she had come to the temple.

"In my seventh year," Elyra answered him. "When I came here, I had a different name. The temple discarded that name and gave me a new one."

"With your permission?"

She shrugged. "Not really, but I was not unhappy with my new name. I liked it, a lot, actually, so I did not protest."

"So you were named by the temple?"

"I was."

"Do you remember your old name?"

"No, I don't remember it at all."

"And your family?"

"I no longer belonged in that family, the family that birthed me. I belonged in this family, the temple's family. So I do not see them unless they come seeking the guidance and counsel of the oracle, and then, they are just souls seeking help, like every other soul who comes here. I feel no special connection to them."

She who watched them saw them sitting side by side on the steps of the temple, night after night, and she saw that this satisfied them initially. But then, after many nights, she saw that it wasn't enough anymore just to sit and talk. She saw him signal the fact by taking her hand and raising it to his lips, then holding it rather than releasing it. She saw desire in Elyra's eyes when he touched her, and she saw the same desire reflected in his eyes.

She saw the effect of his presence in her life on Elyra during the day when she was supposed to be focussed on the people.

Sometimes Elyra was focussed on them the way she had been, but sometimes she was distracted, struggling with her focus and her levels of concentration as she anticipated the moment she would see him again.

She saw them share their first kiss on the steps of the temple, leaning into each other, their kiss gentle, intimate and full of tenderness. Their first kiss was a caress, an exploration, a coming home, and it was deeply satisfying to them both. But then, of course, their kisses changed as their passion and desire flared into life within them. Their kisses deepened, their hands on each others' bodies, their fingers entwined in each others' hair.

And, then, finally, she saw them curled against each other, sound asleep, lying naked under a single sheet in the darkness of Elyra's room, and she knew they had become lovers.

Through all of this, Elijah was beside her, holding her hand tightly in his own. As they glimpsed each unfolding scene, neither of them spoke. There would be time enough for that later. For now, they observed. They merely observed.

And then, without any warning whatsoever, she and Elijah were standing on the edge of a vast room, like a ballroom, its floor decorated with beautiful, patterned tiles, its ceiling high. Blinking in surprise, she took a long moment to get her bearings, and her balance, but when she adjusted to the new scene, she looked around the room, absorbing as much detail as she could to establish what the room was and what it might be used for.

Elaborate, round candelabra hung from the ceiling at regular intervals, perhaps half a dozen of so, and they were all full of lit candles. The light from the candles was aided by the light from torches, in sconces, on the white walls of the room so that the room was well lit. At one end of the room, musicians were playing, and the room was full of beautifully-dressed people, many of them dancing. As such, the room was full of movement and music and colour. Turning questioning eyes to Elijah, she caught her breath at the profound sadness in his eyes. He didn't speak, he just indicated with his head. Following his line of sight, she saw Elyra and Andular standing in a small circle of people, talking. He held her close, his fingers clasping hers.

Watching them, the blood drained from her face – she who watched – and she swayed on her feet. Elijah steadied her with both hands, but still, he said nothing.

"The cloak . . ." she said. "She is not in the temple, and she is not wearing the cloak."

"Yes, mika, the cloak. She is not protected, not hidden."

"Why did you not stop her?"

"I cannot and could not make your choices for you, my dearest, as much as it pains me sometimes. She made a choice. Now she must suffer the consequences."

She watched them both again for a moment, and then she turned frowning, puzzled eyes to him again. "Why does she wear yellow?"

"Because," he said gently, "it is not white."

Looking over at them again, she thought Elyra looked beautiful in her golden-yellow dress. Its bodice hugged her body to the top of her waist, and then the gown fell in soft folds to the floor. The gown was sleeveless, leaving her shoulders and arms bare, and her hair had been elaborately pinned. Far from being hidden, she thought Elyra stood out, whether or not she was aware of it. She drew the eye, and she was, indeed, drawing many eyes.

She who watched grew agitated. Her stomach became a churning mass of nervousness, and in her agitation she would have taken a step towards them to berate them for their foolishness, and to warn them.

What the hell were they doing?

What the hell were they thinking?

Had they lost their minds?

Did they not realise the danger they were putting her in?

But Elijah stopped her with a firm hand on her arm. "No, mika," he said. "We are observers only, remember. We must not become participants. We must not."

Swallowing her distress, she resigned herself to the inevitable and stood passively, watching, although she was still a churning mass of nervousness and her heart was pounding uncomfortably in her chest.

In the end, it was Elyra herself who wandered away from him. She was not paying attention to Andular's conversation, and, in the crowded room, she needed fresh air. So she wandered onto the balcony at the opposite end of the room from where the musicians were playing. Just a moment was all it took. Just for one foolish moment, she left his side.

They, too, who watched followed her onto the balcony, not because they walked out onto it but because Elijah took them there, the way he could take them instantly from one place to another, one scene to another. And so, they both saw that Elyra was followed, the black shadow of her stalker detaching from the crowd and moving stealthily in her wake. He who followed was dressed in black – black trousers and boots, long, black coat, his face wrapped in a black scarf so that only his eyes could be seen. He looked very much like a clichéd assassin in modern movies. The way he followed Elyra, there was certainly no mistaking his intent.

Barely had she stepped onto the balcony before he attacked, as if he knew he didn't have much time. He pushed her, drove her backwards against the balcony's wall and held her in place with a strong forearm against her neck. Taken by surprise, she had no time to defend herself. Holding her still, remorselessly, relentlessly, he removed a fine, curved dagger from beneath his coat and drove it up under her ribs on one side of her body, the blade ripping the material of her dress. Elyra flinched and then stilled in shock, her eyes wide. As quickly as he drove the dagger into her, he pulled it out of her and, again, drove it up under her ribs on the opposite side of her body. This time, he drove the blade high and deep enough to pierce her lung. Almost immediately, she coughed as the breath was forced from her lung. When the black-clad assassin withdrew his blade this time, he released her, jumped over the balcony, and disappeared into the night, melting into it, becoming one with it.

Elyra was still pressed against the wall, but she raised her hands to the wounds in her gut, a look of resigned comprehension on her face. She coughed again, and this time, she coughed up a globule of blood. It fell onto her chest and left a stain around her lips, her mouth. Slowly, as her knees buckled under her, she slid down the wall, no longer able to hold herself up.

She who watched broke free of Elijah's grip, moving like lightning to kneel beside Elyra. Not thinking about whether or not she could or should touch Elyra, and whether or not she would be able to, she reached out and took Elyra's hand in her own.

"I'm here," she said urgently. "I'm here."

Elyra responded, clutching at her hand with a strength that belied her injuries, and her loss of blood. She was struggling to breathe, blood now pouring in a trickle from both sides of her mouth.

"You have . . . . been . . . . watching . . . ." she said, struggling to speak.

"Yes."

Elyra's eyes focussed on hers. "Did . . . I . . . lose . . . my . . . way . . . ?"

The question pierced her – she who watched – every bit as powerfully as the blade that had pierced Elyra. She wanted to scream, "No," but she could only shake her head, in sympathy more so than in denial. Elyra's eyes lost focus. She coughed again, fell over sideways, and then lay very still, her eyes open, empty, staring, and her fingers released their tight grip.

Pressure, born of unbearable pain and a sense of utter helplessness, began to build within her, she who watched.

The pressure within her gained momentum when she was forced to release Elyra's hand and step back as Andular stepped onto the balcony and saw Elyra's still body. The pressure continued to build as she saw him fall to his knees beside Elyra, pick up her still body and cradle her against him.

"No," he said. "No, no, no . . ."

And then he buried his face in her neck and sobbed, his tears mingling with Elyra's blood.

And Elyra's blood covered them both.

He picked her up and, holding her against him, took her back inside. The people immediately around him fell silent and cleared a path for him, a look of horror on their faces. When the entire room realised what was happening, the music stopped, suddenly, and those who were dancing cleared the floor. When he reached the very centre of the room, he fell to his knees, not because Elyra's body was heavy but because the burden of his own grief was too much for him. The people moved back, clearing a wide circle around him, many turning away, unable to bear witness to the rawness of his grief.

"This city will be plunged into darkness," he yelled through his tears. "We are doomed without her."

She who was watching left Elijah on the balcony to follow Andular back into the ballroom, trailing in his wake. When he fell to his knees and a circle was created around him, wide and completely clear of people, she walked around and around and around him, looking at and absorbing every detail of what she was seeing, the pressure building, gaining strength within her. Blood covered both him and Elyra, starkly red against the yellow-gold of her dress. Her body was draped over his knees, her arm hanging loosely on the floor, her head thrown back, exposing her neck. The muscles in his arms stood out like cords of strong rope as he held her body, and both grief and tears ravaged his face, altering it.

Grief, anger, helplessness, guilt, regret. It was all there, etched across his face, reflected in his eyes.

The people around him, hugging the walls of the ballroom, were suffering from near-total paralysis. No one moved to help him. No one moved to comfort him. No one moved to take Elyra from him. Many watched in horror, their hands over their mouths, but many more were turned away and could not watch at all. The king alone moved, galvanised into action, his determined movements highlighting the paralysis of everyone else in the room. He moved quickly. He gave the order to his guards to seal the palace and the city. He wanted the assassin found.

Elijah thought she had seen enough, so he caught up with her in the circle around Andular, and he took her hand, taking her away from the ballroom.

In the blink of an eye, they were back in the interior of the temple. Sunlight was lighting the interior, and the temple was, once again, full of people. But the people formed a long, long line, a silent procession, and they moved slowly, their heads bowed in grief and mourning. Elyra lay on a bier in front of the dais under a white cloth, the cloth pulled down to expose only the tops of her shoulders, her neck and her face. The blood had been cleaned from her face, and she looked peaceful in death.

The two stood side by side, cloaked in the same sadness, watching as the long, steady procession of people paid homage to Elyra. Nearly all of them left flowers or a single flower on and under the bier so that, throughout the day, the flowers piled around Elyra, forming a floral mound. At one point, the steady procession was interrupted when the king walked the length of the great hall with a small entourage of people around him, his cloak billowing out around him, his step determined, and his expression grim. He, too, placed flowers on the bier at Elyra's feet, and he leaned over her to place his hand on her forehead, and then to follow his hand with his lips.

She who watched heard him clearly when he spoke, even though she was standing some distance away from the bier.

"I will stand in your Light all the days of my life," he said. "I will honour your life with every breath of my own, and as long as I live, the darkness will not reign over our people. This is my solemn vow to you, Lady of Light. I will honour you with every breath I take, with every choice I make, with every promise I make, and with every thought that passes through my conscious mind."

As she listened, connecting with his words even though she could not understand the language, the pressure built within her. In response, her breaths came fast and shallow, and a knot burned in her throat.

And then, the king was gone. The long procession of people was gone. The temple was empty and silent, and the torches were once again lighting the space between the pillars, casting Elyra's face in a flickering orange glow that seemed to exaggerate her utter stillness. A single, brown-cloaked soul stood motionless beside the bier, in front of the dais so as to avoid the mound of flowers, his eyes holding and reflecting his very great pain as he looked down at Elyra.

"We were fools," he said. "We were so in love we thought we had become impervious to the danger. I thought I could protect you. This is my doing, every bit as much as if I wielded the blade myself . . ."

And the pressure built to breaking point, exploding within her, burning through her limbs.

She curled her fingers into fists, her nails digging into her palms, and, mustering every ounce, every scrap of strength and energy within her, she screamed at the Universe. She screamed the word 'no' at the Universe, but the word was indistinguishable. Really, she just screamed. Her scream ripped through the silence of the temple, filling the interior and echoing off the granite floor and the pillars.

He flinched violently as if he'd been struck. His body jerked as if he'd been punched, and he turned his head quickly to look behind him, over his shoulder.

Surprised, she stopped screaming, but her breaths were ragged, coming deep and fast, her chest heaving with every inhaled breath.

When he turned his head, he looked right at her. Shocked, she looked back. He wasn't supposed to be able to see her. As his eyes locked on hers, he turned his whole body to face her, and so they looked at each other, perfect reflections of grief and upset . . . and shock. She could not take her eyes from his, and he could not take his eyes from hers. They stared at each other, and she knew, she just **knew** he recognised her.

He spoke, and his words confirmed what she already knew. "You live."

"Yes, I live," she replied, "sort of, in another time and place." And then, knowing he would not understand her words, she nodded. But she couldn't help but add, "The soul goes on, even after death."

Elijah, watching, allowed them this one exchange for as long as he dared, and then he touched her arm with gentle fingers.

"Come, mika, it is time to go."

And they were sitting, once again, opposite each other, cross-legged, with his round, brass table between them. She was still breathing deeply with her upset.

"Eli," she said when she realised where she was, "I feel very ill."

He rose to his feet, nimbly given his supposed very great age, and moved around the table. Leaning over her, he helped her to stand. "I know, mika, my dearest one. Come."

He helped her move to his small bed. When she was lying on it, her eyes closed, he knelt beside her and rested a warm, dry hand on her forehead.

"Rest now, mika, my precious. Just rest. Just rest."

He watched her become calm. Her breathing slowed and became regular. His hand on her arm calmed her, and his other hand on her forehead covered her sight, so that her visions were blocked. She needed a break and he knew that even in sleep her visions would come, so he gave her the respite she needed. Even as he watched, she fell into a deep, perfectly still, restorative sleep. Her conscious mind had, indeed, absorbed all that it could cope with, so it simply turned itself off – a mechanism of self-protection – the mind's response to trauma.

He had no sense of time, so he had no idea how many hours passed before she stirred and opened her eyes. He was still kneeling beside her with his hand on her forehead, and when she opened her eyes on his, she recognised him instantly and smiled. And then she lost her smile.

"He saw me. How is that possible?"

"His sight is as powerful as yours, mika," he said gently.

"But he saw me when Elyra didn't . . ."

"Elyra saw you. Make no mistake about that. She saw you very clearly. She held your hand, did she not? She just did not consciously acknowledge who you really are. She could not, I suppose. But he could, and did. He recognises you every time he encounters you, without fail. Every time."

He had removed his hand as he spoke. Slowly, she sat up.

"How do you feel?" he asked her.

"Groggy, but better," she replied as she ran a hand around her neck and stretched it. "Thank you, Eli. I needed a break from my visions."

"I know."

"How many hours was I asleep?"

"I do not know. I have no sense of the passing of human time, mika. Many, I would say."

"Well," she said as she stood, "I need to return to my hotel. They'll raise merry hell if I don't come back. I think they were very reluctant about setting me up with my own car so I could go driving around the Egyptian desert by myself. They'll feel responsible if I don't return and they think something's happened to me. Besides, I need time to process all that I've seen today before we settle in for one of our in-depth conversations. I want to be fresh for that, not to mention armed with my own ideas and thoughts about what happened back there."

"Of course, mika. You know I understand. I think you are very wise."

She leant over to pick up her cardigan and scarf. "Eli, are you free of the temple now that I have returned and revisited the past?" she asked as she pulled the cardigan over her bare arms.

His smile twinkled at her. "Free as a bird," he confirmed.

She returned his smile as she started to wind the scarf around her shoulders and head. "What will you do now, then?"

"Well, that depends entirely on you, my dearest one. We are bound by profound vibrational energies, you and I. We love Working together, which is as well because we have much to do."

She smiled again. "Good to know," she said. "I'm very glad to hear it. So I will be seeing a lot more of you, then?"

"Indeed."

"Right, then," she said as she leant over the bed to pick up her sunglasses, "I shall see you tomorrow."

"I will have a pot of coffee brewing, ready," he said, and then, given the look she threw him, felt it prudent to qualify his statement. "A **normal** coffee," he added and was rewarded with another of her smiles.

~

Conversation over a Normal Coffee

She didn't bother knocking when she arrived at his small house the next day. She knew she was expected, so she simply lifted the latch on the front door, pushed the door open, and walked in.

He was hunched over his small pot-belly stove. "Just in time," he said without bothering to turn around.

Standing at the end of the small bed, she dropped her bag onto it and then unwound the scarf from her shoulders, slipped off her cardigan, and dropped both with her sunglasses onto the mattress next to her bag. Then she kicked off her shoes and walked in bare feet to sit on the same plump pillow she had sat on the day before. Today, she wore a white dress, its skirt long, reaching her ankles, its small sleeves sitting on the edges of her shoulders like little caps, the neckline low and scooped, and the bodice hugging her figure to the top of her waist.

"How did you sleep?" he asked her, turning to glance at her as she made herself comfortable on the cushion. Unbeknownst to her, a smile twinkled in his eyes when he saw what she was wearing. "White, because it is not yellow," he said to himself in the silence of his own thoughts.

"In fits and starts," she replied, answering his question. "And when I slept, my dreams were full of disturbing images from our vision . . . no surprises there. So I guess you could say I had a downright shitty sleep. How about you?"

He chuckled at her response, and then he answered her. "I do not sleep, mika."

"Which rather begs the question of what you are doing with a bed in your house. I did wonder when I first saw it."

He threw her a quizzical glance. "The bed is for you."

She raised her eyebrows at him, and he chuckled appreciatively at the expression on her face.

"You do not look like you had a bad sleep, you know," he told her. "In fact, you look quite refreshed."

She smiled at him. "I'm just glad to be back here."

He smiled back, and then he turned, taking a moment to stack the tray, and, as he had the day before, he brought it to the table, placed it on the floor, and sat, cross-legged, opposite her on his own cushion. In silence, he handed her tiny coffee cup and saucer to her over the table, and she reached out to take it from him, putting it gently in front of her.

He raised his own coffee towards her. "Shalom, mika."

And she did the same, smiling as she said, "Peace to you, too, Eli."

His smile twinkled, again, in his eyes as he took a sip of his coffee, his smile full of affectionate amusement generated by her response in English. She, too, unaware of his amusement took first one sip and then another and another. His coffee really was very good.

"Did we drink this in the temple?" she asked him as she took another sip.

"Not in the temple, mika, but, yes, we drank this once upon a time."

She looked at him and inclined her head. "Oh." She drew her eyebrows together in a slight frown, but, having taken her there, he now felt it necessary to pull her back to the present. They were not here to discuss **that** incarnation . . . at least, not yet. That conversation was for another time.

"I like your necklace," he said.

"Thank you," she responded, bringing her fingers up to touch it. "I thought you would. They call it the Aquarian Cross," she told him. "The cross of balance, as opposed to the Christian cross which is out of balance."

"Ah, yes," he said, smiling, "that is you, mika – a being of balance. I see why you wear it."

A small but comfortable silence descended on them as they savoured each others' company and sipped the sweet and spicy coffee. And then, he pre-empted their conversation.

"There are two things I would like to tell you before we begin," he said. "First, they caught the assassin. He paid for his crime with his life. He was executed. But, of course, he was completely unable to tell them who had paid him."

"Of course," she snorted. "So the people who really killed her got away with it."

He raised a finger at her, like a headmaster dealing with an errant student. "Only in that life, mika. Only in that life. You are forgetting about a crucial law of the Universe and of existence itself that we call karma."

Again, she snorted cynically. "These people have so much karma I fear they would need to live a billion lives just to work through it all."

"And so they will. So they will."

"I think the queen organised it," she said, sounding pensive. "I have absolutely no proof, of course. But I think she still commanded many people and organised many dark things from her place of exile in the country. They may have banished her from court, and killed her in the eyes of the people, but they did not strip her of her power. She was very angry when Elyra saved Ahmose from the being of darkness that had a hold of him. I have no idea how I know that, but I do know it. I think I could feel her anger. She had worked very hard to orchestrate Ahmose's possession, and Elyra single-handedly destroyed her plans in one embrace."

He considered that for a moment before responding. "Well," he finally said, "that's certainly an interesting theory. It makes perfect sense, of course. She had, indeed, worked hard to become queen in the first place. That much I know for certain. So it would make sense that she would seek control through a son – a son who would, himself, be king one day. She just didn't bargain on the integrity of that son's character, and on the influence on that son of a genuinely honourable king and father."

"Ah. So she underestimated both husband and son, then?"

"Indeed, so it would seem."

"What's the second thing, Eli?" she asked him, sounding somewhat reluctant. She was half afraid of what the second thing might be, although she didn't know why.

"Ah, yes, the second thing. I was really hoping I could show you, but you'd had enough. I do not think you would have handled seeing it, so I pulled you out of the vision. And," he added almost under his breath, "I could not risk him seeing you again. He, Andular, surrendered his position at the king's court and his command of the king's guard and army, and he spent the rest of his years in the temple studying the ancient mysteries. He became a priest. We gave him her room, as a matter of fact."

She swallowed nervously and worked her bottom lip with her teeth. All of a sudden, she seemed to have lost her voice. She couldn't speak.

"I rather think you in your current incarnation may have had something to do with that, now that I think about it," he mused, considering the idea even as he said it.

Finally, she found her voice, but it was weak, a croak. "Because he saw me?"

He nodded. "Indeed. Because he **recognised** you and knew you lived on . . . or lived again, whichever expression you prefer."

She thought about the possibility of that, and of any potential ramifications. And then she asked, "Did he replace the oracle?"

Elijah frowned. "No, mika, there was no replacing her. She was what she was, and she was unique. The city lost its oracle when she died. He became a priest, but he did not interact with the people. In fact, apart from me, the only person he really interacted with was the king. Ahmose visited him often at the temple. They remained close for the entirety of their lives, and Andular still offered the king invaluable advice and counsel. Between the two of them, they did indeed fulfil Ahmose's promise to you. They kept the darkness at bay. They kept the darkness in its place. Never again, during his reign, were they of the darkness able to get a foothold on either the king or the city. Unfortunately, Ahmose's heirs were not as strong nor as capable as he was, and so ancient Khem deteriorated in the decades following Ahmose's death, aided and abetted, of course, by the extremely erratic weather patterns that usually accompany a change in the precessional ages."

She blinked away tears as she listened, determined not to cry.

"And the temple?" she asked, her voice croaky with suppressed tears.

"The temple endured for as long as it could."

Again, silence descended upon them. He looked at her in the silence, knowing the effort it was costing her to hold back her tears. He wanted her to release them. After all, her tears did not make him uncomfortable. And she needed to cry. She needed the internal cleansing offered by the shedding of tears.

"Do you love him?" he asked her.

"Don't you mean **did** I love him?" she countered quickly.

"No, mika, I do not. I mean **do** you love him? I am not asking about Elyra. I know Elyra loved him. I am asking you about you."

"How can I love him? I don't know him," she said, looking at his chest, avoiding eye contact.

He frowned heavily at her as he scolded her. "Mika."

She sighed, a sound of resignation, and she looked up at him as she acquiesced, giving in, surrendering to the truth, just as he wanted her to.

"If I use my conscious mind to answer that question, the answer is no. But I can't use my conscious mind to answer because I feel the answer in every fibre of my being, in my heart. I don't love many people, Eli," she confessed. "But, yes, I love him. And I love you. I adore you, actually. That's about it, really. That's my full quota. Yes, I love him."

"Then," he said, enunciating each word carefully and clearly, "call . . him . . to . . you."

Her eyes widened in surprise. He couldn't have shocked her more if he tried his damnedest. "What? No, Eli. I would be signing by own death warrant if I did," she said quickly. "'Tis too dangerous . . .'"

He shook his head at her. "No, you are wrong. You will not be signing your own death warrant, although I understand why you would think so. Had you called him to you many years ago, yes, you would definitely have been signing your death warrant. But we, you and I, have been changing that, and this conversation is a very significant part of the reason why, and how, for that matter."

She stared at him, aghast that he'd even suggested it, let alone outright commanded her to do what would be most dangerous to do.

But, still, she trusted him, and so the shock that had widened her eyes morphed, as she looked at him, into bewilderment, confusion, and, strongest of all, curiosity. If he had commanded her, then that was, indeed, where the two of them were going – what they were walking and Working towards.

He thought it wise to change the subject temporarily, to give her time for his command to seep into her consciousness without interference from her conscious awareness. Slapping his hands against his knees, he said, "Now, I believe the first thing you would like to discuss is the cloak."

Gratefully, she acceded to the change of subject. "Yes."

When she said nothing more, he decided to steer the conversation where it needed to go himself. "You came to a significant realisation last night, I believe, during your late night contemplations."

She pursed her lips at him in disapproval. "Are none of my own thoughts private, then?"

"Not many. Your realisation?"

"You created the cloak deliberately, didn't you?"

"Did I?" He inclined his head at her as he asked the question.

"Yes, I believe you did. It's perfect, in one sense. It became the symbolic source of the very thing within which and behind which I hide. The shadow dynamic within me that causes me to hide, uses it as such, does it not? My subconscious uses it symbolically to weave an invisible cloak of the black feathers of shadow and ordinariness around me so that I am hidden in every life I live, and in every reality I create around me. So powerful is it, or so powerfully am I able to do this that it is as if I am actually wearing the cloak all the time."

He looked at her for a moment before answering. "Yes, mika. 'Tis just as you say. And, yes, I did create the cloak deliberately, with exactly that purpose in mind."

"Well, in this life, the cloak has caused me very great pain, Eli."

"Only because you have become conscious of it. In every other life you've lived you have not been conscious that you hide in ordinariness and shadow." He contemplated her for another long moment. "You see it as a negative, but you have forgotten that the cloak has allowed you to function in all those lives you've lived outside of and away from the protection of the temple. In that sense, it is anything but a negative.

You only think of it as negative now because you are having to face the dynamic within yourself to dissolve it."

"Yes," she admitted, "that's true enough."

"So, does it have to be stated explicitly that it is time to surrender the cloak, mika? You may come out of hiding now."

"Isn't that dangerous?"

"Not if you heal yourself. And heal yourself you must . . . and you are. 'Tis why you are here, after all."

He waited for her to either perpetuate their current topic of conversation or to steer it into new territory, but she remained silent.

He was about to speak, but she pre-empted him.

"Why do I create my own death in the landscape of my reality whenever I encounter him? Because even though they, of the darkness, had me killed in that life, in Elyra's life, they could not do so without my permission. And I seem to encounter this theme again and again. In other lives I've lived, I did the same thing. I created my own death, thereby separating myself from him. And in those other lives, I cannot blame those of the darkness. I seem to do a damn good job of killing myself, all by myself."

The silence that followed this collection of statements, as true as they were, was full of anticipation and expectancy. She had carried the question half way across the world to ask it of him. Indeed, it was a very significant part of the reason why she was actually there. And it was also a very significant part of the reason why he had taken her back to her own past.

"Before I answer you, my dearest one, I need to ask you a question of my own because your answer will determine where we go from here . . . where **you** go from here. I am referring to the path you will create under your own feet, the higher road or a slightly lower one. Your answer will determine the Work you will do in your immediate future.

"So," he continued, "are you asking me this question with a view to **negating** the need to create the reality of him in the landscape of your life, or are you asking me with a view to **safely** creating the reality of him in the landscape of your life?"

His question stabbed at her, just as the curved dagger had stabbed at Elyra, robbing Elyra of the ability to take the breaths necessary to sustain her very life. And, as if he had, indeed, stabbed at her – she of whom he had asked his question – she felt pain in her solar plexus, sharp, stabbing pain. Her throat burned with the effort of holding in the tears that welled in her eyes, but, this time, she lost the battle. Helplessly unable to contain them, and not completely understanding why they were there in the first place, as she looked at Elijah, the tears escaped, leaving trails of moisture as they rolled down her cheeks. She tried to speak, but the painful lump in her throat prevented it. Desperately, she tried to pull herself together, enough to at least release her throat to facilitate her ability to speak thereby perpetuating the conversation she knew they must have.

"He pulls me away from myself," she said with difficulty. "Look at what happened to Elyra. He pulled her away from her duties and responsibilities, as he did with Viola*, the Roman Vestal priestess, and as he did with Jade#."

"You believe that . . ."

"I believe it because he does," she said vehemently, "because it is so."

"No, mika," he said firmly. "He does **because** you believe it. Or, rather, because you believe it, that is your perception of what happens. Your belief underpins your perception, as belief always does. But in stating that so emphatically, you are only looking at the physical circumstances, and you are, therefore, missing the true point. You are looking at the <u>physicality</u> of those lives, those experiences, not the <u>meta</u>physical." He allowed the words to impact her, knowing they were already working on and in her consciousness, and then he added, "Because, the metaphysical truth is, of course, exactly the opposite. Far from pulling you away from yourself, he pulls you **to** yourself. And therein lies the answer to your question. You create the reality of your own death whenever you encounter him **because** you fear being pulled to yourself, away from and out of your place of safety, your place of hiding. And you create your death because the fear is working to protect itself, thereby protecting you **from** yourself.

"And," he continued without giving her time to respond, "what is your definition of 'duties and responsibilities' anyway? Have you not firmly established that the rules and traditions and the downright silly etiquette surrounding the priestesses of Vesta were Viola's prison – **a prison that kept her from herself.** Is not . . . or was not her primary duty, indeed, her only **real** duty, to herself?"

"So why did I punish myself by drinking a vial of poison in that life?"

"You tell me."

She shook her head, quickly, as if shaking off an errant, unwanted thought. "Because I broke the rules. I did the wrong thing, let an awful lot of people down – the entire population of Rome at the time – and I deserved to be punished. Or at least, that's what Viola thought."

"Yes, so she did because, as I said, her sight was rooted in the physical. And, as such, caught and bound in physical perspective as she was, she did, indeed, do the wrong thing, by everyone. But whose rules was she breaking?"

She of whom the question was being asked did not respond.

"Whose rules, mika?" he asked again, raising his voice. "They were not her rules, but they **were** her place of safety – the very thing that kept her from herself – the very things that bound her up, like being wrapped in mummifying bandages, in the perspective of the Vestal priestess – the character-identity of that life. So whose rules was she obeying to keep herself safe?"

"Theirs," she all but yelled back. "The institution's. The rules were part of their system of control, in more ways than one." And then she softened her voice and said more quietly, "Jade did not break any rules by being with him, so why did she punish herself with death."

"Jade did not punish herself with death," he responded. "She escaped him, irreversibly. He always got her back when she eluded him, did he not? Well, in death she eluded him irrevocably. He couldn't get her back."

Again, his words hit her as if he'd punched her, hard. "Oh god," she breathed. And again, his words generated a fresh wave of tears. "Oh god," was all she could manage to say a second time.

"Jade had created a life of solitude and order for herself," he elaborated, his voice gentle. "The life she had created, after the turbulent life of her childhood, was her place of safety. She was what she wanted to be, and she knew who she was. He threatened that." He paused for a moment to give her time to accept that, and then he continued, "You think she wasn't hiding because she translated the ancient Wisdom, and worked with it overtly and publicly. But she **was** still hiding, mika. She was hiding behind and within the culture of academia. She was an academic, not a priestess, in her own eyes, so she approached and dealt with the Wisdom from the perspective of an academic. And who was it who saw the truth?" He raised a finger. "Who was the one person who saw the truth and responded to it, even though that truth was being channelled through the sister?"

"Him," she said, but the word came out as a strangled croak.

"Him," Elijah repeated by way of confirmation. "Always, throughout the entirety of their interaction in that life, he did not see her as an academic. Brilliant, yes, but not an academic. He **never** saw her as an academic – the way she saw herself. Even Pravesh, as insightful as he was, still related to her on the basis of their academic roles, their academic accomplishments and their academic business. That's exactly why his wife was never threatened by his and Jade's relationship. Blake, Andular's incarnation in that life, saw her as something far more profound than that, far more beautiful, far more powerful, and **that** is what he responded to."

"Oh god," she said on a sob. "He threatened to tear down the disguise of her physical identity, to bring her out of her place of safety, **within herself . . .**"

"Yes, mika," he said quietly, "thereby overturning the apple cart of her whole life. From top to foundation, he threatened to tear down the building of her. Yes, he pulled her off track, but at a depth that you are only now beginning to comprehend. The track she was on – the track she had worked hard to carve for herself – was a track or a path she was clinging to for dear life as a means of staying safe and hidden. He was the powerful spanner in the works, so to speak, and she was helpless to resist the pull of him, as was Elyra, of course. He pulls you out, powerfully . . ."

"Yes," she said, interrupting, "look at Elyra. He enticed her out of the temple thereby jeopardising her safety . . ."

"A perfect metaphor, wouldn't you say, precious Lady? Again, that is the old belief speaking within you." He levelled a penetrating look at her across the table. "You blame him? He certainly did."

She shook her head involuntarily. That he blamed himself had been the straw that broke the pressure building within her when she was in the vision. She hadn't been able to handle it. That had torn her apart almost as much as Elyra being torn from him. The truth was she didn't blame him. She didn't blame him at all.

"I don't blame him, Eli," she said. "I really don't."

"I know. In truth, you never have. Elyra didn't so much punish herself for what she saw occurring in her life after crossing paths with him, she protected herself. As did Jade. And, actually, as did Viola. You may liken it to an egg desperate to keep its shell intact so that the yolk is contained and protected. He threatens to crack and remove the shell, so you, in all your incarnations, act to protect it . . ."

"It's like armour, then," she said, interrupting. "The image, or the perspective I hold of myself in each life, it's like armour."

"It's exactly like armour," he agreed. "As for Elyra, she felt as if she was being drawn along on a strong current she had no control over, being taken away from her 'duties and responsibilities', as you put it. He may have 'enticed' her out of the temple, but it was **she** who wandered away from **him** thereby leaving his protection and giving the darkness exactly the opportunity it needed to do what it so desperately wanted to do. What did she ask you with her dying breath?"

"Did I lose my way?"

"Yes, mika, because that was the belief she held within her – the same belief you still hold within you – the same belief Viola held within her – the same belief Jade held within her. You always believe you lose your way. But in believing that misguided belief, you look only at the physical circumstances in these lives, as I said, and you then create out of the misguided belief you hold thereby creating your own death. But even the belief itself is born of the intact fear within you, and it is the fear out of which you **truly** create. The fear of being truly seen, and of being cut down for it."

She bowed her head at that, and sobbed quietly. Moving, she reached over for her bag, and rummaged through it to locate the small packet of tissues she'd brought with her. "It's always good to come prepared," she muttered when she found them. "Especially when engaging in a conversation with you."

He smiled.

When she was settled back on the cushion, she took a moment to wipe her face and blow her nose, relieved she hadn't bothered with make-up that morning, and then she raised her tear-stained face to look at him, not caring that she looked a mess.

"But therein lies the way out of death, mika," he said when he could see she was settled again and ready to continue. "Therein lies the way to **avoid** creating your death when next you encounter him, as you will when you **call him to you.**"

"How?" she asked, completely failing to see what he was alluding to. "How do I avoid creating my death in my reality when I encounter him again? I don't see that."

"Before we get to that," he said, "ask me the questions you are holding within you. They are important. We've a need to address them. They are foundational, actually, to what we're talking about. One must always make sure the foundations are secure before starting to build, mustn't one?"

She raised her eyebrows only briefly, but then decided not to take issue with the fact that he was perfectly reading her mind. So she asked the questions she was holding within her.

"Can you tell me how it is he always upsets the apple cart of my life whenever I encounter him? I mean, I can see now that he takes me beyond the disguise of the character-identity, or he did with Jade and he threatened to with Viola, but how does he have the power to take me from my place of safety – the place of safety I construct for myself? And how is it I can never resist the pull of him?"

He inclined his head. "Shall we answer the last question first? Did you not just see for yourself how it is you can never resist the pull of him? So, mika, **you** answer that last question for both of us."

She closed her eyes, seeing in her mind's eye the scene from the vision when Andular and Elyra had first laid eyes on each other. "Beauty," she whispered without opening her eyes. "Incredible beauty. He is beautiful."

He smiled, and the smile sparkled within him. "Oh yes," he agreed, the words a breathy whisper that matched hers. "Beauty. Now, answer me this. How is it he can never resist the pull of you?"

She opened her eyes so she could look into his. "Beauty," she replied.

"Indeed. Yes, indeed. And beauty that does not have to be seen visually to be seen, as you experienced in Jade's life. Now, to answer the first of your questions – the question as to how he so easily takes you from your place of safety – the answer is very simple. Reflection. Attraction. And sight."

She looked puzzled as she thought that through. So he elaborated.

"**He** sees and recognises the sheer force and power of **your** beauty, and **you** see the sheer force and power of **his** beauty such that your combined beauty is pulled up and out of you both. **He** sees the sheer force and power of **your** Light, and **you** see the sheer force and power of **his** Light such that your combined Light is pulled up and out of you both. You are drawn to his Light and his beauty and his power like a moth to a flame, just as he is drawn to yours in exactly the same way. Well, actually, I would say you are drawn to each other like powerful magnets. There is no force on earth that can match it, nor is there any force on earth that can negate or obviate it, mika. Except, of course, death and separation. Reflection. Pure, potent, powerful, perfect reflection."

She looked at him, just looked at him, without responding. But his words were generating such an avalanche of thought and realisation that she was struggling to keep up with them. She could vaguely see and sense the truth and power of it, but it was still not an easy thing getting her conscious mind around it.

"Reflection, mika," he repeated, helping her out. "But what is all that truly a reflection of, exactly?"

"So you're saying we're drawn to each other because we are a perfect and pure reflection of what lies at the very heart of us . . . or," she revised, thinking, "of what is the truest essence of us?"

He nodded once, definitively. "Just so. Of who and what you **really** are, underneath the disguise of the incarnated identity. And it is **this** that you pull out of each other. And, of course, that will always have ramifications for your reality. What happened to Elyra's powers of concentration where her work was concerned after she encountered him?"

"She struggled at times. She was distracted."

He nodded, once. "Indeed. She was no longer fulfilled by it. Now there was something else to fill her up, so to speak. Her own truth."

Closing her eyes to concentrate, she whom he called mika could see the dynamic in Jade's life – the disguise of the character-identity, the academic, completely obscuring . . . what? She could see Jade hiding in the disguise and in the disguise's success. She could actually see it. And, of course, she could see how Viola was hiding in the rules and the robes of the Vestal priestess. That wasn't at all hard to see. But Elyra, surely she wasn't hiding . . .

"Yes, she was," Elijah said definitely, nipping that thought in the bud as soon as it came forth, "just as much as was Jade or Viola, or you, for that matter." He leaned forward across the table, narrowing his eyes at her. "See her life anew now, mika. Walk with me through it."

His words, once again, took her back there, into the vision. When he knew she was back there, he guided her vision with his words.

"Like you, she was hiding. But how was she hiding, and what was she hiding behind? Or, what was she using to hide?" He answered his own question. "She was hiding **behind** her role as the oracle, her 'duties and responsibilities', as you put it, interacting with people who could not see her – people who only ever confirmed the perspective she held of herself. She was hiding **within** the robes of the oracle. The temple and the robes and training of the priestess defined her, mika, and they defined her physically. And in defining her physically, they limited her perspective of herself. She was the oracle, and to her, that's all she was. In that sense, the temple and its existence were her prison. Why else did she wear yellow-gold to the court function they attended? She was enjoying a moment of pure freedom. At the court function, she was not the oracle, nor was she a priestess. She was a beautiful woman, a beautiful soul. Did you not see how the people at the ball could not take their eyes from her? Her beauty was bedazzling that night because she was her truth, and she was radiant. She, too, like you, like Jade, like Viola, was hiding from herself. But he saw her, just as she saw him. From the very instant they first made eye contact, they saw each other. But she never made the connection between what she saw in him and what was truly within her because she was so well hidden. She did not know or comprehend just how much he reflected her."

"Did he? Did he know?" "Not when they were together," Elijah replied. "But by the end of his life he knew, with a little help from me. Yes, he knew. As for her, he gave her his hand, which she took willingly enough. But deep, deep down, she was afraid of where he was taking her, so she put a stop to it, very effectively as you saw for yourself. She created exactly what she feared in the landscape of her reality."

"Being seen, and being cut down for it." She sighed, a long, drawn-out sound. "Oh what a complicated psychology."

"Do you think yourself any different from anyone else in that sense? You **are** different from everyone else, but not because of your complicated psychology, but, rather, because you are so damned good at unravelling it. And, mika, unravel it, you will."

She nodded, believing him. "In a very real sense, what I am doing with myself is exactly what Elyra made Ahmose do in our vision. She bade him walk towards the Light. So, too, am I walking towards my own Light."

He smiled. "Just so, beautiful Lady."

Silence filled the small house then as she contemplated all that had been discussed so far, and in the silence, it all began to seep into her bones, so to speak. She could feel it permeating every fibre of her being. And in the silence, a question shimmered into being. He felt it straight away and so pre-empted her.

"Before we deal with the question of why you crossed paths at all in those lives, especially given the fact that you just ended up creating your own death, there is something else about those deaths and the reasons for them that I need you to see, understand and acknowledge, mika. 'Tis terribly important because it will provide us with the key to **not** creating your death this time around."

She nodded intensely, frowning in concentration. "I'm listening," she said unnecessarily because he knew she was hanging off his every word.

"Do you think," he began, "the Process has ever **not** underpinned every life you've lived? Do you think just because you created your own death each time that something went wrong? Or that the Process somehow went wrong? Or that the Process somehow abandoned you? Well," he continued, "yes, you do think that. Is that not exactly what that misguided belief is – you losing your way? So you believe you somehow caused the Process to derail, to go off track, or to stop altogether . . ."

Instead of responding verbally, she looked back over all three lives, and then nodded. That's exactly what she'd thought, every time. And she thought it now.

"Well, in truth, mika, this misguided belief you've held within you, directly born of the very great fear wrapped around your soul, as it is, has been allowed to remain in your psyche intact because **the fear has been allowed to remain in your psyche intact.** The Process has never touched it or stirred it or brought it to the surface of your conscious awareness, there to resolve it. You died, every time, to protect the fear and the belief so that both would continue to facilitate identification with humans as they are in the abyss of darkness and Separation. It was, quite simply, not time for you to be healed, to become whole and complete. It was necessary for you to retain the fear. Remember," he said, "even fear serves Purpose."

"Oh," she breathed. "Oh god." She brought her hands to her mouth as her sight opened up and she could **see** what he was saying. "I see. Yes, I see. We had worked hard to put the fear in me in the first place, not to mention what I had to go through to put it there – something I hope never, ever to repeat[+]. So the Process couldn't resolve it whilst ever we needed it to remain there, and so it didn't. It didn't ever put its finger on the fear. So the fear created death in those lives because it was intact, exerting a powerful influence over my whole psyche, as fear does. And it was allowed in order to facilitate identification, to be as humans are in the abyss of darkness and Separation, as you said. Because of the fear, I am Separated from my Self as they are."

"And," he said, "that brings us nicely to a convergence point in our conversation, does it not? This life. This, your current incarnation. The answer to the question you didn't get to verbalise before – why cross paths at all in those lives – and the very thing that marks this life as vastly different from those other lives." He spread his hands out beside him. "Are we not answering the question as to why you crossed paths in those other lives right now?"

She looked at him blankly for a moment, and then her expression cleared as realisation dawned, or, at least, realisation of what he was driving at exactly. "We crossed paths so that I could do the Work in this life?" she half asked, half stated, sounding very unsure.

"But of course. You crossed paths in **those** lives so that you could see all the dynamics involved, in **this** life. And now we come to the powerful truth of what, exactly, Elyra was, and what she was able to do."

"You said she was not a future oracle, as many oracles are, but, rather, one who was able to see the source of one's shadows in the present. So, if anything, her vision, her sight was directed back into the past."

"That is so," he confirmed when she paused. "And are you not experiencing this quality in yourself right now?"

"Yes, so I am . . . untangling my own shadow dynamics. And so, in that sense, she was able to set people's feet upon the path of their highest potential, by causing them to resolve the shadows within them that keep them **from** the path of their highest potential."

"Just so. So what need had she of future sight when she caused people to reshape their own futures by resolving the shadows of fear that shaped and formed the path upon which they walked, thereby changing those paths, dramatically, too."

"And this is why she posed such a powerful threat to the darkness."

He inclined his head. "Why exactly?" She was right, as well he knew, but he wanted to be sure she understood exactly why she was such a threat to the darkness.

"Because the darkness needs fear to retain control of the human psyche, and she holds within herself . . . sorry," she corrected, "I hold within myself an innate ability to resolve fear, even those buried deeply in the psyche. With resolved fear, comes altered mindset, belief, perspective, and with altered mindset, belief and perspective comes a shift in consciousness, and with a shift in consciousness comes significant change in the fabric of reality itself. And if I can do this on an individual basis, I can also do it on a collective basis."

She did, indeed, understand. He smiled, and his smile sparkled in his blue eyes.

"Yes, my dearest one, that is so. And now, have you not wondered why, as powerful as she was, Elyra remained unaware of the powerful fear dynamic within her – a fear that held such power over her it caused her to create her own death?"

"Yes," she said softly, "I have wondered that. Of course I have wondered that, almost from the moment we first saw her."

"Her sight was blocked, of course. Before she met him, she had no reason to see the fear within her. But after she met him, her powerful sight was still blocked so that she never once processed it, or confronted it, or acknowledged it. Perhaps, had she lived, she would have confronted the fear. In fact, I have no doubt she would have. But she was not given the opportunity, was she? Her life was ended before she had a chance to see the fear and process it. And in creating the fear in the landscape of her reality, she gave **you** the opportunity to see and face the fear."

Again, she stared at him, slightly wide-eyed, as his words penetrated and sank deeply. Yes, he was right. Elyra was given no real chance to resolve the fear and, thus, the fear remained intact and powerful within her such that it eventually caused her to create her death.

He gave her a moment to process the knowledge, and then he asked, "What did Jade, Viola and Elyra all have in common that makes them very different from you?"

She took a moment to answer his question, not because the answer eluded her, but because it didn't. She knew what it was that made her life so different from theirs, and she needed that moment to allow the answer to sit with her, to penetrate.

"Christ alive," she whispered. "I'm consciously aware of the fear. They were not consciously aware of the fear wrapped around our soul like shadowed barbed wire, from where it exerted such a powerful influence on their lives – causing them to hide, each in their own way – and, then, of course, to create their deaths. But I **am** aware. I am aware of its source, its inception, its **con**ception, its nature, its effects, its power, its purpose. And I guess that further answers the question as to why he and I crossed paths in those lives."

"How so, dear one?"

"In Working, as we are now, on the whys and wherefores of how and why I created my death when I encountered him, I can see more deeply into the reasons why I hide, but more significantly, into **how** I hide, and **what** I'm hiding from, and then how I protect myself when I encounter him."

He nodded. "Just so, dear one. Because it is him, and only him, who pulls you out of hiding, so it had to be him you encountered in those lives." He shrugged his shoulders, the gesture exaggerated and, therefore, dramatic. "It could not have been anyone else."

"No," she whispered. "It couldn't. 'Cause no one else reflects me the way he does."

"Just so."

Silence again reigned while she let everything sit with her and within her – a silence he allowed for a long, long moment. He just sat watching her, honing his awareness on what was transpiring within her. But then, he knew it was time to move on. They hadn't yet finished this wonderful Work. They hadn't yet reached the culmination, the reason and Purpose for it all in the first place. It was still necessary to bring it all full circle . . .

"Have you not now been told that human incarnations do not sit well with you, mika?" he asked, breaking the silence. "To have to wear one at all is bad enough, but you have hidden behind and within each one you've lived since those god-awful events of so long ago[+]."

She nodded slowly. "God, yes. They are like ill-fitting suits, my incarnations. But in this life, the incarnation has caused me unimaginable pain because I've felt it not sitting well. And, of course, in the early days of awareness, I misunderstood the pain and searched in the wrong places for a cure."

"Ah, yes. Awareness. And that really does nicely bring us to a point in the conversation we really, really need to be – the very territory we've been Working towards. The Purpose of this life," he said. "So, back to my original question. Do you **negate** the need to create him in the reality of your life, or do you **safely** create him in the reality of your life?"

"I safely create him in the reality of my life," she said softly. "That is my answer to your rather penetrating question, Eli."

He smiled at her. "But of course it is."

She smiled back. She couldn't help it.

"Right, then," he said. "So how do you do that? What is the key to safely creating him?"

He paused for dramatic effect, and, again, she smiled at his dramatics, but she remained silent, awaiting him, not daring to interrupt.

He levelled a penetrating look at her across the table. "There is one life we have not yet discussed in relation to the fear dynamics within you, mika. We have talked about Jade's life, and Viola's life, and Elyra's life, so you are now fully cognisant of the dynamics involved in those lives. But there is one life we haven't yet touched on."

At first, she looked back, frowning in concentration, trying to recall other lives, other memories that might be relevant. And then it hit her, and her expression cleared. "Ah," she breathed. "Mine. We haven't talked about the dynamics of my life."

He smiled, and his smile sparkled in his eyes. In truth, it was the sparkle of anticipation, and she knew it, could see and sense it. "Just so," he confirmed.

"But . . ." she began.

"Please," he said quickly, cutting across her thought before she even had a chance to voice it and holding up his hands like a traffic cop holding up lanes of traffic, "do not tell me we have not yet discussed your life because you have not encountered him and so have not had cause to create your own death."

She stared at him with her mouth open, the thought still hovering unspoken on her lips. That was, indeed, exactly what she was going to say.

"We have not yet discussed your life," he told her, lowering his hands to the table, "simply because we have not yet got to it. We have been busy covering those other lives. And," he added, looking at her pointedly across the table, "you **have** encountered him, mika. In this life," he added for good measure, even though it was not necessary to do so.

She reacted to his words instantly. Or, rather, her heart reacted. It skipped a full beat and was now pounding uncomfortably in her chest as she stared at him for an entirely different reason. She knew exactly to what he was referring. So she had no need of being told when and how. And she was, too, perfectly well aware of the consequences of that encounter. So powerful was the experience that she thought of herself as two beings – the one before the encounter and the one she was now, after the encounter.

"The only reason," he said, watching her closely after giving her a moment to absorb the truth, "you did not create your own death was, of course, because the encounter with him was so brief, he pulled you out only for the briefest of glimpses. A flash of Light, albeit a powerful one, was all it was, was it not?"

Unable to speak, she simply nodded.

"Still, that was enough to make you run. And so you did thereby ending the encounter as abruptly as it had begun."

"Thereby," she added softly," probably saving my own life in the process . . ."

"Yes, indeed. And so, a good thing it was, then, that you ran. Not to mention all the Work you were always going to have to do in the interim, between then and now, without him, Working alone. He could not help you do that."

She nodded slowly, seeing the truth of that. "That was him?" she whispered because she wasn't, in that moment, capable of speaking any louder.

"Of course, mika. But of course. Look closely at all the dynamics at play and you will see they are all exactly the same as those we've been discussing."

She tried to do what he'd told her to, but her sluggish mind could only be with the shock of what she was now being confronted with. Elijah watched her closely, knowing her mind had shut down temporarily while it processed something wholly unexpected. Although, really, she had known the truth, deep down. She'd just been very effectively blocking it. Well, he was determined to **un**block it.

"You have known the truth, mika," he said softly. "You have long known you were making your way back to him. You have just been denying the truth courtesy of the very great fear within you. The fear has blocked your sight, which has, of course, served Purpose, because, until now, the knowledge would have served only to distract you. Why else do you really think you are here with me now if not to prepare you for what is to come?"

She couldn't respond. She could only sit in silence with her heart pounding in her chest.

He inclined his head at her, a smile twinkling in his eyes. "Shall we walk through the dynamics involved, step by step, together?"

She nodded mutely, drawing a smile from him again. It was a rare thing indeed to witness her being so mute, so unable to speak. Normally, she loved speaking, as much as did he, as a matter of fact, which was exactly why their dialogues were so mutually enjoyable.

"All right, then," he said. "How or in what way did he 'pull you off track' as he did in those other lives this time around? What did he pull you out of at the time you crossed paths? What were you hiding behind?"

She took a deep breath, and while she did, she cast her vision back over that time of her life. Like the powerful light of a lighthouse sweeping the territory around it, she swept her vision across that time and the years preceding it, seeing the shadow dynamics that underpinned those years of her existence.

"My life hasn't been nearly as romantic as those other lives," she commented as she looked back at her past.

"That's probably more due to the lack of romance in the human experience itself, mika, rather than in your actual life."

She focussed on him, briefly, raising one eyebrow in disbelief. "I agree with you about the lack of romance in the human experience, Eli, but this life I've lived has been utterly devoid of anything beautiful or romantic. Really – a dry and arid wasteland of existence."

He looked concerned, but her words did not surprise him. He knew she felt that way, and probably with justification, too. She knew what she was talking about, after all, because she had experienced incredible beauty in many of her incarnations, none of which were or had been human. So she was perfectly able to compare a life of beauty with one that lacked it, and to recognise that this one **did** lack it.

"Yes, mika," he capitulated softly, "you are right, methinks. How can there be beauty or romance in any life lived in the darkness and Separation of the abyss, but especially for you who knows different?"

"Very true. Elyra's life was beautiful, I think."

"That's because **she** was beautiful."

She smiled slightly. "And I'm not?"

"You have been far too hidden, mika, to be truly beautiful. Or, I should say, to sparkle with your own unique beauty. Much more hidden than Elyra."

Her smile disappeared . . . completely. "And my reality has reflected that."

"Yes, it has. It has been utterly devoid of any type of reflection. So, to my question."

Again, she took her vision back. "I was living that absolute epitome of mundanity and ordinariness – the recipe of life – career, marriage, mortgage, kids." She shuddered, obviously, as a chill of horror rippled down her spine. "But in terms of what we've been discussing – the perspective I've held of myself in each of those lives I lived – the recipe successfully contained me in this life, but it never sat well with me. In fact, I hated it. But," she said, drawing out the word, "I was on track, so to speak, building a nice career, with a big house in the suburbs, etcetera, etcetera, being a good girl, making my daddy proud."

"Just so," he agreed. "And the reason you hated that persona was that you always were meant to surrender it. And so, mika, what happened after that oh-so-brief encounter with him – Andular's incarnation in this current life?"

"Well," she said, "you said it yourself, Eli. I ran."

"After that, I mean."

He watched her closely while she thought about her response. He knew full well what she was seeing because her encounter with 'him' – the 'him' of their discussions – had been the most pivotal point, very possibly the most significant thing she'd experienced up to that point. She'd awakened in one fell swoop after years and years of utter dormancy. Now, she needed to look at the experience anew, with a more knowledgeable perspective, with and through metaphysical eyes.

"After that," she said quietly, her eyes still unfocussed, "I felt as if I had walked into a brick wall, with no warning whatsoever, and fallen smack on my ass. It hurt, too."

Surprised by her choice of words, he frowned slightly. "A brick wall?"

It was the tone of the question rather than the question itself that drew her attention so that she focussed on him again. "I use the term 'brick wall' only in the sense that the experience stopped me utterly in my tracks. I couldn't keep going the way I had been going. And the impact was so significant I couldn't remain standing. I felt like I collapsed, not just metaphorically. I collapsed psychologically because the experience cracked me open so severely it felt like I'd fallen apart, and so I had."

"I see," he said. "So the egg shell was, at last, cracked open?"

She nodded. "Irrevocably. I couldn't pull it back together again. I couldn't even try to pull it back together again. That's how severely it was cracked open. So I had no choice but to be apart, to come unravelled."

"And the inner contents of the egg?" he asked her.

She smiled, although the smile was part grimace. "That was not pretty. The inner contents of me came spilling out. At first, it was pure toxin that came spilling out – all the toxic stuff of this current incarnation – the toxicity of my abject and chronic ignorance and insecurity, all the toxic programming, the misguided mindsets, a ton of different fears. You name it. If it was yukky, it came out."

He chuckled.

"The worst part, though," she continued, not at all amused herself, "apart from initially not understanding what was happening, was in becoming aware of just how ignorant and full of fear and misguided mindset and perspective I was. It was as if the inner content of the egg had become putrefied in its containment, which it had, and which," she looked at him significantly, "if you've ever smelt a rotten egg, you would know is pretty revolting."

He chortled again, briefly, fleetingly, the sound full of his amusement despite its fleeting nature. "I'm sorry, mika," he said as he sobered. "I do so love your use of metaphor. You know that. But it is, still, a little hard to laugh at the pain of those years. You were in enormous pain. I knew that. I walked it with you, as a matter of fact."

"I know, Eli. I very much doubt I could've walked it without you."

He smiled at her as he nodded his acknowledgement. "And then," he said, changing the subject slightly, "you discovered something that has become inordinately helpful, and, in fact, brought something into your life that had previously been so lacking."

She nodded, smiling. "Writing, and the nourishment of true Wisdom and knowledge."

"So," he said, inclining his head as he looked at her with his eyes narrowed, "you've been rediscovering yourself, your **true** Self. But you are still very much contained, not to mention hidden, of course. You are still very much containing and hiding yourself, beautiful Lady."

She sighed. "Yes," she agreed simply.

"There is an antidote, of course," he said. "And to that end, we need to go back to that night, you and I – that oh-so-brief encounter with a for-all-intents-and-purposes total stranger. So what was it exactly that stopped you in your tracks that night?"

She didn't have to think about her response. She already knew. "My reflection," she said softly. "I saw my reflection, the very thing I fear. Reflection and fear – one and the same. God, no wonder my life was turned upside down from that point."

"Your life was turned upside down from that point because you were cracked open, and so you could now begin the journey into your inner layers, seeing many truths that were formerly hidden and suppressed."

She nodded her agreement. "Well," she said, "it's still coming out. Fifteen years of pain. Oh what a lovely life this has been . . ."

"There is an end, mika," he said softly, not at all without empathy or sympathy. In a very real sense, he had felt every bit of her pain. "I know you think there will not be an end to it except through death, which I know you have longed for. But just as there is always a beginning when it comes to fear, so, too, there is always an end, should we choose to look it full in the face, confront and dissolve it. This you know because you are, in fact, very good at resolving fear."

She could only nod mutely.

"So," he continued, "if I was to tell you I know you will not run this time around, first, would you believe me, and, second, on what, do you think, am I basing that certainty?"

"First, I believe you. And second, Knowledge," she said. "Not yours. Mine. The fear has been pulled into my conscious awareness, and we have been doing a lot of Work with it, as I said before. Fear needs ignorance to survive and thrive. Knowledge breaks up the bedrock of ignorance so that the fear begins to dissolve. Knowledge can and does go a long way towards disempowering fear . . . a long way."

He nodded. "Indeed."

He allowed a moment of silence to fill the room, and then he said softly, "So, mika, be your metaphysical truth in this dry, arid, wasteland of human reality. Let them see who you are. Call . . him . . to . . you. You know exactly **who** to call in because you've seen him in many lives now. And you know him, so do not allow yourself to be distracted by his identity in this lifetime."

"Dear god," she whispered. "Eli . . ."

He sat back on his cushion, not at all inclined to be sympathetic, and raised a finger at her again. "You know, now, the metaphysical Purpose of this life and, therefore, of him. Tell me," he commanded almost harshly. "Tell me."

"Restoration," she whispered. "The restoration of my reflection and, therefore, of me. Healing. Wholeness. Completeness. The complete disempowerment of this god-awful fear that is wrapped around my soul, keeping me severed from my own metaphysical, higher-dimensional truth, keeping me hidden."

He nodded. "And because you know the metaphysical Purpose, mika, you **exist** in that same metaphysical truth. And if you do, so, too, will he. Go beyond the physical circumstances and the physicality of who you are in this lifetime, and take him beyond the physicality of his incarnated identity, too. You can do this. You hover on the edge of your metaphysicality, beautiful Lady. Go beyond hovering now. Take the step necessary to step fully into your metaphysicality. Call him to you. Therein lies the key to **not** creating your death this time around. Focus on the metaphysical truth, exist in it, not the physical circumstances, and you will not create your death.

"Your fear," he continued, "has its roots in the physical. That is why it had so much power in those other lives, mika, because your sight was trapped in the physical, thereby giving it power and form. Your fear has no power on the metaphysical plane. So go there, be there, exist there, in the metaphysical. Exist as your metaphysical Self.

"Closure," he said softly, "like the final chapter of a long, long book . . . or a long, long circle of incarnations. Close the circle, mika. Finish what was begun so long ago."

~

* Viola's story is told in "*Like the Stopper in the Vial*", one of the collection of stories in *Pieces of Me*, and a follow-up is given in "*A Conflict of Scripts*", one of the collection of stories in *The Messiah Perspective*.
\# Jade's story is told in "*Non-Celestial Orbits*", one of the collection of stories in *Altira*.
+ The events referred to in this dialogue that were the source of the fear dynamic in every life discussed are laid out in the third story of this collection: "*The Fallen*."

The End

Faerie

This story is dedicated to the Faery community –
My Faery community –
Who followed me into the human realm
To restore creation,
To reclaim the human experience for the Light.
You are my people, my family,
Beautiful souls, all.
My thoughts and, therefore,
My love and Light are with you still,
As yours are with me.

Story Time

"**A**re you ready?"

She didn't ask them the question because she wanted an answer. Rather, she asked them the question because, in that brief moment between question and response and then during the response itself, she was able to feel, connect with and absorb the energy of eager anticipation that was weaving itself around them all, like a living, breathing thing with a life all of its own. In this moment, just before she began the story, the energy of eager anticipation was pure and perfect and powerful. It hovered in the air, almost shimmering with its own power. She always enjoyed this moment, and, always, without fail, her smile reflected her enjoyment, sparkling in her eyes as she looked at them all eagerly awaiting the evening's story. Once the story was begun, the energy of eager anticipation would morph, transform itself into fascinated fixation, no less powerful, of course, but there is a unique kind of magic in anticipation, don't you think?

In response to her question, hundreds and hundreds of little heads bobbed up and down, quickly, in almost perfect unison, and then pure and perfect silence descended, and they all became perfectly still, appearing to her like rows and rows of little statues. It was in this moment that the energy of eager anticipation was at its most powerful, and so, she took a moment to absorb it, to breathe it in, and to savour the moment.

For you see, faeries love stories. I mean, they really <u>love</u> stories. They love stories in the same way children love candy, although stories are far more nourishing to faeries than candy is to children. Faeries soak up stories the same way a dry sponge soaks up water. Well, actually, I should qualify at this point by explaining that faeries love certain kinds of stories, because there are some downright horrible stories going around, are there not? Fairies do not love stories of darkness – fear, trauma, tragedy, violence, betrayal, abuse, exploitation. Who does? Who would? No, faeries love stories of love and romance, the triumph of good over evil, of heroes and heroines, of courage and bravery, of princes and princesses. They love stories with genuinely happy endings. To faeries, a well-told story **is** exactly like candy – candy for the soul. A good storyteller, as she was, could weave the magic of a story so that each faery hearing it was carried along on the current of the story, riding its highs and lows, lost, temporarily, in the ebb and flow of the events that comprised the whole.

She had an impressive repertoire of stories, an internal storehouse of them, to choose from, many gleaned from those of her lives she had lived in the human realm. Stories of mythology – Greek, Norse, Egyptian – were **her** favourites, and some of the stories she weaved for her faeries were based on her own experiences (although she always changed the endings of those stories, bending the truth somewhat so that she gave her own stories happy endings). She knew, though, that **their** favourite stories were, and always would be, fairy tales. Sometimes, she mentally shuffled through the repertoire of her stories until she came to a story that she felt suited the energy of the evening, like shuffling a pack of cards, fanning the cards out and choosing one. Sometimes, though, like this evening, she knew exactly which story she would tell them. She didn't have to think about it.

Story time was a time-honoured ritual for her and her faeries. At the end of every day, when the sun's light loses its potency and is beginning to give way to the darkness of the night, her faeries would come for story time. As the guardians of nature, faeries have their own work, and they do, indeed, work very hard, so not every faery was present every evening. Sometimes her faeries got caught up with whatever it was that was requiring their energy and attention so they didn't come to hear the evening's tale. Story time was a ritual that was available to all her faeries should they choose to partake, and whether or not they partook was entirely up to them. Usually, there were at least a few hundred of them, but some evenings there could be less, and some evenings there could be more. Regardless of how many of her faeries came, she always told them a story. The story, every evening, was her gift to them.

She was their queen, and they were her people, her petals, as she called them. Her name was Kalistäe but her faeries only ever called her 'Mirri' which, in their language, means 'mother/lady' or 'lady-mother'. In the ancient world, even in the human realm, high priestesses often bore the title "Mirri-Ani" or "Miri-Ani" which means First Lady/ Mother – a way of honouring the ancient language of the Fae realm. The Fae realm has many kings and queens, as many, in fact, as there are bee hives in the human realm, each one intimately connected to his or her own hive, or community. Faerie kings and queens are not like those in the human realm. Faerie kings or queens, as Kalistäe was, do not rule or govern or hold court, nor do they expect to be served by their people. On the contrary, if anything, faerie kings and queens serve their people. That was certainly her role and function in her mind. She was there for them, not the other way around.

The Fae have no need of governance or rulership. They are their own Truest Natures, and they exist as such. So, unlike humans, who need laws to protect them from themselves, and people in government to make those laws, the Fae have no need of laws, or not fabricated laws anyway. There are natural laws governing the Universe, and the Fae, of course, naturally adhere to those. Faerie kings and queens are, perhaps, more like priests and priestesses, conduits of divine love and wisdom, forming the sacred heart of their people, so that their community of faeries exist around them. Faerie kings and queens are to faeries what flames are to moths, and they are what queen bees are to a hive. Kalistäe was the sacred heart of her faery community, and she was a never-ending source of divine love for them. As such, story time was a way for her to send them her love, to infuse them collectively, and for them all to be together, as one. As I said, each story she told them was her gift to them, and the words of her story carried her love to them.

And she did, indeed, adore them. Her faeries, all of them, held within them and, therefore, constantly expressed to her, their consternation over her lack of a mate, a consort, a life partner. Most, if not just about all, faerie queens had their own consorts. Not so Kalistäe. But she always responded to this expressed consternation the same way. With her hands spread wide, a smile sparkling in her eyes, and a dramatic shrug of her shoulders, she would always say, "Why do I need a mate when I have you?". And that was how she genuinely felt. She had everything she needed in her little community of faeries.

Allow me to digress for a brief moment. There are many humans incarnate right now who are from the Fae realm. Many of you know it, but most of you don't yet realise it. As such, it would probably be of great benefit for me to explain what the Fae realm actually is, at least from my perspective, and what a faery's place in it actually is. The Fae realm is not something 'up there' or 'over there', nor is it a kind of 'underworld'. It is, in fact, all around us, and it is everywhere. The truth is, the Fae realm exists within (some of us), and we exist in it or certainly with it. Just as breath is vital for human existence, so, too, is the Fae realm vital for existence itself here on our planet. Unfortunately, humans are so separated from themselves now, and they are so crippled with fear and ignorance that they believe the Fae realm or the realm of faeries is naught but fantasy and imagination, make-believe, stories for children, not adults.

Let me ask you a question. Are humans body only? If humans are body only, then how is it they think and feel? Are they not also mind and heart and soul, even if they are hopelessly cut off and disconnected from their heart and soul? If humans are so much more than just a body, then does it not follow that Gaia, our planet, is also so much more than just a body? Gaia is a consciousness in her own right, and she, too, has a soul. In a sense, the Fae realm exists in and is part of Gaia's soul – the soul of the world. How long have the Fae existed? For as long as humans, or longer? There is a school of thought that believes the Fae have existed for as long as humans have, and that, in fact, the Fae came into existence when humans did. It's an interesting theory. There is certainly no disputing nor mistaking the connection between the beings of the two realms – the human realm and the Fae realm. If nothing else, we look alike. Faeries, gnomes, elves, dwarfs, dryads, sylphs, mermaids and mermen, just to name but a handful of beings from the Fae realm (there are many, many more, of course), all look like humans. Or is it that humans look like them? In a sense, the beings of the Fae realm are the manifestation of the etheriality of human consciousness – the higher aspect of human consciousness. We are certainly intrinsically linked.

The two realms – the human realm and the Fae realm – were never meant to be separated as they are now. That they are is a tragic indictment on the success of the priests of darkness who have usurped human consciousness, taken it over, controlling it and separating it from its own divine source. In fact, the two realms are a vital part of each other, and, as I tell you in "Lady of the Lake", each mourns the loss and Separation from the other. Humans are now heavy and dense in terms of their energetic vibration because they have fallen into lower-dimensionality (a purely material existence, if that helps), and lower-dimensionality is all they know and, therefore, all they see. They are bound by lower-dimensional mindsets. Faeries, not so. A faery's energetic vibration is much higher than humans', and that is precisely why we no longer see them. They vibrate at a level that is beyond the perception of the human lower-dimensional physical sense of sight. If we could but raise our own vibration, humans could see them again, and easily, too. But for those humans who know how to open their inner vision, faeries can actually be seen.

Faeries are highly sensitive and highly intuitive – another reason why we do not see them anymore. They cannot abide the shadow that is individually and collectively wrapped around the human heart, choking it and suppressing its beautiful Light. In fact, a faery will perceive you more so with his or her intuition than with his or her own physical sense of sight. Are you quick to anger, or are you intolerant or ruthless or resentful or bitter or utterly selfish and thoughtless? A faery will stay well away from you . . . as far away as possible, in fact. In the Fae realm, yes, faeries are, as many have stated, guardians of nature, but they also hold within them another important function. They are sparkles of joy, and they fill the Fae realm with their joy, just as birdsong fills the air with joy in the lower dimension, and whale and dolphin song fills the seas of the earth with joy and beauty. Thus, anything that allows faeries to express and experience the joy that they are – music, dancing, laughter, a good story, a caress of pure affection – is vital to a faery, as vital as breathing is to a human.

A word of caution: never, never swat a faery away as you would an insect. You will do unimaginable, possibly even irreparable damage to that faery whether or not you actually hit him or her. That kind of annoyed intolerance could hurt a faery beyond your ability to understand it.

I could spend time answering all those unspoken questions you probably hold within you where faeries are concerned. Do they have sex? No, they do not. To a faery, the beauty in the simple things like holding hands or kissing or touching cheek to cheek generates within them a kind of joy and ecstasy that causes the human orgasm to pale into insignificance. And, faeries are not born, like humans are, and they usually do not die (although it is possible for a faery to become deceased before his or her time). Faeries incarnate, and they disincarnate. Simple. Consequently, they can be incarnate for a lot longer than humans, many hundreds of years, in fact, although they do not count the passing of the years as humans do because they do not fear old age as humans do. Faeries do not age simply because they know the truth. Aging is just a belief. Humans believe they will get old and die, and so they do.

Some people have said faeries are not monogamous in their partnerships. I could not disagree more. This is certainly not my experience of them. I would warn those people to be careful not to imbue faeries with human characteristics. Faeries are a little like birds in that they mate for life because they form intimate bonds as partners that are greatly satisfying to them, and they would not break such a bond, nor would they damage it with an act of infidelity. You have to remember, the human penchant for falling in and out of love is not based on love itself. Rather, it is based on fear. Humans fall in love because they lack, and in falling in love they are trying to attain for themselves whatever it is they think they lack – the characteristic or characteristics held within the person they fall in love with. That is, they are trying to fill a void or a hole within themselves, trying to be whole, and in falling in love with a person, they mistakenly believe that person, or a characteristic within that person, can fill the void. Faeries exist in a state of abundance. They do not lack. Faeries do not 'fall in love'. They love.

Do they wear clothes? Yes. Do they eat? They can, although they eat for pleasure, not for nourishment and energy. Some people believe they love things like bread, honey, cream and milk. Honey, yes, absolutely. It is sweet and natural, but milk and cream? Faeries would not tolerate dairy, and that is precisely why many incarnate as humans in the human realm also cannot tolerate dairy. If you feed a faerie bread, by all means add honey or jam. They would love that. But please, please make sure the bread has none of the god-awful chemicals (like preservatives) we're quite happy to feed ourselves. The chemicals we put in our food and water, not to mention down our drains or sprayed across our fields and gardens are highly toxic to faeries and do very great damage.

The important thing to remember with any being in the Fae realm is that they do not think or conceptualise or perceive as humans do, so it is a mistake to project human thoughts, beliefs, perceptions and focusses onto them. Humans are entrapped in lower-dimensionality, the beings in the Fae realm are not. As such, the Fae know and comprehend so much more than humans could even remotely begin to imagine.

One more thing you should know before we return to our story. Faeries are <u>not</u> children. Faeries are often depicted as children, or child-like, in human art, but this is probably more a symbolic representation of innocence (not naivete, innocence – a state of existence without fear). The faerie consciousness is anything but child-like, and, in fact, a single faerie will most probably hold wisdom within him or her that far, far transcends that of even the oldest of humans. So do not ever make the mistake of thinking that just because a faery is tiny compared to us, he or she is a child. If you hold this mindset, you will severely and significantly underestimate them, to your very own great detriment.

So, with that said and established, back to story time.

Still savouring the energy of anticipation, Kalistäe made herself more comfortable on the carved wooden throne upon which she sat, arranging her gown around her and then laying her arms on the arms of the throne, and clearing her throat in preparation for a lot of talking. She looked up at them. They surrounded her on different levels so that, to look at them all, she had to turn her head and sweep her eyes from left to right, and up and down. A faery would never cut down a tree, of course, but when a tree either willingly or unwillingly loses a branch, faeries can make wonderful things out of the wood. And so it was with her faeries. They had crafted rows and rows of benches, like very thin bookshelves, from branches and twigs. The benches were beautiful, and they looked like a tiny arena around her. Tiny, colourful cushions covered the benches for their comfort so that when she looked at them as a whole, she saw splashes of colour, as if an artist had thrown splashes of different coloured paint onto a canvass that hung suspended in the air. Their hair contributed to the palate of colours, too. Many of her faeries had hair the colour of spun moonlight, but many also had hair the colour of honey, while many more had hair the colour of golden sunlight, and many more had hair the colour of an old oak's dark-brown bark. Some, a precious few, had hair the colour of a raven's feather. 'Tis a misnomer that a faery's hair is like spun silk. A faery's hair is shaggy, like a collection of tiny feathers. Regardless of the colour of the hair on their heads, all heads were still, and every pair of eyes were riveted on Kalistäe expectantly. She smiled her affection at them.

"Tonight," she told them, "I am going to tell you the story of Ariadne."

She wasn't entirely sure why she wanted to tell them Ariadne's story this evening. Perhaps if I take a moment to outline Ariadne's story for you, the reader, you may have an insight of your own into why she was attracted to this particular story on this particular evening. Her faeries had heard Ariadne's story before, many times, in fact. Some people believe faeries have poor memories. A misnomer, and an unfair one at that. Unlike humans who are so bound and locked into a linear concept of time, faeries have no concept of time. Faeries live so much in the moment that the moment is all there really is for them. The future, to a faery, has not yet happened and so will take care of itself, and the past has come and gone. Faeries do remember, but they remember the past as moments, so that if any particular past moment has an impact on the present moment, they will remember it, otherwise what is the point of remembering it? The beauty and the joy of life is in the creation of each new moment, and each moment, in that sense, to a faery is like a blank canvass, full of beautiful, breathtaking, wondrous potential. Humans cannot live that way unfortunately and not just because they are so bound by a linear concept of time, but because they take so much baggage and shadow – fear, judgement, anger, resentment, preconception, misguided belief – from one moment to the next thus negating the wonderful potential of each new moment. Also, of course, humans invariably have unresolved pasts (and not just in their current lives) that dictate their future and control their present – one of the many tragedies of human existence.

So, even though her faeries had heard Ariadne's story before, this new telling of the story, in this new moment, was, itself, new for them. Kalistäe never told the same story the same way anyway. With each new telling of a story there was always some new focus, some new thread of a storyline added or weaved, like a different tapestry depicting the same scene as others but showing that same scene absolutely uniquely.

Right, then, for you, the reader, let us have a recounting of Ariadne's story as Kalistäe would tell it to her faeries this particular evening so that you may know and connect with the story as her faeries would.

Many, many thousands of years ago, there existed on the island of Crete in the Mediterranean Sea a mighty people ruled over by a mighty king. These people, called the Minoans, were a seafaring people with a mighty fleet of powerful ships, and they had built for themselves beautiful palaces and cities made of stone that still exist to this day, although the palaces are now naught but impressive ruins. The region was, many thousands of years ago, prone to quakes that would shake the earth and cause the waves of the sea to pound and even rear up over the coast of their island, so it is not surprising that they paid homage to Poseidon, the god of the sea, water and earthquakes. The legend of Minos, the mighty king of whom I spoke earlier, tells us that in order to settle the question of whether he or another should become king, he knelt at the edge of the sea and prayed to Poseidon to send a bull from the sea so that he, Minos, might sacrifice it thereby consecrating his kingship. Poseidon granted Minos' request, sending a bull from the sea so that Minos' right to rule his people and reign as king was both confirmed and sanctified.

But the bull Poseidon sent was so handsome that Minos could not sacrifice it, and so he substituted the bull for another and kept Poseidon's bull for himself. 'Tis not a good foundation for kingship, is it, to betray a god? Yet, betray a god, he did. Poseidon is not stupid, nor is he so easily fooled. In his rage at being thus betrayed, he caused Minos' queen, Pasiphaë, to fall obsessively in love with the bull. Disguised as a cow, she went to the bull to consummate her love for it, and she bore it a child – a hideous creature, an abomination, half man, half bull. The Minotaur. Minos built a maze, a labyrinth, underneath his palace to house and hide the creature, a reminder of his own very great shame, although I do not think he built the labyrinth because he was contrite.

Minos did not necessarily forgive his queen but nor did he cast her aside, and so he and Pasiphaë went on to have more children, one of whom was Princess Ariadne. Ariadne was, of course, beautiful, as most princesses are. But did anyone notice? Did her father notice? Well, no, because her father's focus was consumed with other pursuits. In his heart of hearts, Minos wanted more power, not just the rule of his own people. He was a conqueror, and so, he made war with Athens, but during the war, his own son was slain, and Minos' heart was full of anger towards the Athenians, even though, of course, the war raged at his instigation. Athenians desired peace and so they made a terrible bargain with Minos to seal that peace. In return for peace, they were to send a tribute of six young men and six young women to Minos every few years. And every few years, when the tribute was sent from Athens, Minos sacrificed these young Athenian people to the Minotaur, the abomination that lived in the labyrinth under his palace.

But the Athenian prince, Theseus, railed against this terrible bargain, and so he convinced his father to include him in the next tribute so that he could go himself to slay Minos' monster and to end, once and for all, the terrible tribute. Reluctantly, his father, the Athenian king, agreed. When Theseus arrived on Crete among the youths of the year's tribute, it was natural that Ariadne should capture his attention, and he should capture hers. He courted and wooed and seduced Ariadne, and he sought and enlisted her aid in his quest to slay the Minotaur. Ariadne fell helplessly and hopelessly in love with the Athenian prince and so she agreed to help him slay the Minotaur. She gave him a skein of wool, or thread, to unravel behind him as he went deeper into the labyrinth so that he could find his way back out by following the thread once he had killed the Minotaur. And he did, indeed, slay the creature. Once the deed was done, he fled Crete in a ship, taking Ariadne with him. But on the way back to Athens, they stopped at the island of Nexos, and when Ariadne fell asleep on the beach, Theseus cruelly left her there, alone, taken from her land and her people, and abandoned. When she awakened, she could see the sails of Theseus' ship on the distant horizon.

Can you imagine how she felt when she awakened and realised what Theseus had done? She was heart broken, devastated. She sat on the beach and cried until she had no more tears left to shed, and it was at this point that the god, Dionysus, came upon her.

Dionysus is a special god, popularly known to be the god of wine and vegetation. The peoples of the ancient world were known to indulge in wine-laden orgies in his honour. But what is probably not so well known is that he is also the Lord of Souls and is associated with the Nether World. As such, he was a favourite of Kalistäe's and also of her faeries, for reasons that, I hope, are obvious to you, the reader. At first, Dionysus sought only to comfort a distressed maiden, but as he came to know her, he fell in love with Ariadne. He healed her broken heart, and so she, too, was able to fall in love again, and so she did, with him. Eventually, they married and had children of their own. She thought it her destiny to be with a prince, and she was devastated when that prince deserted her. But as is always the way, destiny knew better. Ariadne had to be torn from the prince, severed from him, because, in truth, it was her destiny to be with a god. In fact, Dionysus was her true soul mate.

And there endeth Ariadne's story.

As she weaved the threads of the story for her faeries, and as they followed the highs and the lows of Ariadne's experiences, Kalistäe watched and observed their reactions. Many have said of a faery's wings that they are thought forms of energy. This is not inaccurate. In fact, faeries' wings are a part of their very soul, so what a faery is thinking and feeling at any given moment is expressed in their wings. When Ariadne fell in love with the Athenian prince, Kalistäe's faeries' wings were bright, upright and open. When the prince betrayed Ariadne and abandoned her on the beach, breaking her heart in the process, Kalistäe's faeries' wings drooped like flowers in desperate need of water as they felt Ariadne's pain and sadness. Some faeries are tiny, but not so her faeries. Her faeries were as tall as an outstretched hand, sometimes taller, and their wings were taller than them, wide at the top, like a butterfly's wings, and tapering to a graceful point at the bottom. The tips of their wings could thus be seen over their heads, and the bottom of their wings reached nearly to their ankles. Consequently, they could never sit, cross legged, on a flat surface. To do so would squash their wings or bend them, hence the rows and rows of thin benches they had crafted for story time. But the size of their wings also meant that Kalistäe was easily able to perceive both their connection with Ariadne's story and their emotional reaction to it.

So, having heard Ariadne's story, are you able to shed any light on why Kalistäe was so drawn to this story this particular evening? No? Well, why would you when you don't know what is to come? Unless you are exceptionally gifted, which is entirely possible because there are many, many exceptionally gifted souls incarnate in the human experience right now. And, in fact, to give you a slight hint, the story was more for me, and possibly for you, the reader, than it was for Kalistäe's faeries. To give you another slight hint, there is beautiful, profound, incredible meaning in Ariadne's story, and in the symbolism weaved into the fabric of it. All will be revealed once we finish this story. You will understand why this particular story this particular evening. I promise.

A faerie would never interrupt the flow of a story by asking a question in the middle of it, so from start to finish, Kalistäe weaved Ariadne's tale for them, embellishing parts of the tale as she went. Even so, despite the lack of interruption, the ambient light around them was vastly changed by the time she'd finished. The sun's light was all but gone, although the moon's light was yet to take its place. She finished story time with the same time-honoured words she always finished story time with:

"A good night to you, my petals."

As they roused themselves and began to stir, she watched them from her vantage point on her wooden throne, a smile of pure affection hovering in her eyes.

It was, perhaps, as well that neither she nor any of her faeries sensed this would be the last story she would tell them for a long, long, long time. Neither she nor they were aware of any sense that events to come would shake their little community . . . well, actually, would cause it to disperse like dandelion seeds in a strong wind.

Yes, it was just as well they did not know what was to come.

~

The Captain and the Mage

So, the next day, the day after the telling of Ariadne's story, something happened in their small world that had never happened before.

The first inkling Kalistäe had that all was not right in the world beyond that of their forest of ancient oaks was two of her faeries flying towards her holding an envelope between them. The envelope was large enough to require two of them to carry it to her, not because it was heavy but because it would have been too awkward for just one faery to carry. As she watched them approach, the chill of premonition started in the region of her heart and spread outward, through her limbs, causing her skin to tingle with tiny goosebumps. But she was very careful to hide it from her faeries.

When the two carrying the envelope reached her, she took it from them.

"Thank you, Pip, Lill," she said, dipping her head briefly in gratitude. "From where or from whom did you get this?" she asked them.

"Well," Pip replied, "it was left at the edge of the forest during the night, against one of the outer oaks, but we could see no one around, so we do not know from whom it comes."

The envelope was beautiful, a mix of pale yellow and cream in colour, very good quality, and her name was penned across its front in a hand that was well used to writing. She recognised both the envelope and the hand writing immediately, and so, as she turned the envelope over to open it, a myriad of nervous little butterflies gathered and danced within her.

Word travels lightning fast in a close-knit community such as theirs, especially when something out of the ordinary happens, so as Kalistäe opened the envelope, many of her faeries were gathered around her, most of them using their wings to hover around her at shoulder height as they watched her, intense curiosity etched on their little faces. It is no coincidence that dragonflies are associated with faeries in the human realm. To begin with, faeries have a tendency to appear to humans as dragonflies and butterflies in the modern era, but, also, faeries do not flap their wings gracefully like birds. They flutter their wings so quickly their wings become a blur, just like a dragonfly's wings.

Kalistäe broke the wax seal on the back of the envelope, opened it, removed the folded piece of paper within, unfolded it, and read it, her faeries watching her face closely to see and sense her reaction. Remember what I told you about their intuition? Well, it mattered not that she showed no reaction on her face. They could, by now, feel the disturbance within her. They could sense her nervousness and her disquiet, and so they were all aware now that the appearance of the envelope did not bode well or bring good tidings.

"What does it say, Mirri?" Brom asked when Kalistäe remained silent even when she had finished reading the letter contained within the envelope. "Please tell us."

Brom and his life partner, Jezz, were two of the faeries in their community who were always with Kalistäe, always. Never was there any Separation between them and her. They were her confidants, her two little stalwarts, her right hand. Very often, they knew her thoughts even as she thought them, and they acted on her thoughts without her having to voice them. Although all her faeries knew her well, Jezz and Brom knew her best. She privately thought of them as her salt and pepper. Jezz was like a gentle little moonbeam with hair the colour of luminous moonlight. Brom's hair was very dark, like Kalistäe's own hair. He was the impetuous one of the two, always coming up with new and different ideas. More often than not, he spoke for the two of them, not because he was controlling or even dominating but because he couldn't help but voice his thoughts as they came to him. For all that Jezz was gentle and quiet, and he voluble and impetuous, they were both possessed of unwavering strength, courage and wisdom, and these of their characteristics were invaluable to Kalistäe. She privately thought that it was both their differences and their similarities that made them such a perfect pair, and she didn't know what she would do without them. Fortunately she didn't really have to think about that much because they were always just there, with her.

She looked up at them all.

"The Mage has requested my presence at the edge of the forest. He specifies a time and a place. He wishes to confer with me, and what he has to tell me, he would prefer to do so face to face. He needs our help with something, I think, although he does not say so in the letter."

"Oh-oh," Brom said, hovering right beside her, always at her right shoulder, and speaking, as usual, for all the faeries present. "That does not sound good."

"No, this is not good, Brom," Kalistäe said, the tone of her voice echoing her disquiet. "This is really not good. I fear something terrible might have happened. The Mage has not made this request lightly."

You have to understand, Kalistäe's little community existed at a point in human time when humans still knew of the Fae realm and were quite comfortable with it . . . well, some more so than others, I would say. Most were comfortable with it so long as they had nothing to do with it. There were, of course, and always would be, those who feared it greatly. I wouldn't exactly say there was contact between the two, as such, at this point in human time, although there were some humans who did enjoy contact with the Fae, of whom the Mage was one. In fact, Kalistäe and the Mage were like old friends, and had enjoyed contact with each other for many, many humans years. The Mage was a learned man, one who open-mindedly studied the natural world around him with a view to understanding it, one who recognised that to understand the natural world you simply could not ignore a vital part of it. So it was natural that he had, many years earlier, sought out Kalistäe and others of her kind to glean their wisdom. He and she had remained friends ever since. He it was who kept her community of faeries in touch with the affairs of humans, but their contact had, over recent years, morphed into a kind of 'no news is good news' dynamic. The fact that he was making contact now, and so definitely, did not bode well for either the human or the Fae realms. Something was wrong. She could feel it.

The Mage was indeed awaiting Kalistäe at the edge of the forest as promised in his letter, and he had a companion with him. As she moved closer to the edge of the forest, Kalistäe could see a contingent of a dozen or so men with horses some distance away, behind the Mage and his companion, obviously told to keep away. The men were holding the horses and talking among themselves, paying no heed whatsoever to the Mage and his companion. At the very edge of the forest, she stopped, not willing to step beyond it, and the Mage bowed low, formally, with his hand laid flat over his chest.

"Lady Kalistäe," he said, "how very wonderful it is to see you again. It has been too long since last we spoke, I think. Thank you for granting an old man his request."

She smiled at him as he straightened.

"Old, indeed," she scoffed, her smile still sparkling at him. "You are ageless, my old friend. And 'tis very good to see you again, too, Orde."

He was tall, slightly taller than she was, and slim, with long, thick, dark-grey hair and a long, dark-grey bushy beard to match. Neither hair nor beard had felt a pair of scissors for a long time, nor a comb most probably. He never bothered with such trivialities. There were always far more interesting and important things occupying his thoughts. His eyebrows were dark, darker than his hair and beard, and his eyes were grey and always sparkled with his intelligence and his irrepressible humour. He wore a long, white tunic, and a long-sleeved, blue over coat with elaborate red brocade and embroidery around its edges – the uniform of his craft, a little like a priest's robes – and on his feet were leather sandals that had seen better days.

The Mage responded to her smile, his own smile sparkling in his grey eyes for a moment, and then he introduced his companion. "May I introduce Captain Abram," he said indicating his companion with an outstretched hand. "Captain Abram is the captain of the king's army. Captain, this is the Lady Kalistäe."

She removed her eyes from the Mage and looked at the captain, but he was staring at her, as if in a trance, or as if suddenly turned to stone, with his mouth slightly open. He was, in that first, initial moment of meeting her, completely unable to speak, and this from a man who had seen and experienced much in his life. You have to understand, for some humans, the Fae can take some getting used to. While they look like humans, they are also very different from humans. Whereas the Mage was well used to Kalistäe and her kind, the captain was not, this being the first ever contact he'd had with the Fae. To date, the captain had always been focussed on other things, understandably so given his command of a whole army. It wasn't that he had no time for the Fae. He'd just never had cause to make contact with them or to have any dealings with them. The Fae simply did not feature in the landscape of his world, his sphere. Captaining the king's army took up a rather large amount of his time and attention, not to mention space in his overall life and in the rhythm of his day to day life – something that was to change from this moment on (the Fae can tend to have that affect on humans when crossing their path). To him, as he'd watched her emerge from the forest, Kalistäe had first appeared like a mirage, shimmering with light, but nebulous and insubstantial, ethereal, even ghostly, like an apparition. It was only as she got closer to the edge of the forest and to him that she had shimmered into a more solid form, until she appeared so solid, she looked exactly as they did . . . well, not **exactly**, but you get my meaning.

And when she shimmered into a more solid form, she was, to him, so dazzlingly beautiful that he could only stare. Certainly, he had never seen a woman as beautiful as she was. Such is the appearance of the Fae to humans. She appeared tall to the Mage and the captain, tall and slim, with skin like luminous moonlight. Her hair was the colour of the dark-brown bark of the oaks of her forest, and her faeries had arranged it into a pile of curls on top of her head. Her curls were a continued source of fascination to her faeries who all, without exception, had straight hair. She wore an under gown of what looked like silver-grey satin with silver-grey satin slippers on her feet. Over the satin under gown, she wore an over gown of fine, silver-grey gossamer, the material so fine it looked like web. It was part of the gown up the top, over the bodice, but opened like a coat underneath so that, as light as it was, it billowed out behind her when she walked. It was interwoven with sparkling jewels that were, in fact, little sparkles of light, so that she seemed to glitter even when she was solid. The gown as a whole, the satin under gown and its over gown of gossamer, had long sleeves that covered her wrists, and the skirt, too, was long. The over gown of gossamer trailed behind her as she walked, disturbing the leaves of the forest floor in her wake. The bodice of the gown was fitted to the top of her waist, and it sat on the edges of her shoulders so that her neck and the tops of her shoulders were bare. She wore no adornments, no jewellery, which was, itself, a novel thing to the captain who was used to the heavily made up and overly-bejewelled ladies of the king's court. Her eyes were beautiful, compelling, framed by dark lashes, and silver-grey, the same colour as her gown.

The Mage cleared his throat in the somewhat awkward silence that followed his introduction. "Captain Abram," he said again.

The captain seemed to shake himself out of his temporary stupor, and, as the Mage had done, bowed low and formerly.

"Forgive my rudeness, my Lady." Straightening, he added, almost under his breath, "I've not seen anything quite so beautiful before."

Kalistäe responded to both the honesty and the compliment. As she had with the Mage, she smiled at the captain, receiving his compliment with grace.

"Thank you, captain."

He was slightly taller than the Mage, wearing a soldier's uniform – tailored dark-red tunic, black pants and long, black, leather boots, a long, red cloak over his shoulders. He wore a sword belted to his hip, and his dark-brown hair, although shoulder length, was neatly tied back and held in place with a strip of leather. His blue eyes were clear, the colour of the sky on a cloudless day, and they held hers unblinkingly, without fear. She noted the fact with interest as she responded to his greeting. Most humans struggle to maintain eye contact with the Fae, especially when encountering them for the first time. The Fae have a way of looking right into a person and it usually makes that individual squirm with discomfort. Not so the captain. The fact that the captain was able to maintain such steady eye contact with her told her more clearly than words that he was a man who had very little to hide. The captain was a man who was not ashamed of anything he had done.

"Different we may be," she said to him, "but I still understand human nature, very well, in fact. You have not encountered the Fae before now?"

"No, my Lady, I have not."

"Lady Kalistäe," the Mage said, drawing her attention and sounding somewhat uncertain, "are you alone?"

She laughed a tinkling laugh, genuinely amused. "Oh but you should know better than to ask such a question, Orde. I am never alone." And then, she turned her head slightly as if speaking to someone standing behind her and said, "You may come out now. They will not hurt you."

Slowly but very surely, little heads hesitantly appeared over the top of the branches of the trees closest to Kalistäe, and from behind leaves, and from behind Kalistäe herself. Brom and Jezz appeared over her shoulders, hovering initially until they took up their usual places, perched on her shoulders, Brom on her right and Jezz on her left. Some of her faeries settled where they were, sitting on the branch they had previously hidden behind, but many of them hovered around Kalistäe.

Again, unable to help himself, the captain stared. He'd heard the stories of faeries as a boy, not as an adult, but he'd always thought they were just stories – a product of someone's imagination. And yet, here they were, as real as he was. They, too, were beautiful, each and every one, but they seemed uncommonly and downright strange to him.

Again, catching himself, he sent an apologetic smile to Kalistäe. She caught it and returned it, letting him know all was forgiven.

"Ah, yes," the Mage said, sounding very satisfied and chuckling his amusement and his affection for Kalistäe's little community of faeries. "Much better. Much better indeed."

Kalistäe smiled at him again, briefly, in response to his words. But then her smile faded. "What am I doing here, Orde?"

The Mage cleared his throat. "My Lady, 'tis grave tidings I bring, I'm sorry to say. The king has convened the Council of Kings, and I have advised him that I believe the Council to be an exercise in utter futility without your presence. I know it is much to ask of you, but would you accompany us to the capital so as to attend the Council. All will be revealed there. I would not ask this of you if it was not so important. In my very humble opinion, 'tis imperative that you attend and hear what the captain has to say. Your advice and counsel are very much needed at this time, I fear."

"Oh, dear," she whispered softly, like the whisper of a soft breeze. She knew of the Council of Kings. Only matters of extreme concern, matters that affected not just their land but the lands beyond its borders, were cause to convene the Council. Needless to say, the Council had not been convened for many, many generations. All the lands had been at peace, untroubled. There was not the need. The butterflies fluttering within her again made themselves known. "Mage," she said formerly, "you are known to us, and you are our friend. This we know. You would not ask this of me if not for the gravest of concerns. In this, we trust your judgement. I will do as you ask. I will accompany you to the king's capital. I will grant your request. I will attend your Council."

The Mage, in response, closed his eyes as relief, pure and potent, coursed through him. Again, he bowed. "I thank you, my Lady."

Kalistäe turned around to face her faeries. "Belle, Jasper, you will have to explain to everyone that I cannot tell them their story this evening. I am so very sorry. I doubt we will return in time. I will see you tomorrow, hopefully. Stay together and take care of each other. Brom, Jezz, will you come with me?"

"Yes, Mirri, of course," Brom answered for them both. "We would never let you go by yourself, never."

When she turned back to the Mage and the captain, a silver-grey satin cloak covered her gown, its hood pulled up, hiding her hair and partially hiding her features. Her two faeries, Brom and Jezz, were hovering beside her, shoulder height. The captain blinked in surprise but refrained from saying anything.

"I am ready," she said simply.

They did not have overly far to travel. The king's capital, Duavel (pronounced Dwa-vel, with the accent on the 'vel'), could be seen in the far, far distance from the edge of Kalistäe's forest of oaks. Still, the distance was far enough to warrant the use of the horses. Kalistäe sat astride her horse like a man, her silver-grey cloak covering its rump, and her faeries sat, or kneeled, more like, on the tops of her legs for most of the ride, looking out at the land as they passed through it. The captain, riding beside and slightly behind Kalistäe, couldn't help but watch her two faeries, especially Brom who was on the same side as he. Brom's upright wings reflected his fascination of the landscape through which they passed. Like a dog with its head out a car window, its ears upright, watching everything that passes and smelling every scent that comes and goes, Brom was absorbed, fascinated, sometimes fixated on the things he could see from the road – stone and thatch cottages with smoke wafting out of their chimneys, cows in fields lazily chewing the grass, a wagon or cart laden with wooden barrels or sacks of grain passing by in the opposite direction, children playing hopscotch or skipping rope and singing nursery rhymes, orchards of lusciously-ripe golden or red fruit on rows and rows of fruit trees, quacking ducks flying overhead in a v-shaped formation. Things the captain took completely for granted were a source of utter fascination to Kalistäe's faeries, and their fascination made him look at the landscape through a slightly different lens. He liked what he saw. Only as they approached Duavel did the two faeries disappear under the edges of Kalistäe's cloak, staying out of sight of prying human eyes.

Orde rode beside Kalistäe, and they talked about a myriad of different topics, catching up, for the entirety of the ride. The captain's men rode in front, behind and on either side of them, forming a ring of protection. While Kalistäe and Orde talked quietly and the faeries avidly and interestedly watched the landscape, the captain and his men remained silent, vigilant, their eyes constantly scanning the terrain through which they rode, watching for signs of potential trouble.

Once they reached Duavel and passed underneath one of its gates, the riding party stretched itself out, by necessity. Courtesy of both the crowds and the narrowness of the cobbled streets of the capital, they were forced to ride two by two. The captain rode beside Kalistäe when they reached the capital, ever protective, Orde behind them with his own escort. Kalistäe absorbed her new surroundings almost as keenly as her faeries had done. The capital's stone buildings loomed over them and around them. She wondered how humans were able to live in such constricted conditions. In a very real sense, they almost lived on top of each other. She would have struggled to breathe if forced to live the same way. She also observed the faces of the people they passed, noting their lack of curiosity, as if the riding party was a common sight to them. Nor did she detect panic or fear on their faces as they went about their business. Whatever was worrying Orde, enough to request her presence at the Council, either the people were not aware of it or it was not worrying them. She suspected it to be the former of the two possibilities. They passed into an open, paved square, as large as three whole blocks. The square was teaming with people walking in different directions, but the people parted like the proverbial Red Sea, almost unconsciously, for the riding party, obviously used to having to move out of the way for horses. The king's castle, at the top of the square, dominated the space around it, looming over the square like a benevolent guardian. The riding party dismounted at the bottom of the staircase that led to the castle's entrance. Kalistäe's faeries still hid within the folds of the cloak, even as and after she dismounted. The captain's men did not accompany them. They left the captain, Orde and Kalistäe, leading the horses away. The captain escorted Kalistäe and Orde up the stairs of the castle's entrance and then through the corridors of the castle. In any other circumstance, Kalistäe would have paid attention, admiring the beauty of the castle's interior – its polished marble floors, its colourful walls, high, painted ceilings, opulent furnishings, its glittering chandeliers and candelabra, its golden-framed mirrors and paintings, its beautiful sculptures and tapestries – but the tension coiled within her precluded such admiration.

When they reached a pair of heavy, closed, very tall, beautifully-carved, dark wooden doors, the captain hesitated. Before he opened the doors, he felt it prudent to warn her.

"My Lady, you should know, all the lands are represented at the Council, and some have brought with them quite sizeable contingents. The room is well crowded."

She no longer wore the cloak, and her two faeries hovered beside her, one at each shoulder.

"I see," she said. "Thank you, captain. I am grateful for the warning."

As if in direct response, her faeries, staying protectively close to her, settled on her bare shoulders, one on either side as he had come to expect, and they folded their wings close to their bodies, like a concertina fan.

The captain was not wrong. The room behind the wooden doors was enormous, like a large ball room, with a high, painted ceiling, an enormous gold and crystal chandelier hanging in its centre, large, floor to ceiling windows on its outer walls framed by thick, yellow drapes, allowing in plenty of light, a colourful, polished marble floor . . . and it was full of people. The throng of people parted for the captain, and as the people parted to allow them through, Kalistäe could see an enormous, polished wood table in the centre of the room. When they entered the room, the captain lightly and protectively touched her arm, putting his hand under her elbow, staying close to her. As they moved through the people, she and her faeries pointedly ignored the stares of the people. The captain escorted her and Orde to their places at the table, and then he bowed to her and left. He had work to do, for he it was who, with Orde's invaluable assistance, had organised the agenda and the topics to be discussed at the Council this day.

The table, she discovered once she took her place at it, was elliptical, and it was even larger than she'd first thought. In the centre of the opposite side from where she was stood the king, whom she had met through Orde on a number of occasions. When she looked over at him, he bowed formally as Orde had done, with his hand laid flat over his chest.

"Lady Kalistäe," he said over the din of conversation that was filling the room, "my gratitude to you for attending our Council. I can assure you, your counsel is very much needed and will be greatly appreciated."

She bowed her head in return. "Morghan, your majesty, you are most welcome. I hope I justify your faith in my ability to offer you appropriate counsel."

"Oh you will," he said definitely. Like the captain, Morghan's near-black hair was shoulder length but, unlike the captain, he wore it loose. Today, he looked every inch the king. He wore his crown atop his dark hair, and his mantle was opulent, complete with ermine collar and sleeve edges. His doublet was richly embroidered and he wore a large ruby ring on one finger. The formality of his dress was unusual for him. He preferred more informal clothes, no matter where he was or what he was doing. The formality of his dress, she knew, was part of the theatre, but it also symbolised his intent to rule over the proceedings today. King Morghan had called this Council, and King Morghan was in charge.

With Orde and Kalistäe now present, Morghan called for silence and asked the throng of people for their undivided attention. Despite the crowd of people filling the room, near-total silence descended.

The king thanked everyone for their attendance, and then he took the time to introduce all those who were standing at the table. As this was the Council of Kings, only kings or queens and dukes and princes stood at the table, with the exception of Orde, Morghan's Mage and most valued adviser, and Captain Abram, commander of the king's army. I will not bore you by naming all the kings and queens present (although there was only one queen and we already know her), but I will tell you who they were or, rather, which lands they ruled. The king of Moab ruled the land to the north. The kings of Elba and Bressar ruled the lands to the east, and the king of Isae ruled the lands even further east. The Western Isles, of which there were more than a dozen, sparkled like green gems in the sun-drenched, sparkling seas to the west. Each isle was independent, or ruled itself in its own right, although not all were kingdoms. Some were dukedoms and some were principalities. Of course, although officially independent of each other, they were all bound by trade and treaties and agreements, not to mention marriage, so that they were many, but they were also one. It would be tiresome to name every one of the Western Isles, so I will name the largest, Corynth, and the smallest, Thora. Without exception, the ruler of every isle was present.

And then, the one king I will name other than Morghan, King of Pereia, the land within which the Council of Kings was taking place, was Amoranth, one of the five kings of the elvish lands to the south. As if Orde's and Morghan's request for her presence was not enough of an indication to Kalistäe of the seriousness of the situation, coupled with the fact of Morghan's very formal dress and the presence of every ruler of every land, the presence of one of the elvish kings was very revealing and very worrying indeed. Kalistäe felt chills in her entire body when Amoranth was introduced and, behind him, representatives from every elvish land, although he would obviously speak for them all. The elvish kings never, never left their own lands to come into the lands of the humans. They no longer interacted with humans at all. So the fact that so many of the elven folk, and one of their kings, had come here to take part in the Council was unprecedented in their time. When he was introduced to the Council at large, Amoranth turned towards Kalistäe and bowed low.

"Lady Kalistäe," he said, "it gladdens my heart to see you here."

She bowed her head in acknowledgement and when they both straightened, they maintained eye contact for a long moment, exchanging words silently, in the depths of their minds.

"It is that bad, then?" she asked him.

"Worse," he said. "Darkness has come to our lands and yours, Kalistäe. It threatens the well-being of us all. Listen closely and know that what is spoken of today is merely the tip of the iceberg. We have long felt it, but of late it has been gaining power, and we can no longer ignore it."

"Why have I not felt anything?" she asked him.

"I know not, my Lady," he replied. "I know not. Perhaps you did not want to sense it, because I think, of all those present today, you are the one upon whose shoulders this burden will fall heaviest."

She looked sad as she nodded her acknowledgement of his words.

And so, throughout the long morning, she did exactly as Amoranth instructed. She listened closely, and she observed many things both overt and subtle. Often, as the captain presented his reports and followed these with first-hand witness accounts, the other rulers interrupted to ask questions or seek clarification. Not so Kalistäe or Amoranth. The two listened, their attention never wavering, without saying a word. Kalistäe did not even make comments to Orde who was standing next to her and who already knew of the incidents being reported on and presented, nor did he make any comment to her, although often-times he glanced at her in an attempt to gauge her reaction if not her thoughts. He would not interrupt her observations or the flow of her thoughts. She would detect subtleties that everyone else would miss. He would not disturb her concentration.

As I said, Captain Abram had prepared detailed reports which he presented to the Council, but he did not just present reports. His reports, if anything, although thorough and detailed, were an introduction to what followed each one. He had organised numerous individuals to provide first-hand accounts of the sorts of incidents that were occurring throughout all the lands. And so, the Council of Kings heard from mothers and fathers whose children had vanished, sons and daughters whose parents had disappeared, brothers whose sisters were missing, and sisters whose brothers were missing. In all and every case, no trace of those who had gone missing had ever been found – no body, no blood, no torn or ripped clothing, no signs of a struggle. Children had vanished from cottage gardens, husbands and brothers had left for daily chores and never come home, mothers and sisters had left to attend the local market and never arrived. The witnesses, in recounting their own stories, often did so tearfully. They came from every land, not just Pereia. Some had travelled far to tell the Council their sorry tale.

At one point, one of the kings asked the captain a pertinent question.

"Are these disappearances increasing in number, captain, or are they occurring surely but steadily?"

"A good question," the captain replied. "They are increasing, and have been over a number of years. At first, reports of missing persons were sporadic, seemingly random, and rare enough not to raise any concerns. The incidents could be blamed on hungry wild animals or on unfortunate accidents. Not so anymore. They are now occurring too regularly, too consistently, and far too prolifically to be attributed to mundane causes like wild animals."

"Are they occurring in specific places, or in some places more so than others?" the same king asked.

The captain shook his head. "No, your majesty. People are disappearing from everywhere, from isolated places and from crowded places, from villages and from cities, during the day and at night. They are disappearing in every land, although not so prolifically in the Western Isles. The one thing I can report is that no person has yet vanished from inside his or her own house, although people have vanished from within other buildings, like taverns. To date, every individual who has gone missing, regardless of age, has been outside their house for one reason or another."

Kalistäe and Amoranth exchanged looks, speaking silently in their thoughts for the first time since the Council began.

"Threshold," she said simply. "Whoever is doing this is bound by the power of the threshold."

"So it would seem," he replied. "An interesting but valuable observation of the captain's."

It is not just a strange quirk of legend that has a vampire barred from entering a house without an invitation. Vampires are genuinely wholly unable to enter a house without being personally invited because entities of darkness cannot penetrate the barrier of the threshold. Practitioners of magic will tell you that there is real power in the threshold created around a home, and that power is strong enough to prevent dark entities from entering. I tell you true, and this is true regardless of whether you believe in magic or not. What do you think forms the basis of the power of the threshold? Love, familial bonds, trust, care. These have real power. It would be worth remembering that. It would also be worth remembering that fear, hatred, violence, abuse, distrust all erode the power of the threshold because these break the familial bond, or the bonds of those living in the house. True. The fact that the perpetrators of the disappearances were bound by the power of the threshold signalled to Kalistäe and Amoranth that the perpetrators were not ordinary humans, and that there was magic involved, black magic, probably the blackest magic.

The two of them held eye contact for a moment longer as the entire Council silently and collectively digested the captain's answers to the questions posed, and each person present was confronted with the deeper and more far-reaching ramifications. Whatever was going on, it was escalating, a confirmation, Kalistäe knew, of Amoranth's belief that this darkness was gaining power. The disappearances were sinister, of that there was no doubt, and worrying, but at this early stage, Kalistäe had heard nothing that allowed her to know who or what might be behind them. That there **was** something behind them all was a certainty, but as to what it was, she could not sense at this early stage, although an as-yet-unfounded suspicion was beginning to take root within her.

And then the captain presented another report and the Council heard from individuals who had either witnessed or themselves been subject to the effects of a new kind of recreational smoking drug, like tobacco but not tobacco, that was insidiously robbing those who smoked it of their sanity, in some cases permanently. It induced frightening hallucinations that continued to plague the victim long after he or she had sobered, when there was no more trace of the drug in their system. The hallucinations could, apparently, come at any time whether the individual was awake or sleeping, and they completely distorted the victim's perception of reality. In some cases, the drug had induced extreme paranoia, and the individual had hurt people as a result. Some victims had found the experiences too much to handle and so had taken their own lives. Others had fully recovered, and yet others were struggling to handle the hallucinations that were plaguing them so that they were struggling to live normal lives. In every land, the drug had been outlawed, and the laws introduced in an attempt to stamp out the drug were harsh. Despite the risk, the prevalence of the use of the drug was increasing and spreading. It was, apparently, highly addictive so that people were still using it long after they desperately wanted to stop. And, of course, its effects were not just individualised. It was fast becoming a serious threat to the economic stability of each land, and any and all attempts to locate the source of it had so far failed, although it seemed to be more prevalent in the east than the west. It was, as yet, to make any sort of impact on the Western Isles. Other than that, the captain reported that there seemed to be no epicentre of supply, or none that could be identified.

Kalistäe sought Amoranth's attention again, and the two held eye contact as they exchanged silent words.

"Again, the Western Isles are not as touched by this problem as those of the eastern lands. Water, do you think?"

Amoranth did not answer straight away. "Water?" he repeated when he finally did respond. "You think the water is forming a natural barrier that is difficult for them to cross?"

"It would seem so."

Someone else asked another salient question of the captain, drawing their attention.

"And you think this new drug is related to the disappearances we heard about earlier, captain?"

"I do, yes."

"For what purpose is it being used, do you think?"

"Destabilisation, I think, your majesty, at a collective level, and a deliberate fostering of both dependence and a disruption to normal cognitive function at an individual level."

Again, the Council digested this in complete silence. The captain had obviously thought long and hard about the underlying whys and wherefores of the appearance of the drug, and no one was prepared to discount his conclusions.

"Do you have proof of the connection between these two concerning problems, captain?" The question came from somewhere else around the table.

The captain shook his head. "Nothing tangible, no. Just gut instinct."

Again, the entire Council was silent. The captain was respected, and so was his instinct. No one doubted he was right.

The next report and associated eye witness accounts presented to the Council were concerned with strange lights and noises in isolated places, like forests and in the middle of fields. Some brave individuals had managed to get close enough to witness strange rituals, intoxicated people dancing naked around an altar or a fire and screaming unearthly screams of ecstasy and pain. Twice, witnesses told of long, silver knives used to cut the throat of a captured animal so that its blood could be collected and consumed, and one witness told the Council the sacrificial victim had been human. During this account, Kalistäe and Amoranth again exchanged a long look and, with it, silent words.

"Blood sacrifice," she said. "They are speaking of rituals involving blood sacrifice."

"Indeed," he replied. "Such is the power of the black magic attacking your lands."

"Now, at last, we have something that genuinely links all these incidents – an underlying agenda. Black magic, just as you say."

"Yes, Kalistäe, black magic."

"You think those who have disappeared are being used as fodder for their rituals of black magic?"

"I do."

"By the gods," she breathed. "Who would do such a thing?"

"Who indeed."

Throughout the presentation of the reports and the witness accounts, Kalistäe's two little faeries inched slowly closer and closer to Kalistäe's neck until they were pressed against her.

"Are you all right, my petals?" she asked them at one stage.

This time, Brom remained silent – telling in and of itself – and it was Jezz who responded.

"'Tis quite horrible, Mirri," she whispered. "Quite horrible. 'Tis hard to comprehend."

"Yes, Jezz, my blossom, it is. It is indeed."

But something was beginning to niggle at Kalistäe as her suspicion grew. A chill dread had taken up residence deep within her, and she had a terrible feeling that she just might recognise the hand that was guiding these collective incidents. She hoped, hoped she was wrong, but if not, then she would need to connect with the overall intent of this dark agenda, and that was not going to be pleasant . . . not pleasant at all.

And then Captain Abram presented the last of his reports, perhaps the most disturbingly chilling of them all. There had been a number of incidents, again, in every land, involving either single or multiple murders, or massacres where there seemed to be no motive whatsoever, and of which the offenders had no memory whatsoever. In each case, the individual who had committed the murder or massacre had no idea why they had done it and nor could they remember a single moment of it, a truth born out by the fact that none of them tried to run or hide or evade authorities. They could not remember how they got there, wherever the scene of the murders was, and, once they came to, they had no notion of why they were there.

When the captain presented his report, he confirmed that, in each case, under the laws of the lands, those who had committed the murders had, themselves, been condemned to die. In most cases, they had already been executed, but there were some, a handful, still awaiting execution.

"But," the captain said as he finished his presentation, "I can't help feeling these people are as much victims of these incidents as the victims themselves. In every case, they are as perplexed and bewildered and downright confused by their own actions as they would have been had they not committed the crime and been accused of it."

Among the last of the witnesses the captain presented to the Council was one such individual. They brought him in with his hands bound in front of him and his feet shackled in chains so that he had to shuffle to the table. The captain first gave an account of what had happened, outlining the events of the fateful night to the Council. The man had gone to his local tavern late at night when there was only a dozen patrons left. He had with him a long, curved, silver knife, and in a frenzy, he had stabbed the tavern keeper and every patron still in the tavern – thirteen men in total. Some of the patrons had been big, strong men – men who did physical work for a living – and their blood had been spilled so violently that the tavern was all but covered in it, like paint. The man had overpowered them easily even though he was not, himself, big and burly as some of them had been. The man then gave an account of what he had experienced from his own perspective. Various ones of the Council's kings questioned him, but, really, to no avail. He could not remember anything either just before, during or straight after the incident. Apparently, the last thing he remembered was going to bed next to his wife as he did every night, and the first thing he remembered afterwards was coming to, standing outside his local tavern, covered in blood with a bloodied knife in his hand. The knife was not his, and he didn't know where he'd got it from. He didn't recognise it. Giving his own account, he seemed like a gentle man, a common farmer, a family man in his mid thirties. The captain brought in other witnesses, people who swore the young farmer had never exhibited even a slight tendency to violence. He was a good man, a family man, a stalwart of the local community, and his actions were entirely out of character.

When it was obvious there were no more answers to be gained from the young farmer, the captain's men were about to lead him away, back to his jail cell where he would see out the last of his days.

"Wait."

The single word sliced through the room, the silence and, indeed, the Council like a hot knife through butter. Every head in the room turned towards Kalistäe, and the soldiers who had hold of the farmer froze. The one word held her power. She had made sure of that, but she had spoken not one word throughout the entire proceedings. The impact of her speaking now after silence was as powerful as the power imbued in the word.

She inclined her head. "Captain, would you allow me to question this man? It may take some time, but there are answers here that may be of value to us."

He motioned for the soldiers behind the man to desist. They obeyed, releasing him. "Of course, my Lady. Please, ask of him what you will."

"I pray the Council indulge me," she said to the Council at large.

"Please, Lady Kalistäe," Morghan responded on behalf of the Council, "ask this man what you will."

Kalistäe nodded her thanks and then looked at the farmer. "What is your name?"

His head was bowed and he wouldn't look at her. "Ethan. My name is Ethan."

"Well, Ethan, would you look at me, please?"

Reluctantly, he looked up. He had no choice but to look at her not just because of the forum and the context but because her command was compelling. He looked over the length of the long table at her, and when he did she locked her eyes onto his so that, try as he might, he could not look away. His story had greatly disturbed Kalistäe largely because throughout his telling of it, she had sensed that he felt more sorry for himself than he did his victims, or his victims' families. And so, relentlessly, she held his eyes with her own, probing, delving into his unconscious memories. Silence stretched between them, and, in fact, over everyone in the room. No one around the table or behind those who stood at the table moved or spoke. Some even held their breath, glad, in this moment, they were not in the poor farmer's shoes.

The silence and the long, probing look into his eyes paid off. Kalistäe found what she was looking for.

"You are proud of your little farm, are you not, Ethan?" she asked him, breaking through the silence and deliberately emphasising the word 'little' by imbuing it with slightly more of her power.

Ethan, the simple farmer, flushed, angry, and his tone when he replied also held his anger. "My farm is not little. It is thriving and prosperous."

She inclined her head at him. "And," she added, "it has been in your family for generations. You inherited it from your father, and he inherited it from his father, and so on, back through the generations. Is that not so?"

"That is so," he confirmed.

"Then how did it make you feel when a stranger, a first-generation farmer, purchased the land next to yours . . ."

Foolishly – I say foolishly because it is only a fool who would interrupt a Fae being when he or she is speaking, cutting across his or her words – the farmer interrupted her, and when he did, he sounded belligerent. The gentle man standing before the Council giving an account of his lack of memory had disappeared, or so it seemed to every member watching the interchange.

"I made him feel welcome. I did. But he did not try to fit in. He never made any effort to be neighbourly, an' he did things the rest of us'd never do."

"The consequence of which was the establishment of a very successful farmstead. He, this neighbour, naught but a first-generation farmer, built up his farm so successfully in just a handful of years that his farm threatened the viability of yours."

Again, her words carried her power, and her voice sounded ever-so-slightly harsh. Both Jezz and Brom hid their faces against her neck. They had never before heard their queen speak to another so harshly.

The farmer flushed again and said, "I was addressing that."

"But oh the shame should you fail, oh the shame." Again, she inclined her head at him. "You told the Council nothing unusual or out of the ordinary happened in the days and weeks leading up to the events of that awful night."

"Yes, ma'am, that is so."

"Then I want you to tell the Council what happened on the night of the full moon two months before the massacre."

He shook his head. "I don't remember that night . . ."

"Yes you do. Speak."

She locked her eyes on his. He swallowed nervously as the vision of that night filled his mind. He'd completely forgotten about that night, forgotten it so completely it was as if it had never happened. But as he looked deep into her eyes, he suddenly remembered it . . . all of it. It came flooding back into his conscious mind as if she had opened a door to allow the memory to flood in.

He licked dry lips and swallowed nervously. "I went to the tavern after dinner and I had a bit too much to drink, and I talked to a few friends about my worries 'n what the intruder was doing to mess things up for the rest of us."

"That's what you call him, the neighbour? You call him the intruder?"

"Yes, ma'am."

"What happened in response to your criticisms? Did anyone else hear you other than those to whom you were speaking specifically?" She and he both knew he'd spoken loud enough for the whole tavern to hear him, but that was not important so she let it go.

"There was a man in the corner of the tavern. I'd not noticed him, but then I did notice him, and he beckoned to me. So I went over and he told me he could help me with my problems."

"What did this man look like?"

The farmer thought. "He was . . ." He stopped talking, unable to bring the memory of the man into focus. He raised his bound hands and waved them over his face. "He was just like any other man, but he was kind of in shadow. I couldn't see him properly."

"What was he wearing?"

Again, the farmer tried to bring the memory into sharper focus but couldn't. All he could see was black shadow. "Black. He was just wearing black, like a cloak with a hood. Except he had this kind of medallion thing." He used his bound hands to indicate the region of his chest.

Kalistäe and Amoranth exchanged a silent look. Her worst suspicions were confirmed.

"Priests of Si'il," she said silently.

He nodded, slightly, subtly.

"What are they doing here?"

"You tell me, Kalistäe. If the Si'il are here, they want humans under their control and they will not stop until they **have** humans under their control. And even then, they will not stop."

She nodded her agreement and then looked at the farmer again. "How did he help you, Ethan, this stranger in black?" she asked out loud.

"He gave me some gold coins. He said the money would help me to di . . . di . . . div . ."

"Diversify?" Kalistäe asked, helping him out.

"Yes, that's it. Diversify. And he said once I did, I would become competitive again."

"And what did he get out of this deal?"

The farmer shook his head. "Nothing. He just said I could pay him back when I started making money again, as I would if I di . . . div . . . did what he suggested."

"A total stranger gives you gold and asks nothing in return, and you don't think this strange or out of the ordinary?"

The farmer worked his bottom lip, biting it with his teeth. "To be honest, ma'am, I didn't remember it. I didn't remember the whole night. I didn't remember talking to him."

"And the gold? Where did you think that came from, then?"

He shrugged.

"You didn't care, did you? You cared only that you had it, and you could spend it. It made you feel successful again. It made you feel important. It made you feel like you could beat him, this first-generation farmer who had moved next door and was showing you up, making you feel like a second-rate farmer."

For the first time, the young farmer looked guilty, contrite. He lowered his head. "Yes, ma'am, it just felt good to have it. It felt like I was back in control."

The room was utterly still and silent as every person listened to the conversation. The captain was frowning, and so was Morghan.

"How long did you spend with this shadowed stranger that night, Ethan?"

Again, he shrugged, his head still lowered. "I dun know, ma'am. I dun know. I dun remember."

"Can you guess?"

"Hours, I would say. Many hours, though I've no notion what we talked about for so long. I remember the tavern being all but empty when I went home."

"Captain," she said, shifting the conversation for a moment, "do you still have the knife used in the massacre?"

"Yes, my Lady."

"Could I see it, please? I believe it to be the same as those used in the ritual sacrifices we heard about earlier."

"Yes, my Lady." He turned and nodded to one of the soldiers behind Ethan. The soldier turned on his heel and disappeared into the crowd of people behind the farmer. The captain frowned again as he turned back to Kalistäe. "You don't think this was a kind of ritual sacrifice, do you?"

"I don't think it, captain, I know it. Why do your own dirty work when you can manipulate others into doing it for you? When you know what to look for, you will find seemingly trivial but important and connected facts regarding the times and places of these murders and massacres."

"Like what, if I may ask?"

"Like the fact of them taking place on either the full or new moons, when the power of the subconscious is either very strong or hidden, whichever best serves their purpose. Like the fact of them taking place at or near a convergence point of the ley lines that criss-cross the lands. Like the fact of them taking place at significant times during the year – equinoxes, solstices, just to name two, when very specific energies are available and accessible. Like the fact of them taking place relatively close to a larger town or city so that word of the massacre spreads, and many, many others get to hear about it."

Again, the Council was utterly silent, but this time, the silence held an element of shock and fear. It was obvious, now, that these random murders were not random at all. Rather, they were like specifically targeted attacks, and they were part of an overall, very dark agenda.

"Ethan," Kalistäe said, breaking the silence, her voice gentle at last, "look at me."

He looked up and, as much as he desperately did not want to, he looked into her eyes once again.

"He promised you the world, the stranger in black. He promised you success and wealth, everything you wanted, but he had no intention of delivering on his promise. Instead and in return, he has taken everything from you, your farm, your family, even your life. Do you understand that?" When he just looked at her, not responding, she continued, "For a few gold coins, you bartered away your soul. You were jealous and resentful, and you were terrified of failing. He used these of your shadows as leverage to control you because you gave him permission to control you when you took his gold. You unwittingly sealed a bargain. And with that control he inflicted horrible pain and devastation on your village. You think you gave him nothing in return for his gold, but you gave him yourself, your body and your mind, two things that should never, never be bartered away. A high price to pay, do you not think?" When he still didn't respond, she continued. "Answer me one more question. The first-generation farmer who bought the land next to yours, was he among the victims that night?"

Tears were coursing down the farmer's face, unchecked. Unable to speak, he nodded, slowly.

"When are you to be executed?" she asked him.

"A week from today, ma'am."

"Then I would advise you to make the most of the week you have left, Ethan. Contemplate my words and make yourself face the truth. You were not the victim here. You are very much responsible for what happened. You have to find a way to face the truth of that. 'Tis the only hope for your soul."

The farmer nodded, although his head was bowed and the nod was difficult to see.

When the farmer had been led away, Kalistäe addressed the Council.

"Gentlemen, you are . . ." she shook her head. "I'm sorry," she said, "**we** are under attack. I recognise the hand that is guiding these incidents, and I saw in the farmer's memories what it was who manipulated him that night. You are right, captain, in your assessment of the connectivity of every event, every incident. They have an agenda and they are working towards it as if they are ten paces ahead of everyone else, which they are. They are priests of utter darkness, and they are not of this world, this dimension. They are not human, nor are they Fae. They are something else entirely, and they are pure evil. They are generating fear, and they are using that fear against you. As for the murders, they are using the fears within those individuals against them. They are using personal fears and the satiation of want to manipulate."

"What can be done to stop them, Lady Kalistäe?" In asking the question, Morghan was voicing the question that hovered over the entire room.

She exchanged a long look with Amoranth. "Before I answer you, Morghan, I would like to see for myself one of the sites spoken of in the reports earlier, one of the sites of the rituals."

The king nodded. "Of course."

"I will take you myself," the captain said.

"Thank you, captain," she said, and then turned towards Orde. "Will you accompany us, Mage?"

"Wild horses could not keep me away," he replied.

She smiled briefly, and then addressed the Council through the king. "When I have seen a site of their rituals, I will know more about what it is they are trying to achieve specifically."

"Good," Morghan said. "This Council is suspended. We will convene again tomorrow, and I, for one, would very much like to know what you find, Lady Kalistäe. Until tomorrow then, this meeting is adjourned."

~

Kalistäe leaned against the door frame, folded her arms across her waist, and watched, a smile curling her lips and sparkling in her eyes. 'Twas the doorway to Orde's study she leaned against. His desk was covered in stacks of books and papers, and Brom and Jezz were sitting on one such stack of books listening in rapt attention to Orde as he talked. They were sitting, cross-legged, their wings open and upright, on top of the books, their hands resting in their laps and their faces rapt, their eyes wide with wonder. Orde was, of course, thoroughly enjoying his captivated little audience. He was, in fact, in his element. So much was he enjoying talking to his audience that he was using his hands to talk, magnifying the drama of his words. Faeries don't usually interrupt a flow of rhetoric with questions, but both faeries were shooting questions at him in the natural pauses in his rhetoric, not that there were many of those, but when there were, the faeries couldn't seem to help themselves. Consequently, the ebb and flow of the conversation was changing direction constantly. Kalistäe was glad of the distraction for them after the horror stories at the Council session that day. Had she known what was to be discussed, she would have thought twice about bringing them with her. This, she thought, still smiling as she watched their avid little faces, was just what they needed. She was grateful to Orde.

She watched them for a while and then she turned away and walked out onto the balcony. Orde had a suite of rooms in the king's castle, and she and her faeries were his guests for the night. The riding party would leave very early in the morning to ride out to one of the sites of the rituals spoken of at the Council so that they could be back in time to present their findings.

The balcony outside Orde's suite of rooms was long and thin and beautiful, its floor covered in small, perfectly square, decorative red tiles, and its balustrade solid to about waist height then comprising many arches made of brick. Through the brick arches, she could see the king's capital spread out below, and she could see the spectacular colour of the sky as the sun disappeared below the horizon. The sky was all pink and orange, and it had bathed the city in the same pink-orange light, highlighting the curled, red roof tiles on many of the buildings throughout the city. It really was beautiful, like the painted canvass of a master painter.

The sound of boots on the tiles behind her interrupted her reverie. The captain joined her, standing beside her and looking out at the sky as she was.

"Beautiful," he said simply.

"Yes, it is."

"Sadness does not become you, my Lady," he said quietly.

She smiled without removing her eyes from the glorious sky. "I am glad to hear it."

"Am I right in thinking your sadness a confirmation that these strings of seemingly unconnected incidents are as dire as we believe them to be."

"Yes, captain, you are right. I suspect you are not often wrong, actually." She turned towards him. "You did very well today. You really did. Your observations were very helpful. You've obviously thought long and hard about what is occurring."

He turned towards her, too, smiling his acceptance of the compliment. "Thank you, my Lady. I cannot take full credit, of course. I had a lot of assistance from a lot of people, especially Mage Orde." His smile disappeared. "How is it you know these dark priests, Kalistäe?"

She noted his use of her personal name, without the title in front of it. She liked the way he said her name. But in answering, she broke eye contact with him, looking out, again, at the spectacular sky.

"I wish I did not know of them," she said softly. "I am Fae, but I am also a Guardian. The Guardians and the Watchers are as one, and we are Guardians of life itself. As Guardians, we uphold the only real natural law in the Universe – the Law of Love – and so we go where we are needed, to do whatever is needed, whenever it is needed. The dark priests of Si'il were once Guardians, too. They were once of the Light, but they turned to the darkness, and the darkness now defines them in every way." She shook her head. "I confess I do not know how a being can turn from the Light to the darkness. I simply cannot comprehend it." She looked at him again. "But do you not see, we are the same, but we are also opposites, each of us the antithesis of the others? And because we are the antithesis of each other, we are become mortal enemies. They were once Guardians of life itself, but now they abuse and exploit life. They take, and they destroy life. They will bleed humans dry, leave nothing but dry, empty husks where once life pulsed."

"By the gods," he breathed. "Why us? I mean, what do they want with us?"

"Control," she said. "What else? They want to feed on you, like vampires. But they don't want control of individuals. They want control of human consciousness." She spread her hands wide. "They want control of the whole thing."

He raised an eyebrow. "Is that all? Total control," he repeated cynically.

"I suspect I know what the underlying intent of their agenda is, but I will be more certain tomorrow . . . I hope. We shall see. Either way, captain, they are an enemy you cannot see, and to fight them . . ." She shook her head, not wanting to break the spell of beauty that was all around them courtesy of the spectacularly beautiful evening.

He watched her closely as she talked, and, again, she noted his ability to maintain eye contact with her. It was remarkable, really. He had a way of looking into her that was almost Fae in both nature and ability. When she finished speaking he continued to look at her, and, in the silence that fell over them, she inclined her head in silent question, wondering at his thoughts, for she would not be so rude as to delve into them without his express permission.

"You have ruined me for any woman I know and for any woman I am likely to meet in the future," he said. "You are so beautiful, every other woman appears plain beside you."

She took a moment to recover her equilibrium. "Well, then," she said, stepping towards him, into him, and raising her hands to his chest, "I should be sorry about that, but I am not . . . strangely."

She stood on the balls of her feet and gently touched her lips to his. It took only a moment, full of his surprise, before she felt his arms come around her, and then he deepened the kiss. She allowed him to take control of it, and she moved a hand up, curling her fingers around his neck. He pulled her against him, not hard but gently, and she allowed herself to melt into him. For how long they kissed, neither could tell. Time became utterly suspended as they surrendered completely to their kiss and to the sensations it generated within them both.

And then, she pulled her lips away from his, gently, and she smiled into his eyes.

"A gift, given. A memory," she said softly, and he could feel her breath on his lips. She removed her hand from his neck and laid a finger over his lips. "Now, all you have to do is close your eyes and remember, and there will I be."

And then she was gone, like the breath of a breeze, and the captain was left with the scent of her all around him and the echo of the sensation of her lips on his.

~

Circle of Darkness, Circle of Light

Leaving their horses with the captain's men, the captain, the Mage and Kalistäe walked towards the site, or, rather, towards the altar they could see. The altar looked like it had been placed in the middle of nowhere, but both Kalistäe and the Mage knew better. Once again, when Kalistäe left her horse behind, she mentally shed her silver-grey cloak so that she walked, between the Mage and the captain, in her silver-grey gown, holding the long skirt clear of the ground, the fine gossamer material of its over gown trailing on the ground behind her, disturbing leaves and grass and twigs as she walked. Both her faeries were perched on her shoulders, one on the right, one on the left, their wings folded against their bodies, and their little bodies and their faces were taut with tension. Even this far from the altar, they could feel the malevolence of the energy that hung over the site. A contingent of the captain's men held and stayed with the horses, but this time, none of them spoke and they watched, interested, as the captain, the Mage and the faery queen walked away from them, approaching the site spoken of the day before, at the King's Council, the site at which the witness thought the sacrificial victim had been human.

When still some distance from the stone altar they could all see, Kalistäe suddenly spread both her hands out beside her to physically stop the captain and the Mage walking any further.

"Stop," she said suddenly, urgently. "Do not take another step."

Both the Mage and the captain stopped where they were, almost involuntarily obeying her, so that the three stood together facing the stone altar, although it was still some distance from them. The captain

119

could see no reason for Kalistäe's sudden command and the sense of urgency conveyed in the tone of that command. All he could see ahead of them was a clearing roughly, not perfectly, ringed by the tall trees of the forest, in the centre of which was ground covered in dirt and dried leaves, and the altar of stone. The altar was long, with a slab of stone placed on top of a stone base. It certainly looked like an altar upon which anything, either animal or human, could be sacrificed. But, although the captain could see nothing to warrant Kalistäe's urgent command physically, he could feel the atmosphere. The air here in the middle of the forest should have been fresh and clear, carrying the scents of the forest. Instead, the air was heavy, stale, and carried the smell of stagnancy and decay, even death. He even thought he detected the faint tang of the smell of blood.

To Kalistäe and her faeries, the site looked very different visually, although they, too, easily detected the smell of decay, and they, too, felt the heavy stagnancy and staleness of the air.

"Can you see it, my petals?" she asked her faeries.

"Yes, Mirri. We can see it." Again, Jezz answered for both her and Brom, Brom being too occupied with what he could see to answer. He was staring at the site with his mouth slightly open and his eyes wide with surprise. He'd never seen anything like it. He didn't know such a thing was possible. And it was so utterly out of place here in the beauty of the forest, among the tall, ancient trees.

"See what, if you don't mind me asking?" the captain asked, watching Brom intently, knowing the little faery was seeing something he could not see.

"Can you see it, Orde?" Kalistäe asked the Mage.

"Aye, my Lady, I can see it," he replied. "It looks like thick, heavy, black mist hugging the ground, hovering over it, rolling over itself, like a bubbling, boiling cauldron of thick soup. I can smell it, too," he added, holding his hand up to his nose as if to block the foul smell, and grimacing in distaste.

That, the captain could relate to. He, too, grimaced at the foulness of the smell and held a hand up to his nose.

Kalistäe nodded her agreement of Orde's description of the black mist and then, for the captain's sake, she swept her hand around the edge of the clearing from where she stood, following a circle around the altar with her hand, as she spoke. "There is a circle of darkness here, unimaginable, dark, malevolent energy," she told the captain. "We are standing at its very edge. One more step and we would be standing in the darkness, and we would have broken the circle, sending the energy spiralling out of it. At the moment, the circle is containing it. You would be affected by it were you to step into the circle, Captain Abram."

"Don't use your physical sight, Abram," the Mage said. "Use your inner vision. Cast your eyes slightly above the site, and let your eyes lose focus."

The captain did as the Mage instructed, frowning when he glimpsed darkness out of the corner of his eyes, darkness hovering over the ground like thick fog. Automatically, he tried to focus on it with his physical vision, but when he did so, he lost sight of it. So, again, he did as the Mage instructed, and, again, he could just perceive an impression of darkness, dark shadow hovering over the site in a circle, with the altar at its very centre.

"How would it affect me if I stepped into it?" he asked his companions.

"It would generate dark emotions within you," Kalistäe replied. "You would most likely become angry or just plain afraid, and you would probably end up in some kind of altercation with one of your men, or with one of us. It would make you aggressive. You'd feel like you wanted to punch someone. It could also make you feel ill."

"Why risk it here, Kalistäe?" the Mage asked. "These rituals are usually conducted behind closed doors, so to speak. Why risk being seen by conducting the rituals out in the open where they can be witnessed by innocents?"

"The site is too strategically important," she replied. "This is not just a convergence point of two ley lines, Orde. This is a convergence point of three. And the energy moves in this direction." She swept a hand from front to back, indicating behind her. "And we all know what is behind us, do we not?"

"Blood of the gods!" the Mage swore vehemently. "Duavel. They are using this site to send their dark energy into the capital."

"Just so," Kalistäe confirmed. "And the energy here is far, far too strong and potent and powerful for it to have been generated with just one ritual. They are using this site regularly, very regularly. I would say many of your missing persons have met their deaths here on the altar, captain, although you will find no trace of their bodies."

"How so?" the captain asked her, frowning.

She glanced at him. "You really want to know?"

He nodded, although somewhat reluctantly.

"They do not just drink the blood of their victims," she said quietly. "They consume their organs, and they burn the bones and grind them into dust so that the dust can be sprinkled and spread all over the site. Thus is the dark energy held in place. The dark energy is not hovering over the ground. It is hovering over bones turned into dust."

"I won't ask you how you know all this," he muttered. "I don't think I want to know."

"I know because I know," she said. "I know because I know what they are, and I know what they do to control, to retain control and maintain it. I know because I know how ritual magic works. I know how it can be harnessed for good or for evil. The fact that this," she lifted her hand to indicate the site, "will come back on them three-fold seems to bother them not at all. I confess I do not understand that mindset.

"And I know," she continued, "because I have encountered these beings and their minions many times before." She took a deep, concerned breath. "The physical act of death in the form of ritual murder is bad enough here because it generates such dark, dark energy, but what really concerns me is what these horrible rituals are doing to the souls of their victims. That, I hardly dare think about."

"Can you clear the site, Kalistäe?" the Mage asked her.

"Yes, I can," she said. "And so I will."

"And when you clear the site, will it help the souls of those who have been sacrificed here?"

"I do not know, Orde. I truly hope so. I hope it releases them. Really, I do."

She raised her hands in front of her, and it looked to the captain as if she was using them to weave air, to tie and sew nothing. He tried to catch an impression of what she was doing, but gave up and watched her and her faeries instead. All three, and Orde, were concentrating on whatever it was she was creating with her hands. The captain watched them watching her fingers. They all had intense expressions on their faces, and their eyes all followed whatever it was Kalistäe was doing with her hands.

What the captain could not see was that Kalistäe was weaving a net of silvery-grey Light-energy with her fingers. She was making it larger and larger, adding to it like one who knits more and more wool into a scarf. And then, when she thought it large enough to cover the site, she spread it out and cast it out over the entire site, just as a fisherman casts his net over the water to catch his fish. When the net was over the entire site, she lowered it. She should have let it go, so that it was lowered and could settle on the site by itself, free of her . . . or, rather, so that she was free of it. Instead of letting it go, though, she held it for a moment longer. The net, whilst ever she held it, was still part of her, connected to the deepest part of her, so when it settled over the site and made contact with the energy of darkness that pervaded the site, she felt that energy, and, with it, the malevolence that was an intrinsic part of it. The malevolence came through the net of her energy, through her fingers and into her, striking at the heart of her. And when it came into her, she felt a cold, dread chill fill her body, and a moment later, a rush of pure nausea swept through her – her own energy system's innate reaction to something alien introduced, like swallowing something that is poison to the body. The body automatically tries to purge the poison, and so, too, Kalistäe's own energy system automatically tried to purge the darkness. She shivered, swayed and staggered backwards. Instinctively, the captain reached out to steady her, holding her arm with one hand and sliding his other hand around her waist to support her.

"Whoa," he said softly. "I've got you. I've got you."

When the net of her energy dropped onto the site, both faeries watched it swallow and consume and dissolve the darkness, and then both followed the path of the Light with their eyes, because the energy of her Light, once dropped, was not contained within the site but, rather, moved along the energy lines of the earth that were connected to the site. The captain, holding Kalistäe steady, saw Brom turn on her shoulder, quickly, facing behind her, squatting on his hands and feet, his wings opening and coming upright as he followed something along the ground with his eyes. Whatever it was he saw, his eyes were wide with wonder, and a broad grin split his face and lit his eyes.

"Wow," he said, drawing out the word. "See how fast it goes, Mirri. Mother Gaia is swallowing it up. She loves it. See it clear the ley lines of the dark energy. 'Tis beautiful."

Kalistäe didn't respond. She was still fighting the nausea, although it was starting to dissipate as her energy system processed and dissolved the darkness that had been introduced.

"Well," Orde commented on the other side of Kalistäe as he looked at the site, "that was easier than I thought it would be."

Kalistäe's faeries launched themselves off her shoulders, their beautiful wings a blur as they flew directly into the area around the altar, and immediately began clearing away the little pockets of darkness that were left, casting little nets of their own. The darkness simply dissolved in their nets of Light-energy. Orde followed them into the circle around the altar, no longer mindful of stepping into dark energy. The dark energy was gone.

"The site is clear," he said. "What a difference it makes. You can feel the clearer, lighter air, and that horrible smell is all but gone."

"Almost," Kalistäe responded. "It is almost clear, Orde, but not quite. There is still human blood on that altar. To clear the site completely, the altar will have to be removed and burnt."

"That can be arranged," the captain said definitely.

"Orde," Kalistäe said, drawing the Mage's attention. She was holding on to the captain for support. "There was an arrogance in the energy, a kind of supreme confidence. They know they will not fail. There is a source . . . a reason for their arrogance. Something happened, something pivotal, something powerful."

The Mage, standing a short distance from her, looked at her and then bowed his head. "Ah, yes," he said quietly. "I think I might know what that is. I've always known that what happened was too significant not to have more far-reaching consequences. I've dreaded those consequences, I have to confess, awaited them, actually. Now, it seems, they are upon us. They were preparing the way for their own dark agenda." He looked up at her again.

"What happened?" she asked as tiny goosebumps spread over the skin of her body, and chills ran over her scalp and down her back like an unseen waterfall. His words had stirred within her a dread suspicion, like a door of knowing gently clicking open in her mind. A part of her knew what **had** happened because she knew she would be there. In a very real sense, the past was her future. In fact, she would be directly involved . . . a sacrificial victim.

"Many, many years ago," the Mage said, "when I was but a small boy, there was a direct and coordinated attack on the priesthood. Someone, or something, moved against the priesthood, Kalistäe. 'Twas the last time the King's Council was convened, as a matter of fact. But it was convened too late. The damage was done, and there was naught they could do about it. No one knew whose mercenary army it was that moved against the priesthood, and it all happened so fast that no one could stop it. But move against the priesthood they did. The priesthood was all but wiped out."

"Are you all right, Kalistäe?" the captain asked, concerned, as she swayed again.

She'd gone awfully pale, paler than usual, her eyes were wide – wide and full of pain – and her breaths were erratic, shallow and fast. Images assailed her, pouring in through that open door in her mind. "By the gods," she whispered.

She turned her eyes towards the captain, looking at him directly, and she shook her head, slowly.

"The Elohim priesthood was the beating heart of the human experience," she said, "and the heart is the very thing that binds the physical and the spiritual – the material realm and its true source. I know what their intent is." She raised her fingers to cover her lips. "'Tis worse than I could've imagined. Even had I sat and contemplated the worst possible scenario, I could not have come up with what they have planned."

The captain frowned, concerned not so much at what the dark agenda was, but rather at how it had affected her.

"I need to address the Council, Abram. I'm afraid humanity is doomed, utterly doomed, until such times as Free Will is removed from the human experience. But that will not come for many, many aeons into humanity's future. Until then, humans are in serious trouble, very serious trouble indeed."

~

"Members of the King's Council," Kalistäe said, "I was able to connect with the malevolent intent of the darkness that is attacking us. To explain to you what their intention is, I must tell you a little about your own history, but from a perspective you've probably not heard before. I pray the Council indulge me."

They were, once again, standing around the polished wooden table in the enormous ball room, and the room was, once again, full of people. Despite the number of people packed into the room, probably a few more than the day before, the silence was so total, so complete that if not for Kalistäe's voice, it would have been possible to hear a feather drop onto the polished marble floor.

"The Council will hear whatever you have to tell us, Lady Kalistäe," King Morghan said, speaking on behalf of the entire Council. "Please tell us whatever you deem is necessary for us to hear. Time matters not. However long this takes is how long it takes."

Kalistäe smiled at him, and her smile sparkled in her eyes. He found it utterly impossible not to return her smile in kind.

Then she took a moment more to breathe deeply, trying to calm her beating heart. She was not nervous to be speaking to so many people. That bothered her not at all. What would be difficult was the thorough revisiting of the past – a past that directly involved her in every way possible – a past that was her own future. For today's session of the Council, the Mage stood where he'd stood the day prior, on her left, and the captain, ever protective of her, stood on her right. She could feel the heat of his body, and she drew strength from his presence beside her.

"When the human experience was originally created," she said, "the Guardians gave humans a gift – a gift that was meant to be a blessing, but has now, I fear, become a curse. Humans are simply not equipped to handle it. Human consciousness is not developed enough to handle it.

"Free Will, gentlemen, and ladies. I'm talking about Free Will. Choice. And I refer not to the kinds of choices you make in the context of the infrastructure of your day to day lives – what you will eat for dinner, what you will wear for the day, whether or not you will make love to your wives at the end of the day. I am referring to the choices we make to follow the path laid out for us by destiny, the script of our own souls, the reason and purpose we are all here in the first place, the blueprint of which is written on our hearts. Free Will is your undoing. Free Will has become the means by which many, many humans are straying so far from the paths of their destinies, in their current lives and in their past lives, that they are doing themselves very great harm. Courtesy of Free Will, the dark priests have gained a foothold on and in human existence, and, with it, through it, they are controlling and manipulating human consciousness.

"It was because of Free Will that the farmer, Ethan, could choose and act against his own Truest Nature, his soul. In fact, his choices and actions were highly contradictory to his own Truest Nature. And in so doing and so choosing, he has lacerated his own soul, bound it up in karmic obligation and imbalance, and he has trapped himself in the eternal cycle of birth, death and rebirth here in the human realm. And, of course, he has hurt others, not just his victims, but their loved ones as well, and his loved ones, too. I fear the consequences, for him, will be dire well beyond this life he lives only for one more week. And he still has to face the fear that caused him to choose and act as he did in the first place. Not only is the fear still very much intact in his soul, but he has given it even more power over him by choosing to act out of it thereby giving into it rather than facing and resolving it.

"This you must know. The dark priests need humans, but they need humans to be trapped here, in the eternal cycle, reincarnating over and over again, as Ethan is now destined to do. The dark priests cannot fulfil their plans without humans. They will feed on human suffering, and dark human emotions, yes, but, worse, they will use and manipulate human consciousness to form the fabric of the reality they want to create for themselves, here, in this dimension. Humans are creators, after all, but they can and will be manipulated to create realities according to the dictates of the dark priests.

"And why?" She asked the collective question herself, to save the Council the trouble.

"Because they wish to exist outside of the Divine Mind. 'Tis not, in truth, possible to exist outside of the Divine Mind, but they believe they have found a way to do so. 'Tis the way of illusion. If something **seems** to be, then so **must** it be, must it not?" She shook her head. "'Tis so in the way of illusion. Illusion is illusion, after all. Focus on it, see only the illusion, exist in it and as part of it, and you will become disconnected from the truth. This is their intent.

"And that brings me to the 'what' that is the crux of their dark agenda."

She swallowed and tears filled her eyes. The captain moved closer, subtly, and lightly touched her arm behind her so that those around the table could not see the gesture.

She looked around the table and made no attempt to either stop her tears nor to wipe them away. Her two little faeries wrapped their arms around her neck and buried their faces against her, their wings drooping like flowers in desperate need of water.

"I am so very sorry," she said. "Had we known this would be your fate, we never, never would have gifted you the power of Free Will. Never. We have condemned you to untold suffering."

She took a deep breath. "Separation. That is their intent. Separation."

In the silence that followed, a deliberate silence that she allowed to persist because they needed to absorb the one single word even though she could see from the expressions on their faces that they did not understand, with the exception of Amoranth, the elvish king, who nodded slowly and then bowed his head and closed his eyes. He knew.

"When Orde was a small boy," she explained, "something happened that I know many of you know about even though you were not yet born yourselves. The dark priests moved against the Elohim priesthood, all but wiping it out. The priesthood was also gifted to you to serve as the beating heart of the human experience, to guide you and direct you, keep you on the path of your collective destiny, and to keep you connected to Divine Will and Purpose. And when humans moved against them, even manipulated as they were, the deaths of the Elohim priesthood tore the fabric of human reality asunder, ripped it apart. 'Twas a symbolic act that held incredible power, as the dark priests knew it would, and it paved the way for their dark agenda. The physical, material realm of the humans was now ripe for the dark manipulations that would sever it completely from its source, its soul, the truth of its higher dimensionality. Separation. The Separation of humans from the Divine Mind. The Separation of the two realms – the human realm and the Fae realm – that form the whole of this creation. And, worst of all, the Separation of human conscious awareness from its own higher consciousness – that which humans call 'the soul'.

"The incidents reported on in yesterday's session of Council are all designed to weave the fabric of human reality with threads of absolute, utter fear, so that the fabric of human reality will comprise fear – shadow and darkness – itself. But for fear to exist and thrive, the dark priests must create a bedrock of supreme and chronic ignorance, hence the massacre of the Elohim priesthood. The dark priests will expunge whole tracts of human history from the collective human consciousness so that you do not remember your true origins. They will fabricate religious institutions that are nothing more than programmed mind control. This religious dogma will become wrapped around the human heart, turning humans into virtual slaves. The Light of the soul – that incredible spark of divine knowledge and wisdom that forms the true heart of the human experience – can have no expression in a reality based on ignorance and fear. Thus, they can program you to think and believe whatever they want you to think and believe. They can manipulate you to make choices and act any way they want you to. They can capture and hold your focus so that you are consumed with and focussed on whatever they want you to focus on. You will look upon your own world, your own realities, your own lives, your own selves, and you will see only what they want you to see. This is their intention."

Silence followed. And, in fact, the silence filled the room. And then someone asked a question, breaking the silence. People were almost relieved, and many holding their breath released it.

"The rituals witnessed by some and spoken of yesterday," someone around the table asked, "and the massacres by manipulated individuals, like the farmer, what is the direct purpose of those?"

"Humans have already forgotten about the existence of the ley lines of the earth," Kalistäe responded, "so they pay them no heed, and yet, the ley lines are the energetic veins of the earth such that every human is affected by the energy they carry. Obviously, when the lines are clean and clear, this has a profoundly positive affect and influence on human consciousness and culture. Likewise, when the lines are clogged with fear and the energy of dark emotion and dark events, humans are similarly, only detrimentally, affected and influenced. When blood sacrifice occurs at the convergent points of these energy lines, the energy of fear and darkness and the blackest magic travels through the earth, and affects and influences human culture in those areas touched and fed by these affected ley lines. If enough black energy is fed through these ley lines, the energy of fear and darkness will govern human existence – human choice, human actions, mindsets, perspectives, focus. Human existence will, then, express all those dark characteristics associated with fear – violence, corruption, exploitation, conflict, abuse, control, but also psychological illness, like depression. And, then, all the dark priests have to do is maintain their rituals to maintain the dark energy in the ley lines and, with it, the darkness that will underpin human existence.

"And they do not sacrifice at random. They choose their times and their places to perfection to manipulate energy itself. After all, all **is** energy. If they sacrifice women, they stir up negative feminine energy – an energy that is underhand, devious, hidden, manipulative, and undermining. If they sacrifice men, they stir up negative masculine energy – an energy that is aggressive, violent, dominating, subjugating, controlling. Negative masculine energy is used to cause conflict and war. And then, the children. Fear and innocence are polar opposites. Innocence is a state of being, without fear. By destroying the innocence of children, they are destroying innocence itself, and they are sending that destroyed innocence through the ley lines, paving the way for fear.

"Blood sacrifice is powerful. The spilling of blood in a ritual spell is binding. Have you never heard of a blood oath? Such an oath is powerful indeed. But blood holds the life force, and, therefore, it holds a unique kind of power. They are sealing their rituals with blood to bind and to magnify the power of the dark energy generated by the rituals.

"As for the drug the captain spoke of, the drug you all know about, the captain was right in his assessment. Drugs, because there **will** be more, are all about destabilisation that, again, paves the way for control, at every level of society, from the individual to the collective. These drugs impair cognitive function, yes, absolutely, but they are also about dependence and addiction, and they are also about a never-ending source of revenue. Many birds killed with a single stone, you might say."

"Can we stop them, Lady Kalistäe?" Morghan asked the question.

"Oh yes," she answered harshly. "The dark priests can be stopped, Morghan. But for that to occur, humans will have to take responsibility for their own dark emotions. They will have to go within, honest introspection, and they will have to confront their own wounded psychologies. They will have to be prepared to face and dissolve their fears, and they will have to be prepared to choose against the satiation of want and need, obsession and addiction, lust for power and wealth and control. They will have to obviate their ignorance with an open-minded quest for knowledge, particularly higher knowledge, and particularly self knowledge."

Morghan looked at her, shocked for a moment, and then he bowed his head and closed his eyes.

"I see you have as much faith in humans as do I, Morghan," she said gently. "Humans must now walk the long, long road of consequence, and there is little those of us of the Fae realm can do to help."

She looked over at Amoranth, and he nodded his agreement. "We will do what we can," he said. "But the darkness is already gaining power, and we must withdraw to protect ourselves, not from the darkness itself, because it cannot get a foothold on our culture, but from the consequences of its control of the human experience. Humans are brutal when they fear. They will tear each other apart. They will destroy their environment. We cannot be a part of that. We will not be a part of that."

Morghan nodded his understanding, and then he looked over at Kalistäe. "Will you stay and help us, Lady Kalistäe?"

"Alas, Morghan, I cannot." She felt and saw the captain flinch beside her. "I am a Guardian. This darkness must be put in its place, and it cannot be done here and now, at this point in human existence. I have Work to do first, and then I must go to that time when the darkness can be defeated, at that point in human time when Free Will will no longer form the premise upon which the human experience is based. I have much Work to do. Amoranth and I will protect you, those of you who rule your lands. You are the most vulnerable of all. If they control you, they rule your lands. And the elvish priests will clear the ritual sites you know about. But I fear that will give you only temporary reprieve."

She bowed her head, and then she looked up at them all again.

"I am sorry. I would stay if I could. You must know that."

King Morghan bowed to her. "We know that, Kalistäe. We wish you every success in your endeavours to put this darkness in its place. May the gods of every culture go with you, my Lady, and keep you safe. Thank you for your wise counsel. It is now up to us to do what we can to keep the darkness at bay for as long as possible."

~

"How is this your responsibility, Kalistäe?"

She, the captain and the Mage were again standing at the very edge of Kalistäe's forest of ancient oaks. The riding party had, for the return journey, ridden from Duavel in complete silence. Even the two faeries had not looked at the landscape as they rode through it this time. The captain had thought they were asleep in Kalistäe's lap, but when he'd ridden closer at one stage, he'd seen they were awake. Their little faces held a worried expression and their wings were drooping. They were sad, and sadness does not sit well with faeries. Sadness is, in fact, the very opposite of what they truly are – joy – and so sadness is painful for them in a way humans fail to understand. It makes them ill. Now, at the edge of the forest, they were hovering behind Kalistäe, waiting for her to join them, and watching her say goodbye to the captain and the Mage.

Again, a contingent of the captain's men were holding the horses a short distance away, talking among themselves and not paying any attention to those standing at the edge of the forest.

"You cannot deal with this yourself," the captain said when she didn't answer his question.

"I can deal with it," she said. "And I must. If not me, then who?"

"This is not your responsibility," he said again.

"Then whose is it?"

"Not yours."

Orde watched and listened in silence. He knew how the captain felt, but he also knew the captain's arguments were futile.

"This is who I am, Abram. I am a Guardian. I must do what is needed, and I must go where I am most needed. I must. Unlike you, I do not have the luxury of choice. I serve the Light and, as such, Free Will is not a part of my Truest Nature. I must go and do as the Light wills."

"Who will protect you?"

"I will have no protection, initially." She refrained from telling him what she knew would happen to her. He did not need to know about that. But she could tell him what the consequence would be. Perhaps that would give him some small comfort. She softened her next words. "There is no greater protection than being truly hidden, as I will be."

She turned to go, but, quick as lightning, he reached out and stopped her with a hand clamped around her wrist. "Kalistäe, don't . . ."

In holding her wrist so tightly, he forced her to take steps that brought her closer to him. And so she was able to look deeply and directly into his eyes, her own not without empathy and sympathy and compassion.

"If this situation was reversed," she asked him softly, "and it was my hand encircling your wrist to stop you from going into battle at the head of your army, in service to your king, to fight a mortal enemy, would you allow me to stop you?"

He looked at her for a moment more, and then, slowly, he loosened his hold, and finally he released her, shaking his head. "That's not fair," he said.

"Remember my gift to you," she whispered, ignoring his comment. "Remember."

He shook his head again. "'Tis not enough."

Slowly, she backed away from them, holding her gown clear of the ground. "Perhaps we shall meet again in the human realm," she said to them both. She looked at Orde. "Farewell, my friend."

"Farewell to thee, my Lady," he responded, bowing slightly with his hand laid flat on his chest.

She smiled at the Mage and then looked at the captain. "Remember my gift. 'Tis more powerful than you realise, Abram."

And then she turned and walked into the forest, her faeries flying at shoulder height beside her. To the captain, she became, again, a shimmering mirage of Light, and then she disappeared from his sight altogether.

But in the forest, she stopped, unseen by them, and looked back at them. The Mage put his hand on the captain's shoulder – a gesture of profound sympathy and understanding – and said something she could not hear.

Seeing the gesture, and the captain's response, Kalistäe bowed her head, her heart full of sorrow.

"Mirri," her faeries said, "what is it?"

"There is a strange connection between the two of us," she answered them, gesturing with her hand to indicate the captain whom they could still see outside the forest. He hadn't yet moved to rejoin his men. "I feel his pain as if it were my own. Perhaps it **is** my own. But he is human. I am Fae. We cannot be together. And if I stay with him, I will not be able to do the Work I **must** do. You, my petals, are in danger from the darkness every bit as much as are humans. We must restore this creation. We must."

"You are bonded, Mirri," Brom said. "And 'tis not karma that binds you."

"What do you mean, Brom?"

"You each hold a piece of the other's heart," Jezz said. "'Tis why the essence of you is so alike. No wonder you will not take a consort, Mirri. He **is** your love, your lover."

Kalistäe frowned at them. "Why do I not know that for myself?"

"You are blocking the knowledge of it," Jezz replied, "if not the sense of it."

"But you feel something powerful for him, do you not, Mirri?" Brom asked her.

She nodded. "Yes, I do, although I do not understand it. Why would I block the knowledge of it?"

Jezz shrugged her little shoulders. "So you can walk away . . . perhaps. 'Tis not your destiny to be together just yet."

Kalistäe considered that. "So," she said slowly, "if he holds a piece of my heart, then he and I have crossed paths before?"

Two little heads bobbed up and down quickly, and they both answered in unison. "Yes."

"And," Kalistäe added, "no doubt we are destined to cross paths again."

The two little heads bobbed up and down again, quickly, and, again, they answered in unison. "Yes."

"Right," she whispered, and she turned away from the sight of the captain and the Mage to walk deeper into her forest of ancient oaks, her mind already shifting to focus on what she had to do now. "We need to gather everyone together. I must speak to them all."

~

"Darkness is taking over the fabric of human reality," she said, wasting no unnecessary time getting to the point. Her community of faeries had, of course, responded to her call and were once again filling the arena of little benches. She could not sit. She was too fraught with tension to sit still, and so she walked back and forth as she talked to them. "Darkness has usurped the human experience, and it is insidiously and systematically taking control, with the sole intention of separating humans from the Divine Mind. Their reality will become hellish."

She stopped walking to look at them. "I wish I could stay here, with you all, in this beautiful world we have created for ourselves, deep in this ancient forest." She raised her hands, spreading them out beside her. "I feel such contentment and peace and calm here with you all. 'Tis why I have never felt inclined to take a consort. I simply have not needed anyone or anything else. Here, in our forest, I can take the deepest and purest of breaths. But, alas, I cannot ignore what is happening beyond the boundaries of our beautiful forest. The darkness threatens us, too. The darkness is, in fact, as serious a threat to the realm of the Fae as it is to the realm of the humans. I must go there. I must do what I can to reclaim and restore human creation. It breaks my heart, but I must leave you, my petals."

Silence fell. Complete silence descended and, with it, complete stillness, apart, that is, from the gradual drooping of each little faery's wings.

And then Brom spoke up. "We are coming with you, Mirri." His voice was flat, not asking, but telling, brooking no argument and merely stating an absolute certainty. Hundreds and hundreds and hundreds of tiny heads bobbed up and down in agreement.

Kalistäe looked surprised. "Who is coming with me?" she asked in surprise and watched as every little hand was raised – a veritable forest of tiny arms raised all around her. Tears filled her eyes and she took an involuntary step back, lifting her hand to her chest in a futile attempt to still the jump of her heart. "Oh, my petals," she whispered, "bless you. But I cannot ask you to come with me. The human reality will be hellish. It will be the opposite of everything you are." She looked at Jezz and Brom, sitting together, holding hands, on the arms of her throne. "You will be separated from me and from each other. Our community will be scattered."

Again, as usual, it was Brom who answered for the entire community. "We have already decided, Mirri. We will not let you go there alone. We are coming with you. We know what the human reality will become. We know what we're doing, just as you know what you're doing. We are your family, your people, and where you go, so, too, do we go."

Kalistäe's tears filled her eyes and overflowed. She looked around at her community of faeries, her petals, her adored people, and she saw the same unwavering resolve on their faces that she heard in Brom's words, and in his voice.

She bowed her head to them. "So be it, then. I will not try to dissuade you. Know that you have my deepest gratitude and love. But this I vow to you. I will return here to tell you another story. Watch for me in the human reality. I will send you a signal, when I am ready, and I will call you to me so that, even there, we shall be together again, as one."

Hundreds and hundreds and hundreds of little heads bobbed their understanding and acknowledgement of her promise and her instructions.

Leaning down, she outlined a circle with the fingers of one hand. Although nothing was actually there, on the floor, everyone present saw the circle of Light clearly. When the circle was complete, it held Kalistäe's blazing Light. She stepped into it, and then she looked up at her petals one last time, and, raising her fingers to her lips, she gifted them a collective kiss.

"Carry my love and my Light in your hearts, my petals. And I will see you soon."

She became blazing Light, and then she became indistinguishable from the Light in the circle, disappearing in it. And then, as if in a powerful and full waterfall of sparkles of Light, her faeries flew into the circle after her, poured into it, each disappearing until nothing remained but an arena of tiny, empty benches, an empty, wooden throne, and an ancient forest, empty but for its beautiful, old oaks. And the forest was full of silence.

~

An Addendum

Many, many beings from the Fae realm are here, in the human realm, incarnate. When Kalistäe and her faeries came here, they did not first disincarnate from the Fae realm, and so, they hold their Fae essence within them, still. It forms the core of who they are even though they are all human because they are all incarnate in the human realm – very much like a double incarnation. Although each of us who have come here from the Fae realm have done so for reasons of our own – some have come to champion specific causes, like saving or cleaning the environment, and some have come to experience for themselves the Separation and the fear that characterises the human reality, while others have come for a myriad of different reasons – we are all bound by a common Purpose, a common covenant: to end the Separation of the realms. To end Separation itself. To restore creation.

And there is only one way we can truly achieve this. We must end the Separation within ourselves. We are an army, yes, but we will not fight the darkness as one side of a battle faces and fights the other side. Rather, we are here to fight the darkness within ourselves, and to master and conquer the separated, lower-dimensional human reality, again, within ourselves. Materiality has almost completely devoured human consciousness, consumed it, digested it. We, too, have become a product of the material reality, a part of it. This is what we will fight, allowing our own higher consciousness to awaken and rise, once again, from the quagmire of the material reality that has consumed our own conscious awareness, rather like the proverbial Phoenix rising from the ashes of its own funeral pyre, reborn, renewed, regenerated. It is our own lower-dimensional identities that are burnt to ash on that funeral pyre.

Have any of you seen The Matrix – my favourite movie? The scene when Neo awakens in the pod, surrounded by pink, gooey gel, to see the horrible truth of his existence is a perfect analogy for what we all must now do. Breaking free of the goo that covers us like muck – a perfect metaphor for lower-dimensional existence – is merely the first step. Freeing our minds of the programming, the tricks and the lures, the temptations and the distractions – all mechanisms of anaesthetisation and manipulation deliberately weaved by the dark priests into the very fabric of this reality – this is the hardest part. But we are strong, and we are powerful, and we <u>are</u> Light. We can do this. We will do this. We have already succeeded.

But how do we end the Separation of the realms? I mean, really. Well, first, we have to peel away the layers of illusion within – our own shadows and fears. Then, we must learn to look out at our reality, at the landscape of our life, and know that we do not exist in that reality. Reality is the <u>result</u> of thought, not the <u>source</u> of the thought. We exist within, in a place within that is spectacularly beautiful. It is the place within that is the source of our thoughts, and, therefore, the source of our reality. Know that it is there. See it, that place. Go there, clear it out, and then be there. And then watch the impact of this beautiful place within on your outer reality.

But first, of course, we must come forth from our mundane lives. We must shed those ordinary identities as a cicada sheds its old shell, leaving it sitting as an empty husk on the bark of a tree. These ordinary identities no longer serve us, and, in truth, they are as empty as the empty, discarded cicada husks.

So then, what of Kalistäe? What happened to her? She is here, Working, and she has not forgotten her promise to her petals, her faeries. In fact, she has written them a whole new story, a fairy tale. Actually, truth be told, she has written them two stories. She loves the stories, and she knows her faeries will love them, too. One of the stories is, in fact, the signal she spoke to them about, the signal that will allow them to know she is ready, and she is calling them to her. She longs for the day when her Work here is done and she can tell her faeries her new stories. Or, even better, regardless of whether or not her Work is done, her community of faeries gravitates to her once again and she can tell them her stories in <u>this</u> realm.

So what of the captain? Has she encountered him again? Yes, of course, many times, and I have written these stories because they form part of the storehouse of my own memories. Their overriding story is yet to be resolved, though. I hope their story is resolved in this life I'm living now because, to be very honest, I don't want to have to come back here. I will if I have to. 'Tis the nature of who I am and what I do, but I would rather not.

And so, there is but one more thing to address and resolve before I close this piece off and finish it: Ariadne's story. Why did Kalistäe tell her faeries Ariadne's story on that last night they were all together?

Well, for me, of course, and, most probably, for you, too.

As stories of myth always are, Ariadne's story is rich in symbolism – the language of the soul. But the most powerful symbol in her story is that of the labyrinth. The labyrinth symbolises the labyrinth of the human psyche, and for those of us who are here to awaken the spark of our own divinity, to reconnect with it and give it wonderful expression in our realities, the labyrinth of our own psyches is absolutely unavoidable. It must be navigated.

To begin with, if we examine Ariadne's life before Theseus came into it, given what we know of both her mother and her father (and here I won't elaborate but will, instead, leave you to draw your own conclusions about her parents, individually and together), I strongly suspect Ariadne was all but invisible at her father's court. I doubt she received very much attention. Minos would, perhaps, have noticed her when it suited him to do so, which probably wasn't very often. His court represents for all of us the lie of the landscape around us in this reality before we know anything different, when we are, perhaps, victims of our circumstances, in many different ways, and when we are at the mercy of the pitfalls of lower-dimensionality, feeling very ordinary and insecure, not quite fitting it. This court is not nourishing. Its priorities and its focusses are meaningless, and maybe we're unsure of our place in it. At this court, we almost certainly have no real sense of Self. And in place of a true sense of Self, we try to become defined by lower-dimensional constructs, whichever constructs define acceptability in the particular court we find ourselves in.

Ariadne may have been unhappy at her father's court. We'll never know because no version of the myth tells us this is so. Regardless of whether or not she was happy, she still betrayed everything she knew – her family, her people, her land, her culture – for a cause that was not hers. And why? Because, with no sense of her own Self, no anchor in her own truth, her own essential being, she became invested in Theseus, and in Theseus' labyrinthine journey, **his** cause. Theseus was Ariadne's escape into a supposedly better court. But she was only swapping one court of physicality for another, and she had to learn the hard way, escape does not get us very far. In fact, it gets us nowhere. We must transcend – grow beyond our own shadows and fears and misguided mindsets. She was easily seduced, of course, as many of us are by the prospect of a better life, a better identity as defined by physical constructs. So when a heroic, handsome prince, who embodies all the impressive constructs of the material reality, promises her a new life if she helps him, with no sense of her Self and her own destiny, why would she not become entwined with him and his destiny? This symbolises the power of physical reality to seduce us, to consume our focus, to cause us to lose ourselves in pursuits that do not serve us and do not express our Truest Natures. The pursuit of wealth and success are obvious examples of this.

For some, this aspect of her story symbolises the loss of one's own centre to the lover, or the lover relationship. That is, the fact of us losing ourselves in another, or in a relationship, whatever form that relationship takes (I've seen some, for example, lose themselves in the parent-child relationship, women becoming clichéd 'mothers' at the expense of themselves). I'm sure many of us can relate. But for most of us, this aspect of the story symbolises the loss of our own centre and our own inner sense of Self to the constructs of physical reality, or to the pursuit of those constructs (and by constructs, I mean all those things we try to pull around ourselves and into our realities to be acceptable, to belong, to fit in: wealth, fame, career, job, physical beauty, the recipe of life: marriage, mortgage, impressive house, children, whatever it is we relentlessly pursue).

When Ariadne was left on the beach, alone, abandoned, used, betrayed, devastated, this became her trigger, cracking her open, getting her attention, in one sense, forcing her to realise the constructs of physical reality were somehow damaging her, keeping her from herself. The constructs we seek in physical reality do not in any way provide us what we truly need. Instead, they smother our sense of Self and, with it, our self expression. The trigger, or the triggering event for this process is often a physical trigger – a divorce or loss of job, for example – or maybe we just begin to realise that the constructs we've used to define ourselves are meaningless, and they are not making us happy. We have become what we are not. But in becoming what we are not, we do not know who or what we actually are. The constructs we pursue are empty, meaningless, and the pursuit of them is the same. We realise they do not define us as we've been taught to believe, and the realisation causes a bewilderment and a sense of loss. I confess I've had to experience quite a few of these severance experiences, sitting alone on the beach of my psyche watching as the future I thought I would be living sailed off and disappeared over the horizon of my life. My own inner transformational Process has had to pull me away from many, many things.

So what does define us? Who are we really? Alone, on the beach, with nothing left and nothing around her, Ariadne had everything she needed. She had everything she needed within to, finally, navigate the labyrinth of her <u>own</u> psyche, there to begin to connect with her own inner sense of Self.

Because what truly awaits us at the heart of the labyrinth, despite the shadows and demons and monsters we will and must fight along the way, is our own stairway to heaven. Our Selves. Not sensed, but known and experienced. And, of course, ultimately, expressed. And we know Ariadne succeeded in reaching the heart of the labyrinth of herself because Dionysus, her true soul mate, that divine reflection of her true Self, entered the landscape of her reality. And he could not wait to sanctify the intimacy of their union with marriage. So will it be for us when we reach the heart of our own labyrinth.

For each of us, heaven – our own version of it – will be different. But, for each of us, when we reach it, it will become weaved into our reality. I promise you. And the more of us who can achieve this, the more powerful we will become, as a group, at changing human reality – the very fabric of human reality itself.

So, what will your version of heaven be, I wonder? What is your heaven? What will you see weaved into the fabric of your reality when you start to connect with your own version of heaven?

What is mine, my version of heaven? Well, for me, there is no greater heaven than being connected with my true Self . . . than being, and being with my Self. When I am connected, I do not need anyone else . . . at all, just as Kalistäe didn't. I am everything I want. I know this because I have existed in my own personal hell, not knowing and not being who I really am. Hell for me – something I've come to know very well because I have existed in it for so long – is being disconnected and separated from my Truth, and hidden. As Kalistäe, I was as I am, and it never occurred to me I could be otherwise. Now I know I <u>can</u> be otherwise. I guess that makes Kalistäe my heaven.

~

The End

The Fallen

I will not die,

Because I have been dead for aeons of human time.

And so I know what true death feels like.

I know what it is to exist as death itself.

'Tis a living hell –

A hell of disconnection, Separation, ignorance, isolation, fear.

I would not wish such an existence on my worst enemies.

And yet, 'twas those same enemies who created this existence,

Deliberately, consciously.

Thus must I now set this creation right once again,

And return it to the Light.

Because I can.

Watch out.

I am resurrected.

I will end this hellish existence now and forever more.

The First Sign of Stirring

There was, somehow, always silence in the clearing. When the sun was shining and birdsong filled the rest of the forest, silence filled the clearing. When the sky was heavy with thick, dark clouds, and a strong wind was stirring the leaves in the ancient, tall trees that circled it, silence filled the clearing. When the dark of night reigned and the moon's light caressed the leaves in the trees, turning them silver, silence and stillness filled the clearing. In summer, when tiny animals were out foraging among the trees in the forest for nuts and seeds and other tasty morsels and they scampered into the clearing, their movements slowed and they foraged silently. In autumn, when golden leaves fell from the trees, they did so silently. In winter, when snow flakes fell, covering the ground in a blanket of white, they did so silently. But then, when has anyone ever heard snow make a sound when it falls? Rain is a different story, is it not? When has anyone ever heard heavy rain fall silently? And yet, when rain fell in the clearing, it did so silently. The thick raindrops should have pattered the leaves, but they did not. Somehow, they fell onto the leaves silently . . . somehow. When the gentle breezes of spring stirred up the carpet of leaves on the forest's floor, causing them to whirl and eddy, in the clearing they swirled on the air currents silently.

Even when the clearing was full of beings, tall and graceful, short and squat, tiny and dainty, their stature mattered not at all. Their footfall was somehow always silent as they walked, despite the fact that a thick carpet of leaves always covered the forest floor in and around the clearing. The long material of their gowns and cloaks disturbed the carpet of leaves as they walked, but while such disturbances should have made some sort of noise, never did a swishing noise so much as touch the silence. And so, too, should their conversations have marred the absoluteness of the silence, but, somehow, even when they spoke, the silence remained untouched, undisturbed, absolute. They spoke in hushed tones, of course, but still, regardless of the number of conversations, the silence was always pervasive, and it always covered the clearing like a shroud.

And the silence was different in the clearing – different from the silence that prevails just before a storm – different from the silence that fills a church when the priest makes an appearance or when the heads of the entire congregation are bowed in prayer – different from the silence that always fills a library – different from the silence that fills a house in the dead of night when all its occupants are sleeping soundly. The silence in the clearing was different because it was thick and heavy with reverence, and it was tinged with an air of sadness. Even nature Herself honoured the reverence in the silence and was a part of it.

Anyone stumbling across the clearing by accident could and would be forgiven for thinking they had inadvertently stumbled into a scene from a fairy tale. Although human feet never trod in the clearing – no human had ever set foot in it, in fact – any human who came upon it would believe he or she <u>had</u> somehow managed to step into the pages of an ancient fairy tale. The beings who came to the clearing and spoke in hushed tones knew better, of course. They knew the scene in the clearing was not from a fairy tale, and they understood the reverence in the silence and the air of sadness. They understood both very well indeed.

For, you see, a woman lay in the very centre of the clearing on a beautifully-sculptured table of white marble, under a covering of glass, and she lay perfectly still as if in death or as if she herself was a statue made of smooth marble. Indeed, her skin was smooth and pale, like marble, and her eyes were closed. Dark lashes fanned against the pale skin of her cheeks, and her pale hands were crossed, fingers curled, over her breasts. She lay under shrouds of silk, but her face and shoulders were uncovered so that she was easily seen under the glass that covered and protected her. She was dressed in a beautiful gown of pale, pearl silk that left her neck and shoulders bare but covered her arms to her wrists. The layers of its skirts were long, covering her feet, and some of the silk had fallen off the marble table, under the glass, almost touching the ground, like a beautiful table cloth. Rows of beads of pale moonstone circled her wrists and her neck and adorned her hair. On the pillow upon which she rested, her hair framed her pale face in a collection of dark-brown curls. The beads around her wrists and neck were perfectly still, and her chest did not rise with every **in**haled breath. Nor did a cloud of condensation appear on the glass that covered her with every **ex**haled breath.

There was no breath.

Only one feature marred the perfection of her, for she was supremely beautiful, even in death and despite her absolute lack of animation. Just above her crossed hands and her curled fingers, an ugly, vivid, red scar ran down her chest from the base of her neck and disappeared under the silk material of her gown. Well, truth be told, although it looked like a scar, it wasn't really. The wound in her body had been cleverly sewed up to appear like a scar, but it was still an open wound. The wound had never healed or resolved itself into a scar. It had never been given the chance to heal because the wound itself had taken her breath away, quite literally. The wound ran the entire length of her chest, between her breasts, from neck to navel, and it covered the place on her body where her heart should have been. Underneath it, there was no heartbeat because there was no heart at all. Her chest cavity was empty. Her chest cavity was a void, an empty space. Someone – some foul, evil being – had taken her heart in an act of pure, malevolent, evil violence.

I told you this was no fairy tale.

The act of violence that had taken her life, the Lady who lay upon the table of marble, had been a black magic ritual of such foul corruption, such evil, malevolent intent, that its power had torn at the very fabric of human reality. There had been many witnesses, and many of those witnesses had loved and adored her. It was they who saved her body after the priest of darkness tore her heart from her body and then left her to die. Those who had witnessed and who loved her sewed up her wound, cleaned and bathed the blood from her, dressed her in a gown of silk, arranged her hair, adorned her with the bracelets and necklace of moonstones, and preserved her on the table of marble, under a protective covering of glass, in a clearing deep in the forest where her people could take care of her. Over the aeons she'd lain in her resting place, the energy of the clearing had changed so that, gradually, the clearing itself had filled with a reverential silence that nothing could touch or penetrate. Those who had saved and preserved her could be with her here, still, and so they came often just to be so, hence the beings who sometimes filled the clearing with their presence, if not their conversation. She was with her people still, despite all that had occurred. Had she but known it, the knowledge would have filled her heart with joy, even though her heart was missing.

And so, we, as observers, have come upon the scene of the Lady on her table of marble in the clearing at that time when the light of day is just beginning to lose its strength, making way for the darkness of night and the moon's light, if, indeed, the moon's light was to bathe the clearing this night. That remained to be seen. The clearing was all but empty, but two loyal companions kept the Lady company. Both had made themselves perfectly comfortable beside the table of marble. One – a magnificent, white unicorn – sat on the carpet of leaves beside the marble table with her long legs folded under her. Her head was bowed slightly, not with sadness but because she was relaxed and content and still and calm. With her head bowed, the horn of pearl spiralling from her forehead did not point to the heavens as it usually did. Her name was Isadore, and her contentment as she sat in the clearing beside her Lady was perfect in its absoluteness.

And so it was, too, for the other of the companions. He sat beside Isadore, right next to her, in fact, cross-legged, on a stool of wood with a book resting on his crossed legs. He was not tall, perhaps about the height of a ten-year-old human boy. Being Fae, as he was, he looked like a human boy, but he was no boy. He was, in fact, far older than the oldest human living, and no human would ever match him for wisdom and knowledge and experience and insight. His black hair was cropped short and looked ruffled, as if someone had run their fingers lovingly through it, exposing the slightly pointed ears that were common among the Fae. He wore dark trousers that ended just below his knees, a white shirt with long tails, and a navy-blue vest. His feet were folded under his legs, but they were not bare. On the contrary, he appeared to be wearing ballet slippers, although they were not, in truth, ballet shoes at all. His name was Cory, and although it was impossible to know it right at that moment courtesy of his concentration on the pages of his book, his movements were always inherently graceful, like those of a dancer in motion, so it was perhaps appropriate that his shoes looked like ballet slippers.

The two companions were content to be with their Lady, and they were content to be with each other. They were united in their devotion, and so they were perfectly attuned, each to the other, perfectly connected. The end of every day, come rain, hail or sunshine, warm or cold weather, saw the two here, in the clearing, beside their Lady. The uncanny, reverential silence always surrounded them and shrouded them as it did the clearing. They barely noticed it, so used to it were they. Cory always stayed until the darkness of night well and truly filled the clearing, and then he left, reluctantly, but Isadore always stayed beside her Lady for the duration of the long night.

And so, the Lady's two companions sat together in the silence, Isadore with her head bowed and Cory with his eyes on the pages of his book. Together they sat as the ambient light in the clearing gradually changed with the setting sun, and the forest around the clearing was slowly plunged into darkness.

Before darkness reigned supreme, however, something happened that had never happened over the aeons and aeons the two had sat beside the Lady at the end of every day. Something unheralded, unprecedented. Something quite remarkable. A small noise penetrated the silence, pierced it actually.

Clink.

Although both companions heard the noise, because the noise was very, very distinct in the clearing where silence reigned so supremely, Cory didn't at first register it. Only when he saw Isadore's ears twitch and come forward out of the corner of his eye, did he realise what he'd heard and raise his eyes from the pages of his book. Isadore raised her head, her ears forward, every muscle in her body suddenly alert and tense, no longer relaxed.

"I heard it, too, Isadore," Cory said as he slowly, gently, closed his book and put it on the stool beside him.

Slowly, supremely elegantly, like a dancer in motion, he unfolded his legs, put his feet on the clearing's floor, and stood. Isadore watched him, her brown eyes fixed on him as he first looked around the clearing, a frown creasing his brow as he wondered at the source of the noise. And then, finding nothing untoward or out of place, nothing that could be the source of the noise, he stepped slowly, elegantly, closer to the marble table upon which lay his Lady, and looked down upon her as she lay in perfect stillness.

He wasn't expecting to see anything. He just looked because he was standing, and because the noise was so remarkably out of place in the silence of the clearing, and because he always looked at her when he stood. He always looked at her whenever he could because he loved to look at her. Was he in love with her, his Lady? Very possibly, for is that not what you do when you are in love? Look . . . whenever you are able? It had, in fact, been his very first sight of her as she lay so still on her marble table that had triggered such loyal devotion within him. A single look. That was all it took, and he was smitten. And before that, it had been the stories told of her among his people that had aroused such curiosity he had been compelled to come and see her for himself.

Now, as he looked at her, his Lady, this time, his attention was caught anew and he leaned closer for a better look, his frown deepening the crease in his brow. And then he froze. He stared, quite unable to absorb what he could see, and as he stared, his mouth opened as if he would have talked. But no words came forth from his lips. Affected by his supreme tension as she was, Isadore unfolded her own legs and hauled herself to a standing position. And then she, too, looked down upon her Lady. Cory looked up, into her brown eyes, for a long moment, his own beautiful blue eyes wide with surprise and wonder, and then he turned and ran. He ran out of the clearing so fast he left a large cloud of disturbed leaves in his wake. He ran through the forest like the wind, so lightly his feet barely touched the forest floor. He ran and ran as if his own very life depended on the speed with which he ran. And when he burst out of the forest, still he ran . . . .

~

Cory's flight interrupted another nightly ritual involving two companions. The two were sitting in a large room with a high ceiling, most of its walls covered in floor to ceiling bookshelves packed full with beautiful, old, leather-bound books. Its floor of white, polished stone was a near-perfect reflection of the flames in the big old hearth that dominated one wall of the room, also the main source of light in the room. Shadows lurked in the corners of the room and played with the books on their shelves. Courtesy of the flames and the red-brown leather of the books on their shelves, the light that vied with the shadows for dominance in the room had a distinctly orange cast to it so that the room had unwittingly become a canvass of red, brown, and orange colour.

The two companions sat in front of the fire, one on a lounge covered in colourful cushions and the other in an over-sized single chair. Both were comfortable and relaxed as they spoke, the muted tones of their conversation filling the room just as were the shadows of the night. On the table in front of them, crystal glasses were made colourful with the amber liquid that half filled them, the amber liquid turned bright red-brown-orange by the flames of the large fire. One of the companions appeared younger than the other, although that was not the case at all. His long legs were stretched out in front of him, his booted feet crossed at the ankles. His long, dark hair, half tied back and held in place with a thin, black ribbon, appeared blue-black in the fire's light, and his deeply-blue eyes also appeared dark in the muted orange light. The other, apparently-older companion drew on a long pipe, filling the space around him and his companion with sweet smoke. His long white hair was unbound and remained unchanged in colour, even in the muted light that filled the room. His long beard was, like his hair, white as the driven snow, and his light-blue eyes twinkled with an inner, unearthly light, again, even in the muted light of the room. Both companions had the slightly pointed ears, beautiful hands, long fingers, and the jewel-coloured, crystal-like eyes that are typical of the Fae, but the ears of the older were hidden under his mane of white hair.

And so, it was into this warm, relaxed, contented atmosphere that Cory ran, bursting through the closed, thick, wooden door, causing it to swing back violently on its hinges. He flew into the room and stopped short beside the lounge and its companion chairs, skidding and sliding slightly on the smooth stone of the floor. The two who were seated on the lounge and its chair, their conversation abruptly halted by the interruption, looked at him, neither shifting his position. He stood before them with his mouth open as if he wanted to speak but no words were coming out. His finger tips were entwined in front of him, working together, his eyes were wide open, and he rolled his feet, shifting from one to the other and back again as if he was struggling to stand still and wanted only to be on the run once again. The tension within him was palpable, rolling off him in waves. That alone would have been enough to shatter the peace and calm of the atmosphere in the room, but he was so twitchy, wholly unable to stand still.

The silence stretched out between the three occupants of the room as the two who were seated waited for Cory to speak, but to no avail. Finally, the older of the two companions removed his long pipe from his mouth, inclined his head, and said, simply, "Cory, what is it?"

Cory swallowed and although he managed to speak, his voice was naught but a hoarse whisper.

"She moved." Fingers still working, he swallowed and tried again, although the words came out in an identical hoarse whisper. "She moved."

The younger of the two companions did not move, but he said, "What do you mean, Cory? She cannot move. She is dead."

Again, Cory swallowed, his eyes still open wide like little saucers. "I was reading, and Isadore was dozing." He spread his hands out, splayed out beside him, the gesture elegant, his movements fluid and graceful. "The clearing was full of silence as it always is, but a sound," and he raised one hand, using his thumb and forefinger to indicate a small amount, "just a small sound penetrated the silence. Isadore's ears twitched. She heard it, too, so I put my book down and stood to see what could have made the noise. Nothing in the clearing had moved or was out of place. But when I looked upon my Lady . . ." He could not finish. His throat was tight with raw and pure emotion.

"What, Cory?" the older of the two asked, leaning forward. "What did you see?"

Wholly unable to speak, Cory crossed his hands over his breast as his Lady's had long been crossed over her breast, and then he moved his left hand down across his waist. "She moved," he whispered again, "and the beads on her wrist clinked. That was the noise."

The older of the two companions lowered his pipe to his lap, frowning, and both companions exchanged a long look, the younger uncrossing his legs and sitting up straighter on the lounge.

"You'd better show us, Cory," the older said on behalf of them both.

~

Cory led the two companions through the forest and into the clearing at a much more sedate pace than he'd exited it. The older of the companions carried a long, white staff that matched, perfectly, the white of his long tunic, and all three carried orbs of light, like the crystal balls of fortune tellers, only these were opaque and emitted luminous, bright, white light. They were not heavy and they sat in the palm of a hand quite comfortably. With their orbs of light, the three formed a silent procession of light as they walked through the forest, bathing the trees in white light as they passed them by. When they entered the clearing, both companions bowed their heads to Isadore, the younger with a hand over his chest, and greeted her by name, both noting that she stood so close to the marble table upon which lay her Lady that she was touching it. That, in itself, was highly unusual. Normally, at this time of night, she was sitting on the carpet of leaves, dozing, content just to be beside her Lady. Both companions sensed the tension within her, a tension that was a perfect match for Cory's.

The older of the two companions stood at the end of the table, and the younger stood on one side, Cory on the other, next to Isadore. And so all three saw that Cory had been perfectly right. The Lady's hands were no longer crossed over her breast, and were, in fact, no longer touching at all. Nor were the fingers of her left hand curled, but were, instead, laid flat across her waist. Now that the fingers of one hand were laid flat, the elegance of her hands and her long fingers was apparent.

"By the gods!" the younger of the two companions said breathlessly as he put his orb on the glass and rested his fingertips on it, leaning over to get a better look.

"By the gods indeed," the older of the companions repeated quietly. "Could it be? She stirs." He looked over at Cory. "Are you sure you did nothing to cause her to move? You did not knock the glass by accident?"

Cory threw the old man a look that expressed his response to the questions more eloquently than words.

The old man chuckled. "No, perhaps not. Silly questions, Cory. I apologise. I'm just seeking a more mundane reason for her movement so as to avoid disappointment should it turn out to be nothing." He bent over and put his orb and staff on the ground beside him. When he straightened, he said, "We need to remove the glass. It is time, methinks"

The younger companion looked up at the old man quickly, frowning, about to protest, but then thought better of it, nodded, and picked his orb up off the glass, putting it on the ground beside him. Cory looked to the younger of the two companions for guidance and, when he saw the other nod his approval, put his own orb on the stool of wood behind him and then helped the other two release the clasps that held the glass in place, and then all three used those same clasps to lever the glass covering up and away from the Lady. They walked with the glass and gently laid it on the ground at the clearing's edge. When the Lady was free of her glass covering, Isadore touched her snout to the Lady's forehead in a light caress. This was the first time she had touched her Lady in aeons and aeons of time. But she broke contact quickly and tossed her head high, snickering in distress, the movement causing her white mane to ripple like a wave down her neck, and she stamped one of her front feet. Her agitation communicated itself to the other three, each of whom had resumed their positions at the table.

"Isadore," Cory said urgently, laying a soothing hand on the unicorn's white coat, "what is it?"

In response, Isadore tossed her head again, and then, gently, she leaned over and touched her snout to the wound on the Lady's body.

The younger of the two companions, watching Isadore, reached over and picked up the Lady's hand, holding it in both of his own so that his hands were wrapped around hers, the thumb of one hand interlocked with hers.

"She's remembering," he said softly, his voice almost a whisper. "She's remembering, and I cannot help her. She must do this on her own, as she has done everything else on her own."

The older of the two companions moved then to put a comforting hand on the younger one's shoulder. "Be at peace, Gabriel, my old friend," he said. "Be at peace. Your strength will infuse her, and your love will communicate itself to her. Rest easy, my old friend, rest easy. Do not despair. She will feel it if you do."

"Who is remembering?" Cory asked quickly, sounding confused. "Isadore?"

Gabriel, the younger of the two companions, looked at Cory. "No, Cory, not Isadore. Isadore shares her thoughts when they touch. Ever was it so."

The strange silence once again filled the clearing as Cory stared at the younger of the two companions.

"But you said it yourself, Gabe. She is dead. How can she have thoughts?"

The older of the two moved then. He came around the table of marble, knelt in front of Cory and put his hands on Cory's shoulders. "Nay, my friend, not dead, just dormant . . . separated from herself. They had not the power to kill her even though they took her heart. No one holds that kind of power. She cannot be killed. She has lain here dormant, missing herself in a sense, not dead, awaiting the time when she will stir and come to life once again. How did you think she could lay here so perfectly preserved?"

Cory looked at the younger companion in confusion, and then he looked back at the old man. "Well, I thought they had done something to preserve her when they sewed up her wound, and I thought the glass preserved her."

The old man shook his head. "No, Cory, 'tis not so."

"So . . ." Cory found he could not say the words, and he looked at the old man, tears filling his eyes. "So . . ." he tried again, and again he faltered.

"So," the other said, helping him out, "she always was destined to stir, to rise once again, Cory, and to walk again upon this earth whole and complete and restored. We have never told you because we had no notion of when she would stir, and we did not wish to raise hopes that could be dashed."

Cory looked over at Gabriel, the younger of the two companions. Gabriel nodded his agreement with the old man's statements, silently, once.

Isadore, feeling the strength and potency of Cory's emotions, laid her snout on his shoulder, offering comfort. Without thinking, Cory reached up a hand and laid it on the unicorn's snout. There were not many souls who were allowed to touch the unicorn, but he was one, Gabriel another, the old man yet another.

The old man stood then and moved to resume his position at the end of the table. Cory, too, turned to face the table, his eyes on his Lady, a hand still laid upon Isadore's smooth coat for comfort, whether his or hers it was hard to tell. Perhaps for them both. The older of the companions bent over to lift his staff and his orb in his hands once again, and he held his orb high so that light covered the marble table and they could see, clearly. For many long hours they all kept a silent vigil beside the Lady, ever patient, not speaking, their eyes never leaving the Lady on the stone table. If she was truly stirring then she would move again, and this time they would be ready. They would see it. And then they would know for certain, beyond doubt, she really was stirring.

~

I watch myself constantly,
And I observe the way I live now,
As if I am standing outside of myself —
A dispassionate observer.
Held up against the norms of human existence,
My yearning for solitude, the simplistic way I live,
My Hermit-like, reclusive existence,
My shunning of all their tricks and lures and traps,
And the way I so easily see through their manipulations,
Are just not normal.
But I am not one of you,
And nor have I ever been one of you.
So what is 'normal' for you is not 'normal' for me.
In fact, the way you live now is painful to me,
A pain that is exacerbated when I watch and observe you.
You are so chronically ignorant.
But I cannot judge you for that,
Because so, too, was I, once upon a time.
I have worn an ordinary human identity so many times.
But no longer.
I know who I am now,
So I know why the human identities do not sit well . . . at all.
I am returning to my true form, and I am coming home.

The Shadow of an Open Wound

It was a night just like any other. The night was cold, it being the second day of winter, so she lay under her quilt feeling the heat of her electric blanket against her back. As she rubbed hand cream into the skin of her hands she thought about the day's reading. So fast was her Process taking her on now she found it necessary to read the cards every day. And the day's reading had been a particularly powerful one. As was usual for her at the moment, the Swords were doing their wonderful, powerful work, so she knew false, misguided mindsets were being cut away, and she knew those mindsets were associated with her physical identity. She knew she was shedding it, like removing a suit of clothes, one item at a time, or like a snake shedding its old skin, little bit by little bit. She had shed so many misguided and false mindsets associated with her physical identity that she felt as if all the goals, dreams and ambitions; wants, desires and obsessions she'd held close for the last fifteen years had been stripped away, peeled away, swept away. It was as if her metaphysical, higher-dimensional Self had sent a bowling ball into her psyche, scattering all her physical wants and mindsets and dreams like ten pins. None of them remained standing now. A perfect strike. In that sense, she was stripped bare. But it felt good.

So what was left? That was the question she had discussed with them, those who Worked with her in the deepest recesses of her mind, that very day. She had told them that even though those old dreams and wants were false, or egoic, and were, therefore, not in any way connected to her true destiny, they had still provided her with endpoints, outcomes to Work and walk towards. In that sense, even though the path under her feet she thought she was walking was false, not at all real, it had still been a path, even if it was only an illusion, and even though it had generated despair within her far too often when it didn't eventuate. Still, she had known where she was walking and what she was walking towards, so she'd known where she was putting her feet with each step taken . . . or she **thought** she had. Sometimes, ignorance really was bliss. Well, now the illusion of those false paths had been stripped away, but she could no longer define or describe or even understand the path she **was** walking. Where was her Process taking her? Or what was it taking her to? This is what she'd spoken to them about that day.

And they had responded, although not in the usual way.

In the afternoon, she'd heard no voice in her mind as she so often did when they responded to her questions. She'd just felt the epiphany, the realisation. It was just there, filling her mind, filling **her**, pervading every cell in her body, so that she just knew. And with the knowledge came the realisation that she **did** know where she was walking, and, of course, with knowledge comes understanding, even though she would still have to wrap her human mind around it.

The cards saw it, of course. They always saw her Processes, and today they had told her the energy of the Tower was pulling down old thoughts and desires and wants and beliefs . . . no surprise there really. The surprise was in the power of it, if anything. But the reading also spoke of shadows of the past being banished. She knew already that it was so. Last night, she had dreamed of people from her past in this, her current life, as she always did when the door in her mind that guarded her memories opened up. But since she had all but transcended her shadows of this lifetime, she knew that the memories the cards spoke of were from other times and spaces and places. And all of it was part of the same Process – the Process revealed to her by her epiphany.

And so, the epiphany? The path she really **was** walking (as opposed to the one she **thought** she was walking . . . or, perhaps more aptly, the one she **wanted** to be walking) was quite simple. She was walking into the truth of herself, as opposed to the illusion of herself. She was walking into her metaphysical Self, as opposed to the physical being she'd long thought she was. And that meant fully being. Or being, fully . . . whichever you prefer.

I told you it was simple.

Transition – the most powerful transition it was possible to make in a single lifetime. This was the Work of the ninth stage of initiation, a stage no longer connected to the seven stages of incarnation. And no one knew but her . . . which made perfect sense because no one could do this but her. Those who **could** help her already **were** helping her, powerfully, hence her epiphany, which they had, no doubt, given her. Certainly no one in this physical reality was capable of helping her because they were not even capable of seeing the truth of her or of seeing truth at all. Their judgements were very clouded. That tends to happen when your eyes are permanently closed. There is an awful lot you don't see. Well, her eyes had been opened. And now the cards and her epiphany had helped her open her eyes even more.

She was shedding the character-identity she was in this lifetime, but at the same time, she was becoming her true identity – her metaphysical, higher-dimensional Self. Strip away the illusion and what remains? Truth. She was shedding her physicality, stepping out of and away from it, and morphing into her metaphysicality. It was rather like changing characters half way through a stage play, but gradually, subtly, not all at once, so that the mind could make its own adjustments along the way . . . well, keep up, really. And that wasn't to say her personality was changing, although, also, it was. Nor was her physical appearance changing. Rather, she was changing that with which she identified – a character that answered to a different name, so to speak.

She knew, specifically, which memories it was time to Process, too. She sensed it, somehow. Well, truth be told, she'd known for a while that pieces of these particular memories were missing, and so she'd also known the time would come when she would have to address that by finishing the Process that was addressing the memories. She needed to see them through to their bitter end, and to then understand what effect they had on her.

Perhaps, on the other side of those painful memories, there was the truth waiting to be claimed, a truth she had long hidden from. So, it was time, then.

She reached over and turned out the light, and then, just as in a darkened cinema that facilitates focus on the images on the movie screen, so, too, did the darkness facilitate her own visions now. She let them come, and she readied herself to watch.

~

At one stage, during their silent vigil, the old man spoke an incantation, lifting his staff and his orb higher, his eyes riveted on those of the Lady on the table of marble.

"Come, Ushara," he commanded, "walk towards me. See the Light and walk towards it. Know who you are. Remember. Come to me. Raise your vision. Lift your awareness. Remember. Let the veil of forgetfulness fall away. Let your vision clear." He kept muttering the words over and over, at first loudly and then quietly, almost under his breath.

The Lady did not stir, nor did she move in response to his words. She lay on her table, as still as the marble underneath her. But he knew, despite her stillness, that she had heard him. He could feel her response.

~

Expecting to see the temple under the flattened mountain – the site of those terrible memories – she saw, fleetingly but powerfully, an image of herself lying on a slab of marble in a clearing ringed with ancient, tall trees. She was lying in a pose of death, one hand across her waist and the other over her breast, and she was lying under shrouds of beautiful cloth. She could see the wound on her chest because she knew it was there, but it was not open because they had sewed it closed. She recognised the image of the Lady in the pose of death but not the context – the clearing in the forest. She had seen the same image before, but in a darkened cave. The change of context, darkened cave to forest, was symbolically significant, she knew, and it spoke to her of the power of the shift in her consciousness from when she'd first seen the image, burdened with her ignorance as she had been, to now.

And then she knew why she was seeing the image in her visions. He was pulling her there.

At the end of the table upon which she lay, at her feet, a man stood radiating powerful Light. He held an orb in one hand and a long staff in his other, and he held both high. His blue eyes bored into hers intensely. And although the orb obviously gave off light of its own, its light was eclipsed by that of the old man's. She knew him. She knew him well, actually. She could not hear him speaking, although she could see that he was, but she knew what he was telling her.

"Keep walking. Walk towards me. Remember who you are. Remember . . ."

She wanted to tell him she got his message. She wanted to tell him she knew and understood, but she had no way of reaching out to him.

~

Finally, when the dark of night well and truly reigned, and their silent vigil was stretching into many hours, their patience was rewarded. Just a small movement, so slight as to be barely noticeable, although each one of those who watched saw the movement clearly. The fingers of her right hand, the hand still crossed over her breast, uncurled, slowly, gently, until her fingers were straight. But instead of lying flat over her breast, her fingers were elevated, as if she was reaching, reaching, reaching out her hand . . .

Seeing the movement, Isadore again touched her Lady on the forehead, and, again, tossed her head high, snickering and shaking her head in distress. She liked not the images she was seeing in her Lady's mind.

"I know, Isadore," Gabriel said. "I know. She is stirring and so, too, will the memories of the past be stirring. If she is to remember who she is, she must walk through those memories. Such terrible memories. Such terrible, terrible memories . . ."

He, alone, knew well how terrible those memories were because he, too, had been a part of them when they originally occurred. Long, long ago had he processed the memories for himself, but even so, they still had the power to cause him incredible pain – pain, he knew, she would have to walk through, too.

~

Lying in the darkness of her bedroom, her visions took her from the clearing in the forest straight to the time and place she expected. It was logical, after all, to go there first. So she saw, again, as she'd seen before, the beautiful, ornately-carved, full-length mirror and the curved silver knife*. She had Processed this memory thoroughly, so she understood the images, and she knew what she'd done to cast the ritual spell using the knife and the mirror*. She saw the pool of shattered glass at her feet, and she saw the drops of blood falling onto the glass from the wound in her open hand, a wound she had put there deliberately, as part of the ritual, using the knife. She saw the blood staining the blade of the knife, and the beautiful mirror in front of her was empty of its glass so that she could no longer see her own reflection.

Now, though, the story changed, as it always did when she was ready to Process more of the memory as it had happened.

~

"Kiaara."

She heard the voice calling her name, and she recognised it and the sound of his booted feet on the stone floor of the porch outside her room. Heart pounding, eyes open wide, she dropped the knife and searched around for something to wrap around her hand to contain the bleeding. He must not see what she had done. He must never know. He must never, ever know.

And then, her hand wrapped, she went out to greet him and to stop him coming into her room so he wouldn't see the mirror and the knife. He would know if he saw them.

He smiled when he saw her, and when she was close enough, he raised his hands and slid his fingers behind her neck, his thumbs caressing her cheeks. He bent down so he could kiss her. And so he did. His lips caressed hers, and she returned his kiss. When he pulled away he saw her bandaged hand. Blood had soaked her makeshift bandage, and the deep red was starkly clear against the white bandage. He frowned, concerned.

"You're hurt," he said.

She tried to pull her hand away. "It's nothing. Just a silly accident. I picked up broken glass . . ."

He wouldn't let her pull away. "Let me see."

He held her hand while he unwrapped the bandage, and when he saw the wound, his frown deepened. "This looks bad. Let me send one of my surgeons to have a look at it."

"No, Ambrose, it'll be fine. It's just a shallow flesh wound. Nothing vital was . . ."

Her voice broke and caught. She couldn't finish the sentence, and she struggled to suppress a sob. Nothing vital was severed. That's what she was going to say. But that wasn't true . . . wasn't true at all. In fact, something so terribly vital had been severed, its absence would cause her unbearable pain. The wound on her hand formed part of a ritual spell that had severed her from her own reflection, of which he was a vital part. She had severed herself from herself, and she had severed herself from him. How could she tell him what she'd done? How could she tell him what she'd done to herself, and what she'd done to them in the process? She could not. She simply could not.

Ever sensitive to her deepest thoughts and feelings, he pulled her against him. "What is it?" he asked her, his lips against her forehead. "Something's very wrong. I can feel it."

She closed her eyes against the pain that washed through her, and she melted into him, savouring the strength of him, savouring the warmth of him, savouring the solid, dependability of him, and savouring the feel of his arms holding her. He was a tough, battle-hardened soldier, a Ranger, a commander of a whole army, the king's army, in fact, and the king's personal guard. As such, he was one of the most powerful men in the land. None held the trust of the king as did he. He was a man of honour, and, as such, none had earned the trust and respect of the king as he had. His body held the scars of battle. She knew those scars well. Many, many times had she touched them with her own lips, so she knew that he knew what it felt like to be wounded. But he would need all the strength he possessed to deal with what was to come. All she could hope for was that, one day, he would understand why she had done what she'd done this day, and she hoped he would forgive her. She hoped she could forgive herself for what she'd done to them both this day.

"Will you do something for me, my love?" she asked him, not raising her head.

"Of course. Anything. You have but to ask. You know that."

She pulled back so she could look at him. "Will you remember me always . . . always? No matter what. And will you remember that I love you, deeply, passionately, truly?"

He frowned again and raised a hand to caress her cheek. "Kiaara, you're scaring me. What's going on?"

She laid her uninjured hand over his. "Something terrible is going to happen. Something terrible . . ."

The images changed. Her visions took her from him, at least as they'd been together there in the temple in the days before those terrible events.

In the images she saw now, she was a witness, not really there, because she hadn't been there originally. These were his memories, not hers, but she was able to stand outside of it all, looking on, such was their connection.

She saw a dozen or so of his men running, running desperately through the castle's opened gate and then through the large, grassed courtyard, knocking things over and pushing people out of the way in their haste to get to their captain. He raised his head when he heard the scuffle of their approach and their desperate, yelling shouts and cries. She heard, too.

"They're moving against the priesthood . . . they're moving against the priesthood . . ."

She saw him turn a ghastly, ghostly shade of pallor. "Who is? Who is moving against the priesthood . . . ?" he yelled.

But he was already moving, grabbing his sword, his cloak, and running towards his horse.

She heard his men yell at him. "An army. We don't know whose army. We don't know who commands it. We don't know . . . . It's been seen . . ."

He didn't wait for his men. But they followed him anyway. They would have followed him into the pits of hell if he'd ridden there to do battle with the devil himself. They would have followed him into any battle, and so they followed him now into this one. They all vaulted onto the backs of their own horses, even though some of those horses hadn't yet been saddled, yelling at their comrades to join them. Men all over the courtyard dropped what they were doing and ran towards the stables. Other men came running from beyond the courtyard, alerted by the cries or, with the well-honed instincts of soldiers, knowing something was wrong and they were needed. And so, a long stream of men flowed out of the castle's gate in the wake of their captain's panicked, hasty departure, the men at various stages of dress, but very few of them fully and properly prepared and armed for battle, although all of them had their swords with them.

She saw them all, and him in particular, running his horse at breakneck speed, something he would never have done normally. He valued his warhorse even more so than he did his long sword. She knew, somehow, that her own words were ringing in his ears as if she was speaking them to him right there.

"Something terrible is going to happen . . ."

The scene changed again.

~

She balked at the images she saw now, her mind rejecting them, shutting down on them, causing her to cringe and curl up in pain.

"No . . ." she moaned into the darkness. "No . . . Oh god, no . . . ."

~

Her entire body convulsed as if someone had sent a bolt of electricity through her. She didn't open her eyes, but the fingers of both hands straightened and then curled, stiffly, as if she was in great pain and she was bracing against it. Without having to touch her mistress, Isadore tossed her head and snickered in distress. The motion caused Cory's hand to slide from her coat. Unable to help himself, his heart thumping with fear and his eyes full of tears, he reached out to his Lady and wrapped a hand around her forearm. All he could do was hold her, let her know he was there. Her fingers had moved out of Gabriel's hold when she moved them. He re-wrapped his hands around hers and bowed his head, his eyes closed. There were tears on his cheeks, too. The memories were flooding his mind even as they were flooding hers.

"Help her, Salomon," he said, his words anguished. "Help her."

The old man responded, not needing to be told twice. Again raising his staff and his orb, he intoned an incantation, this time with his eyes closed, and no longer using words the others understood. "Nadrach amal porthos, mika . . . you are not alone, dearest . . . Vité radiät . . . See the Light . . . Vité radiät . . ."

~

They are searching the temple's rooms for her. She knows it. She can hear them, and she knows it is her they seek. She is standing in front of the empty mirror, and there are tears in her eyes and on her cheeks. She closes her eyes briefly, fortifying herself with her courage, and then she opens them, resolute. To save her people, she goes to those searching the temple and surrenders herself even though she can hear her people begging her not to. She could run and save herself. Instead, she tells those of her people she sees to run and save themselves, shaking her head in response to their anguished pleas that she join them. She cannot join them. She cannot run. The rabble army will search until it finds her, she knows, and more of her people will die as a consequence. But the Elders have asked her to do this. She cannot run from her promise to them. Her people know not that she has made a promise to the Elders.

Hands tied behind her back, she is pulled outside by a strong hand on her upper arm, and then she is hauled down the steps of the temple, her captor uncaring that she stumbles and trips. His vice-like grip on her arm holds her up and keeps her from falling to the ground. She is calm even though she is deadly afraid, and tears are coursing down her cheeks and dropping off her chin like rain.

She wants to tell them it was she and her people who had given them life, not so they could destroy and kill and maim, but so they could learn and evolve and grow and create. Their actions were not causing them to grow but, rather, to stagnate, and she knows they are burdening their own souls with such debt – the heavy, heavy burden of karmic debt. She stays silent. They will not listen because they cannot hear. They are in the grip of the blood lust. They are mad with it. They are like wild, savage dogs given a first taste of blood. She has never seen it before, but she has heard of it. It breaks her heart to see human men behave in such a way, with no thought for human life, no thought for the pain and hurt they are causing, no thought for the trauma they are inflicting. Their faces are twisted masks of madness and blood lust. She wonders what they think they will gain from their actions – power, riches, status, title, land . . . ? The dark priests will not deliver on their promises. They never do. They never have to. This she wants to tell them, too, but, still, she stays silent. There is no point. They will not and cannot hear her. They don't want to hear her. They want only to destroy her.

The scene around her is happening as if in slow motion. She feels as if she and everyone around her are moving in slow motion. She sees some of her people trying to reach her, their hands outstretched towards her as they are held back by strong, violent arms, their open mouths screaming their terror, their faces contorted with grief and horror, and wet with tears. She sees the rabid dogs of this mercenary army plunge swords and daggers into innocent, defenceless chests and bellies, some pulling the swords loose only to plunge them back in again and again. Her people. Her people under violent attack. Her people in pain. Those of her people the wild soldiers are killing are not armed, nor are they trained for battle, and they have no way of defending themselves. Reprehensible. The mercenary soldiers are killing for sport, for pleasure . . . they are killing for the love of it. Murder, pure and simple. Cold-blooded murder. Genocide.

There are bodies all around her as she is pulled through the temple and then down its steps, some lying on the temple's stone floor, some fallen down the temple's steps. Many are fallen. Those she loves have fallen. All are lying in a pool of their own blood, their robes and tunics torn and soaked in their blood. Some lie still, staring at nothing, their glassy eyes open and as still as their bodies. Faces that were once animated, alive with personality and the joy of living are now empty and still. Eyes that were once filled with laughter are now frozen in horror. Mouths that spoke and smiled are now opened in a permanent, silent scream, no sound escaping their lips. Their bodies have become naught but empty vessels. Her throat constricts and burns with her grief as she looks upon the broken, torn bodies of her people, and she struggles to breathe.

And then, through the carnage, she sees the leader of this rabid, mercenary army. She knows who he is because he stands still in the middle of massacre, facing the temple at the bottom of the stairs, soaking up the screams of terror and agony. He is cloaked, hooded, cowled, covered from head to toe in his black robes, and his silver medallion is starkly clear against the black of his robe. He holds his hands out beside him as if his open hands are helping him to soak up the energy of trauma and terror. His head is thrown back in ecstasy and his eyes are closed. His mouth is open in a macabre grin so she sees his rotten, black teeth, and she sees, too, the grey-green puckered skin of his hands and face. He is not trying to hide what he is. He is not human, although his body once was until he corrupted it, but he and his kind have long wanted control of the human experience. Today, she knows, they will get it. Today, humanity will be plunged into the abyss of darkness, no longer existing in the Light.

Behind the dark priest, at the edge of the stone courtyard in front of the temple's steps, she sees columns of stone, a dozen or so, erected at regular intervals. The columns are not normally there so she knows the rabble army has brought them and placed them in front of the temple to serve the malevolent agenda of the dark priests — sacrifice, ritual sacrifice. Some of her people are being dragged to the columns and bound to them like common criminals. She watches as the dark priest raises his voice and his hands, intoning words of dark magic, dark energy. She feels the dark energy swirling around them all, and she watches the effect it has on the wild dogs of the mercenary army. It energises them and spurs them to more violent action. Some of them laugh maniacally.

The priest gives a signal, a wave of his raised hands, on both sides of him, as if he is conducting an orchestra, and she watches as those of her people already bound to the columns are silenced with a knife run across their throats. She watches then as they gurgle and struggle for breath, blood oozing from their mouths and the wounds in their throats, covering the skin of their faces and chests in thick, red blood. They make no sound other than the gurgling struggle for breath because they cannot scream. The knife wound damages their throat, making speech and sound impossible.

There are beautiful mosaic pools of clear water in front of the temple's stone courtyard, and she watches as the blood of those sacrificed runs across the stones of the courtyard and drips into the pools of water. So much blood. She has never seen so much blood. The blood mingles with the water, and so the pools of water quickly become red with blood, the stones of the courtyard stained with it. Pools of blood.

She is hauled, dragged to a column of stone in the very centre of the others, the very centre of the courtyard where it connected to the temple's walkway, in front of but between the pools of water, the column obviously marked for her. Her hands are untied and then rebound again behind the pillar of stone, locking her in place. They bind her throat to the pillar so that she is forced upright, and she struggles to breathe. The binding on her throat is bruising her, hurting her, crushing her neck.

The dark priest stands in front of her, leering at her, and he removes his hood so that she can see him clearly. He is ugly, putrid, and the stench of his corruption fills her nostrils. He smells like death and decay, like rotting flesh. His eyes are glittering black, with no white, no colourful iris, and no pupil. It is as if his whole eyes are a glittering, black void. His teeth are rotten, his head is hairless, and his skin is pitted and pockmarked. His fingers are long, and his nails are black and have been filed to a point, like black talons. There is poison under those nails, she knows — the poison of corruption — but he has no intention of killing her with poison.

He wants her to fear him. He wants to soak up her fear of him. But she is distracted. She hopes her lover does not come now, and she is watching for him. She does not want him to witness her death, to see, and to forever more hold the memories within him. She would spare him that agony. Her worries are consuming her thoughts so that she barely notices the priest, and her reaction to the priest, or lack thereof, angers him. She stares ahead as if she does not see him, her eyes steady and unblinking. There is no fear of him in her eyes, and he becomes enraged. He snarls at her, and so it is in a rage that he raises his arm and brings it down again, knife in hand. She jerks. Her whole body jerks with the strength of the strike, and her eyes widen in shock and pain. Her breath catches in her throat. He uses all his considerable, unnatural strength to pull the dagger down, down, through her body. From neck to navel he opens her up. And then he drops the knife and uses both hands to prise open her rib cage. Reaching into her body, he wraps a taloned hand around her beating heart and pulls it out, and then he turns and holds it high for all to see. The sleeve of his black tunic falls to his shoulder and everyone can see her blood running down his raised arm, coating it. He lowers the heart and, turning to face her, he grins his ugly, macabre grin at her and then sinks his teeth into it, taking first one and then another and then another bite out of it . . .

~

On the table of marble in the clearing, the Lady did not move, but blood welled in the wound on her body. It soaked into the beautiful material of her gown, staining it bright red, and then it formed rivulets, like tears, that ran from the wound over her pale skin.

Isadore tossed her head again, and stamped the ground with a foot. The three who kept a silent vigil watched the blood welling, and then Gabriel closed his eyes and bowed his head again, completely unable to contain his sobs. Salomon, the older of the two companions, moved. He laid his staff on the ground and he went to put a comforting hand on Gabriel's shoulder. But he offered no words of comfort. There were no words of comfort to be offered.

Cory just froze, and he could not tear his eyes away from the sight of the bright, red blood. "Oh no," he said, and his words held his anguish and echoed the distress in the others who kept watch over the Lady. "Oh no."

He took a handkerchief from a pocket in his vest, and he reached over to clean the blood from her skin, but the action proved futile. For every rivulet of blood he wiped away, another took its place.

~

She is alive for long seconds after her heart is removed from her body, and although shock and trauma rob her of normal cognitive function so that she is no longer fully aware of what is happening, she sees what the priest is doing to her heart and the image imprints on her psyche, forming part of the memories. She sees him eat much of her heart. And then her breath flows out of her and the light goes out of her eyes. Her head falls forward slightly, not fully given the binding on her throat, and she sags like a rag doll.

What happens next, she sees not from within her body, but outside of it, standing as an observer in the middle of the carnage, next to her own body.

Her lover rides into the temple's grounds with his own men, and she watches his face as he sees her and knows he is too late. He jumps from his horse, pulls his sword from its scabbard and screams in grief and rage as he cuts down the rabid dogs of the priest's mercenary army. He and his men show no mercy, and they are seasoned fighters, well trained and battle savvy. The mercenary dogs are no match for them. Very soon, the bodies of the mercenary soldiers are lying among the bodies of her own people. The captain's men leave none of the mercenary dogs alive. So much for their reward, she thinks. Their reward is death in this life, and now each of them must traverse the human experience laden with the burden of their karmic debt. What they have done this day will be reversed on them. It will be done to them. Such is the nature of karma – an unavoidable universal law.

She watches her lover fight his way to the priest, and she sees that the priest does not try to run or escape. She wonders why because she knows it is not in their nature to martyr themselves. But then she realises the priest will form another body for himself, such is their higher-dimensional power. No doubt he already has one prepared. When her lover reaches the priest, the priest grins an insane, maniacal grin at the captain, his black teeth stained red with her blood and his black eyes glittering with malice.

"You may cut me down, Captain Ambrose," he says through his grin, "but you are too late. The damage is done." He throws his head back and laughs insanely. "Our will is done," he yells at the sky. Again, he laughs, and then he looks again at the captain, bringing his hands, coated in her blood, up, holding them together, prayer-like, against his chest, and he bows his head, although his eyes stay on those of the captain. "Our will be done," he says and grins.

The captain screams his rage as he raises his sword and strikes the priest's head from his body. The head falls from the body and rolls, its maniacal grin now frozen on its features, and the body continues to stand for a second or two, and then it crumples at the captain's feet. The captain drops his sword, takes his dagger from his belt and cuts the bindings around her neck and wrists, and then he catches her body as it falls. He, too, falls to his knees, not with the weight of her but with the weight of his grief, and she watches as he closes the eyes of her body with his fingers, those same fingers that have caressed her so many times. He takes his own cloak from his shoulders and wraps her in it. And then he holds her to him and sobs against her, rocking with his grief.

Not one but two hearts are broken this day.

She watches, and she is filled with grief herself, despite the fact that she has no body, no conscious mind. She becomes the grief. She knows, because she is privy to all her memories now, that this is a pattern formed in this moment that will play itself out between them in many, many lives, the same tragedy repeated over and over again. She wonders what will break it, what will set them both free . . .

And she knows that after this day, shadow will be wrapped around her own soul, like a spiral of shadowed barbed wire buried deeply in her soul.

What happens when you are cut down just for being what you are? You stop being what you are, do you not? Except that you are, and you cannot not be what you are. So what then? You hide what you are. When you are, and that is the truth of you, the only way to stop being what you are is to hide the truth of yourself, from others, yes, but especially from yourself.

Severed reflection.

What better way to hide the truth than to hide it from yourself. If you are hidden from yourself, you cannot be, because you do not know what you are. She holds the truth of her within herself, and she holds the truth of him within her. And he holds the truth of her within him. So she will now be severed from the reflection of her that he casts.

Severed reflection.

One of the hands of her body falls out of the captain's cloak onto the stones of the temple's courtyard, and she sees the open wound there, a wound she put there, deliberately. It has not had a chance to heal.

Severed reflection.

She falls to her knees beside her lover who is cradling her own body against him. What is done is done, and cannot now be undone.

Severed reflection.

She has torn herself apart. She has torn them apart. From this day forth, she will be a stranger to herself, estranged from herself. There is nothing in heaven, in hell, or on earth more painful or more torturous.

And humans say the Fallen are evil, responsible for all the woes of the human experience. If only they knew the truth, for 'tis exactly the opposite. Humans are responsible for all the woes of the human experience because they chose to exist in the abyss of darkness and Separation. That is what they did with the gift of Free Will. If only they knew the sacrifice the Fallen had truly made, and all because they had not the heart to let humans fall into the abyss alone, with no way out, and no one to guide them. For, you see, that's why the Fallen fell — so that humans would not wallow in the abyss alone.

~

Now that I know I am not one of you,
And now that I know what I am,
I know it is not in my nature to have
Or to exercise Free Will.
Free Will is an illusion,
And I am not one to be beguiled or seduced by illusion.
It has taken me a long time to realise the truth of that,
And to understand it.
But now I understand why I am as I am.
And, at last, I understand where I am walking,
And what I am Working towards.
I have walked this path always, without knowing it.
But now I know.
Restoration. Healing. Wholeness. Completeness.
The power of the symbolism of me returned to what it once was,
Returned to what it is, and what it should be.

The Temple Under the Flattened Mountain

She opened her eyes in the darkness. The visions had stopped. They just ceased. There was nothing more.

"God-damn," she muttered as she rolled over under her heavy quilt, knowing there was nothing she could do if they'd stopped of their own accord. She couldn't make them come, but she wanted to see what happened to the captain as she sometimes could in her visions. She wanted to know he'd gone on, and how he'd gone on without her. She needed to know he had been all right. Nothing. "God-damnit," she muttered again.

How she wished she could reach out across time and tell him they would meet again. They would be lovers again, many times. If he could just hold on . . .

But there were questions she needed to answer for herself. Vital questions – questions that, really, now defined the path she was walking. How could she heal the wound in her chest as she lay on that marble table, because she knew she **had** to heal it, and she knew only she could do so? And how was she supposed to heal and restore her severed reflection? A while ago, she had walked into that territory where she had started to see the events that caused her to be severed from it, but now she had to go a step further. So how was she supposed to do that?

And, now she knew what it was her heart truly desired. Her heart wanted to be whole again. Her heart wanted to be restored. Her heart wanted to be healed. Her heart wanted to beat, freely, to the rhythm of its own unique song, and it wanted to drink in its own very great beauty.

So how was she to achieve this? How . . . ?

~

"It's stopped."

Silence followed as all three looked at the wound on her chest. Cory lifted the kerchief he was using to clean the blood from her skin.

"Gabe," he said again when neither of the two companions responded verbally, "the wound has stopped bleeding." He never addressed the older of the two by name. He loved the old man deeply, he was just very intimidated by him. So by addressing Gabriel, he was addressing both of them.

Salomon was perfectly well aware of the fact that he intimidated Cory, so he understood that Cory was addressing him as well by saying only Gabriel's name.

"Yes, it has, Cory," he responded on behalf of both himself and Gabriel.

Indeed, the blood still pooled in the wound on her chest but it had stopped welling and was no longer forming rivulets that ran over her pale skin.

Gabriel focussed on the wound, and he lifted a hand away from hers to wipe the tears from his cheeks.

"What does it mean?" he asked the old man who was still standing beside him with a hand on his shoulder.

"I do not know," the old man said quietly. "I wish I knew, but I do not."

As if in response to his words, Isadore again touched her lips to her Lady's forehead. And this time, she did not toss her head or stamp her foot. Instead, she stayed as she was, her snout gently touching the Lady on the marble table, a lingering kiss.

All three companions watched her, and though none of them spoke, they all knew the Lady's memories were no longer distressing Isadore. All three wished they, too, could know what was passing through the Lady's mind. They wished they could know . . .

~

She thought she would just fall asleep and hoped her dreams weren't full of nightmares after what she'd just seen. Her visions had exhausted her, so sleep would have offered a welcome reprieve from the intensity of what she'd seen. But, to her surprise, the visions started again, and they were clear, strong and powerful, pulling her focus, demanding she pay attention. Obviously her Work with them tonight was not finished. Surprised, she turned over again onto her back so she could watch the images against the backdrop of darkness that filled her bedroom.

~

She wandered around the market, basket on her arm, humming a contented tune to herself, occasionally smiling at and greeting people who passed her or who served her behind the stalls. She was wearing a light dress of turquoise, its sleeves covering her arms to her elbows, the neckline low and scooped, and the skirts long. Around her neck she wore a silver chain with a silver heart on it that sat just above her breasts, just above that place in the body where the heart beats its rhythm. The necklace was her gift to herself when she realised she had saved up enough money to be able to afford little luxuries like a necklace. She'd purchased it at the market, of course. Her weekly wanderings through the market were her treat to herself on her one day away from the dusty rooms and the dusty tomes of the library where she worked to copy the copious numbers of ancient books and scrolls and parchments that filled the library's shelves.

She wandered around the market by herself because everything she did, she did by herself, and she wandered slowly and aimlessly from stall to stall, in no hurry at all. The sun was shining brightly in a bright-blue, cloudless sky, and its reflection on the bright-white sand that covered the town's centre square where the market was set up was glaring. She didn't mind. She could feel the sun's warmth on her skin, and it felt nice. The market was teaming with people, and there were many stalls displaying many different items. Around the edge of the town's centre square, she could see tall buildings that gleamed bright white in the sun's light, including the library where she worked six days of the week. She paid the library and its companion buildings no real attention, though. There was too much of interest to look at in the stalls she was wandering past.

And then, suddenly, from behind her, something was placed roughly over her mouth, and a strong, pungent smell filled her nostrils, a smell she didn't recognise and one that brought tears to her eyes. A strong hand held the cloth in place over her mouth and nose, and a strong arm was clamped around her waist holding her against a solid male body behind her. She struggled to breathe, and she unconsciously dropped the basket on her arm to bring her hands up, trying to pull the hand that held her away from her mouth. But her efforts were futile. The hand didn't budge, and her vision wavered and blurred. Then she could feel herself falling . . .

She woke up lying on a dirty, dusty floor. She didn't know where she was, and her hands were bound together behind her back. She struggled against the bindings but to no avail. They were tight and they held her wrists together implacably. With her arms behind her back, her position on the floor was awkward, and the muscles of her arms were screaming in agony. Her cheek was against the dirty wooden floor, and the dirt was scratching her skin, so she tried to haul herself into a sitting position, but jolting movement made it impossible, and she realised she was in some sort of wagon. So she gave up trying to move. Around her, all was darkness, but she could see darker forms near her and knew she was not alone. The darker forms, she thought, also had their arms behind them, and most of them were in sitting positions, leaning against the wall of the wagon. No one spoke. No one moved, and she thought they must have been asleep. Had they been taken as she had, against her will, taken by surprise and overcome? Strangely, she wasn't afraid. But she was cold, inside and out. Goosebumps covered her skin, and the light material of her dress did little to shield her from the chill of the night. And within, a determined resolve was forming, like a solid thing in her chest. Whatever they wanted with her, these people who had taken her from her town, her home, they would not get it.

She must have fallen asleep again because, again, she woke up. She was lying on her back at one end of the wagon, and the position was causing her own body to crush her hands underneath it. Although the darkness of night was all around her, light was coming into the wagon through an open door, and the wagon was no longer moving. The light was orange and it was flickering so she thought its source must have been a fire. A man was looming over her in the darkness, and in the muted light she could see his hair and beard were black. His eyes appeared to her like dark pools in the muted light. He must have moved her, and it was the movement that had awakened her. He was bending over her, trying to push her dress up her legs with one hand while he held himself over her with his other. Again, strangely, she felt no fear, just a kind of inner knowing.

Calmly, not bothering to try and struggle, she looked up at him in the muted light of the wagon and said clearly, "Where that hand touches me, it will burn. Your hand will burn where it touches my skin. Do you hear me? Do you understand?"

He stopped briefly, surprised that she spoke his language, and surprised that she knew which language he spoke because he spoke a different language from the one she spoke in her land, her town. And then, recovering from his surprise, and completely ignoring her, he continued to try and push her dress up her legs. He was succeeding, too, running his hand up the bare skin of her leg when his body jerked as he bent over her, and she heard a voice behind him.

"Ahmed, you god-damn idiot. They're not ours. You know it's forbidden. You know this. Do you want to get us all into trouble? How do you know she's not a virgin? You know how prised they are. She could earn us good money."

"Just a bit of harmless fun," her attacker muttered. "Just want to feel that lovely body against me again." But he allowed himself to be persuaded and pulled back from her.

Left alone, and with the lack of movement in the wagon, she was able to roll herself into a sitting position, and was able to shift, or shuffle backwards, along the dirty wagon floor, so that she could position herself to see out the open door. Fire was, indeed, the source of the flickering orange light in the wagon. Their fire was huge and roaring, like a small bonfire rather than a camp fire. She could see the men sitting around it on small, wooden stools, and her attacker made the mistake of taking his place around the fire so that he was in her line of vision. Concentrating on him, she focused her will and held a vision of his hand in her mind's eye. In her vision, his hand was red and blistered. She had no idea how much time passed before she saw him stand to pick up his plate, not realising it was so close to the flames it had grown hot from the heat of their large fire. She heard him scream, and heard, rather than saw him drop the plate. Satisfied, she released the vision, relaxed her head back against the wall behind her and closed her eyes.

~

Frowning up at the darkness in her bedroom, she wondered what this vision was and what it meant. Was it a memory? It didn't feel like a memory. It felt different somehow. And what did it have to do with everything she'd already seen this night? Where was she in the vision? And when? Was this before or after the terrible events that had brought down a powerful priesthood and plunged humanity into the abyss? So many questions. No answers. Yet. Well, the only way to get those answers was to continue to allow the visions to come. The answers were always in the visions.

~

She was sitting in the same position, her bound hands still behind her, leaning against the wall of the wagon, her legs stretched out in front of her, and the wagon was, once again, full of darkness and the same muted, orange, flickering light from the slavers' fire. They had travelled for days, moving during the day, stopping at night. She was hungry and thirsty. Her tongue felt as if it was too big for her mouth, and her mouth felt gritty, as if she'd swallowed sand. The last time the slavers had given them water to drink was well over a day ago, and she and the other captives had had no food from their captors at all, and this despite the fact that the slavers ate well every night once they'd built their fire. Nor had the slavers allowed any of the captives to leave their makeshift prisons, so the wagon stank of sweat, unwashed bodies, and human refuse. She felt dirty, soiled . . . and cold. She'd forced herself to move when she could, lifting her legs, moving her feet and her hands behind her back, trying to prevent the numbness from setting in, but it was a battle she was losing.

Again, the door of the wagon was open and she was able to see the slavers sitting around their fire eating from their metal plates. She didn't know why they opened the door at night. There were barred windows on both sides of the wagon that had no glass in them, so it wasn't for air that the slavers opened the door. She watched them talking and laughing as they ate, completely uncaring that their captives were cold, hungry, thirsty, in pain, uncomfortable. She watched, too, as they passed around a flask, taking big mouthfuls before passing it on. Watching them, she thought she would have given anything to take a sip, too, just one sip.

For the next couple of hours, she watched the men and listened, her focus honed on them, her concentration not wavering once, even slightly. It never occurred to her that the focus she was able to maintain for that length of time required incredible mental discipline. She didn't think about it. She just did it. So she watched and listened, and wondered. Did they think their captives could not understand their language? Obviously her attacker had not informed them she could speak their language, or maybe he just didn't think it was important. Did they think they could not be heard? She suspected so. What was she to them? A captured slave? So as a slave, she had no intellect, no ability to think for herself, and certainly no ability to understand their language. She was, to them, naught but a mindless thing, cargo. Well, unfortunately for them, that wasn't the truth of what she was. She knew and understood many languages. She had a gift for language, and the market town she had long called home, given its location near a junction of the borders of three lands, was a cosmopolitan melting pot of many different cultures, all of which spoke their own language. She had learnt them all. So she knew the language of the slavers, and she knew exactly what they were saying. They were arguing, at first good naturedly, but then, with every pass of the flask around the circle of them, their argument became louder, more heated and more indiscreet. They were arguing about which of the captives were to go to whom, and they kept mentioning three names. Three names. Three individuals to whom each of the captured slaves would go. She concentrated on the names, saying them to herself over and over and over so she wouldn't forget them: Windsor, Lichfield, Marlborough.

From their conversation, she gleaned snippets of information that she was able to piece together to form a whole picture, and the whole picture allowed her to understand her situation. They were, indeed, slavers, and having filled their quota, they were returning to deliver the slaves to those who would pay handsomely for them – the three names: Windsor, Lichfield, Marlborough. She knew the three paid handsomely because of the way the slavers were dressed and because their camp, every night, was opulent. And because she wore, still, her necklace with its plump, little silver heart. The slavers hadn't touched it. They were not interested in it at all. So she knew, now, she would go to one of the three who would pay the slavers well for her, the three whose names were being drunkenly bandied around, tossed around the conversation like balls.

What did the three want with her and the other captives in the wagons? She didn't know where she was, in which land, but she knew slavery was outlawed in every land. No one, regardless of wealth, kept slaves because, in every land, keeping slaves was punishable by imprisonment and the confiscation of all lands and assets. So if the three kept slaves, how did they hide them? Or did they? And if they didn't bother hiding them, what did they do with them?

Again, there was no fear in her. Strange. Nor was there any emotion in her. She wasn't angry at her captors. No emotion, just cold resolve and knowledge. This caravan of wagons with its captured slaves would never reach its intended destination. She would make sure of it.

Concentrating on the flames of the fire, she focussed her will, summoning a clear vision in her mind's eye. And again, with incredible mental discipline, she held the vision for the rest of the night, relentlessly, shunning sleep.

And the next morning, when sunlight took the intensity of darkness away from the inside of the wagon, her vision became reality.

~

Frowning slightly in the darkness of her bedroom, she wondered at her ability in this vision. Again, she asked the question silently. Was this a memory? It didn't feel like a memory. But she was summoning visions, sending out her will, and making the visions manifest in reality, and she could feel the absolute certainty she held within herself that her visions would become manifest. Power. She could feel it – a power that felt alien to her as she existed in this, her current reality. So, who was she in this vision? Who was she, because she could not be just a simple scribe, working at copying ancient texts for a living? Not with knowledge and power like that. So who was she?

~

The soldiers had separated them all. The slavers knelt on the grass beside the remains of their camp fire, near their wagons, and their hands were tied behind their backs. They were kneeling in a line, next to each other with their backs to her, so she could see, at last, that there were nine of them. She, too, was kneeling on the grass among the other captives, most of whom were men and children, and her binds were cut, so her hands were free. She knew the slavers had weapons in the long pockets of their trousers, although she didn't know how she knew. She hadn't seen the weapons, and she hadn't seen the slavers put the weapons in their pockets. She just knew they were there. She waited for the soldiers to search them, but they didn't.

Watching the soldiers, she knew which one was in charge. He wore the command comfortably, and he gave orders that were obeyed without hesitation or question. So she tried to get his attention. It wasn't hard. Again, she concentrated her vision, and focussed her will, sending it out to the soldier giving orders. Unblinking, she focussed her eyes on his, waiting for him to notice her . . . which he did. When he looked over at her, she raised a hand and pointed a finger directly at the slavers, then made a downward sweeping motion with her hands beside her, indicating pockets, and then she raised her hands again, and made a motion of one hand, extended forefinger, held over her opposite forearm, indicating the slavers had guns. The soldier looked surprised for a split second, and then he moved towards the slavers, giving orders as he walked. A handful of them, him included, searched the slavers and retrieved the weapons – beautiful, ornate, but deadly shotguns. When they searched the wagons, the soldiers found cones of gunpowder.

"Are you a witch, then?"

She took her eyes from the soldiers and turned her head in the direction of the voice that had asked the question. One of the captives kneeling on the grass behind her – a man, older than she – was looking at her. His question held no judgement, and nor did his eyes.

"The one who tried to attack you burnt his hand, just like you said he would," the captured man said as if he felt the need to justify his question. In fact, the slaver's hand was still bandaged.

"Yes," she said simply. "But I am no witch. I simply put the thought in his mind and kept it there until he created it."

The captured man nodded, as if her explanation made perfect sense to him, which it did not. He'd really only understood her first word – yes. "And the soldiers?" he asked her. "Did you do that, too?"

"Do what?"

He shrugged. "Cause them to find us."

"Yes," she said again. "I did that, too. I held the thought in my own mind until I created it. But I am no witch."

"Well, then," he said quietly, sounding slightly disbelieving. "I thank you, ma'am. You have saved us all."

She smiled slightly and nodded at him. And then she turned, again, to watch the soldiers. The one she had motioned to, their commander, looked over at her and acknowledged her help only with the briefest of nods, and then he looked away and continued issuing commands to get the caravan organised for movement.

~

She was sitting on a chair in front of a perfectly square but plain wooden table. The chair on the other side of the table was empty, so she sat in the room by herself. The room was small but clean, and the table and chairs were its only furniture. Its walls were grey stone, its floor, smooth wood, and its ceiling of beamed wood was high. A door on the left of her was shut, and there was only one window high up in the wall to her right. The window was thin in height but wide, and, although it was high so that she couldn't see out of it, even if she'd stood on the chair, it was large enough to let in a decent amount of light.

She was clean again, properly clean, and she was no longer hungry or thirsty. The soldiers had escorted them all to a city, and although it was larger than any city or town she'd ever been in before, she didn't know its name. She'd tried to catch it, but without success. The soldiers had treated them well enough, but were obviously reluctant to talk to them, or maybe they just thought there would be a problem with a language barrier, so no one told the captives where they were being taken. When the caravan with its escort of soldiers had arrived in the city, the slavers had been escorted under heavy guard to the prison cells under the city's castle, and the captives had been taken to the city's hospital. There they'd been given proper meals and water, their wounds and injuries were tended to, they were given hot baths with soap, and a warm bed for the night. They'd taken her own dress away, it being dirty and ripped, so she wore a borrowed gown. The dress was green, a nice shade of green, she thought. Whoever had chosen it for her had chosen well because it was a perfect fit. Its skirts were long, as were its sleeves, and its neckline was scooped and laced up at the front. Underneath it, she wore a shift of pale cream that was seen around the edge of the neckline of the dress and contrasted nicely with the green material. Her wrists were bandaged underneath the sleeves of the dress where the slavers' bindings had cut into them, and there was lavender cream on the bruise on her cheek where she'd lain on the dirty wagon floor whilst under the influence of whatever it was the slaver had put over her mouth. She touched the plump little heart on its silver chain, taking comfort from the fact that, after everything she'd endured, she was still wearing it. After being looked after in the hospital, early that morning, she'd been escorted to this little room under the castle. It felt good to be alone again, really alone, so she was comfortable and content as she sat in the room, waiting.

After a long, long time sitting in the room by herself, the door opened and a man came in laden with rolled scrolls, pens, and an ink bottle. He was quite short, she thought, for a man anyway. His nose protruded from his face more so than most noses, and on it was perched a pair of thinly-framed spectacles. His hair was pulled back into a neat pigtail, and his doublet, which was quite nicely elaborate, seemed just a little bit too large for him. He seemed harried and flustered as he placed his writing implements on the table in front of her.

"I'm so sorry to keep you waiting," he said as he organised pens, ink and scrolls, and took a seat opposite her. "Many people to interview, you know." She watched him in silence, unmoving, with her hands in her lap. Finally, he was ready. She knew he was ready because he picked up one of the fountain pens, dipped it in his ink bottle and looked at her over his spectacles. "Do you speak the king's language?" he asked.

"Yes, I do," she said clearly, her words carrying a faint hint of an accent, although she'd never heard the language called 'the king's language'. She knew it as Pereian.

He looked mightily relieved. "Well, thank the gods for small mercies," he muttered. He wasn't good with other languages so he'd struggled somewhat with the testimonies of the other captives. "May I begin by asking you where you're from?"

"Birrel," she said simply.

His pen failed to touch the parchment underneath it. Instead, he looked at her again over his spectacles. "Birrel?" he asked, looking somewhat puzzled. "I'm afraid I've not heard of it."

"It's a fairly large market town on the south-western border of Elba," she explained.

He looked somewhat horrified. "Elba? Oh, my dear," he said, "you are a long way from home, I'm afraid."

She raised her eyebrows. "I am? Well, where am I, then?"

"This is the king's capital, Duavel (pronounced Dwa-vel, with the accent on the 'vel'), in Pereia."

"Oh," she said, unsure as to how, exactly, she felt about being in an entirely different land, and then wondering how in the name of the gods she was supposed to get back home.

"What is your name?"

She hesitated. Her name? What was her name? By the gods, her name. Everyone had a name. So what was hers?

He watched her, pen poised, his eyebrows rising as it became apparent she couldn't remember her name.

And then a name presented itself, even though she knew it wasn't the name she'd carried in this lifetime. She said it out loud. "Kiaara."

~

In the darkness of her bedroom, she blinked in surprise.

"What the fuck?"

Kiaara was the name of the priestess who'd been viciously, violently executed. Was this earlier in Kiaara's life? But no, she'd always carried a different name in this life she was seeing. She even knew it: Louise. So why couldn't she remember it, and why had she given the scribe Kiaara's name? How did she even know that name?

~

She watched while he carefully recorded the name she'd given him on his parchment, and then he looked at her again over his spectacles. "Now, Kiaara from Birrel," he said, "would you mind telling me what happened to you?" She told him, leaving nothing out except the part she'd played in helping the soldiers find them, watching him the entire time while he scribbled and scratched at the parchment with his pen, every now and then dipping it in his bottle of dark-blue ink. And then she told him about the slavers' argument as they'd sat around their camp fire, getting drunk, and she told him the three names she'd carefully memorised – Windsor, Lichfield, Marlborough – completely unsure as to whether or not the names would mean anything to him.

Pen suspended over the parchment, he looked up at her, not bothering to look at her over his spectacles, but this time, looking at her through them.

"Pardon me?"

Patiently, she repeated what she'd heard, and finished, again, with the three names.

He dropped his pen, highly agitated, not noticing the ink splodge that appeared on the parchment, and he stood, scraping the chair behind him as he did so.

"Ah, please, excuse me." And he turned and hurried out of the room, shutting the door behind him.

Strangely, she didn't stay with herself in her vision. Instead, she followed the scribe as he scampered like a small rodent along the long, dark hallway outside the room.

"Where's Captain Ragnar?" he asked someone as he passed them by, in a very great hurry.

The person he'd asked pointed towards large, green, double, wooden doors. "He's in the courtyard sorting through the slavers' wagons."

The scribe hurried in the direction of the doors and then, equally as hurried, he pushed them open and scampered outside, into a large courtyard where the slavers' wagons had been parked in a wide circle. Watching her visions, she recognised the courtyard even though she'd only seen it but briefly when Ambrose's men ran to tell him of the atrocities being committed against the priesthood. She wasn't surprised. She knew the land, recognised it, because she'd been there many times, not just in the life she'd lived as the doomed priestess.

Items retrieved from the slavers' wagons – chests, lanterns, stools, maps, weapons, clothes, a variety of implements – were strewn all over the grass in the courtyard around the wagons. The scribe dodged them all, heading for the soldier who was, once again, issuing commands, organising at least two dozen soldiers, all of whom were emptying the wagons and sorting through everything they were finding.

"Ragnar," the scribe said as he reached the leader, not realising, in his agitation, that he'd forgotten to use Ragnar's correct title, "I need a word."

The soldier barely paid him heed. He waved a hand in the scribe's general direction and said, "Not now, Johann, I'm busy . . ."

"Yes, now," the scribe yelled. And then, realising how he'd just spoken to the captain of the king's army, and noting the reactions of the soldiers around the captain, all of whom stopped what they were doing to throw him a disapproving look, he cleared his throat. "It is a matter of some urgency, captain."

Now she was back in the small room, sitting by herself at the table with the scribe's writing implements spread over it. The door opened, and the scribe entered the room again, pushing his spectacles further up his nose as he glanced at her. The leader of the soldiers who'd caught the slavers followed the scribe into the room, the same soldier to whom she'd motioned a warning of weapons hidden. The scribe took his seat again at the table, and introduced the soldier as the captain of the king's army. Acknowledging him with a slight incline of her head, which he neither acknowledged nor responded to, she watched him lean against the wall with his arms folded, obviously none too happy about being pulled away from whatever had been holding his attention. His impatience was obvious in his taut muscles and his folded arms, not to mention the expression on his face. He seemed to her to be cantankerous and intolerant in nature. She was certainly yet to see him smile, not that she'd seen much of him since motioning the warning to him. She watched him lean against the stone wall, thinking he obviously didn't devote a lot of time to his personal grooming. His eyes were vividly, beautifully blue, but the rest of his appearance detracted from their beauty. His beard was long and unkempt, unusual for a soldier, especially one in charge. His hair had been pulled roughly back, held in place by a strip of leather, but bits of it had escaped, and it, too, looked unkempt, lank and greasy. His leather boots were polished, though, and his tunic was elaborate, decorated with blue and silver brocade, and looked new. Although his fingers were long, his nails were dirty and broken or torn. All of this she noted, both inside and outside of the vision, and she couldn't help but note the difference between him and Ambrose, her lover, because both of them held the same position – captain of the king's army. They were polar opposites, at least in terms of their appearance and presentation. She wondered how alike or different they were in terms of the characteristics that had made her love Ambrose deeply, passionately – inner strength, courage, integrity, honour, intelligence, sensitivity, well-honed instincts where people were concerned.

The scribe drew her attention by asking her to repeat the story she'd told him earlier, which she did, finishing it with the three names she'd so painstakingly memorised.

The captain didn't uncross his arms, but he narrowed his eyes at her.

"Those are men of title here at the king's court. You should be careful about making accusations against powerful men such as they . . ."

"I make no accusations," she replied calmly. "I am merely repeating what I heard of the slavers' argument."

He pushed himself off the wall, straightened and motioned to the scribe. "Do not record their names, Johann. At least, not yet. We need to speak to the slavers, methinks."

Again, the vision did not stay with her in the room, but, instead, followed the captain and the scribe along the same dark hallway. The captain, sensibly, obviously thinking on his feet as he went, collected a few more witnesses in the form of his own men along the way to the cells underneath the castle. And then she watched him question the slavers.

An argument ensued among them, some of them wanting to talk while others wanted to remain silent.

"You fools," one of them spat at the others, "we're dead men. Do you not realise? That was the deal. If ever we were caught, they would cut us loose."

"Cut us loose," another remonstrated. "That doesn't mean we're dead."

"Idiot. They'll make damned sure we don't talk . . ."

The captain, realising he wasn't getting the information he required, regained their attention and shot questions at them.

"I think you misunderstand, man." This was the one willing to talk, the one who'd called the others fools. "You think they are our customers," he said, referring to the men of title whose names she had painstakingly memorised, "but you are wrong. They are our employers. We work for them, travelling the different lands looking for people for them. They tell us what they want, and we get it for them."

A shocked silence followed as the captain, the scribe, and the captain's men registered the magnitude of what they'd stumbled into. Two of the men whose names she'd given them were dukes at the king's court, the other an earl, each of them members of the intimate circle of nobles that surrounded the king, powerful men, all.

"If you are getting slaves for these men, then where are they?" the captain asked the slavers. "None of those men keep slaves."

The slaver who was willing to talk, shrugged his shoulders. "Beats me, man. We just get them people. We don't know what they do with them."

"They don't use them as slaves." The slaver who'd spoken had sat in the corner of the cell with his arms folded, watching and listening, but sitting in a heavy, morose silence. He'd neither spoken up nor tried to silence those who wanted to speak up. Now he had the full attention of everyone in the large cell, soldiers, scribe and slavers.

"What do they do with them, then?" the captain asked him.

"They sacrifice them."

A shocked silence followed. The captain put his hands on his hips. "They what?"

"No, man, you're wrong," one of the slavers said.

"They sacrifice them," the slaver repeated. "I've seen it with my own eyes. I followed them one night." He shrugged. "I was curious, even if you weren't," he said, addressing the other slavers. "Not only did I see it with my own eyes, but I can tell you Marlborough does it himself."

"Does what?" the scribe asked.

The slaver motioned with a hand across his throat. "He cuts their throats, and then he drinks the blood." His lips curled into a sneer, or what looked like a sneer. "But he makes damn sure they're real scared first. That's the way he likes them . . . scared. Why else did you think we weren't to take good care of them?" he asked the other slavers.

The captain ran a hand through his hair. "God's blood. What about Windsor and Lichfield?"

The slaver shrugged. "Don't know about them. I just assumed they'd be the same. The three of them seem to work together."

The scene changed. Now she saw the captain and the scribe standing in a dark corridor, outside the slavers' cell.

"You're not thinking of taking them on, are you, captain?" the scribe asked.

"Of course," the captain replied. "They are not above the law. What they're doing is a violation of their power. They need to be called to account."

"They'll cut you down rather than allow themselves to fall from grace. And they have the power to do it."

"We have witnesses, Johann. The king and the court will have to listen to us."

The scene changed again. This time, the captain was standing in the cell again, with the bodies of the slavers all around him, some on the stone floor of the cell where they'd fallen, some still sitting on the benches around the cell's edge. "Get Tanner," he commanded someone behind him, tight lipped. "I want to know how these men died."

The scene changed again. The room was large, its walls the same grey stone of the small room with the wooden table, its beamed ceiling high. The bodies of the dead slavers were laid out at different angles on a huge table in the middle of the room. To fit them, the surgeon had been forced to lie a couple of them over the legs of the others. He wore a thick, leather apron that covered him from neck to ankle, and his arms were covered in thick gloves that were coated in blood and gore up to his elbows. On his nose, he wore glasses that looked more like a modern diver's goggles. The glasses made his eyes appear overly large. The bodies on the table were in various stages of dismemberment.

The captain was leaning against the wall just inside the room's only door.

"God's blood," he said, screwing up his nose and bringing a hand to his mouth, "how you work in here with this stench, I'll never know, Tanner."

The surgeon's nose was pegged, so he didn't bother replying. Instead, he said, "I cannot tell you how these men died, Ragnar. Some of them have various medical ailments that would've caused them some discomfort." He pointed to one. "This one has stones in his kidneys . . . painful. 'Tis probably just as well he died before he could pass them." He pointed to another. "This one has an ulcer in his stomach that would have made him quite ill. This one," he pointed at a third, "has tumours in his bowel, and this one has extensive scaring on his liver." He looked at the captain through the thick lenses of his glasses. "He obviously enjoyed a little too much of the drink in his time." He looked back at the bodies and made a motion with his gloved hands to indicate all the dead. "But none of their ailments would have caused such a quick death, overnight, and all at once. It's as if their hearts just stopped beating in their chests for no apparent or good reason."

"What about poison?" the captain asked. "Is that a possibility?"

"Well, yes. It is. In their food perhaps?"

"Or sprayed? There was a weird smell in the cell when we found them."

"Inhaled? Yes, yes, it's definitely a possibility . . ." He leaned over the bodies. "Yes, Ragnar, look at their noses. They're all the same. Red, as if burnt." He looked up at the captain again. "I've checked their blood for poison already. In fact, that was one of the first things I checked, but I'll check again. See if I can find traces of any lesser-known poisons." He looked pointedly at the captain. "You know, Ragnar, if there was poison in that cell, you could be affected."

"I'm fine."

"Maybe so, but if you start to feel dizzy or ill, you come see me right away."

The captain raised his eyebrows at his surgeon. "If I've been affected by poison, Tanner, there's probably not a whole lot you can do about it."

Tanner grunted. "Not so, captain. Not so. I have amassed an impressive array of antidotes . . ."

The scene changed again. This time, the captain was talking to the scribe, Johann, in a small room, the walls of which were covered in floor to ceiling book shelves full of books. The scribe sat at a wooden desk in the centre of the room, also piled high with stacks of books, parchments and rolled scrolls. Writing implements covered the desk where the stacks did not.

The captain was leaning on and over the desk, his hands splayed. The scribe was obviously intimidated as the captain loomed over him.

"We need the woman," the captain was saying. "She's a vital witness now."

The scribe grimaced. "Well," he said reluctantly, "that could be a problem."

The captain narrowed his eyes and didn't bother responding verbally. It was enough.

"Well, with all that happened yesterday," the scribe explained, "I forgot about her. I didn't realise until last night, so I went straight down to see if she was still in the room. She wasn't. She was gone. I searched the castle and the grounds, but to no avail."

The captain straightened. "Search the city. I'll let my men know you need their help. I want her found. See to it, Johann." He pointed a finger at the scribe. "Do not disappoint me on this. Do not . . ."

The scene changed again. She was back in the room, at the table, by herself. She'd been sitting for so long at the table, her feet were tingling. So she stood and started pacing, back and forth, back and forth, and then she sat again. And at the point she sat again, the visions assailed her. So powerful were they that they usurped her physical sense of sight. She no longer saw the room around her. Instead, she was surrounded by the empty, partial ruins of an ancient temple under a flattened mountain. She saw steps leading to the temple itself, and in front of the steps, a courtyard of stone, at the edge of which stood columns of stone.

With the vision came knowledge. She knew why she was there, why she'd been taken from her simple life in a town she didn't really belong in, among people who were not capable of reflecting the truth of her back to her. She had been in the town, working as a scribe, because she had been hidden, dormant, awaiting that time when she would be required to awaken, to remember the truth.

She knew where she had to go.

She breathed deeply and quickly with the depth of the emotion that welled up within her. She was going home.

~

"Ah . . . Gabe?"

Gabriel and Salomon were talking quietly, or, rather, Salomon was talking quietly to Gabriel, but when Cory said Gabriel's name, Salomon stopped talking and Gabriel opened his eyes, raised them and looked at Cory.

"The blood's gone," Cory said.

Gabriel and Salomon both looked at the wound on the Lady's chest. Cory was right. The blood that had stained the skin of her chest and her beautiful gown was gone, vanished as if it had never been there. Even the kerchief in Cory's hand was once again crisp, clean, pure white.

Cory looked to the other two for answers, the question filling his eyes, but all three remained silent. Gabriel continued to look at the wound without the blood, and Salomon looked over at Cory, shook his head and shrugged his shoulders, the expression on his face almost apologetic. He knew what the question was that hovered in Cory's eyes, but, alas, he had no answer to give.

~

"Oh, I get it," she whispered into the darkness of her room.

Now she understood. Transition. As Louise she had been a simple albeit talented scribe, living a simple life in a simple town that wasn't really home, although whilst there she had thought it was. Now she knew why she'd given Kiaara's name to the scribe. The further the caravan had travelled away from Birrel, towards the temple, Louise had disappeared and Kiaara had taken her place . . . taken her **rightful** place. What had she thought earlier? It was rather like changing characters half way through a stage play. She was right. She knew where she was going. She was going home.

This wasn't a vision of memory, as such. It was a vision of metaphor . . . of Process.

~

"Here, lass, wrap this around ye. 'Twill protect ye from the chill evening."

Gratefully, she accepted the blanket, wrapping it around her shoulders and relishing the warmth it offered. "Thank you, Jacob. Will you not be cold yourself?"

"Nay, lass. I'll be just fine. Dun ye worry abou' me."

Earlier, once she'd known where she was going, wanting to waste no more time sitting alone, she had stood and walked over to the door in the little room with the stone walls and the perfectly square wooden table. She wasn't sure they hadn't locked her in even though she was not their prisoner. When she tried it, it was unlocked, so she walked out and, eventually, after trying a myriad of different corridors and doors, she walked out into bright sunlight, and then she walked out of the castle's grounds. She had met Jacob after getting horribly, hopelessly lost in the city, with its cobbled streets and alleys that all looked the same to her. She'd never been in a city like it. It was so large, it was intimidating, and its streets and alleys felt like a maze. All she wanted was to find a way out of it, but in the right direction. She'd asked numerous people if they knew where the flattened mountain was, but no one knew what she was talking about. After she'd asked the dozenth person with no success, she'd leaned against the wall of yet another white building and tried to stop herself bursting into tears. That's when Jacob had found her.

"Hey, little lady, why so sad?"

She'd looked up to see him peering at her in concern. He had a kind face, plump, rosy cheeks, and kindly, twinkling eyes. A kind soul.

He was older, too, with a thick, grey beard, and she had trusted him on sight.

"I'm a little lost," she explained.

"Ah, I see. Well, then, where do ye wish to be?"

"I'm looking for a mountain with a flattened top," she explained. "But no one seems to know where it is."

"I see," he said again. "Well, ye ain't gonna find it here, in the city. Of that, I can assure ye."

Despite the seeming hopelessness of her situation, that had made her smile. He smiled back, and his smile twinkled in his eyes.

"Tabletop Mountain," he said. "Sounds to me like ye might be looking for Tabletop Mountain, lass."

She'd unfolded her arms and straightened, looking at him hopefully. "You know of it?"

"O' course I know of it," he said. "I see it every day from my own place. Mount Vernon is its real name, but we locals only ever refer to it as Tabletop Mountain." He looked at her, bemused. "It's far from here, ye know, lass. Ye couldna' walk to it by the day's end from here. I tell ye what. Ye help me deliver m' barrels, 'n I'll buy ye and me a bite to eat, then I'll give ye a lift to yer mountain."

He was standing beside a sturdy wagon, his two donkeys, their heads bowed, waiting patiently, and on the back of his wagon was a stack of different-sized barrels, some big enough to hide in, some no bigger than a hand, and a whole stack of others of every size in between. She smiled, mightily relieved and grateful for his help.

Her smile held her gratitude. "Deal," she said. "I will help you with your barrels, and I would be most grateful if you could give me a ride to my mountain."

"Jacob," he said, bowing towards her. "My name's Jacob, little lady. And your name?"

"Kiaara," she said. "My name is Kiaara."

And so, she and Jacob had travelled around the city in his wagon delivering his different-sized barrels to various taverns and inns and shops, and picking up empty ones, or, with the larger barrels that were so big they were impossible to move, pouring out their contents into bottles and jars. When his deliveries were complete, they ate in one of the taverns, and then left the city through the city's western gate.

The soldiers on the gate greeted Jacob by name and commented on the fact that he had a new friend. Jacob told them a small lie, explaining that she was his niece. One of the soldiers nudged his comrade.

"That's what they all say," he said with a wink at Jacob.

Jacob flicked the reins, looking embarrassed, and as the wagon moved forward, he felt it necessary to apologise. "I am sorry, Kiaara. Soldiers will be soldiers."

She smiled. "It's quite all right, Jacob. We know the truth so it matters not what they think."

By the time they were travelling out of the city, along the Western Road, the sun was beginning its descent towards the horizon and the afternoon air grew crisp and chill. After the cold of the nights in the slavers' wagon, she shivered and wrapped her hands around her arms in a futile attempt to keep warm. Jacob handed her the reins of his wagon and reached behind him to pull a thick blanket out from under the seat. She was grateful, but the gesture made her realise she'd left the castle with nothing but the dress she wore, and with nowhere to stay overnight. She really hadn't thought anything through, but that was probably for the best. Thinking things through would've made her stay right where she'd been, in the small room, obviously forgotten, not knowing how to move or where to go.

By the time they pulled the wagon to a stop in front of a large, white house with a big porch, the windows in its two storeys full of light, and a couple of lanterns burning on its front porch, the dark of night had well and truly taken hold.

"We'll have some dinner here," Jacob informed her, and then he pointed beyond the house. She looked in the direction he was indicating but all she could see was darkness. "My place is over there," he said. "I assume ye've no place to stay tonight, lass."

"I'm afraid not," she confirmed.

"Well, no matter," he said affably. "There's plenty of spare beds either here or at my place. Yer mountain's over yonder, but ye won't see it tonight. Ye'd best wait 'til tomorrow."

She and Jacob had dinner in the white house, sitting around a huge table in the company of a handful of adults and so many children she was hopelessly unable to determine which children belonged with which adults. The room they ate in was full of the warmth of the fire in the large hearth, full of the light of the dozen candles and lamps around the room, and full of the warmth, comfort and welcome of a large family. She sat at one corner of the table, with Jacob beside her, and the table was covered in bowls and plates of food – freshly sliced tomato and basil, olives, soft, white cheese and hard, yellow cheese, crusty, white bread, plates of roasted meats and vegetables, bowls of flavoured olive oil, fresh and dried fruit, hard-boiled eggs. Over dinner, she learned the house was the centre of a thriving farmstead, and everything on the table was grown or produced at the farm. The farmstead was owned and run by three brothers, all of whom, with their families, were seated around the table, although only one brother and his family actually lived in the house. The other two brothers and Jacob had their own houses on the land, but they always ate their evening meal together. Their main produce at the farm, she was told, was their primary source of income, and that was where Jacob came into his own. He took the olives, olive oil, and wine in his barrels to the city where they had regular customers. He made the trip at least once every week, sometimes more.

"Ah," she said at one point, smiling at Jacob as she whispered to him, "no wonder the soldiers on the gate knew you."

His smile twinkled back at her. "Aye, indeed, no wonder."

As is usually the case with large, happy, contented families, everyone seemed to talk at once so that the room was as full of conversation and chatter as it was heat and light. Many of the occupants of the table talked at her, and she found it impossible to concentrate on one conversation at a time. It was as well no one required a reply from her, so she ate, relishing the delicious, fresh food, and nodded when she felt it appropriate.

After dinner, the women stood and rounded up the children. They took the chatter with them as they all left the room, and she was entirely unable to prevent a sigh of relief to be sitting in blessed silence once again. Jed, the eldest brother and the one who lived in the white house with his family, poured liquid from a decanter into small glasses and handed them around, placing one in front of her.

"So then, lass, what brings ye to these parts?"

She took a sip from her glass, holding its liquid on her tongue while she tried to decide whether or not she liked it.

"Um," she said, swallowing the liquid and deciding she did like it, "I'm looking for a mountain with a flattened top, and Jacob has told me it is here . . . somewhere."

"Oh aye," Jed said, "that it is. 'Tis over yonder," and he waved a hand in the direction of the mountain. "Ye can see it clearly from the farm. And what would ye be wanting with our mountain, then?"

She took a moment to register the absolute silence as everyone who remained sitting at the table awaited her response, all eyes turned upon her, including Jacob's.

"I'm looking for an ancient temple," she said quietly, "and I know it sits under the flattened mountain . . ."

Even before she finished the sentence, the quality of the silence changed. She felt it. They all looked at her, their eyes wide with fear, or alarm, unless she was misreading their expressions. For a long moment, no one moved and no one spoke, and the silence grew heavy and awkward. She felt uncomfortable.

Finally, Jed broke the silence. "Are ye sure ye know what y're doing, lass? 'Tis not a good idea to go near that place. We stay well away. There are ghosts there, ye know. Terrible things happened in that place . . ."

"She knows."

Every head swivelled in surprise to the other end of the large table. Kiaara had barely noticed the old woman who sat at one corner of the table, so silent had she been until now. She was so old she was hunched over, bent over like a stalk of wheat in a strong wind. Her hair was as white as the driven snow, and her eyes were milky white and sightless. Her hands, resting on the table in front of her, and face were heavily lined and wrinkled, and her hands were bent and gnarled and knobbly.

"She knows, Jed, my boy," she said again, and her voice was strong – as strong as her mind obviously was. She turned her eyes on Kiaara again, and somehow, Kiaara knew the old woman could see her. "Is that not so, girl?"

"Yes," Kiaara said, "that is so. I know what happened there."

"Aye, I thought as much. Ye can stay here tonight, and I'll take ye m'self tomorrow. Billy," she said, turning her sightless eyes to the boy sitting around the corner of the table, next to her, and laying a gnarled hand on his arm, "will ye take us, lad?"

"Of course, grandmama," he said, laying a hand over hers. "I wouldn't let you go there on your own. We'll take the old wagon. Might be a tad uncomfortable but it'll get us there."

She nodded. "Good lad," she said. And then she turned her sightless eyes to Kiaara again. "If ye've nowhere else to rest yer head, lass, ye can stay in my room tonight. We'll make up a mattress for ye."

"Thank you . . ." Kiaara said, unsure as to how to address the old woman.

"Ashanti," the old woman said.

Kiaara bowed her head towards the old woman. "I thank you, Ashanti."

Silence again filled the room, settling over the table like a heavy blanket, and the men folk continued to look at the old woman, their expressions perplexed.

"Ashanti does not say much," Jacob explained, leaning towards Kiaara and lowering his voice so as not to be overheard. "Except to Billy. She really only speaks to Billy. I think she just spoke more words to you than she has to the rest of them in a year."

"Ah, I see," she said softly, and she looked over at the old woman, assessing, wondering.

"Are you a priestess, Ashanti?" she asked the old woman much later. She was lying on a makeshift mattress at the end of the old woman's bed. The mattress was plump and comfortable, as was the pillow under her head, and she was warm under a pile of blankets. The room had been plunged into darkness when Ashanti leaned over and blew out the candle beside her bed, but Kiaara was brimming with questions, not at all inclined to sleep, as the old woman well knew, hence the offer of a bed in her room.

"Nay, lass, I am no', or no' in the way ye think."

"But you have the sight?"

"Oh aye, I definitely have the sight. 'Tis just as well, eh? Since m' eyes went bad, the sight has been strong with me. I see many things, things most people do no' understand, except Billy. He's m' favourite grandchild. The others are all silly little starlings."

Kiaara chuckled softly in the darkness. She thought so too after only one dinner with them.

"Aye, lass, I see ye get m' meaning. Painful, is it no'? The sight always skips a generation in m' family. My grandmama had it, I have it, and Billy has it. So I see yer Light, lass. Even now, in the darkness of the room, I see yer Light. I seen it when we were sitting at the table. It was all I could see. So I says to m'self, why is she here? 'N then ye told Jed of the temple 'n it all made perfect sense.

"See, I was but a wee lass," she continued, answering Kiaara's unspoken questions as she continued to speak, "when m' own grandmama told me the stories of what happened at the temple. She herself was but a wee lass when it all happened, but she never forgot. Until she breathed her last, she still remembered like it had happened the day before. She still mourned, lass, she still mourned and grieved. Though she was but a wee lass, she'd wanted to be a priestess in the temple, but the priesthood were pulled down, destroyed, 'n she were robbed of the chance to be a priestess. 'N as ye saw for yerself tonight, those of us who've long lived in these parts, we've never forgotten, 'n we keep away from the temple, even now, after so long."

"I can understand that," Kiaara said. "The shadow of trauma and terror and grief would still hover over it, like an echo, but just as real nonetheless. Even the most insensitive of souls would feel it, I think."

"Aye, lass, 'tis so. 'Tis so. 'N we dun like to be reminded. We've ghosts of our own, ye know. Ye see, the people cowered 'n hid when they should 'ave come to the temple's aid. They should 'ave protected it with their own very lives if it came to it. But they did not. They did nothing."

Kiaara could hear the bitterness in the old woman's voice.

"Is that what your grandmama told you?" she asked.

"Nay, lass, it's what I know for m'self. Dun forget, I see in m' visions. I've seen wha' happened for m'self. For many years, as a wee girl, no' understanding the sight, I had nightmares I won't ever forget."

"Could you tell me what you saw? And could you tell me what your grandmama told you about what happened?"

"O' course, o' course. Well, as to what I saw, 'n see still if I wish to recall the visions, I see the army of cut throats and murderers paid by powerful men to cut down the priests 'n priestesses of the priesthood 'n all those who lived 'n worked in the temple with them. I see the blood lust in their eyes 'n in their blood-thirsty grins. I see them goin' on their killing spree, cutting 'n slashing 'n stabbing. I see blood on the stones, on the steps, on the floor of the temple, 'n I see the fallen lying in it. I see their empty, staring eyes, 'n I see the pools at the temple's entrance filled with their blood.

"But," she continued, "'tis what my grandmama told me that has always stayed with me strongest even over what I seen for m'self. She told me about the High Priestess who could've run but did no'. She stayed to save her people 'cause she knew it was her the dark priests were really after. They weaved their dark magic, 'n he, the one who killed her, cut her open, pulled out her heart, 'n he ate it, right there in front of her. Blood on his hands, his arms and his teeth. M' grandmama told me the dark priests knew they had to snuff out her Light 'cause then the priesthood would truly die, 'n so it did, never to rise again as it was in those days. 'N do ye know why, lass? 'Cause," she said, answering her own question, "she was the priesthood's connection to the Elders. She was one o' them, ye see. She **was** them, here, in the flesh, 'n as such, she was a powerful symbol. That's why 'tis her the dark priests were after. They used their dark magic to cut down the symbol of what she was and what she stood for. She died right there, in front of her own people."

Silence followed, and then the old woman said, "But this ye know, do ye no', lass?"

"Yes," Kiaara whispered, "this I know."

"Ye remember, then?"

"Yes, Ashanti. I remember like it all happened yesterday."

"Ah. I'm sorry, lass. 'Tis a horrible memory to have to bear."

"Yes, 'tis."

"Have ye born it all yer life, then?"

"No. It's only been with me since the vision of the temple came to me today. With the vision came memory, but it's as if the memory has always been there, and all that had to happen to make me remember was the door opening in my mind, which it did, today."

"Ah, I see. That's good, then, that ye havena' born it all yer life. Many of her people died that day, as ye know, but many more survived. They took her body. Did ye know tha', lass?"

"No, I didn't know."

"Oh aye, they took her body 'n left this realm, left it for good. They took her away so they could take care o' her, and so no human would hurt her anymore, 'n so no human hand could be laid upon her again. 'N they themselves left this realm, left humans to themselves."

Kiaara sighed, unable to help herself. "Can you blame them? Ever is it so, Ashanti, that the choices of the few have always had such widespread consequences that affect the many in this human realm. 'Tis never the many who decide to go to war. 'Tis only ever the few, but the many are forced to suffer the consequences. And never more so did the choices of the few have such terrible and far-reaching consequences for the many than with the events that tore down the priesthood. And perhaps the greatest tragedy of it all is that the many still don't know what really happened to them that day."

"Aye, lass, well said. Ye are right, o' course. The darkness got a hold of it all, did it no'?"

"Yes, it did."

The two women were silent for a long moment, both lost in their own thoughts, and then the old woman broke it.

"M' grandmama always told me she, the High Priestess, would return to walk again in this realm. 'M grandmama could see it right from when the Lady died, through to her own death. 'N she always said the return of the Lady would herald great change. 'Sweet child,' she used to say to me, 'She will walk again in this realm as She truly is. If She returns in yer time, ye promise me ye will do all ye can to help her.' So I promised, 'n it were no empty promise. I meant it. Even on her death bed, she made me repeat the promise, 'n so I did, so I did."

Kiaara was silent.

"'Ave ye returned, then, lass? 'Tis ye, is it no'?"

"Yes, 'tis me, and, yes, I have returned. Or, rather, I should say, I am return**ing**. I am coming home, Ashanti, after wandering in the wilderness of the darkness for so long, not remembering who I am. I am coming home . . . at long, long last."

~

Billy had been right. The old wagon was bone-jarringly uncomfortable, despite the cushions they had laid across the seat. Every time the wagon went over a bump or a hole in the road, she felt as if her bones rattled in tune and in time with the rattle of the wagon. The three of them – Billy, Ashanti and Kiaara – were squashed together on the wagon's seat. She had a hand under the old woman's arm to steady them both. Despite the discomfort of the ride, she still noticed the landscape they were passing through – orchards of fruit trees full of brightly-coloured fruit, olive groves, vineyards, fields full of ripe crop, fields of lush grass upon which plump cows, woolly sheep, and goats were munching contentedly.

"This land is very fertile," she commented at one point.

"Oh aye," Billy said. "'Tis very fertile, and we can grow anything here." He held the reins with one hand while he motioned with his other, "These farms virtually feed the city by themselves."

"Duavel?"

"Aye, the king's capital."

She could well believe it, such were the bountiful fields and orchards they were passing through. The landscape was beautiful, actually, full of vibrant colour. The green of the trees and grass glistened in the morning sunlight like emerald silk. And over all of it loomed the mountain without a peak. In the haze of the morning sunshine, the mountain looked deeply, darkly blue, a benevolent guardian, passively watching over this part of the land. Although they ambled in their wagon, taking their time, she watched the mountain, in the distance at first, but getting ever closer. And with every passing league, she became more and more nervous as they got closer to the mountain.

When they reached the outer edge of the temple's grounds, the mountain loomed large, not close enough to cast a shadow over the temple, but close enough so that it dominated the landscape and provided a beautiful backdrop for the temple itself, as if nature had wanted to provide the perfect background to highlight and bring out the temple's very great beauty. Billy pulled on the reins and brought the wagon to a stop.

The three of them did not move. Kiaara cast her eyes over the temple, noting and marvelling at the incredible accuracy of her vision. The temple was exactly as she'd seen it in her mind's eye.

"Is it as ye imagined, then?" Ashanti asked her.

Despite her nervousness, Kiaara smiled, and the smile was in her voice as she answered. "Are you a mind reader, too, Ashanti?"

The old woman chuckled. "I can feel yer thoughts in yer stillness."

"Ah. Well, my vision was remarkably accurate. I saw it perfectly."

"'N how does it compare to yer memories of the temple in the past?"

Again, the old woman's astute question caused Kiaara to smile. "Well, it's not as pristinely white as it once was." In fact, from where she sat, the temple looked as if it was covered in thick layers of dirt. The walkway to the temple was paved in the same white stone as the courtyard, but you would not know it if you were not familiar with the layout of the whole complex. Both the walkway and the courtyard were covered in thick layers of dirt and dust, buried, really. The walkway was supposed to be big enough for a carriage to pass along it comfortably, but, even though a carriage could still pass over it, the edges of it were impossible to discern. From her vantage point, she could see the gardens around the walkway and the courtyard were overgrown. Without the priesthood and all those who had lived there and taken care of it, the temple had been reclaimed by Nature Herself. Maybe, she thought, as she looked it over, grazing it with her eyes, Nature had taken care of the temple on their absence, protected it.

"Kiaara," Ashanti said, "are ye afraid ye'll see their blood . . . or their bodies perhaps?"

Kiaara breathed deeply and tears filled her eyes. "Yes," she said simply.

"Ye needn't worry about their bodies, lass. Every one of the fallen were given proper burials. The folk around these parts were able to give them that, if not the help they needed on the day. There are no bodies here. Not sure about the blood, though. Surely, after all these years . . ." She petered off, not finishing the sentence.

"It looks as if layers of dirt and dust are hiding the blood. I hope so. All right," she said, extracting her hand from under the old woman's arm. "It's now or never. If I don't do this now, I won't ever do it."

"Ye go, lass, do what ye must. We'll wait here. Ye signal us, let us know when ye're ready for us to join ye."

"All right. Thank you for this, Ashanti," she said softly, as, heart pounding, stomach a churning mass of nervousness, she stepped down from the wagon. "I'm glad you're here."

~

She was perfectly still as she lay on the table of marble, as she had been for aeons of time, but the quality of her stillness had changed, and those who were watching over her could sense it. There was a quality of heightened awareness in her stillness that communicated itself to those who were with her, as if she was watching intensely or waiting. Her hands were seemingly relaxed against her, one across her waist with Gabriel's hands wrapped around it, one over her breast. But all three who kept a silent vigil beside her could feel a tension in the air around her. It was as if she was holding her breath, even though there was no breath, or maybe she was bracing for an impact she could see coming towards her . . . or was she moving towards it? Isadore was, once again, touching her lips to the Lady's forehead, and, through the connection, Isadore, too, had picked up the tension. It was obvious in the tautness of her muscles and the stance of her body as she touched her Lady . . . and watched what was passing through her Lady's consciousness.

"The gods dammit," Gabriel swore, frustrated. "Where **is** she? What is she doing? Why is she tense? What is she waiting for?"

Although his questions were rhetorical, not really requiring a response from the other two, Salomon still gave him one. "I wish I knew, my friend. I wish I knew."

~

Slowly and very hesitantly, Kiaara turned towards the temple and began walking along the walkway towards the main building with its steps leading to its columned portico.

"Billy, lad, ye keep yer eye on her," Ashanti said quietly. "So long as she stays upright, whether standing or kneeling, we'll leave her be, but if she falls . . ."

"Aye, grandmama, I'll go get her."

"Good lad."

Unaware of the interchange behind her, Kiaara walked along the walkway, moving closer, ever closer to the courtyard.

"The gods damn it . . . damn it to hell," she swore under her breath, although the words sounded loud in her own ears. At the edge of the courtyard, the columns of stone, erected by the mercenary army to serve the malevolent agenda of the dark priests, remained standing. How had they survived? Of all the things to remain . . . "Curse it," she muttered. The columns would be the first thing she removed. She would make sure they disappeared, forever.

The beautiful mosaic pools of water that should have been in front of the courtyard on either side of the walkway were now naught but slight indentations in the dirt and dust. They had been two feet deep once upon a time, large rectangular pools that two men could have lain in across ways, one lengthways, full of crystal-clear water, their blue and white mosaic tiles stunningly beautiful. Now, the tiles were buried, hidden under layers of dirt and dust and fine, dark, gritty sand. She could see no evidence of the pools and their tiles at all, other than the indentations, and she hoped the layers of dirt had protected them, shielded them from the elements, and from time itself, the passing of the years.

She tried to ignore the column of stone in the centre of the others, where the walkway joined the courtyard, as she first approached it and then reached it. But ignoring it was simply not possible. And she wasn't there to ignore it anyway. The memories of the past had to be faced today. Making sure she did not touch it, she stopped beside it without facing it and turned her head to look at it. It was worn, no longer smooth and polished as it had once been. She wondered where the dark priest had got the columns, and then she decided it didn't matter. She waited for the memory to assail her, but, although the image of being bound to it and of what happened afterwards was there, in her mind's eye, so that she could see it clearly, it was just there and aroused neither emotion nor pain. Surprised and encouraged, she turned her head away from the column and walked into the centre of the courtyard, towards the temple's front steps.

And there, unfortified as she was, and unexpected as it was after the lack of her response to the column of stone to which she had been bound, the memories came at her, assailing her, swamping her, swirling around and within her like a whirlwind. The strength and power of the memories and the grief they aroused within her nearly brought her to her knees. Somehow, she managed to keep standing, but she wrapped her arms around her waist in a futile attempt at self protection, and she bent over as if she was throwing up the memories as they came at her.

Her people brutalised. Beautiful souls violated. Her people fallen. Her people under vicious, violent attack. She saw their faces twisted with grief and horror. She heard their screams of terror and pain. She smelt the metallic tang of blood spilled, so much blood, and saw pools of it starkly red against the pristine white of the temple's stone. She saw the fallen lying in their own blood. She saw arms reaching, reaching, reaching for her.

She couldn't catch her breath. Her throat burned with the grief, with unshed tears, with the need to scream . . . scream her agony to the Universe. The weight of it all grew too heavy to bear and it caused her to drop to her knees, her eyes shut tight against the images, the pain, the unbearable grief, and the knowledge of what was torn down that day.

And then, as quickly as they came, the memories vanished, leaving her feeling drained and exhausted and breathless, and leaving her mind strangely empty. Heart pounding, she recovered her breath, slowly, and then, opening her eyes and straightening, still on her knees, she knew what she had to do. Standing, she looked at the ground and held her hands out, drawing, with her fingers, a large, imaginary circle on the ground around her, turning around and around so that the circle formed in her mind's eye.

"Billy, lad," Ashanti said, seeing in her visions what Kiaara was about to do, "ye might want to look away."

"Out of respect, grandmama?"

"Nay, lad. The Light might burn yer eyes. Look away but dun close yer eyes. Ye'll see m' meaning."

The circle strong, Kiaara kneeled in the centre of it. Holding her hands out, palms up, she closed her eyes and spoke, loudly, passionately.

"This temple was once filled with Light and Love and learning, with communion and community and fellowship, with calm and contentment, peace, serenity and tranquillity, with Wisdom and knowledge. This temple was a place of connection. So shall it be again. I reclaim this temple for the Light. So shall my Light banish the darkness of grief and trauma and terror, and emptiness, desolation and isolation. Thus shall my Light roll back the shadows, pushing them out." She turned her hands over and pushed them out, as if pushing against a wall. "Begone shadow and darkness. Begone. My Light reigns here again. My Light fills this temple once again."

She held the vision in her mind's eye, and then, as she had done before, she sent out her will, and her Light.

Billy, watching but not watching from the wagon, saw a burst of Light rolling out from the epicentre of her, and then the Light rolled past him. It was like a wave, large, powerful. And once it rolled past him, the atmosphere, which had been heavy and dark and stagnant, and more than a little frightening, was cleared, like fresh, clear air after a heavy storm.

"Wonderful," his grandmama said beside him, the smile in her voice infectious. "Can ye feel it, Billy?"

"Aye, I feel it. It feels light, as in not heavy, and it feels clear and clean and fresh. It feels pure, like you could take the healthiest of breaths."

Ashanti chuckled. "Aye, lad. That's a good description."

Kiaara sat a moment longer with her eyes closed and her hands out, breathing in the different atmosphere. Her people were too well trained and too knowledgeable to be trapped here after death – ghosts they're called in the modern era – but the events of that day were so traumatic and violent and unnatural that there could well have been some of them trapped in the temple by the intensity of fear and emotion they experienced that day. Her Light would touch them if they lingered, and it would help them release the shadows keeping them trapped. Her Light would free them. She was glad to be able to do that for any of them who had remained, trapped.

Opening her eyes, she dropped her hands into her lap and sat a moment longer, looking up the steps at the portico. She needed to walk through the temple. She needed to see it all. She needed to walk through and connect with all its rooms and buildings and gardens and courtyards again, its energy, its ambience, and each one of her memories associated with each part of it. Standing, she turned and signalled to Billy that she was all right, and he and Ashanti were free to join her. Then she turned and walked up the temple's steps.

Like many of the temples in the ancient world, the central building in the temple's complex of buildings comprised three sections, each with their own particular function and purpose. The central building had formed the central hub of temple existence. The first section was a large hall with a polished stone floor, although the floor was dirty and dusty so it was impossible to tell how polished it was now, and a high ceiling in the centre of which was a large glass window that allowed in the sunlight. The window, too, was dirty, but not so dirty that it blocked the sun's light. So, even in its current state, the main hall was filled with light. This was the section of the temple that had been open to the public, and it was for any visitors or for anyone wishing to avail themselves of all the temple had to offer: advice, guidance, and counsel, healing, teaching, study and learning, prophecy, retreat, divination, meditation, contemplation. To the left of the large hall was a series of doors that led to different rooms, like classrooms, or therapy rooms. She didn't walk towards those. Instead, she turned in the opposite direction. On the right side of the main hall, a series of doors led to segregated courtyards, each separated by arbours of wood that had once been full of creeping, climbing rose bushes. She stepped down into the first courtyard, smiling when she saw the blossom trees were still there, looking healthy, although the rose bushes on the arbours had long ago died off, and the arbours themselves were in various states of disrepair, most of them fallen over.

There had once been a mosaic table and matching chairs in this courtyard, but the courtyard was now empty of its furniture. Smiling, again, at the memories that drifted through her mind, she moved to sit on the stone bench under the blossom trees. She had received the king in this courtyard many times. These courtyards were reserved for important or special guests. But the king had not been important to her because he was the king. He had been important because he bore a great responsibility, and he bore it well. He took his responsibility as the king seriously, understanding it, knowing what was required of him and giving it, willingly. He had been a regular visitor to the temple, and she had worked with him every time he came. Consequently, she had come to know him well, and they had formed a unique and valuable friendship. She had always enjoyed her work with him. He had been a truly honourable man, open-minded, courageous, intelligent, wise, willing to face and resolve his own shadows. The land had thrived under his kingship, as well it would given the honour and integrity with which he ruled.

It was to one of those visits that Ambrose had accompanied him, and that was the first time she and Ambrose had met. Sitting on the bench, under the blossom tree, she laughed softly at the memory. He hadn't said much during the conversation, and he had been wholly unable to take his eyes from her. It had been more than a little disconcerting, not to mention distracting, feeling his eyes on her so intensely. When he and the king had risen to go and they'd started to walk away, Ambrose had said something she couldn't hear. The king had responded by throwing his head back, laughing heartily, slapping Ambrose on the back, and saying, "You're smitten."

A couple of days later, Ambrose had ridden out to the temple by himself to seek an audience with her. Thinking he had come to apologise for his behaviour, she had agreed to see him and had led him out to the courtyard. Instead of sitting at the mosaic table, they had sat next to each other on the very same stone bench upon which she was now sitting. Her smile deepened and sparkled in her eyes as she remembered.

Never one to waste words, he'd come straight to the point.

"Is it forbidden for one such as me to be with one such as you? I've a need to know if so because I will have to find a way to forget you exist."

She had smiled at him back then. "Why would it be forbidden? Underneath our respective roles and responsibilities, we are still individual souls. I am a woman, and you are a man. It may be a little awkward being together given our devotion to, and the demands of, our roles and duties, but it is not forbidden."

He'd looked surprised at first, and then, enormously relieved. "So how does one such as me ask one such as you to dinner?"

She'd laughed at him. "I believe all you have to do is say, 'Will you have dinner with me?'" Still smiling, she'd added teasingly, "Yes, I really think that aught to do it."

He had stayed at the temple for dinner that night, and in the weeks following, they had become lovers. They had been lovers for nearly twenty years. Until the day she had died, every time they had been together had felt like the very first time they had made love. Neither had ever demanded of the other that he or she relinquish the roles they held that often times kept them apart. Perhaps that's why their love had endured so powerfully, so passionately. They had both retained the essence of themselves, neither losing themselves in the relationship.

Her smile vanished, and she stood, restlessly, as pain rolled through her. She didn't know what had happened to him, and she wanted to know, desperately. She needed to know. She couldn't see anything of him after he'd held her body against him and sobbed – a man broken. All she knew, although she couldn't see it, as such, she just knew, was that they had wanted to take her body, but he wouldn't let go of her. They couldn't make him let go. But her visions would not reveal anything beyond that, and her memories of him would not be at peace until she knew.

Leaving the courtyard and its rather unique memories, she walked back into the main hall, and then she walked through it, into the second section of the main building. This section was as large as the main hall, with a similar window of glass in its ceiling, but it had been only for the priests and priestesses and all those who had lived and worked in the temple. Like the first hall, this one was empty, its furniture long ago gone, taken most probably. To the left, through large double doors that had long ago disappeared, was the temple's extensive and impressive library. Many of the texts and books in the library had been very, very old, and, as such, they were irreplaceable and beyond value, although, of course, their value had not been at all about money. Standing in the library, relief vied with disappointment within her. The ancient texts were gone, the library's shelves empty of its old, beautiful books. She wondered where they were and hoped they were safe somewhere, hidden, treasured, valued, as they should have been.

Feeling saddened by the loss of the books, but hopeful, too, she walked back into the hall and then walked through it to stand in front of the doors that led to the sacred heart of the temple.

The third section of the main building was only for the highly initiated. It being the sacred heart of the whole temple complex, its energy held an element of danger for anyone not properly trained to handle it. Behind the dual doors she stood in front of, this third section took the form of a large, circular room, fully enclosed but with columns of polished granite around the edge of the circle.

Its roof was domed, and in the centre of the dome, a circle of glass connected the room with the heavens, at night allowing in the moon's light, during the day allowing in the sun's light. For one Processing something in the unconscious mind, something demanding attention, the moon's light was always best. For one Processing something consciously or in one's conscious awareness, daylight was always best. For her, the experience of the room had been unique and different, and not everyone who lived in the temple was aware of what happened when she went in there. She always went into the room alone, but she was never alone when she was in there. The Elders always appeared, surrounding her, standing between the columns of polished granite. And she'd spoken with them, communed with them, was One with them.

Now, swallowing nervously, she tentatively reached out a hand to open the doors, because the beautifully-carved, double wooden doors were still there, shielding the inner sanctum of the temple from its other sections. But she couldn't turn the handle to open the doors. Her hand would not obey her. Letting her hand drop back to her side, she knew she couldn't go in there, not yet. She wasn't ready. Disappointed in herself, she turned her back on the temple's sacred heart and walked away.

Outside the main building, she wandered among the buildings that surrounded it, all of which had performed different functions in the day to day existence at the temple. In the building that housed the rooms of the priests and priestesses, she stood in her own room, relieved to find it empty. Had the ornately-carved, full-length mirror been there, she felt she may have smashed it to pieces, even though what happened was not its fault. In the room, memories of Ambrose assailed her again because they had spent many nights together here, but the memories generated so much pain within her that she shut down on them, and walked out of the room.

After that, she wandered through the temple's beautiful gardens, now overgrown, with no order to them at all, nor any of the vibrant colour that she had loved, and nor was there any of the sweet fragrances that had always wafted around anyone who walked through them. The vegetable garden, too, was now naught but a tangled mass and mess of weeds. The neat rows of vegetables were nowhere in evidence. In the orchard, to her surprise and delight, the fruit trees were still producing fruit. The orchard itself was overgrown with long grass and weeds that had, somehow, not managed to strangle the fruit trees. There was rotten fruit littering the ground under the trees, but the fruit on the trees looked healthy and edible.

Billy and Ashanti joined her in the orchard. Ashanti lightly touched her arm.

"Are ye all right, lass?" she asked gently.

Kiaara covered the old woman's gnarled, knobbly hand with her own. "Yes, I am. Lots and lots of memories, but I have endured and survived them with my sanity intact."

"Good. 'N so, I've a need to know. What will ye do to restore the temple first, 'cause I know that's yer intent?"

"Aye, that's definitely my intent," Kiaara agreed. "First, I need to remove those curs-ed columns from in front of the courtyard. They need to go. They are columns of death, marked with blood sacrifice, and the temple will not be completely free of the shadow whilst ever they are there. Do you think you could help me, Billy? Would the horses be strong enough to pull them down and then carry them far away?"

"Oh aye, I would say so. And yes, it would be my very great pleasure to help you remove them."

~

There are no stories in this reality, or very few, tragically,
Like the fairy tale stories of old,
With their tragedies and triumphs,
Their heroes and heroines,
Their backdrops of beauty and vibrant colour.
There are no stories because humans live a recipe
That is dictated to them
By the mechanisms of manipulation employed by the dark priests.
Humans live recipes instead of creating their own stories,
Recipes that silence the beating of their hearts,
So that they live a flat-lined existence.
There has been no story in my reality.
And yet, my heart beats, now, its own unique rhythm.
So why have I not created a unique story in my reality?
Because, although my heart beats,
It is not whole, complete.
It is damaged, fractured, wrapped in the shadow of fear,
Severed from itself.
It is time for my heart to be restored.
I am coming home.
And then, convergence ... convergence of vision & reality.
Beautiful.

Breath

It was a night just like any other. The night was cold, it being the third night of winter, so she lay under her quilt feeling the heat of her electric blanket against her back. As she rubbed hand cream into the skin of her hands she thought about her visions of the night before. After she saw herself walking through the temple, absorbing it all and revisiting memories from the past, she'd fallen into a restless sleep and dreamed dreams full of fractured images that had no continuity or coherence to them at all. She'd awoken feeling tired and drained, and then, of course, she'd thought of little else throughout the entire day. She'd allowed herself to think about the visions, though, because she needed to Process them, knowing full well they would continue tonight. Truth be told, she was eager to get back to them. She wanted to be there, in the ancient temple that felt more like home than any place she'd ever been in this, her current incarnation.

Reaching over, she turned out the light and readied herself to watch . . .

~

The temple was a hive of activity. Old and frail of body she might be, but Ashanti was well respected in the local community, and she had rallied them all. Really, Kiaara thought as she stood on the temple's bottom step looking at all the activity, her amusement evident in the smile on her face and in her eyes, Ashanti had called them to arms, and they had answered the call. Not bad for people who had long stayed away from the temple. A group of women were sweeping the interior of the main hall, and using buckets and scrubbing brushes to bring the temple's beautiful floor back to life. Kiaara had not yet had a look to see if old blood stains were still in evidence. She was leaving the women to it, and would cross that particular proverbial bridge when it was time to cross it. Another group of women and children were clearing away the long grass, the weeds, and the rotten fruit from the orchard, and men on ladders were pruning the fruit trees. Another group, Ashanti among them, was clearing the vegetable garden of its tangled mess of weeds, and replanting it with seeds from their own gardens. Another group of men had brought ladders that allowed them to climb up onto the temple's roof, and so they had. They were walking around the roof, checking for damage, making repairs where they could, and cleaning the large, glass windows. Another group of men was clearing away the old arbours and their dead rose bushes from the segregated courtyards, salvaging any old wood they could, and using new wood to reconstruct and rebuild the arbours. She couldn't see them, nor could she see the men on the roof, but she could hear both groups talking to each other as they worked. In front of her, she could see the handful of men using shovels to clear the dirt and sand out of the two mosaic pools. She was watching them closest of all because she fully intended to get into the empty pools herself and use a bucket and scrubbing brush on the tiles when enough of the dirt had been cleared to allow her to do so.

And then, last but definitely not least, Billy was supervising a team of men, Jacob among them, who were using the unhitched horses from Billy's old wagon to pull down the columns of stone. Kiaara had watched them pull down the first column, holding her breath anxiously. She had told them all, especially Billy who, with his gift of sight, would be most susceptible, not to touch the columns. They had heeded her, taking her warning seriously, so they were all wearing thick gloves. She wanted them to burn the gloves when they were finished, but she suspected a good clean in hot, soapy water would suffice. Stone, she knew, the earth's flesh, was a natural conduit for energy, and because the columns had been used specifically for blood sacrifice and black magic rituals, more so than just those that had occurred on that fateful day, she suspected, residual dark energy would still be caught in the stone of the columns, even after so many years. Enough souls had been affected by the dark energy of the priests' black magic. She did not want anyone else to be affected by it. Although Billy and his team of men had inspected the columns initially, no one had been sure of how easily or not the columns would come down. The fact that the columns had survived this long, she thought, did not bode well for them coming down easily. But when Billy tied long rope around the first of the columns, and then harnessed the solid strength of the horses to pull on the ropes, the column had shifted easily and then toppled over with a resounding crash. All those in the vicinity, whether on the temple's roof, standing around the columns or standing in the mosaic pools, had stopped what they were doing to clap and cheer. She had joined them, her smile brilliant and full of her relief, and she had signalled her thanks to Billy. So far, they'd pulled three of the curs-ed columns down, rolling them along the courtyard to its edge where they intended to pile them up and then load them onto the old wagon and take them far, far away. She had asked Billy to bury them if he could, as if he was laying bodies to rest in deep graves.

From her position on the step, watching the various activities around her, she saw the light dust cloud in the distance, and knew what was its source long before the source of it actually came into sight. Knowing what it signalled, she realised she had been expecting it, and so, her focus shifted. She waited and watched.

He rode his horse at a gallop right into the temple's grounds, bringing it to a slow canter and then, in a walk, to the beginning of the temple's buried walkway. At first, she was distracted by the very great beauty of his horse – black and sleek and powerful – a warhorse if ever she'd seen one, bred for strength and stamina and power. But then, when he left his horse at the end of the walkway, not bothering to tether it but, instead, laying a hand on its neck and speaking to it, she focussed on him. The horse stood where he left it, waiting, not even tempted by the abundance of bright green grass at the edge of the walkway. When he turned towards the temple, he saw her straight away. She knew he saw her because their eyes locked, neither of them looking away or breaking eye contact, and so they both stood still, looking at each other, for how long, she could not gauge. Long seconds, at least.

When he started walking towards her along the temple's walkway, she watched him, his long cloak billowing out behind him as he walked, and as he drew closer to her, the blood drained from her face and she brought a hand up to her throat, her breath catching, her heart pounding. He had cut his hair since last she'd seen him, cropped it short, and he'd trimmed his beard, neatly.

The change in his appearance, had she but known it, was entirely due to her. Not one at all prone to the indulgence of self deception, he'd known, when he leaned over the scribe's desk and ordered a search of the city, that his motives were not as pure as they seemed. He'd wanted to see her again, and not just because she had become a valuable witness. Women interested him not at all, and that's not to say he was attracted to men. He enjoyed women sexually, but beyond the sexual gratification they offered, they bored him. They were all the same to him, with only slight variations on an overall theme, depending on their status in life, or, more aptly, at court. The women he tended to gravitate to now were so-called 'women of the night' because, in them, he had observed a freedom from social etiquette, rules and conventions. They were free to be themselves, no airs or graces or pretensions, no image to maintain, no need to watch what they did and said. And, he'd discovered, after a multitude of awkward experiences, that paying for sex always left him free of nasty entanglements. Everyone knew where they stood. So, he kept away from women generally, and he certainly kept well away from the women of the king's court.

Somehow, in some way he couldn't yet fathom, she was different. Right from his initial contact with her, even though that contact had been from a distance when she had motioned a warning to him of the weapons hidden in the slavers' pockets, he'd recognised there was something different about her, although he hadn't acknowledged it until after he'd spoken to her in the scribe's impromptu interview room. In two encounters, as brief as they were, she had managed to achieve what no woman had ever come close to achieving where he was concerned. She had aroused his curiosity, and he wanted to know what it was about her that made her different.

As she watched him coming closer, all she could see walking towards her was Ambrose.

"Are you all right?" he asked her as he drew closer to her. "You look as if you've seen a ghost."

"You look so much like him."

"Who?"

"Ambrose." When he looked at her blankly, she added, "He was captain of the king's army . . ."

"Captain Ambrose?" he asked, surprised. "Who lived . . . what . . . a hundred and fifty years ago, give or take? You knew him? But that would make you . . ."

"Reincarnated," she said flatly, dropping her hand to her side. "How did you find me?"

She was standing on the first of the temple's steps, so when he came close enough to be standing right in front of her, they were facing each other, almost perfectly eye to eye. And he stood close, closer than was usual for an encounter between two people who knew each other not at all. He had to stop himself reaching for her, and the need to do so puzzled him. He didn't understand it.

"The men on Duavel's western gate noticed you," he said, answering her question, "which was just as well, and they knew Jacob, knew where he lived, and then," he looked around him, noticing all the activity for the first time, "the people around here seem to know you by name. Everyone I asked knew exactly who you were and where you were."

She barely registered his response to her question. She was distracted, her mind full of another thought as she registered the significance of his earlier comment. "You know of Ambrose?"

"He's a hero of mine. It's because of him that I hold the same position today. I've studied his battle strategies and tactics extensively, and I've read and re-read his journals . . ."

"He kept a journal?"

He narrowed his eyes at the tension in her body and the intensity in her eyes as she asked the question. He was close enough to her to feel the one and see the other. And, this was not the conversation he'd been expecting to have with her. "He did," he answered her. "The entire collection of them is still in the castle's library."

Reluctantly, although also entirely unable to stop herself, she asked the question. "What happened to him?"

A flicker of irritation crossed his face. Why were they talking about another man? "What do you mean?" he asked. "Are you wanting to know how he died? He died from a wound sustained in battle when he was not yet fifty, too young by far for a man of his calibre."

Her legs suddenly turned liquid, refusing to support her, so she sat heavily on the steps and put her head in her hands. God's blood, she thought, the pain rolling through her, he'd outlived her by barely a handful of years. Was that a good thing or a bad? She didn't know, couldn't think.

The captain moved to sit next to her on the steps of the temple, close but not touching her, puzzled by her reaction, but beginning to put two and two together to form the right picture.

"Kiaara," he said. "Not **the** Kiaara who features so prominently in his journals – the same Kiaara he loved?"

"Yep, the same one," she said, her head still in her hands, her eyes closed against the shock and pain that was coursing through her in time with the pounding of her heart. She felt ill, too, slightly queasy.

"But you were . . ." Again, he looked around him, suddenly realising where he was. "The massacre of the priesthood," he said slowly, "happened here. If you are her, then you were killed . . . violently . . . here."

She opened her eyes, raised her head and dropped her hands onto her lap. "I was," and then she motioned with a hand, pointing a forefinger at the column still standing in the centre of the temple's walkway, "bound to that column."

"You remember it?" He asked the question as if he only partly believed her, or as if he wasn't sure she was telling the truth.

"I remember it, all of it. I was there, after all."

"Right, but people normally don't remember things that happened to them in other lives. In my experience, people tend to have enough trouble dealing with the memories of their current lives."

Despite her distress and anguish, the comment made her smile. She turned her head, the smile sparkling in her eyes, to look at him. "You included?"

He took a moment to respond because her smile made his breath catch in his throat and increased the rhythm of his heartbeat. "No," he replied. "I don't struggle with my own memories."

For a long moment, they sat in silence watching the activity around them, both feeling unnerved and unsettled, he by his reaction to her, and she by what she now knew of Ambrose's life after she had left it. The activity around them had barely ceased while the local folk registered the captain's presence and then, accepting it, continued with their allotted tasks.

"He should have stayed to protect you," the captain said after a while, still watching the activity in front of him. "You warned him, did you not? You warned him something was going to happen. He should've stayed to protect you."

Her heart skipped a painful beat and she turned her whole body towards him to look at him. "Is that what he believed?"

"It's what he believed, and, having read his journals, it's what I believe."

"Oh no," she said, sounding anguished. "He couldn't protect me. There **was** no protection. If he'd been here, he would have died . . ."

"He was a soldier, Kiaara," he said harshly. "Far better he die trying to protect the woman he loves than live with the regret of having done nothing."

She turned away from him and put her head in her hands again. "By the gods," she whispered. Did she do the wrong thing all those years ago in not telling him the truth? But how could she have told him? He would've done everything in his power to prevent what simply had to be. But he had lived the last years of his life blaming himself for what happened. By the gods. Had she known he would blame himself . . .

"He never knew," she said, "because I never told him, I gave permission for it all to happen. There were forces at work that were never going to be stopped. It was all meant to happen, at least to me, as horrible as it was. He could not have prevented it." The conversation was distressing her too much. She needed to change the subject. So, again, she dropped her hands and raised her head, but she didn't look at him. "I know why you're here, Captain Ragnar. You want me to be your witness. What happened to the slavers? Why can't they be your witnesses?"

He leaned forward and clasped his hands, his elbows on his knees. "Dead, to a man. Poisoned."

"But you still want to go after the three men who paid them?"

"Of course. They should be called to account."

"Even though they kill without a qualm and with no second thought? Captain of the king's army you may be, but they can still arrange your death. They'll make it look like an accident . . . a fall from your magnificent horse maybe . . ."

"I'll take the risk."

Now she turned her head to look at him. "And are you prepared to take the risk with my life, too?"

His lips tightened, and he didn't respond. She watched his profile, and within her, a dawning realisation of what must be done now first blossomed and then gained momentum and conviction. Briefly, she closed her eyes as the realisation hit and washed through her, and then, opening them again, she asked him, "Are you devoted to your king as Ambrose was devoted to his?"

He turned and looked at her. "No. I will give my life to protect him, but only because it is my job to do so. In my opinion, he's not worthy of it. He is weak and ineffectual, easily manipulated, bending this way and that depending on which voice is whispering in his ear at any one time."

"Do those men control him, the men whose names I memorised?"

He nodded.

"Is that why you want to go after them?"

He shrugged and looked away from her. "Maybe it's one of the reasons. What they were doing is a travesty, though, an absolute abuse of their power. You know they were sacrificing the people the slavers were getting for them?"

She nodded. "I suspected it. Which of the three do you want to go after most of all, if any?"

He answered without hesitation. "Marlborough."

"Because . . . ?"

"Because one of the slavers saw with his own eyes what Marlborough does to those people."

She absorbed that, not tempted to ask what it was Marlborough did to the captured victims. She thought she could well imagine. "I will not be your witness, Captain," she said. "I am not interested in calling him to account according to the laws of this land, nor am I willing to become entangled in this land's system of justice . . . if you can call it that. But there may be another way to call him to account – a way that will harness the fundamental principles of darkness and Light – a way that transcends the laws of men. But you need to know two things if we do this. First, if we remove this particular head, you know there are twenty more waiting to take his place. Second, if we go down this road, there will be consequences."

He had turned and looked at her again while she spoke. His eyes were of the clearest blue, just as Ambrose's had been, and it was, to her, more than a little disconcerting. Furthermore, there was a strength and a warmth she could feel in the energy radiating from him that reminded her of Ambrose's. Sitting close to him as she was, she could feel it, and she could feel it wrapping around her and infusing her as Ambrose's always had. She had to remind herself he was not Ambrose. Ambrose was gone.

"What consequences?" he asked her, narrowing his eyes at her, interested.

"They will come after me. And if you are involved and they know it, they will come after you, too. You will lose everything you've worked so hard for – your position at court, your command, your position as captain of the king's army, possibly even your life. Are you prepared for that?"

Still looking at her, watching her while she talked, he smiled, and she realised it was the first time she'd seen him smile. His smile took her breath away, just as hers took his breath away.

"Absolutely," he said. "None of it actually means a whole lot to me. In that sense, I don't really have anything to lose at all." But, he thought, as he looked at her, I suspect I have a whole lot more to gain if I do this.

~

She opened her eyes and sat bolt upright in her bed.

"Oh god," she said, her eyes open wide, but seeing nothing in her room, even in the dim light emitted by her bedside clock radio.

She knew what Kiaara was planning to do, and she knew, too, given the nature of this particular vision, what it meant for her . . . what she was being told. But of course. It had to be this way. It couldn't be any other way. The fear. She had to recreate the same circumstances, and then, she had to look her fear full in the face. Stand in courage and confront. It was the only way to truly resolve the fear that was wrapped around her heart, choking its Light, severing her from herself.

~

She hesitated, one hand on the handle and the other on the door, and she put her forehead against the door. Around her, in the temple, the hive of activity continued. The people were enjoying their work, they were enjoying working together, and the atmosphere in the temple reflected their enjoyment. The temple was full of it. The captain had ridden back to the city where he fully intended to organise the few things they would need to set her plan in motion. It wasn't a complicated plan, so there wasn't much he needed to organise, but, still, he wanted to be sure of certain details, not least of which was the duke's presence at the next court function, planned for a handful of days hence. After he left, instead of getting into the mosaic pools to clean their tiles as she'd planned, her conversation with the captain prompted another course of action. She needed to speak to the Elders. It was time, whether or not she was ready. It was time. She needed to reconnect with them. Or perhaps she needed to reconnect with the part of herself that was a part of them.

Nervous again, heart pounding, not knowing what to expect, as she leaned her forehead against the door with her hand on the door's handle, she remembered the last time she'd been in the temple's sacred heart, the round room with its columns of polished granite. She had communed with the Elders, and she had known, then, what was needed, what had been planned all along, what she had to do, and what it would mean.

"The darkness has a hold on the human experience now," they told her, "and the human experience has begun its descent into the abyss. We will not prevent it, Ushara. Into the abyss humans must now fall because it is, ultimately, their choice to do so, and they must experience the consequences of those choices. But we cannot allow them to fall into the abyss alone. They are our creation, and we will not abandon them, no matter their choices, and no matter how low they fall. And they **will** fall very low, Ushara. They will not understand

that they have fallen low, nor will they understand the ramifications **of** falling low. We cannot allow them to wallow in the darkness, isolated, cut off, alone . . ."

She closed her eyes at the memory because the memory caused the now-familiar pain to wash through her.

This time, she turned the handle and pushed open the door. The room was as she remembered it, and it was remarkably clean given the fact that it had existed in a state of absolute abandonment for well over a hundred years. She turned and shut the door behind her, careful to make sure it was properly closed. And then she walked into the centre of the room and stood, waiting, not bowing her head, not closing her eyes, just standing. She didn't know if they would come. She was who she was, but she was a different person, too, no longer the High Priestess of the temple. She didn't have to wait long to find out, though, because they appeared almost as soon as she took her place in the centre of the round room. As was their wont, they surrounded her in a perfect circle, standing with their hands clasped in front of them, one sandalled foot slightly in front of the other, the hoods of their sapphire-blue cloaks covering their hair and partially hiding their features.

She would have spoken to them, but they spoke first, as many, but with one voice.

"This is our daughter with whom we are well pleased."

She bowed her head at that, lowering her eyes.

"Welcome home, beautiful Lady," they said.

She raised her eyes again. "Thank you. 'Tis good to be home, very good indeed. 'Tis good to be standing among you once again. It has been a while . . ."

"Aeons of human time – time that is but a moment for us. Why do you doubt the course of action upon which you are set, Ushara? Is it your ability you doubt, or is it your readiness you doubt?"

Connected to her, as they were, they did not ask the question to elicit a response. They knew the answer, more so than did she. Rather, as was their wont, they asked the question to generate the introspection she needed to keep walking.

"Both, I think," she replied, "but more so my readiness. I have been hidden from myself for so long, lost in the disguise of ordinariness and physicality. 'Tis not a simple thing to suddenly drop the disguise and become as you are."

"And what is that? What are you?"

"I am as you are."

"And what are we?"

"Powerful beings of Light."

"And so, what are you, then?"

She smiled. "A powerful being of Light."

"Just so, Ushara. And you have always been so, always. You did not change. You did not become something else. You did not become something other than what you are. Underneath the disguise, you have always been what you are. You are not so much becoming, as you are remembering the truth of what you really are. You have existed in a state of forgetfulness with nothing around you to remind you of the Truth. That was the true Purpose of the ritual spell you cast so long ago."

"You say I did not change, and in one sense you are right, of course. But in another sense, I did change. I have existed in fear. I have existed in a place of fear, and I have existed with fear wrapped around my heart, my soul. That is not who or how we are."

"We do not exist **with** fear or **in** fear, but we still know what fear is. We still know what it is to experience the wounds of the soul. That is why we know how to Work with fear. We know how to make fear serve Higher Will and Purpose. The fear did not change who you are, Ushara, not really. Not in truth. It has dictated your reality in the many lives you have lived because it served Purpose that it do so. And so has the fear itself existed within you because it has served Purpose for it to do so. But the fear does not alter the truth of who you are. It only alters the way you see yourself because, again, it has served Purpose that it do so. Has the fear prevented you remembering the Truth of late?"

"No."

"No," they echoed in agreement. "How easily you walk through it, the fear, even though it has existed within you for so long, and even though it exists deeply within your psyche. When the fear no longer serves Purpose, as it no longer does, how easily you wipe it aside. **That** is the Truth of the power of you."

Silence filled the round room as she contemplated what they said, and in contemplating, she realised it was true. The fear had not prevented her remembering the Truth of who she was, even though she still could not see clearly. But her sight, her perception, was changing moment by moment, rapidly.

"You have been a physical being," they said, breaking through the silence and her thoughts, "and you have been a physical being separated from your Higher Truth. **That** is **not** who you are. But, of course, your separated physicality has been only an illusion. It still did not change who you are. Only your own perspective of yourself changed, and **is** changing now as the layers of illusion are peeled back to reveal the Truth."

She smiled, and she looked at those in front of her, filling her vision. "The Truth that you reflect back to me."

As one, they nodded, and their collective smile reflected hers. "Just so," they agreed. "So, go, and, in the knowledge of who and what you are, wrap your arms around this duke and see the power of your Light."

Her smile faded. "And what of the captain? Will he be safe? I will not put his life in danger."

"Why not? You will put your own life in danger again, but not his?"

"He has suffered enough because of me." And even as she said the words, she knew the truth, and she knew who Ragnar was. Really, it was obvious, and not just because he looked so much like Ambrose. "All he did was love me, and he has suffered greatly because of it."

"You think he regretted his love for you? You think he regrets it now?"

She shook her head.

"Loving you was and still is his greatest pleasure and his greatest achievement. He does not regret it. His love for you is a part of him, an intrinsic part of who he is. His love for you makes him great, Ushara. So you hesitate to set in motion the circumstances that will free your heart of the fear because you would protect him? Even though he would not thank you for it?"

"No, I will not hesitate, not for a moment. I know what must be done, and I will do it. I just don't want him to be hurt again. I guess I don't want him to be caught up in the circumstances . . ."

"But caught up, he is. He was ensnared the moment he laid eyes on you as Kalistäe, at least in terms of his human incarnations. He was always going to aid you once he saw you and knew your intent. Always. 'Tis his choice, Ushara, and now you must honour that choice, as noble as it was, and see this through, with him."

She didn't respond, but she knew, of course, that they were right. The Elders are never wrong simply because they see Truth. Their eyes are never bound or even influenced by illusion. Always, the Elders see illusion for what it is – a falsity.

They allowed the silence to reign for long enough so that she could absorb their words, and then they broke it.

"Ushara, Lady of Light," they said, "do you remember how you came to be in the temple as its High Priestess?"

She inclined her head as she tried to remember, but, strangely, her vision was blocked. "Was I given to the temple as a babe?" she asked them. "I always thought so."

"You do not remember," they replied. "You are blocking the truth and confusing that life with others you lived. In those other lives, yes, you were given to the temple as a babe or as a young girl. Not so in Kiaara's life. Do you remember what is built on top of the flattened mountain – the mount with no peak?" The question generated an image in her mind's eye. She saw the ruins on top of the mountain, and she saw the ruins of one structure in particular, the pattern on its circular mosaic floor deliberately rendered dormant with a slash through it, a cut. In fact, the dark priests had specifically targeted the buildings on the mountain that day, just as they had specifically targeted the priesthood in the temple below it. Two things had been in their sights as their primary targets that day. She had been one, the round temple on top of the mountain the other, because its function had been so special, so powerful. In destroying the temple on the mountain, they had stopped her kind from coming into the human realm as they are . . . or so the dark priests thought . . . or so was their intent.

"By the gods," she whispered.

"Yes, now you remember. You came into this dimension through the temple, the round temple that served such purpose, and you came here fully formed. You have forgotten, Ushara, that incarnation is an aspect of being human, so it is not natural for you to be incarnated, just as it goes against your Truest Nature to exercise Free Will. Free

Will sits as well with you as does incarnation. That is to say, not well at all. This is why your incarnations, each and every one, have never felt right. What is it you are always saying about them? They feel as if you are wearing ill-fitting clothes. You were not incarnate in that life, although you took the form in a human body, but after the events of that terrible day, you fell into the abyss with humans and effectively became as they are, incarnations included. You, too, became caught in the cycle of birth, death, and rebirth. It is time, now, for you to remember the Truth, Ushara. You shy away from the Truth because of the fear and because of the forgetfulness, because both have served Purpose. No more. You are not one of them, and you never have been. Remember the Truth of who you are. Look beyond the incarnation and return to form. Return to your true form, Ushara, Lady of Light."

~

"Do you attend these court functions regularly?"

"Only in an official capacity, when I'm on duty, guarding the king. Otherwise, I keep well away. They're full of people trying to ingratiate themselves with the nobility. It's painful to watch."

She smiled at that. "I can imagine."

"Well," he said, "very soon you won't have to imagine. You'll be able to see for yourself."

The captain was right, of course, given the fact that they were standing in front of two enormous, beautifully-carved, wooden doors behind which could be heard the faint strains of violins playing. Earlier, she had been attended in his rooms, like a typical court lady with her personal attendants. He had vacated his rooms to give her the privacy she needed to get ready for the ball. The two women who had attended her had helped her into the gown the captain had procured for her, arranged her hair in the latest courtly fashion, and expertly applied touches of make-up to her face.

"Not too much," she had said as they began to apply the make-up. "I don't wish to look like a painted doll."

"Aye, m' lovely," one of the women had said in response. "We get yer meaning, love. They forget they will be talking 'n laughing through the night, so their make-up cracks around the mouth 'n eyes 'cause they're wearing far too much. Do not fear, love. Make-up should be applied so that it enhances what is already there, not so it puts there what is **not** there."

She'd laughed at that. "Well said."

When the captain had returned to his own rooms to collect her, he'd opened the door to his room and stared at her for long seconds, and then, his eyebrows raised, he'd raked her from head to toe with his eyes, absorbing, drinking in the sight of her, assessing every detail. Feeling self conscious under the weight of his intense scrutiny, she'd raised her eyebrows in silent question. "Well," she'd asked, "what's the verdict?"

"You look beautiful," he said simply. "But you don't really look like you."

She'd smiled at that, not unhappy with the comment. "I don't need to look like me," she'd responded. "I just need to look like I belong among them."

"Right. Well, you definitely look like you belong at court, looking like that."

Indeed, so she did. The neckline of the gown he'd procured for her was so low it left her neck and shoulders completely bare and showed a goodly portion of her breasts. The bodice was tight, making her waist appear small, and pushing her breasts up, holding them firmly in place. Her cleavage was impressive in the gown. The material of the over gown was sumptuous, green, gold and cream brocade. Its skirt was long and sweeping, and it opened in front of her so that when she walked, cream silk and lace was evident underneath the skirt. The sleeves hugged her arms to her elbows but then flared into long cuffs, inside of which was the same cream silk and lace that was evident underneath the skirt when she walked. The gown must have cost him a small fortune, and the tailor had altered it superbly so that it fitted her like a glove. It was certainly the most beautiful gown she'd ever worn. Well, actually, in her simple life as a scribe, she had never worn anything as decadent. Despite the sumptuousness of the gown, the arrangement of her hair, and her expertly-applied make-up, the only adornment she wore was her plump little silver heart on is chain. The heart sat between her breasts, and its chain drew the eye downward. She was exposing more of her breasts in public than she ever thought she would, but she didn't care. She would've walked into the ball room bare breasted if it served the purpose of attracting the attention of the duke, although she would have drawn a line at walking into the room completely naked. Thank the gods, being partly bare breasted would suffice . . . hopefully.

The sumptuous gown, her courtly hair style and make-up served a purpose and was part of her plan. Beyond that, it was all meaningless. Her attire was a costume, and she certainly felt as if she was about to step out on stage. In a sense, that's exactly what she **was** about to do, and the costume the captain had chosen for her was done so to make sure she drew attention to herself, drew the eye of those whose eyes could be thus drawn. She just hoped the duke liked what he saw because it was an essential component of her plan that he do so.

"Remember," she said to the captain as they stood outside the door to the ball room, "I need him to dance with me. Dancing is the excuse I need to stand close to him and hold him, which is ultimately what I need to do."

The captain nodded. "He'll dance with you. I'd bet my life on it. He cannot resist a beautiful woman, especially one he's never seen before. He'll dance with you."

"Has he no duchess, then?"

"His duchess died in childbirth many, many years ago, and he has not bothered to replace her. He has legitimate sons so he has no need of a duchess."

She nodded. "So he just has a string of mistresses instead?"

"I would not call them mistresses," Ragnar said. "They do not last long enough to earn the title of mistress."

"Delightful," she muttered as they both turned to the door, the captain with his hand on the door's handle.

The room behind the wooden doors was enormous, a large ball room, with a high, painted ceiling, an enormous gold and crystal chandelier hanging in its centre, large, floor to ceiling windows on its outer walls, all of which were framed in opened, heavy, yellow drapes, a colourful, polished marble floor, and a balcony at one end that was full of musicians playing different musical instruments. The room was full of people. Despite the crowd, it was the chandelier that drew her attention first. Strikingly, stunningly beautiful, it blazed with over three dozen tall candles, the light of which caused the hundreds of pieces of cut crystal in the chandelier to sparkle and twinkle. Although there were candles in sconces all around the walls of the room, the chandelier was the primary source of light in the room.

As they moved deeper into the ball room, her hand through his arm, people greeted him, and he, in turn, introduced her. For an hour or so, they mingled, moving through the crowd of people at one end of the room. At the other end of the room, under the balcony of musicians, people were dancing. At one point, she watched the dancing, observing the movements of the dancers, knowing, or hoping, she would have to emulate them.

"Do you dance?" she asked the captain, interrupting his conversation.

"Not if I can help it," was his succinct reply.

The speed of his reply, as much as the reply itself amused her. "Coward," she teased him.

He responded by smiling, genuinely amused. She was, at least in part, right.

Every so often, as they shook hands or curtsied, talked and mingled, moved through the crowd, she would catch Ragnar's eye, hers questioning. Where was the god-damned duke? The continued absence of the duke meant they were stuck there, making meaningless, inane conversation – a form of torture as far as she was concerned. But every time she caught Ragnar's eye, he responded the same way, shaking his head slightly, and she knew the duke was nowhere in sight.

And then, just as she was beginning to wonder if she should have employed her powers of visualisation, although that would have been difficult not knowing what the duke looked like, their conversation was interrupted, rudely, by a voice directly behind them. Even with her back turned, she could not miss the supreme arrogance in the voice.

"And who is this tasty morsel?"

She and Ragnar turned around to face the owner of the voice, and the owner of the voice immediately helped himself to her hand, bringing it up as he bent over it to place his lips on the back of it. When he'd done so, he straightened and looked at her.

"I don't believe I've seen you at court before, lovely lady. Where **did** Ragnar find you? Not in the gutter, I hope."

The rudeness. The sheer, unadulterated rudeness. She inclined her head at him.

"Does it look to you like Ragnar found me in the gutter?"

The owner of the voice raised a sardonic eyebrow. "One can never tell these days."

Ragnar intervened before anyone else had a chance to say something they might regret.

"Kiaara, may I present his grace, the Duke of Marlborough. Your Grace, this is Kiaara."

She and Ragnar exchanged a brief but meaningful look, and then she turned her attention on the duke and curtsied low, knowing he would be given a good view of her breasts.

"Your Grace," she said as she went down.

But she curtsied not just in compliance with court etiquette. It gave her time to make a mental adjustment before she fully engaged with him. In hearing his name over and over again that night as the slavers argued around their huge fire, she had unconsciously formed a mental picture of what this duke would look like. Assuming he would be prone to the excesses of an indulgent nature, she had pictured him with a huge, portly stomach, thinning hair, and too many chins. She couldn't have been more mistaken if she'd tried. In the flesh, he was tall, a head taller than her, and thin, almost gaunt. He was at least two decades older than her, with iron-grey hair that was immaculately pulled back and held by a black ribbon. For his age, though, he was remarkably unlined in the face, and his immaculate presentation helped, too – polished black boots, an expensive-looking, tailored, navy-blue coat, and a crisp white shirt with flared cuffs that were longer than the sleeves of the coat. His fingers were long and elegant, the nails manicured, and he was clean shaven. His eyes, though, were exactly as she'd thought they would be: black and cold.

"May I have the pleasure of the next dance, my dear?" he asked her, and then, to Ragnar, "You don't mind if I steal her away, do you, Ragnar?"

Ragnar bowed slightly. "Not at all, Your Grace. Be my guest." But then he stood straight, as tall as the duke, looked the duke in the eye and added, "Just make sure you bring her back."

"But of course," the duke replied, bowing slightly himself.

Again, she and Ragnar exchanged a look as she moved away from him, her hand in that of the duke. 'Twas a look that bespoke a different message from them both, he warning her to be careful, she expressing her surprise at how easy it had ultimately turned out to be to ensnare the duke. But she knew, somehow, that he'd been watching them for a while from somewhere unseen, biding his time, waiting for just the right opportunity to approach her. Or, more likely, he'd been assessing her, making sure she was worth the effort – making sure she was not just some silly strumpet in a pretty dress.

On the dance floor, she stood too close to the duke so she could wrap one arm around him, her other held in his. She stood so close her breasts were pressed against him. The action was misconstrued, of course, but she did not care. Although he did not yet know it, he did not have the luxury of time to pursue her. They did not speak as he whirled and twirled her around the dance floor. He was a man who did not waste time, or words, on women. He knew he didn't have to. His wealth and title, his position at court, his close connection to the king, and his grasping, demanding nature all combined to ensure he did not ever expend energy or effort on seducing women. If he wanted a woman, she was his for as long as she entertained him. It was that simple. Kiaara was glad he did not talk because it allowed her to focus, and focus on, for that matter, her inner vision. And so she gave it form and held it for the entirety of their dance. At the end of the dance, he bowed to her, and she curtsied, as was custom, but as he straightened, he reached into his coat and produced a crisp, white handkerchief.

"Is it my imagination," he asked her as he straightened, mopping his brow with his handkerchief, "or is it overly hot in here?"

"It is quite warm," she replied, wrapping her hand around his arm so that he could escort her back to Ragnar.

By the time they reached Ragnar, the duke was looking decidedly ill. He was sweating profusely, and the skin of his face was changing colour, turning an ashen shade of grey. He said nothing as he released her, and he swayed on his feet. Then, she and Ragnar watched as he collapsed in front of them. He fell to the floor, crumpled, really, as if his legs had just ceased to support him. Seemingly full of concern, she moved quickly, dropping to her knees and bending over him, untying his shirt in the pretence of giving him air to breathe, although she knew air would not help him. But she bent over him, and locked her eyes onto his.

"Your heart is black and shrivelled," she said in a low voice so that only he could hear her, "and now it has failed you. Everything you have done has led you to this. Death." She inclined her head and smiled into his eyes. "Was it worth it?"

He was in enormous pain, struggling to breathe, and his lips were turning grey, but, still, he managed to ask her, "Who . . . are . . . you?"

"I am Light," she said. "Dangerous Light for one such as you. And by the way, Ragnar found me in a caravan of captured slaves. I was to be one of your sacrificial victims . . ."

She didn't have time to say any more. Ragnar bent over her and, with a hand under each of her elbows, he pulled her away from the duke and all but lifted her to her feet, and then, with an arm around her waist, a hand under her arm, he escorted her around the edge of the ball room, towards the balcony of musicians, and out through a door near the balcony. She allowed herself to be thus compelled. On the large terrace outside the ball room, elongated rectangles of light covered the stone, the light spilling out through the ball room's large windows. Ragnar walked them both past the rectangles of light, to the light's very edge so that they were partly hidden in the darkness of the night. He turned her to face him, his hands on her upper arms.

"Did you just kill a man with your embrace?" "Semantics," she replied ambiguously.

"Meaning?"

"Do I look like a killer to you?"

He dropped his hands, letting her go. "In my experience, killers are not normally as beautiful as you."

"I am not a killer," she said. "What do you think happened in there? Did a man just dance with a woman? Yes," she said, answering her own question. "But that wasn't all that happened. That was merely a physical thing, certainly all the duke saw and knew until it was far too late. Underneath the physical, there is always a deeper truth. What happened in there, in truth, was that a man of utter darkness danced with the Lady of Light.

"'Tis a fundamental principle of dark and Light," she continued, "that darkness cannot exist in the presence of Light. Does not light always banish the shadows in a room when you bring a lantern into it? I wrapped him in my Light, and I saw that his heart was full of shadow. Actually, his heart was black and shrivelled, as I told him just now. When your heart is full of shadow, and that shadow is banished by Light, there is not a whole lot left. Had there been any good in him, he may have lived. But he was heartless, soulless, cold. Unfortunately for him, there was no goodness left, and so his heart failed him. If I killed him with my embrace, then I had a lot of help from him."

He didn't say anything. He just looked at her. Even though they stood at the edge of the light spilling out onto the terrace from the ball room's windows, they could still see each other clearly. He took a step closer to her so that he was all but touching her, and he reached up to lift the silver heart in his fingers. "Why do you wear this?" he asked her.

"Because it is whole and undamaged, unlike mine."

He looked into her eyes, and she looked into his. He put the heart back against her, but he didn't take his fingers away. Instead, he lightly ran his fingertips over her breast, up the skin of her chest, over her collar bone, up over her shoulder and around her neck. Her whole body thrummed with desire even though his touch was light. Unconsciously, she leaned towards him even as he leaned towards her. Their kiss was not the light caress of many first kisses. Rather, they kissed each other deeply, passionately, hungrily, as if they would devour each other.

When he pulled back, they were both breathing quickly. "Have you had enough of the ball?" he asked her.

"I had enough of the ball when I'd been in it . . for a single moment," she replied.

"Such a way with words," he muttered as he kissed her again. When he pulled back, he said, "Then might I suggest we retire for the night."

He had a room in the castle, or a small suite of rooms more like, and his bedroom was impressive – large, square, the same walls of grey stone that she was familiar with, a polished wood floor that was covered in a thick, red carpet, a four-posted bed of dark, carved wood, a high, beamed ceiling. But it was the view of the city that truly captured attention, especially at night when the lights in the city were scattered throughout the darkness. The windows in the room were large and they met at one of the corners. She stood looking out over the city through the windows.

"The city looks beautiful at night," she said.

He didn't comment. He wasn't at all interested in the view of the city. She'd heard him moving around as she'd stood looking out over the city, but it was only when he came to stand behind her that she realised he'd been undressing. Wearing only a thin tunic and his trousers, his feet bare, he stood behind her and kissed the skin of her neck, below her ear, his hands snaking around her waist to hold her against him. Even through the thick material of the outer gown and the layers of its skirts underneath it, she felt his arousal, and her body responded. He released her, and moments later, she felt his fingers untying the laces of her gown. When it was loose, he lifted the gown and its skirts up, over her head. When she was free of it, wearing only a shift, he tossed the gown onto the floor beside them, and turned her around. But instead of kissing her as she thought he would, he knelt in front of her and lifted one of her feet onto his raised knee. He undid the laces of her boots and pulled the boot and the silk stocking underneath it from her foot. He released her foot and then lifted the other one, untying her boot and pulling it off. But instead of releasing her foot as he had done with the other one, he ran the fingers of both hands over her foot and up her leg. Just his touch could set her body thrumming and humming with desire. Her breathing quickened. When he stood, he continued to run his fingers up her leg, taking the thin material of her shift with him. And then he kissed her, deeply, passionately. She felt she might lose all semblance of control, but he broke the kiss, picking her up bodily. He carried her over to his bed, and she flopped back onto the mattress. Before he came with her, he pulled his tunic over his head, threw it away, and then dispensed with his trousers.

When he joined her on the bed, he leaned over her and, again, ran his fingers up her leg, taking the material of her shift with him. He ran his hand up over her thigh, her hip, her waist, pushing the material up impatiently. Putting a knee between her legs, he leaned over her and, touching her breast with his hand, he took the nipple of her breast in his mouth. Her body arched of its own accord. She had no control over her response to his touch, no control at all. Gasping, breathing hard, she pushed her fingers through his hair, holding his head. He reached down and cupped her, and she moaned and opened her legs. Knowing she was ready for him, he moved, pushing himself inside her. But instead of moving, he held himself off her.

"Who are you making love to?" he asked harshly. "Him or me?"

"You," she gasped. "You are here. He is gone."

She moved her hips. If he wasn't going to move inside her, then she would make him move. He sucked in his breath, lowered himself, kissed her and complied, moving inside her, pushing himself into her, deeper, ever deeper. The pleasure built within her until it exploded. She arched forward and then back, and he, too, convulsed, crying out against her. And then he collapsed on top of her.

The way humans have sex in this reality, now, is, really, little more than physical stimulation. This is especially so given the use and abuse and the exploitation of sex and sexuality in the human reality. As with everything here now, humans do themselves no favours by not honouring the sacredness of sex. And, as physical stimulation only, the pleasure derived from sex does not and cannot in any way compare to the pleasure experienced when sex is an expression of soul connection, not just between two people, but within each of the participants. But then, sexual pleasure is taken into a whole new arena when a man makes love to an initiated priestess. Women are natural conduits of higher-dimensional energy, and that energy is intensified by feminine sexuality. In a very real sense, her pleasure heightens his pleasure in ways impossible to fathom or describe.

But the fact of women being natural conduits for higher-dimensional energy is the very reason the dark priests have worked so hard to suppress and control the sacred feminine, and to convince humanity that initiated priestesses are black witches. Do you not see a common theme in the main religions of the world today – religions that are complete fabrications of the dark priests – religions designed to entrap human consciousness? Each of those religions, to varying degrees, suppresses women, and female priests are still not accepted. This is because females as priests, even trapped in the mind-imprisoning dogma of institutionalised religion as they would be, are a threat to the systems of control. God help us all if feminine intuition should begin to guide humans to a better existence . . . !

In the aftermath of their love-making, she held him against her, holding him with her legs and wrapping her arms around him.

"Ragnar," she said, "you **are** him. The same, but different. Just as I am her, the same, but different. Damaged innocence. Both our hearts were broken that day."

He shifted his position on top of her, taking more of his own weight, but he didn't pull himself out of her.

"You know why I believe you when you say that? Because there's something in me that recognises you. I think there's something in me that recognises every other woman I've ever met in this life is not you."

He rolled off her, pulling himself out of her. She got up, and when she returned to the bed, he was sitting propped up on pillows against the bed's head, under the blankets. She would've slipped under the blankets with him, but he asked a question, and the question caused her to change her mind.

"What did you mean when you said you gave it all permission to happen that day?"

The question stopped her in her tracks, literally. She stopped walking toward the bed and looked at him. And then, she walked around the bed and went to look out the large windows of his room, looking out at the city, her back to him. She didn't want to tell him the truth, but she owed it to him if nothing else. It was a risk. He might not understand, but he also might understand, and that scared her.

She turned around and moved to sit on the edge of the bed beside him, facing him, curling her legs under her. He shifted in the bed to accommodate her. She leaned on one arm, over his legs.

"To understand what happened, I have to go back, before that day, and give you some background knowledge. Do you mind?"

"Not at all. I want to hear whatever you have to tell me. And I'd prefer it if you held nothing back. I want to know the truth, all of it."

She nodded. "So be it, then," she said, lowering her eyes, not because she had something to hide, but because she didn't quite know where and how to begin. "The temple performed many functions," she said, raising her eyes again to look at him, "including the obvious ones of guidance and counsel, divination, healing and teaching. But its most important function was that of connecting the people to," she lifted her hand and waved it towards the canopy of his rather impressive bed, "well, to the heavens, for want of a better word. To the higher dimensions, is the correct term." She paused to gauge his reaction. He was watching her closely, and listening.

"Go on," he said when she hesitated.

"As its High Priestess, that connection was my most important function, and so, whenever I went into the temple's sacred heart, its inner sanctum, the Elders came, and I communed with them. The Elohim Elders are powerful beings of Light, and they created the human experience. Of course, in creating it, they watched over it, and they watch over it still. I am **of** them, in the sense that the essence of me is the essence of them, and I came from the higher dimensions to act as a conduit for their energy, connecting humans to the Elohim, to the Light, to the higher dimensions, to the divine guidance of the higher dimensions. You have to understand the relationship between me and them. I did not, and I do not serve them, in one sense, and nor are they my masters. It's more that if one of us has a thought, we all have that thought because we are ultimately one, and we serve the Light."

Again, she paused, wondering if he understood. He did.

"So what was the thought they had that you had, too?" he asked her.

Again, she lowered her eyes, this time because his question caused the pain to roll through her. She closed her eyes against it. He watched her closely, and he saw that the memory caused her pain, so he touched her arm. Just a light caress. He touched his fingertips to the arm she was leaning on.

She raised her eyes to his again, and he could see the pain in them. "When the Elohim Elders created the human experience," she said, "we gifted humans something that was supposed to be a blessing, but, instead, has turned out to be a curse – Free Will. Choice. Because of choice, the dark priests – utterly corrupt, evil, higher-dimensional beings of darkness – were able to get a foothold on and in the human experience. They began to control it, controlling humans themselves, and they were pulling humans into the abyss of darkness and Separation. We had given humans Free Will, and we could not take it away from them just because they were making terrible, horrible choices. Nor could we prevent humans falling into the abyss for the same reason. We could not protect them from the consequences of their wayward choices. The only thing we could do was allow ourselves to fall into the abyss with them, so that they would not wallow in the darkness alone, with no way out."

"You say 'we'," he said. "How many are you talking about?"

"That's a good question," she replied. "When I say 'we', I am referring to the Elders. But there were many who knew, who followed me, who did as I did. I do not know how many, but I know there **are** many. Many of the Fallen were a part of the horror of that day. Many fell that day, with me, voluntarily, as I did . . . including you," she added softly. "But the problem with being Light is that you cannot fall into the abyss of darkness as you are." She shrugged her shoulders. "'Tis simply not possible, as Light, to live in darkness. So, to fall, to become darkness, to become Separated . . ."

"What did you do?"

"I wrapped my heart in fear, so that the darkness of fear would hide my Light. Fear was the only way I could exist in darkness. I cast a ritual spell that severed me from my reflection, because my reflection holds Light and it would have banished the fear. In casting the ritual spell, I gave permission for the events of that day to form a part of my reality, and those events lacerated my soul with the fear, wrapping my heart in darkness. I allowed it to happen. I gave permission for it to happen, and I was cut down just for being what I am – a powerful being of Light – which is the fear. So in all the lives I've lived since, I have hidden the truth of myself from myself, Separated from myself, so that I could exist in darkness, my Light hidden. So that I could exist with humans as one of them, in the state they, too, were existing in. Do you understand?"

He nodded.

"Ambrose came to the temple the day I cast the spell." She raised her hand, palm up and open, and looked at it. "I used a knife to cut my hand because blood is binding and it adds great power to a spell like that. In that sense, I sealed the spell with my own life blood. But I hid the truth from him." She dropped her hand and looked up at him again. "You see, in severing my own reflection, I was severing us because we are each other's reflection. Had I known he would blame himself . . ."

He wrapped his hand around her arm, tightly. "Ye gods," he said, "you have balls of steel. You knew what would happen to you and you went through with it anyway."

"I did not know the priest was going to tear my heart out and eat it in front of me," she said. "Thank the gods. I'm not sure I would've had the courage to go through with it had I known that. But the whole thing was not about courage," she said. "It's what we do. We do what is needed, where it is needed, and when. It was about doing what was necessary for humanity. No more, and no less."

He leaned forward, reaching up and sliding his fingers behind her neck to pull her to him, and he kissed her, deeply. Then he moved, rolling her over and coming with her so that she lay under him. Again, his hand moved over her body as he kissed her, and she arched in response to his touch, unable to help herself, as she kissed him back and threaded her fingers through his hair.

And then he raised himself and looked down at her. "And now? This business with the duke, what was that about really?"

"When fear is wrapped around your heart, the only way to remove it is to face it, confront it. My fear has to be faced so that my heart can be set free, once again, to beat its own unique rhythm, as it should. What I did to the duke will effectively announce my presence to those who are able to understand what I am, to those who will always want to cut me down . . ."

"Being cut down for being what you are," he said.

She nodded. "Yes. There is fear in you, too."

"I know," he said. "I will die rather than lose you again." As he spoke, he pushed himself inside her. "Do you hear me? I will die before I will lose you again." And before she could respond, he kissed her and moved inside her . . .

~

"Gabriel. Salomon."

It wasn't that Cory said Gabriel's name in full, nor even that he actually said Salomon's name at all that got their attention. It was the way he said their names, like a school teacher warning errant school children to behave themselves. They both looked at him. "Something weird is happening to her wound," Cory told them.

They both looked at the wound on her chest, and then Salomon moved around Gabriel to lean over the wound for a closer look. The skin around the wound was moving, forming tiny threads across the wound itself.

"Ye gods," Salomon declared, laughing, "it's healing." He threw his head back and laughed, his laughter holding and expressing a myriad of different emotions. "She's healing her wound."

"That's not the only wound she's healing," Gabriel said, and he turned her hand over. The wound on her hand had always been hidden in the position of her hands as they lay curled over her breast. Gabriel knew it was there, but he'd felt it as he held her hand with his own. When he turned her hand over so that the others could see it, they all saw the skin around the wound on her hand moving in the same way the skin around the wound on her chest was moving.

Cory turned quickly to pick up his orb of light, and then he turned back and held it over his Lady so that they could all watch the movement of the wound on her chest. The skin around it closed over the wound so that it became a large, lumpy scar on her chest. But even that continued to change.

They watched the wound on her chest and the one on her hand as both disappeared, as if both had never been at all. When the wounds were gone, they all looked at each other, wondering what, in the name of the gods, would happen next.

~

An incessant pounding on the door of the room woke them both. He rolled away from her so he could look at the door.

"Come in," he said.

When the door opened, a man came in whom she had never seen before, but whom Ragnar obviously knew well.

"Griff . . ." he said, sitting up and then getting out of bed, not at all bothered by the fact that he was naked. She watched him as she sat up in the bed, hugging the bedclothes to her protectively, wondering how it was that men were so uninhibited when it came to their own naked bodies whilst women were completely inhibited about being naked in front of anybody at all. Really, the answer is obvious – yet another of those dark manipulations where women are concerned. Glossy magazines , skeletally-thin models, and digitally-altered images all contribute to women looking upon themselves with overly-critical, judgemental, self-condemning eyes. That they do so, of course, dictates a poor self image, and that, in turn, interferes with and hinders their ability to experience their sexuality uninhibitedly. Just another aspect of the successful suppression of the feminine psyche.

"Sorry to disturb you, captain," Griff said, "but you need to know. The duke's son is accusing your lady of murder most foul. Witchcraft. They're saying she killed the duke with witchcraft, and they're baying for her blood."

"What a hypocrite," she said vehemently, drawing the attention of Griff. He looked over at her, grinning at her, unashamedly liking what he saw. She was obviously naked under the bedclothes because her shoulders were bare, and her hair was a dishevelled mess, framing her face in a mass of messy curls.

"Hypocrite or not," Ragnar said seriously as he pulled the thin tunic over his head and tied his trousers, "we need to get you out of here. Griff . . ." he started to say.

"Yes, captain, I know," Griff responded, knowing what his captain was going to request of him and reluctantly dragging his eyes away from the lady in the bed. "Dagonis is being saddled even as we speak. I'll meet you downstairs."

In the aftermath of Griff's departure, they both dressed with undue haste. He helped her put the gown back on, tying the laces behind her, and she sat on the bed, putting her stockings and boots back on, and tying them while he moved around the room, collecting those things he knew he would need, not least of which was his long sword in its scabbard. She did not possess the skill to arrange her hair as the two attendants had the day before, so she removed the pins that were still in it, ran her fingers through it and shook it out. Unbeknownst to her, he paused as he buckled his sword around his hips so he could watch her, wishing they could have lingered in bed.

When she stood, he covered her shoulders in a navy-blue cloak. "You'll need this," he said as he pulled the hood over her hair and tied the cloak in place. Before she could move, he held her in place with his hands on her upper arms and he looked into her eyes. "No matter what happens now, we stay together. Even if we die together, we stay together. Agreed?"

She nodded. "Agreed."

Satisfied, he put his own cloak around his shoulders, pinning it in place and then he moved to open one of the deep drawers in the chest of drawers against the wall at the end of the bed. Pulling out a small chest, the width of a man's forearm, the height of a hand span, he looked over at her, answering her silent question. "The king is very lax when it comes to paying his staff, but he never forgets to pay those of us who protect him. I'll be damned if I'll leave this so the vultures can help themselves to it."

When they left his room, they navigated the castle using hidden tunnels, stairways, and passages, most of them hidden behind panels or tapestries or bookshelves. One of the advantages of being the captain of the king's guard was the privilege of knowing about the secret passages that were hidden throughout the castle, in its walls. Ragnar knew them intimately. Often times, she followed him, holding her skirts clear of dirt and dust, out of little more than blind faith because the passages and tunnels were dark, and neither of them had a torch.

When they finally stepped out into bright sunlight, Griff was waiting for them, holding the bridle of the magnificent black horse she'd seen when Ragnar had ridden into the temple days before. She stood beside the horse, waiting while Ragnar secured his chest behind the saddle.

"They're saying you killed the duke with a hug," Griff said, looking at her with a mixture of awe, respect, suspicion and just a little fear. He, like Ragnar, was a soldier, so there wasn't much he feared, but, like every human, he did fear what couldn't be explained rationally, simply because he didn't understand it. "Is that true?"

She smiled the sweetest of smiles at him, all wide-eyed innocence. "If only I possessed that kind of power," she said. And then she explained, "All I did was dance with him. Death by dancing." She shrugged her shoulders exaggeratedly. "Is that even possible?"

"And that's all you did?" he asked her suspiciously.

"Well, I didn't cast a spell on him if that's what you're asking me. I promise you that."

Ragnar interrupted the interchange. "Griff, thank you," he said as he turned away from his horse to face Griff. The two men gripped each other's wrists in a soldier's firm handshake. "I've never said this, but I'll say it now. You are a fine soldier and a good friend." They released each other and Ragnar put a foot in the stirrup, hauled himself up and swung a leg over the saddle. Looking down from the lofty heights of his warhorse, he added, "And I believe you're in charge now."

She, too, put a foot in the stirrup, and both Ragnar and Griff helped her up onto the horse. It was a long way up. She needed all her strength to haul herself into the saddle. When she was sitting behind him, she wrapped her arms around Ragnar.

"Captain," Griff said, looking up at his captain, "I've a need to know. Is she worth it?"

Ragnar looked down at him in response, and smiled. His smile alone was sufficient answer, but he said, "Oh yes, she's definitely worth it."

Griff nodded, satisfied. He trusted his captain above all other men. If his captain trusted her, then she was, indeed, trustworthy.

As the horse moved forward, Ragnar turned his head to address her. "Hold onto me with your arms, and hold onto the horse with your legs," he instructed her. "Don't resist his movement. Roll with it. Let your body move with him."

She did as she was bid. They had no choice but to leave the city by the western gate, which was unfortunate because it meant those who were seeking them both would know where they were going. Once past the gate, Ragnar urged his horse into a gallop, and it was only when the city had grown small with distance that he eased the horse into a canter.

When they reached the temple, Ashanti and Billy were waiting for them on the temple's steps.

"We've set up your old room, my Lady," Ashanti said. Ever since Kiaara had walked out of the round room after speaking with the Elders, Ashanti had ceased referring to her as 'lass' and, instead, addressed her as 'Lady' or 'my Lady', as had Billy. "'N we've fodder 'n water, 'n a warm blanket for yer horse, captain." And then, addressing them both, she said, "Ye've a day and a night before they come for ye. So, I'll see ye tomorrow, then. Enjoy yer day."

"Tomorrow?" Kiaara asked her, sliding off the horse. "Wouldn't it be sensible for you to stay away tomorrow?"

Ashanti waved a gnarled hand in the air. "Bah," she said. "Sensible is boring. Dun forget, Lady, there are more wrongs being made right tomorrow than just the one."

Kiaara smiled at her. "Ah, yes," she said. "So there are." She walked towards Ashanti and lifted one of the old woman's hands in her own. "Thank you, for everything. Your grandmama would be proud. You have truly honoured your promise to her."

The old woman smiled in response and covered Kiaara's hand with her own. And then Kiaara watched as the old woman walked up the temple's walkway, towards Billy's old, uncomfortable wagon, leaning heavily on her grandson. Kiaara would have preferred it if the old woman stayed away tomorrow. She would've protected them all if she could. But, of course, Ashanti knew best, and she was right. There was far more than just one fear being faced in the convergence of events that was fast closing in on them all.

Ragnar, holding his horse's bridle in front of his horse, was not watching the old woman leave with her grandson. He was watching Kiaara. "You don't want her to come here tomorrow, do you?"

She looked at him. "Of course not. I want them all to be safe. But she's right. The people around here have fears to face, too."

"What fears?"

"They should have come to the temple's aid on the day of the massacre. Instead, they cowered in fear and hid. And, for generations, they have regretted their actions."

"Ah," he said, sounding enlightened, "no wonder they came out in number to help you restore the temple."

She smiled. "No wonder. But the temple served them well in its day, in many different ways, not just spiritually, but economically, financially, and they remember that." She motioned with her hand, indicating the land surrounding the temple. "This land still benefits from the energy generated around the temple back then. 'Tis still very fertile." She dropped her hand and inclined her head at him. "We have the whole day to ourselves, I do believe, and I think I know how we can spend it."

He raised an eyebrow at her, his imagination already starting to work overtime. "Do you now? Well, do tell."

She smiled and walked straight past him without touching him, and then she turned when she realised he wasn't following her, and beckoned to him. "Trust me, you're going to like it," she said.

"Oh, I trust you."

She led him and his horse around the side of the temple's main building to the buildings at the back of the temple where her old room was located. They fed and watered Dagonis, unsaddled him and freed him from his bridle. They left him untethered, but he followed them when she led Ragnar through the landscape behind the temple's outer buildings. Ragnar heard the sound of running, cascading water long before he saw it. The running water, when finally he laid eyes on it, was too small to be called a river, but too large to be called a stream. Bright, green grass covered the river bank, and tall trees grew up on both sides of the water, providing shade. Dagonis immediately helped himself to the grass, his head lowered.

It was a beautiful day, and, for them, it was a day of beauty . The sun was alone in a bright-blue sky, and its warmth was caressing. They spent the day swimming, eating food from the hamper provided them by Ashanti, making love on one of the blankets from Kiaara's room, lying naked in the sun, and talking of many things. The day didn't go fast. Nor did it go slow. It was a day of perfection, an oasis of bliss in a desert of uncertainty and fear.

That night, they lay on a mattress in her room, under a pile of soft, warm blankets, the light from a brazier filling the room with warm, orange light. He was curled against her, one leg under hers and an arm across her waist. She lay on her back savouring the feel of his body against hers, his leg under hers, his arm heavy across her waist, and his breath soft on the skin of her neck. From the regularity of his breathing, she suspected he was very close to sleep. She, on the other hand, was struggling to sleep. Every time she closed her eyes, images that hadn't yet happened, images of what the next day might hold, filled her mind, and she felt her fear.

"Aren't you afraid of what tomorrow might bring?" she asked him.

He stirred against her. "Of course," he murmured sleepily. "But I'm not thinking about it. If I think about what tomorrow will bring then I will miss the beauty of this moment, and I won't be relaxed. I'll be tense . . . as you are."

She laughed softly. "You're a philosopher, too, I see."

He smiled against her. "I am many things – soldier, scholar, philosopher, and now I am a lover."

She turned in the bed, slightly, so she could put her lips on his forehead. "I would like to know what else you are, Ragnar. Do you understand? I want us both to live through tomorrow."

He didn't respond.

In the morning, once they dressed, Ragnar made sure Dagonis was tethered behind the temple's outbuildings so that the horse would not be stressed by what he might hear, and then she and Ragnar sat together on the temple's front steps, their fingers entwined, waiting. The sun was warm, caressing them both as they sat.

"If it comes to it today," he said, "I will die, and you will live."

"I thought you were thinking that," she said quickly. "No."

"Yes."

"No," she said forcefully.

"Yes," he said implacably.

"Wasn't it you who said we stay together even if we die together? Why do you want to die and have me live?"

"Because I will do everything in my power to make sure they do not cut you down as they did so long ago. I will die rather than see that happen."

She didn't respond verbally, but she held his hand in both of hers, closed her eyes and put her forehead on their clasped hands.

It was not even mid-morning when they saw a cloud of dust in the distance. They both stood, watching, their fingers still entwined. As the dust cloud came closer, Ragnar seemed to recognise what was generating it . . . or who, more like. Frowning, he stepped down, releasing her hand, and walked a couple of paces away from her in anticipation of meeting the source of the dust cloud. Out of the dust cloud, there emerged three dozen or so fully-armed soldiers. They rode their horses into the temple's grounds and then dismounted. Griff gave the reigns of his horse to the soldier beside him, and he walked along the walkway to meet Ragnar.

"Captain," he said when he reached Ragnar, bowing his head slightly. "They're mobilising part of the army. Why they need an army to take on two people, I'll never know. 'Tis overkill if ever I heard of it. So, some of us thought we'd even up the odds a little."

Ragnar threw his head back and laughed heartily, and Griff grinned broadly, enjoying his captain's amusement. But then he sobered.

"We fight **with** you, captain," he said seriously, "not against you. 'Tis that simple."

The soldiers took their horses behind the temple to join Dagonis, and then they came to stand in the courtyard, in front of Ragnar and Kiaara, forming two lines on either side of the courtyard, behind the temple's empty mosaic pools.

Not long after the soldiers formed their lines in the courtyard, Billy and Ashanti, in their old wagon, led a sizeable group of local folk into the temple. Very few were armed with swords, but they were all armed with axes, cudgels, hastily-prepared lances, whatever they'd been able to get their hands on, and they, too, took their places around, not among, the captain's men.

Kiaara was standing on the temple's steps, and she smiled as she watched them take their place. Ragnar, standing in the courtyard in the centre of his men, below her, turned around and raised an eyebrow at her. "What was that you were saying about Free Will?"

She didn't bother to reply verbally, but her smile deepened.

The final group to join the impromptu army in front of the temple did so silently, moving to take their place among those assembled there like dancers in motion. They looked human, but the slightly pointed ears and the crystal-like eyes common among the Fae marked them as different. The Fae cannot abide the touch of metal, so their weapon of choice was the bow and arrow. Those already assembled nodded or smiled their welcome, though none spoke, and all stood together as one, companions in arms, standing should to shoulder, united against a common foe. The Fae swelled their numbers dramatically, more than doubling the impromptu army.

One of the Fae, his long, white hair held back from his face in a long, tidy plait, came to stand in front of Kiaara. He bowed to her formerly, with a hand over his chest.

"Ushara," he said, "we cannot allow you to face the darkness alone, not this time." And he handed her a bow and a quiver of arrows. "Your weapon of choice, I do believe."

She smiled at him as she stepped down to take it from him. "I thank you, Amoranth," she said. "'Tis very good to see you again, old friend."

He smiled at her. "'Tis very good to see you again, too. It has been a while, and you have been busy."

Many of the souls standing together, awaiting yet another army of darkness, had been present on that fateful day the Elohim priesthood had been massacred, either as witnesses or as victims, and many of the Fallen stood among the Fae. But there were many more standing among the impromptu army who were there simply because they served the Light. The Light required their presence, so they were there.

The dust cloud that heralded the approach of the army was so large it was more like a dust storm than a dust cloud. It dominated the horizon for an age before the army itself came into view. Every being standing in front of the temple, awaiting the army, watched, none moving, none speaking. What emerged from the dust cloud were hundreds of horses and riders. And they assembled, the cloud of dust around them, at the very edge of the temple's grounds, as if, as a collective, they did not really want to touch any part of the temple. When the army had assembled and settled, the two groups faced each other in almost-perfect silence, no one in either army moving or speaking.

And then, a horse and rider broke rank, and then another and another. Both armies watched as a dozen more or so of the captain's men broke with the army assembled at the edge of the temple's grounds, dismounted and led their horses along the walkway.

"They forget," one of them muttered by way of explanation to the captain and his men standing in the courtyard, "we've seen you fight. I'd sooner face the devil than face you lot in a fight."

They, too, led their horses around the back of the temple's main building, and then they, too, joined Ragnar and his men in the courtyard, facing the army assembled at the edge of the temple's grounds.

Again, the two armies seemed to settle, and they faced each other in near-perfect silence, no one moving or speaking. Only the horses tossing their heads with fear and tension broke the absolute stillness. The tension was palpable and hung in the air over both armies. Kiaara was still standing on the temple's steps, her bow at the ready with an arrow knocked against the string, her fingers holding it in place, her lips tight with determination. This time, they could try to cut her down, but she would put up one hell of a fight. And, although he did not know it, she would put up the same fight for Ragnar, too. He would die today over her dead body . . . figuratively speaking, of course.

And then, in the uncanny silence and stillness, another horse and rider broke rank, moving forward to stand in front of the army assembled at the edge of the temple's grounds. He was young, barely in his third decade of life, but he still wore his arrogance like a piece of clothing, just like his father. Kiaara could see it from where she was standing.

"Captain Ragnar," he yelled across the distance between them all, "no one need die here today. We only want the woman. Surrender the woman and we will let you all live. Hand over the woman and you can all return to your lives as if none of this ever happened."

Ragnar responded by drawing his sword from its scabbard, and his men followed his lead so that for a moment the air was full of the sounds of swords being drawn.

"You want her," Ragnar snarled at the youth on the horse in front of the assembled army, "come get her yourself and suffer the consequences. We will not surrender her."

"Fool," the boy yelled back. "So be it, then . . ."

Kiaara felt them coming. She felt them approaching from behind her because their energy, their essence, preceded them and it touched her like a caress. She couldn't help but turn and look. Ragnar, too, felt the disturbance, the distraction in Kiaara, and he, too, turned to see what had drawn her attention. The Elders walked, in a perfect line, through the main hall of the temple, and then they stood on either side of Kiaara so that she and they formed a perfect line. The one standing next to her on her left put his hand on the bow she was holding and moved it downward, lowering it. He smiled a radiant smile at her and said softly, "Put away thy weapon, beautiful Lady. You've no need of a weapon here today."

Then, as one, with their one-but-many voice, they addressed everyone in both armies. "Ushara, Lady of Light, is our daughter with whom we are well pleased," they said, as they had once before. "Ushara will never again be surrendered into anyone's hands. She stands as one of us. She stands as One **with** us."

And then they moved, walking through the impromptu army assembled in front of the temple, moving towards the other army. You have to understand, it is impossible to describe the Elohim Elders with human words and human language. They are beings of Light, entirely alien, for want of a much better word, to the human experience. Tall? Yes, tall is a word that applies to them, but other than that, no word adequately describes them. They hold the appearance of males and females, but being male or female is more an impression than anything else. This day, they wore their sapphire-blue cloaks because their cloaks made it easier for those assembled there to look upon them, but, really their form is impossible to describe, certainly in any way that does them justice.

As they passed through Ragnar's men, the soldiers stared at them, mouths open, weapons unconsciously lowering. And it wasn't just the sight of them that elicited such a response either, it was the feel of their energy, their Light. A brush with the Light of the Elohim has indescribable effects on the individual experiencing it. For the individual touched by the Light of the Elohim, he or she is never the same again. He or she will experience a massive shift in consciousness and, with it, profound changes in mindset, belief, perspective, focus.

The Elders walked, or seemed to, because their feet didn't really touch the ground, beyond the courtyard, through the temple's grounds, and stopped, still in their perfect line, in front of the youth sitting astride his horse in front of his army. The Elder who had placed his hand on Kiaara's bow was the one who stood directly in front of him.

"Get down off your horse, boy," he said, gesturing with a hand as he spoke.

The youth did as he was bid. He had no choice, after all. When he stepped away from his horse, the horse turned and cantered away, not in fright, more in release, as if it had been given the freedom to do as it pleased, and so it went home.

When the boy stood in front of the Elders, the one who had spoken stepped forward and put both his hands on either side of the boy's head, over his temples, above his ears. Almost immediately, the boy started screaming. He screamed with such terror that his voice became hoarse, and then he broke free and ran. He ran through his army, and, in actual fact, was never seen or heard of again.

As one, the Elders raised their hands. "Disperse."

Immediately, the army assembled at the edge of the temple's grounds began to disperse, but it wasn't so much the riders that obeyed the command of the Elders, it was the horses. Some of the riders tried to pull their horses back, but with no success at all. The horses turned away and began walking or trotting or even cantering back to Duavel, and there was not a damn thing their riders could do to stop them. In a matter of mere moments, the army that had been assembled at the edge of the temple's grounds was gone as if it had never been, or as if it had been but a figment of everyone's imagination.

Only one part of it remained, and Kiaara, watching, marvelled at the fact of them not running like everyone else, because it is, after all, a known fact of darkness and Light that darkness cannot exist in Light. A group of black-cowled priests, perhaps a handful or so, stood their ground against the might and power of the Elohim Elders. The two groups, those of the Light and those of the darkness, faced each other in silence for a long, elongated moment, like a line of pieces on a chest board.

And then one of the Elders spoke. "Your control was only ever illusion, but now, that illusion has vanished as if in a puff of smoke. We reclaim human consciousness and the human experience for the Light."

One of the black-cowled priests spoke, its voice sounding like a dry crackle in an equally dry wind. "We shall see."

The same Elder responded. "Oh, I doubt that," he said.

As one, the Elders began to move towards the black priests. Kiaara frowned as she watched. The black priests did not move even when they began to disintegrate in the Light of the Elohim. Eventually, they were naught but dry dust that was caught and scattered by the late-morning breeze. The message from the black priests was clear enough – they would not relinquish their control of humanity without a fight, and even when they lost that fight, as they would, they still would not cease in their attempts to control it. Well, she wished them luck. They would need it. The Elders turned around to face the temple, and again they raised their hands, palms up, their hands open.

"This temple is restored," they said, and so it was. The walkway and the courtyard were, again, paved in the pure white stone, free of the dirt and sand that had buried both. The gardens were ordered and manicured. The mosaic pools were clean and full of crystal-clear water. Even the steps Kiaara was standing on were no longer worn with time.

The Elders walked back to the temple, stopping, briefly, in front of Ragnar, and the one who had spoken to the duke's son spoke to Ragnar.

"Captain Ragnar," he said and bowed slightly. "Usha, Lord of Light, 'tis very good to see you again."

Unable to help himself, Ragnar bowed back, smiling, his free hand laid over his chest. "Thank you. 'Tis good to see you again, too."

And then the Elders moved past Ragnar to stand in front of Kiaara, mounting the temple's steps to do so.

"Beautiful Lady," the one said, "you must needs come home now. You need to be with your people, and you need to rest. You have done much Work, but your Work here is over for now. You will come here again at will, just as you always did. You will never abandon the human experience. You will continue to watch over it. But for now, you must needs come home."

She nodded. "What about Ragnar?"

He smiled at her and raised a hand to caress her cheek. "Do you not know, beautiful Lady, he ascended the human experience long, long ago. He awaits you, at home, where you belong." And he moved aside slightly, unblocking her line of vision. Behind him, she could see that Ragnar was gone as if he had never been.

She bowed her head in acquiescence, but there was one more thing she needed to do before she went with the Elders.

"Ashanti," she whispered, holding an image of the old woman in her mind's eye, "I must needs go to be with my people for now, but know this. I will return. That is my promise to you and your people. I will return. And I will always watch over you."

She felt Ashanti's response deep, deep within. "Go, be with your people, my Lady. Thank you for all you have done for my people. I shall await your return."

And then Kiaara turned around and took her place in the line of the Elders. Together, they walked back into the temple's interior.

~

The three who had kept a vigil beside the Lady all night were watching her closely, so they all saw the rise and fall of her chest as she took first one and then another and another breath. There was no warning. She didn't move at all other than the rise and fall of her chest. She just simply started to breathe. Cory's eyes opened wide, like saucers, and he simply couldn't help but lean over her and put his ear against her chest, grinning broadly when he felt and heard her heart beating in her chest.

And so it was that she opened her eyes and looked straight into his. He jumped back as if he'd been caught doing something naughty, but she smiled at him.

"What is your name?" she asked him.

"Cory, my Lady."

"Well, I thank you, Cory. I have felt your loyalty and devotion. I thank you for your companionship. Your presence has felt like a warm fire on a chill night." She looked up at Isadore. "You too, my beautiful," she said. "I have felt your companionship. It has sustained me. It has cocooned me, and I paid you homage by remembering you in my words and visions."

Isadore moved forward and touched her lips to her Lady's in a light kiss. When she pulled back, her Lady laughed softly and raised a hand to caress the beautiful, smooth, silky coat of her neck.

And then the Lady turned her head and looked at Salomon. "I got your message, my old friend. Actually," she corrected herself, "I got all your messages, I think, for there were so many. I thank you, too, for your guidance and counsel and your steadfast companionship. But I must needs ask. The books . . . ?"

Salomon had moved to stand right beside her while she had spoken to the two companions on the other side of the table from him. Now, he threw his head back and laughed heartily.

"The books," he said. "That's the first thing she asks me. The books!" He looked at her again, his laughter still in his eyes, and he laid a hand on her arm as he bent over and touched her forehead with his lips. "The books are safe, beautiful Lady. Did you really think I would just leave them to their own fate in the human realm? Never. When humans are ready, we will return them, but until that time, they are safe here."

She smiled. "I should have known. You are right, old friend. I should have realised you would not leave them to their own fate in the Separated human realm. Humans have been in no fit state to even understand them let alone value them."

"I know," he said softly, smiling into her eyes. "Welcome home, mika."

She returned his smile. "I did it. I cannot quite believe I did it."

"Oh, yes, you definitely did it."

And then she looked beyond Salomon. She looked at Gabriel so that their eyes locked as they had in so many lives in the human realm. Salomon moved back so that Gabriel could take his place beside her. Without speaking, he leaned over and put his lips on her forehead.

She frowned. "Do not kiss me there," she said, sounding ever-so-slightly outraged.

"And where am I to kiss you?"

"Need you ask . . . really?" She removed her hand from his and touched her forefinger to her lips. He laughed softly before he leaned over her again and complied, putting his lips on hers in a lingering, feathery-light kiss that she returned.

"Will you help me sit up?" she asked him when he pulled back.

He helped her to sit, and when she sat, she swivelled and swung her legs off the table, putting her feet to the ground next to Cory who was standing watching her transfixed. She glanced at him and smiled, genuinely amused by his reaction to her. With the new position, her hair, which had never been pinned, only placed, fell down her back in a cascade of curls, and the moonstones in her hair fell from her, dropping onto the table of marble beside her with a ping and onto the ground around it with a plop. She watched them fall around her like soft-pink rain, and then she looked at them on the table and the ground around her. She loved moonstones, always had, so she took a moment to acknowledge, with gratitude, the fact that those who had dressed her had adorned her with the jewels. And, in looking down, she seemed to become aware of what she was wearing. The silk of the gown was wrapped around her shoulders, forming long sleeves that covered her arms to below her wrists. The swathes of silk formed a tight bodice and then fell in folds around her legs, the skirts long. She looked down at herself, fingering the silk of the gown uncertainly.

"What am I wearing?" she asked her companions. "'Tis quite beautiful, but very impractical."

Isadore, ignoring her Lady's comment about her gown, folded her two front legs under her so that her body was lowered. Her Lady slid off the table and, as if it was a time honoured ritual the two of them performed regularly, which, in truth, it was, swung a leg over Isadore's back. Isadore raised herself once again. Sitting astride her unicorn, the skirt of the Lady's gown covered Isadore's rump, and it just so happened that the gown was the same colour as Isadore's beautiful, spiralling, pearl horn. Impractical the gown may have been but together the Lady and her unicorn looked majestic, as if they fitted together perfectly, which they did.

In the clearing, the darkness of night was losing its potency, just beginning to give way to the light of a new day. She looked down upon the three who had kept a vigil beside her this long night and she smiled a dazzling smile at each one of them.

"Shall we go home?" she asked them.

Each one of her companions responded to her with a dazzling smile of his own.

~

In the darkness of her bedroom, she saw all, and she breathed a heartfelt sigh of relief. She knew what it meant. No more Separation. No more fractured, ignorant existence. Healing. Wholeness.

Completeness. Home. She was, at long, long last coming home. She was returning to form, the truth of her metaphysical Self. Home.

~

* The details and specifics of the ritual spell cast, and the whys and wherefores of why I cast it, described here, are outlined and, therefore, Processed, thoroughly, in *The Living Death*, one of the stories in the collection entitled *Transcendence* (published only on my website: www.thelady.com.au (Transcendence)).

The End